Praise for
Northern Lights

"Linked themes of the great outdoors, of the frontier, of pitting oneself against nature and against aboriginal inhabitants of various species."

Times Literary Supplement

"Excellently done, slipping in and out between impressionism and straight narrative and very excitingly conveying the reality . . . of men past the end of their endurance."

Listener (UK)

"Haunting . . . survival, courage, and heroes are examined beautifully and simply."

Publishers Weekly

Books by Tim O'Brien

Northern Lights

Tim O'Brien

broadway books ▲ new york

For Ann

With gratitude to the Arrowhead people,
who will know perfectly well that there is no such town as Sawmill
Landing, that Grand Marais doesn't sponsor ski races,
that these characters are purely fictitious and that this is just a story.

BROADWAY

A hardcover edition of this book was originally published in 1975 by Delacorte Press. It is here reprinted by arrangement with Delacorte.

Broadway Books titles may be purchased for business or promotional use or for special sales. For information, please write to: Special Markets Department, Random House, Inc., 1540 Broadway, New York, NY 10036.

BROADWAY BOOKS and its logo, a letter B bisected on the diagonal, are trademarks of Broadway Books, a division of Random House, Inc.

First Broadway Books trade paperback edition published 1999.

Designed by Nicola Ferguson

Library of Congress Cataloging-in-Publication Data
O'Brien, Tim, 1946–
    Northern lights / Tim O'Brien.
      p. cm.
   ISBN 0-7679-0441-9 (pbk.)
    1. Vietnamese Conflict, 1961–1975—Veterans—Minnesota—Fiction.
  2. Wilderness survival—Minnesota—Fiction. 3. Brothers—Minnesota—
Fiction I. Title.
PS3565.B75N67 1999
813'.54—dc21   99-28842
                                          CIP

99 00 01 02 03 10 9 8 7 6 5 4 3 2 1

... and, lo, there was a great earthquake;
and the sun became black as sackcloth of hair,
and the moon became as blood. And the stars
of heaven fell unto the earth even as a fig tree
casteth her untimely figs, when she is shaken of
a mighty wind. And the heaven departed as a scroll
when it is rolled together; and every mountain
and island were moved out of their places ...
For the day of his wrath is come.
And who shall be able to stand?

REVELATIONS

Heat Storm

Blood Moon

Elements

Shelter

Shelter

Elements

Black Sun

Heat Storm

Blizzard

. . . and, lo, there was a great earthquake;
and the sun became black as sackcloth of hair,
and the moon became as blood. And the stars
of heaven fell unto the earth even as a fig tree
casteth her untimely figs, when she is shaken of
a mighty wind. And the heaven departed as a scroll
when it is rolled together; and every mountain
and island were moved out of their places . . .
For the day of his wrath is come.
And who shall be able to stand?

REVELATIONS

Heat Storm   Blood Moon

Elements   Shelter

Shelter   Elements

Black Sun   Heat Storm

Blizzard

One

Heat Storm

Wide awake and restless, Paul Milton Perry clawed away the sheets and swung out of bed, blood weak, his fists clenching and closing like a pulse. He hadn't slept. He sat very still. He listened to the July heat, mosquitoes at the screen windows, inchworms eating in the back pines, the old house, a close-seeming flock of loons. What he did not hear, he imagined. Timber wolves and Indians, the chime of the old man's spoon in the spit bucket, the glacial floes, Harvey hammering at the half-finished bomb shelter, ice cracking in great sheets, the deep pond and Grace's whispering, and a sobbing sound. He sat still. He was naked and sweating and anaemic and flabby. Thinking first about Harvey, then about the heat, then the mosquitoes, he'd been sailing in a gaunt nightlong rush of images and half-dreams, turning, wallowing, listening like a stranger to the sounds of his father's house.

He sat still.

Harvey was coming home.

There was that, and there was Grace, and there were the mosquitoes crazy for blood against the screen windows.

"Lord, now," he moaned, and pushed out of bed, found his glasses, and groped towards the kitchen.

He returned with a black can of insecticide. Then he listened again. The bedroom was sullen and hot, and he was thinking murder. Carefully, he tied the lace curtains to one side. He ignored Grace's first whisper. He pushed the nozzle flush against the screen window. Then, grinning and naked, he pressed the nozzle and began to spray, feeling better, and he flushed the night with poison from his black can.

He grinned and pressed the nozzle. His fingers turned wet and cool from condensed poison, and he listened: mosquitoes and june bugs, dawn crickets, dawn birds, dragonflies and larvae and caterpillars, morning moths and sleeping flies, bear and moose, walleyes and carp and northerns and bullheads and tiny salamanders. It was dark everywhere. The black can hissed in the dark, ejaculating sweet chemicals that filled the great forest and his father's house. He sprayed until the can was empty and light, then he listened, and the odor of poison buoyed him.

He sat on the bed. Harvey was coming home, and he was dizzy.

"Bad night," Grace whispered.

"Lord."

"Poor boy."

"Poor *mosquitoes*."

"Shhhhh," she always whispered. "Shhhh, just lie back now. Come here, lie back. You're just excited. Phew, what a stink! Come here now. Lie back."

"Killed a billion of them."

"Shhhh, lie back."

"No use. What a night. Lord, what a crummy awful night."

"Relax now. I heard you all night long."

"Mosquitoes, the blasted heat, everything." He sat on the bed. He was still holding the defused can of insecticide. Poison drifted through the dark room.

"Poor boy. Come here now. Here, lie back. Lie back." Her hand moved to his neck. "Here now," she whispered. "Lie back and I'll rub you. Poor boy, I heard you tossing all night long. Just lie back and I'll give you a nice rub and you can sleep and sleep."

"I'm going for a walk."

"None of that. You just lie still and I'll rub you." Her hand brushed up his spine and rested on his shoulder. Vaguely through the cloud of poison he heard the hum of returning insects, thousands and millions of them deep in the woods, and he began scratching himself. He was flabby and restless. "I'm going for a walk."

"Poor, poor Paul," she said. She removed his glasses. "There now. Just lie back and I'll give you a rub. There. There, how's that now? Better now? Poor boy, you're just excited about Harvey coming home, that's all, that's all. Just lie back and I'll rub you and you can sleep."

"What time is it?"

"Shhhhh. Plenty of time. Still dark, see? You just lie still now."

"Lord," he moaned.

"A nice rub?"

"I'm going for a walk."

"Shhhhh, none of that. Let me rub you."

"Damn mosquitoes."

"I know."

"Scratch. There." He lay back. He grinned. "Guess I killed myself some lousy mosquitoes, didn't I?"

"I guess you did."

"Massacred the little buggers."

"Hush up. You killed them all. You're a brave mosquito killer and now you can just go to sleep. Roll on to your tummy and I'll scratch you."

He turned and let her scratch. He felt better. The room sweated with the poison. He lay still and listened to the returning mosquitoes, the dawn insects, listened to Grace murmur in the dark: "There, there. Is that better? Poor boy, I heard you all night long. Just excited, that's all. Aren't you excited? Harvey coming home and everything, I don't blame you. Poor boy. Now, how does that feel? Better now? You just go to sleep."

"What time is it?"

"Sleep time," Grace said. "Plenty of time."

Her fingers went up and down his back. He felt better. "There, there," she was whispering, and Perry grinned and thought about the poison sweeping like mustard gas through the screen windows. He felt better. He pressed his nose into the sheets, lay still while she massaged his shoulders and his neck and his scalp. "There, there," she was whispering, softly now, her hand moving lightly. She whispered like a mother. She smelled of flannel. He felt much better. Gradually, she stopped rubbing and after a time he heard her slow breathing. Her mouth was open and she was asleep. Her teeth were shining.

Then he tried to sleep. But soon he was listening and thinking again, thinking about Harvey.

He tried to imagine what great changes the war might have made in his kid brother. He wondered what they would first say to each other. It was hard to picture.

All night, he had been thinking.

There would be some changes. The wounded eye, for sure. It was hard to imagine Harvey with a wounded eye. Harvey the Bull. The blinded bull. It was hard to picture. In a stiff and static way, he remembered his brother through a handful of stop-motion images, a few images that had been frozen long ago and captured everything important. All night the images spun in his head: Harvey the Bull; Harvey digging the bomb shelter; Harvey off somewhere in the woods with the old man; Harvey playing football; Harvey the rascal; Harvey boarding the bus that would take him to a fort in California and from there to Saigon or Chu Lai or wherever.

It was annoying. The few sharp images were all Paul Perry really had. It was as though he'd lived thirty years for the sake of a half-dozen fast snapshots, everything else either forgotten or superfluous or lost in the shuffle, and all night long the few sharp images flopped before him, gaunt summary of three decades, growing up on the old man's sermons and winter stories, learning to swim as the old man watched without pity, college, marriage, returning to Sawmill Landing, the bomb shelter and the old man's death, a job, winter and summer and millions of pine and Norway spruce and birch, billions of bugs. All collapsed around the few images. But even the images offered no natural sequence. They were random and defiant, clarifying nothing, and Perry spent the long night in myopic wonder, trying to sort them into an order that would progress from start to finish to start.

He lay still. The mosquitoes were back. On the far wall, the first light formed patches against Grace's dressing mirror.

Again he swung out of bed. He dressed quietly and carried his shoes to the kitchen. Outside, the sky was chalk colored. It would be another dry day. Sunday. Standing on the porch, he urinated into Grace's green ferns, then he laced up his shoes, hurried across the lawn, passed the bomb shelter without looking, followed the path by memory to Pliney's Pond.

There he sat on the rocks.

He practised melancholia and self-pity.

He scooped a handful of green water from the pond and let it trickle through his fingers, indifferently inspecting it for life. Harvey the Bull, he was thinking. The blinded bull. It was hard to picture. Hard to tell where it all started or even why. He took more water from the pond. Swirling it in his hands, he captured tiny capsules of cellulose, tiny larvae and mosquito eggs.

He waited for the sun to rise.

The forest stood like walls around the pond. Roots of older trees snaked along the rocks and disappeared deep into the water.

"Pooooor me," he moaned.

It was hard to tell where it started. He squinted into the algae, dipped in for more water, let it dribble through his fingers.

It may have started that October in 1962, the October when Harvey quit high school football in order to finish the old man's bomb shelter. It was one of the images: the October in 1962 when the old man's prophecies of doom suddenly seemed not so crazy after all. When the Caribbean bustled with missiles and atom bombs, jets scrambling over Miami Beach and everyone in Sawmill Landing sat at their radios or hunched over coffee in the drugstore, saying: "Maybe the old gent wasn't so crazy after all." When people were asking one another about the hazards of nuclear fallout, asking if it really rotted a man's testicles, does it hurt, would it reach into northern Minnesota, would the winds be from the north or south or does it matter? That October in 1962, eight years ago, when the Arrowhead blazed with red autumn, when Harvey dug a great hole in the backyard, poured cement, strung lights from the pines in order to work in the night so as to finish the bomb shelter for the dying old man.

It may have started then.

Or it may have started further back.

As kids.

He couldn't remember.

That day when he dressed up in his father's vestments, practising to be a preacher, to follow the old man into the pulpit of Damascus Lutheran Church. It may have started or it may not have started. It may have been the afternoon when the old man ordered him to swim in Pliney's Pond. "Jump in," the old man had said without pity. It may have started then, at the moment when he waded bawling into the fecund pond, or it may have started another time, that day, that day, or innumerable other days that washed together, that day when Harvey boarded a bus for California and the war. Or the day he married Grace, a day he barely remembered. "Looks like somebody's mother," the motherless old man had once said. Or other days.

That day.

It was the perfect melancholy hour, and he practised silence.

He sat on the rocks and peered into Pliney's Pond. Pushing his glasses close, he leaned forward and scooped a handful of algae from the pond and rubbed it between his fingers until they were stained green.

It may have started or it may not have started. It was partly the town. Partly the place. Partly the forest and the old man's Finnish religion, partly being a preacher's kid, partly the old man's northern obsessions, partly a combination of human beings and events, partly a genetic fix, an alchemy of circumstance.

Harvey was coming home and the sun was already coming up.

He was restless and afraid. It was hard to imagine Harvey with a wounded eye. Harvey the Bull, the old man's pride, the brave balled bullock. Careful not to fall into the stinking pond, Perry sat on the rocks and peered into the waters and listened to dawn respiration. It was Sunday. He sat quietly, practising silence, letting the night restlessness drain, listening as the forest swelled and expelled like a giant lung: oxygenation, respiration, metabolism and decay, photosynthesis and reproduction, simple asexual chemistry, conversion and reconversion.

Finally, when he was ready, he returned to the house. Grace was still sleeping.

The old timbers creaked. He put coffee on the stove, moved into the bathroom, showered, scrubbed the algae from his hands, dusted himself with his wife's baby powder. It was six o'clock. He drank his coffee, watching the sunlight come in patches through the woods. He was sluggish and lazy and soft-bellied. Sipping his morning coffee and sitting at the table, he considered knocking off some sit-ups. Instead he fixed breakfast. When it was ready, he crept into the bedroom and woke Grace. "Breakfast," he said.

"Phew." She emerged from the sheets. "Phew, I had a dream . . . I was dreaming somebody was spraying insecticide. Did you have that dream? Phew." She was a handsome woman. When she smiled, her teeth shined. From September through May she taught school. Now it was summer. "Come here," she said.

"Breakfast's already on."

"I want some nice cuddling. Come here."

"Don't you want some nice breakfast instead?"

"Hmmmm," she said. "First some nice cuddling. Poor boy, you had a bad night, didn't you? Come here and I'll give you some nice cuddling."

Perry shook his head. "Better hurry," he said. "Harvey comes home today, you know."

"Poor boy," she smiled. "Poor Paul. What you need is some cuddling."

He backed the car into the yard, turned past the bomb shelter and drove out towards Route 18. Gravel clanked against the sides of the car. At the end of the lane, he stopped and Grace leaned out to check the mailbox, then he turned on to the tar road and drove fast towards town.

The road swept through state park land. Another dry day. Branches hung over the narrow parts of the road.

After passing Bishop Markham's house, Grace moved over and put her hand on him. "Happy?" she said.

"Sure. Wonderful."

"What's the matter?"

"Nothing. I'm happy. Can't you see how happy I am? Watch out or I'll drive into the ditch."

The road ran in a drunken narrow valley of the forest, bumpy from winter frost heaves, old tar with a single white line painted down its center, unwinding towards Sawmill Landing, where it would pass by the cemetery and the junkyard, disappear for a moment at the railroad tracks, then continue on into town, past the John Deere machinery yard, the silver water tower, into the hub of Sawmill Landing. Perry drove fast. He knew the road by memory: twelve years on a school bus, in his father's pickup, in his own first car, shuttling back and forth between the paint-peeling timber town and the old timber house. The road had no shoulders and the ditches were shallow rock and the forest stood like walls on each side, sometimes hanging over the road to form a kind of tunnel or chute through which he drove fast, opening the window to let the July heat in, lighting a first cigarette. It was a hypnotic, relaxing drive. Without recognizing anything in particular, he recognized everything in general — the sweep of the road down to the iron bridge, the sound of the tires on the pine planks, the slow curve past the cemetery and junkyard.

"If you're happy, then, let's see a nice smile," Grace was saying, snuggling closer. "There, isn't that nicer? You have to smile when Harvey gets off the bus. Okay? You have to start practising right now."

"All right," he said.

"Then smile."

"Okay," he smiled, despite himself. She was like a gyroscope. A warm self-righting center, soothing with those whispers.

"Isn't that better now?"

"Yes."

"You see?"

"Priceless."

"Don't be that way. Be nice."

"I am nice. I'm priceless. Don't you think I'm priceless? Harvey's a soldier and I'm priceless. That's the way it always seems to go. Perfectly priceless."

"Stop that." She pouted, puckering her lower lip. "I'm only . . . just trying to perk you up a little. Here, I want you to start smiling. Shall I turn on the radio? We'll listen to some church music."

"If you want. Sounds priceless to me."

"Poor Paul." She turned the radio dial to find WCZ in Duluth. The car filled with July heat and the sound of pipe organs and a choir.

Perry concentrated on the road.

He felt her studying him, that vast womanly, wifely, motherly sympathy and understanding that both attracted and repelled him, often at the same time. "Like somebody's goddamn mother," his father had said. In college, more than ten years ago, it was her heavy-breasted sympathy that brought them together. She'd taken him in like an orphan, soothed him through four years at the University of Iowa, calmed him when he dropped out of the divinity school and steadied him when he started at the ag school, decadent Hawkeye sympathy that oozed like ripe mud. After all the years with his father, after pursuing the old man's winter tracks, ice fishing and hunting and fiery sermons, after all that Grace had come with her whispers and understanding, and marrying her after graduation had been as easy and natural as falling asleep in a warm bath. By then the old man was dead.

She was still studying him, snuggling close. "Well," she finally said. "Well, Harvey sounded all right on the telephone. Don't you think? I do. I think so. Actually, don't you think he sounded pretty cheerful?"

"I guess so. He sounded the same."

"You see? You see, he's still cheerful and he sounded fine and everything will be perfect. You'll see."

"I guess."

"So you can smile now. You can be cheerful just like Harvey."

"He lost an eye."

"Well . . ." She trailed off as if recognizing the fact but not its importance. The radio played church music. Perry turned the car along the slow curve of the lake. He was nervous and he lit another cigarette. "Well," Grace said, "I'll tell you this. I'm just glad you didn't have to go. I'm glad about that much anyway. Aren't you? I'm just glad you were too old for the dumb thing. I mean I don't know. It's awful about Harvey and everything. But I'm just glad you didn't have to go, that's all."

"Priceless."

Again she pouted, and the road bumped across the rusted railroad tracks, straightened and descended through a tunnel of white pine that opened into the town. Sometimes he got pleasure out of making her worry. "Priceless," he muttered just for that purpose. On the right, an enamel sign said: SAWMILL LANDING. It gave the population as 781, which had been about right until 1947 when the last lumber company had left town, taking thirty families with it.

The road made a sharp turn and became Mainstreet. Perry parked in front of the bank.

Church bells were ringing as they walked to the drugstore.

Except for two dogs, one sniffing at the other, the streets were as dry and motionless as a postcard. Sunday morning. Sunday morning, four dozen cars parked about the stone church, Jud Harmor's pickup in front of the town hall, Sunday morning, paint peeling, pine rotting, the forest growing into vacant lots and abandoned lawns, fallen timbers, Sunday morning and even inside the drugstore everything was quiet:

Grace found a Sunday paper and they sat at the counter. A Coca-Cola clock showed eight minutes to eleven.

Perry kept his head down. He rambled through the comics and Sunday morning headlines. Grace read the Living section. A wall of mirrors faced them, running from one end of the long counter to the other, plastered with ads for ice cream and Pepsi and Bromo Seltzer, reflecting the rows of toothpaste and stationery and mouthwash and Kleenex, reflecting like a long mercantile mural, reflecting Grace who was gazing at him placid and soft-eyed, featureless as warm milk. He looked away. He looked away and continued through the newspaper until Herb Wolff swung behind the counter.

Without asking, Wolff poured coffee and put the cups down and wrote out a bill.

"Coffee?" he said.

"Thanks, Herb."

"No problem." He waited to be paid. Then he rang up thirty cents on his cash register, poured himself a cup of coffee and sat down beside Grace. "So," he said slowly, "so . . . what's up?"

"Not much. How's your pa?"

Wolff shrugged.

"That's good."

"Keeps holding in there," Wolff said. "So. What's up?" He had a deep voice that never stopped surprising Perry.

"Nothing, Herb. What about you?"

They sat without talking. For hours at a time, people sat in Wolff's drugstore without talking. Stirring coffee and looking at themselves in the long mirrors, listening to Wolff's cash register, watching Mainstreet, asking folks who came in: "What's new? What's up?"

Wolff rearranged a pair of salt and pepper shakers. "So. Not in church today."

"Not today, I guess."

"So what's up then?"

"Nothing. We're here to meet the bus."

Wolff raised his eyebrows, waiting for more, then he sighed. "Relatives, I guess."

"That's about it, Herb. When the devil do we get some rain?"

"I reckon next week. That's what everyone's saying." He paused a moment as if trying to frame a difficult question, then very slowly he said, "Relatives, I reckon."

"That's right."

"That's what I thought." Again he raised his eyebrows. He was dressed in a starched lab coat. It didn't seem to Perry that he'd changed at all since high school. Wolff was one of the Germans. There were Swedes and Finns and Germans, and Wolff was pure German — impeccable and stiffly manicured, greedy eyes, a bristling crewcut and a voice that rose like deep magic from his sunken little torso. Wolff was proud of the voice. Back in high school, when it finally changed, it saved him from an adolescence of constant scorn, pity, practical jokes and half-serious innuendo about his malehood. He now loaded the voice with authority, successfully straining out most of the German accent, always speaking slowly and only after long and apparently tormenting thought. "A relative," he said.

"That's about it. You got any more of this coffee, Herb?"

"Right." He sighed, giving up. Wolff refilled their cups and wrote out a new bill and they sat quietly and listened while the Coca-Cola clock ticked. "I reckon you know Jud Harmor's got cancer," he said.

"I've heard that."

"It's true."

"Did Jud tell you?"

Wolff shook his head. "Nope, but I heard it. I hear it's bad, too."

"He's tough."

"He's old." Wolff was playing again with the salt and pepper shakers. "He ought to step down from being mayor if he's got cancer like I hear he's got. I don't say he *has* to quit. I say he *should* quit. It's for the better."

"I guess it is."

When the Coca-Cola clock showed two minutes after eleven, Wolff got behind the counter and began making coffee for the church crowd. He still had the disjointed swagger that Perry remembered from high school, a sailor's roll that joined with his deep voice to defy everything else about him.

"Anacin and aspirin and all that stuff," Wolff was saying, talking to Grace like a teacher. "It's made in these big vats, you know, and all it really amounts to is plain acid. And you know what acids are. Dangerous. You got to be careful."

"Why sell it?" asked Grace.

"Oh. Well, it is a medicine. That's all I'm saying, honey. Aspirin is medicine and people forget that. I'm just saying you got to be careful because it's not sugar. Not candy. Aspirin is a very potent medicine. Aspirin isn't sugar. Sugar is organic, see? Sugar's got carbons in it, but aspirin's plain acid and acid is something you got to be careful of, see?"

Grace nodded. Then Wolff nodded. He straightened his lab coat and checked his watch against the Coca-Cola clock. "So," he said crisply, "bus gets in at eleven twenty. Who's this relative anyhow?"

Grace laughed. "It's no big secret, Herb. It's Harvey. We just thought it would be best not to . . ."

"Harvey?"

Grace smiled.

"Harvey!" Wolff wailed. He held his hands to his mouth like a girl. His voice sailed up an octave. "Harvey? Well this is . . . Harvey!"

"It's no secret," Grace said. "We thought he'd just want to get off the bus without any fuss."

"Geez," Wolff moaned. "Well, this is something. Harvey? Geeeezzzz. You should've told somebody. For Pete's sakes. Harvey. Well, how is he?" Wolff looked about the store. "For Pete's *sakes*! You should've told us. He's coming on the bus? Geez, I got to get some people here."

"I don't think he wants that," Perry said. He decided to cut Wolff off fast. "Let's just let it be a nice easy thing."

"We *got* to!" Wolff wailed. "He's coming home, isn't he? Geez. I got to make some phone calls." He yanked his lab coat down, dusting it and hustling for the phone.

"Herb. Forget it, will you?"

"The whole town's in church." Wolff banged the phone down and went out into the street and came back. "Geez, this is . . . I can't believe any of this. Harvey. I just can't believe it. He's coming home. I mean, we got to get some people out for him, don't we? How is he? I mean, how's the eye and everything?"

"He's fine," Grace smiled. "We talked to him on the phone and he sounded cheerful and fine."

Wolff rubbed his crewcut. "Well, we got to do something. Don't we? Maybe . . . Maybe I ought to run over to the church and make an announcement or something."

"Forget it," Perry said.

"What?"

"Just forget it, Herb."

"But . . . I mean, shouldn't we get some people here?"

"No," Perry said.

Wolff frowned. He looked shaken. "At least the mayor?"

"Nobody."

"Geez," Wolff moaned. "Somebody should be here when he comes. Don't you think? If I'd known about it, why, I'll tell you, I'd've had the whole council here. I'll *tell* you."

"Leave him alone, Herb."

Perry went outside and sat on the kerb.

The streets were dusty.

Jud Harmor's pickup was gone now, but the two dogs were still there, curled in wait on the steps of Damascus Lutheran. Beyond the peeling buildings there was nothing but forest.

He cleaned his glasses and leaned back. Then he cleaned his glasses again. In a while Grace came out and sat with him.

"Wolff still phoning people?"

"Oh," she laughed. "I think I settled him down. He's in there grinding fresh coffee for Harvey."

"Some creep, isn't he?"

"Paul."

"I'm sorry. You didn't see the time in there?"

"Few more minutes." She took his hand. "You all right now?"

"Sure. I'm okay. I'm priceless. I'll bet that damn bus is late."

"Shhhhh. You just relax and start smiling. Have a bright face."

He gazed up Mainstreet to where the bus would turn in and hiss and stop. The street was silent. The heat seemed to absorb sound. Sitting on the curb, he felt like a boy again, waiting to be picked up from school, or waiting in a stifling theatre for the curtain to draw up and the lights to fade and the movie to begin. He felt he'd been waiting a long time. He was restless. The long night had caught up with him and he needed a cigarette. He was restless. He needed a cigarette and the pack was empty. Grace sat silently, twisting her wedding band, toying with his hand until he pulled it away and stood up. Across the street and down a way, he saw the shoddy frame building where he had his own office. The venetian blinds were down, forming a white backdrop for the lettering on the window: PAUL MILTON PERRY, and below his name, painted in orange, DEPARTMENT OF AGRICULTURE, COUNTY FARM EXTENSION. Sucking the Federal Titty. Harvey always stated the unstated.

"Awful hot," Grace finally said.

"Damn bus is late. I knew it."

"Shall I see what time it is?"

"Yes. And get me some cigarettes. And make sure Wolff isn't on that telephone again."

He walked to the end of the block and back again. One of the dogs trotted over to be scratched. The town was dead. He could hear the muffled sound of the organ inside the church. The town did not particularly depress him, but at the same time he often wondered why anyone still lived there. Wolff was there to sell coffee and medicine. The barber was there to cut Wolff's hair into a flat crewcut once a week. The grocer was there to sell food to the barber. The farmers were there, trying to grow corn in the forest to sell to the grocer, and Perry was there to keep the farms going, to tell them when to use fertilizer, to fill out subsidy applications and loan applications, to watch the Swedes try to grow corn on land meant for pine and Indians. He didn't know. It didn't make sense. Once he'd asked his father why they didn't just move on to Duluth, and the old man went crazy, charging into one of his fiery sermons about the virtues of hardship and how Perry's grandfather had built the house out of the forest's own timber and how a town was like tempered steel and how a transplanted tree never grows as tall or as fine as one rooted in native soil. The lesson of the sermon, if not the logic, always stuck with Perry. The old man died and Perry stayed on. And Harvey got drafted. Old Harvey. Harvey was different. Ever since the old man died, Harvey talked about leaving the town, and one day with the help of the draft board he did leave. A confused time. Harvey the Bull. He was a bull but he was no soldier. As kids they hadn't even played war games. Indians were better, better targets for games with their leather jackets, sour faces, bad teeth and greasy hair, Chippewa mostly. They'd stalked the Indians, crawled on bellies in the weeds behind the house, yelped and bellowed. But never war games. Nothing serious. Trapping games and capture-the-flag and forts in the forest, not far from Pliney's Pond, snow forts in winter and tree forts in summer, great camouflage in the fall, but never war games. And no one in Sawmill Landing knew a damn about the war anyway. It wasn't talked about in the drugstore. Then gangbusters, bang, old Harvey gets drafted, good old Bishop Markham and Herb Wolff on the draft board—sorry, Harvey's number was up, something like that, proper optimism and good humour, a little sympathy, proper pride. Perry stayed out of it. Nothing he could do, and the war wasn't real anyway, and, besides, it seemed somehow natural that a rascal and bull like Harvey was the one to go off to the war. In that sleepwalking, slothful departure there had been no time to counter the nagging thought that the speed of it all, the blinding foggy invisible force behind it, was a sure sign that

Harvey would come home maimed. Because no one knew a damn about it. Vietnam was outside the town orbit. "A mess," was what people would say if forced to comment, but a mess was still not a war, and it did not become a war until Harvey went to fight in it. Two Indian boys went with him. Their picture was on the front page of the town paper, Harvey in the center, grinning and posing, his arms wrapped around the two dull-eyed Indian boys. In September, one of the Indians got killed and the paper carried a short obituary with an American flag stencilled in. But even then it wasn't really a war. It wasn't a war until Harvey got himself wounded and the paper carried another front-page story, pictures of Harvey in his football uniform, pictures of the old house, pictures of Perry and Grace, a picture of the dead old man in his preacher's robes, a long history of the family, and for a time the war was really a war, though even then it was all jumbled and formless. No sides, no maps to chart progress on, no tides to imagine surging back and forth, no real battles or victories or defeats. In the tangled density of it all, Perry sometimes wondered if the whole show were a masquerade for Harvey to dress in khaki and display his bigballed outdoorsmanship, proving all over again how well he'd followed the old man into the woods, how much he'd learned, to show forever that he was the Bull.

The dog trotted back to the church steps.

Perry sat on the curb again, cleaned his glasses, leaned back. Tips of high pine poked over the store fronts.

Grace came out with cigarettes and coffee. "Eleven thirty," she said. "Herb says it's always a little late."

"I just wish that bus would get in."

Then he saw it. It was as though it had been there all along, poised in turn around the corner, waiting to be seen. He saw it and heard it simultaneously. It was the giant Greyhound. It might have been the same silver monster that took Harvey to war in the first place.

It swung off the tar road, changing gears and growling.

Herb Wolff hurried out. "There she is, there she is!" he wailed. He brushed his coat and stood erect. "There she is, all right."

The bus cleared the turn.

"Sure wish everybody was here for this," said Wolff. "This is something. *Harvey*! I can't believe it."

Perry took a step and stood alone. The Greyhound's brakes hissed and forms moved behind the tinted windows and Perry searched for familiar movements. The door opened with another strange hiss, and the great grey cave was transfixing dust and trembling. Perry peered into the tinted glass.

Harvey stepped off alone. He carried a black bag with white stitching.

"Well, hey!" he said.

Without seeing, Perry gave him a great hug.

"Hey!"

"Yeah, you look *fine*. You do!"

"And my God, here's Grace! Grace. You're beautiful." They hugged and Grace was smiling and wet-eyed and Perry was grinning.

"Yeah, yeah. You've got some tan there."

"Sure!"

"You look great. You do, I can't believe it."

"Skinny! Look at that."

"Hey, it's old Wolff! How the devil is old Wolffie?"

"This is something. It is. You look great, Harv. You do. This is really something."

"I'm fine. I am. Where's my parade? Shouldn't they have trumpets and flags and things? How's my honey-Grace?"

Grace kissed him again, still clutching his arm. "Happy, happy," she said. "You're so skinny, aren't you?"

"Skinny? Lean and mean. How's my brother? How's brother Paul?"

"I'm fine. Here, let me have that bag. I can't get over it, you look great. Really."

"I am great," Harvey said. "Now where the devil is everybody?"

"Sunday."

"Sunday? Is it Sunday? Sunday! Incredible."

"Give me that blasted bag."

"Come on," Grace said. "Let's get you home. Some skinny hero."

Everybody started hugging again, then Harvey released the bag and Perry took it and they stood in a circle on the street. Harvey's bad eye was barely noticeable. He was tall and too skinny. His voice had the old nasal tinkle. "Sunday!" he said. "Some bloody day to come home on. Where's old Jud Harmor? Thought sure old Jud would be here with bands and ticker tape and stuff."

"He's around. Here, let's get into the car and we'll get you home. You did get skinny, didn't you?"

"Sure, and you got chubby. You look great anyway. And Grace. Grace is still a honey. And even old Wolffie looks good, so what we need is a good drink to celebrate. Hey, Wolffie! You got a nice drink we can all celebrate with?"

Wolff blinked and shook his head.

"No bloody drink?"

"No. Geez, I'm sorry. Really. Nobody said anything about . . . I would've had the whole town here if somebody just . . ."

"No bloody drink? No parade, no drink. Where the devil is everybody? Some awful hero worship."

"Everybody's in church, Harv."

"Some hero worship." Harvey grinned and pointed at his bad

eye. "So, how you like my pretty souvenir? Better than a lousy limp, don't you think?"

"Doesn't look bad at all."

"I'm thinking about patching her up. You know? A little class."

"Doesn't look bad at all, Harv."

"Glad you like it. Now all we need is a drink and everybody's happy. Are you happy, Wolff?"

Wolff vigorously shook his head, grinning.

"Fine. Everybody's happy."

Grace took Harvey's arm and walked him towards the car. Church bells began ringing. One of the dogs began to bark, sitting back on its haunches with its nose up towards the steeple. Perry was trembling. He opened the trunk and threw the bag in and slammed it shut.

"Remind me never to come home again on Sunday," Harvey said.

"Anytime is a good time. You look great."

"Glad I didn't wear my uniform. Look plain silly coming home in a uniform and no parade." Harvey shook hands with Wolff, then stood with his hands on his hips and looked up and down Mainstreet. The bells were ringing loud.

"Let's get you home."

"So long, Wolffie," Harvey said. "You're a helluva man. Good man. War's over, baby."

Wolff grinned.

Perry started the engine and backed up and drove up Mainstreet.

"That weasel," Harvey said.

Perry awoke before dawn. He went to the pond, sat on the rocks, waited for daylight. Then he showered and dressed and had coffee and drove into town. It was still early and the shops were closed. He cruised up Acorn Street, past Addie's boarding house. Her window was on the top floor but it was shuttered and there were no lights. He drove back up Mainstreet. It was Monday, there was nothing much to do. He unlocked the office, rolled up the blinds, sat at his desk. The pens were in their glass jar, papers were in folders, the desk was clean and in order, the folders were filed. He put his head in his arms. His mouth was dry from a night of drinking beer and laughing and listening to Harvey tell about the bus ride from Minneapolis, the hospital, a few things about the war.

After a time he got up to sweep the office. Then he switched on the ceiling fan. He typed out a loan application for a dumb-eyed farmer named Lars Nielson. Then he made coffee. Then he put the application into an envelope and typed the address on to a sticker and stuck the sticker to the envelope, then he drank his coffee. There was nothing much to do. He should've become a preacher he thought. The town needed a good preacher. Stenberg, the crusty usurper. And Harvey was home. And Grace was happy and wanted a child. There was nothing much to do. He drank more coffee and passed the morning at the window, watching the town come to life, watching morning shadows come out of the eastern forest, pass over the town. He was melancholy but it was an entirely rational melancholia, nothing outright crazy about it. He should've become a preacher. And Harvey was home and Grace was happy, except she wanted a child, and the old man was dead, and Perry was thinking that things would have been better if he'd become a preacher. With the old man gone, the town needed a good preacher.

The ceiling fan spun round and round. He typed out soil reports, read the morning paper, then towards noon he gave up, locking the office and walking on to the street to mail the

Nielson application. He felt flabby and restless. It was another hot day. The tips of some of the pines were turning brown. Standing on the post office steps, he looked up the street and wondered what to do next. A tractor turned off Route 18. Black smoke coming from a pipe on the hood obscured the farmer's face. Perry decided to find Addie for a long lunch.

She was not in the library. He browsed the stacks, waiting, finally taking a world atlas into the reading room where he smoked and looked at the maps and pictures. It was something he and Harvey used to do, a passion for maps and exotic unseen places. He sat over the atlas a long time. Except for the fans and a woman stacking books behind him, the library was quiet.

He was not sure how long he slept, if at all, but suddenly he was wide awake, surprised to find himself in the chair. The atlas had fallen to his lap. He'd been thinking about Harvey's bad eye. Thinking or dreaming, he wasn't sure. The eye was brilliant blue, rolling untethered like a marble, opaque and shining as though lighted from within. The dead eye seemed to have its own life, rolling about in the socket, reckless and eager and full of trouble and blue light.

Feeling a little foolish, Perry blinked and rubbed his eyes and returned the atlas to the shelf.

It was nearly one o'clock.

The woman stacking books looked at him suspiciously.

He grinned at her and shrugged. "Just waiting for Addie," he said.

"Snoring, too."

"I'm sorry. You don't know what time Addie's coming in?"

"I guess I know, all right, Mr. Perry," the woman said. She was eyeing his shirt. He looked down and saw a cigarette burn the size of a quarter. "Addie's off today, anyhow," the woman said. "Monday, you know. You oughta know that by now, Mr. Perry."

She didn't smile. "She works Saturdays so she's got Monday off, you oughta know that by now."

"I forgot."

He bought a case of beer and some groceries. Walking back to the car, he came across Jud Harmor. Jud saw him first. The old mayor was standing in front of the town hall, hands in his hip pockets, brown shirt and brown cotton pants, the straw hat pushed back on his skull.

"Been lookin' for you," Jud said.

"Hey, Jud." Perry shifted the groceries to his other arm and prepared to listen.

"I been lookin' for you."

Perry nodded and waited. There was a bright sun on Jud's face. Under his chin, a large cancer splotch cut down the throat and disappeared under the old man's shirt. He was lean and tough-looking and sly-looking and he looked like Perry's father sometimes. At a certain age, all the old men began to look alike.

"Anyhow," said Jud, "I been lookin' for you. Wolff says Harvey's back."

"Yesterday."

Jud nodded, looking up Mainstreet.

"Came on the bus yesterday," Perry said. "He called a few days ago — last week."

Jud nodded, still surveyed the hot street. "Guess somebody should've told me."

"Sorry, Jud. We were just thinking he'd want to ease back in. You know? No big show or anything."

"Somebody should've told me, anyhow. I should've been there."

Perry nodded. "Sorry."

Jud squinted up the street. There was no traffic. The two lonely dogs were sleeping on the steps of Damascus Lutheran.

"Anyhow," said Jud, "I should've been there. Harvey being a hero and all." He laughed into a cough.

"Oh, I wouldn't say he's exactly a hero, Jud. I wouldn't say that. He got his eye hurt and that's about the end of it really."

"Shit," the old mayor said, "you think I don't know that? Bound to happen sooner or later. Like your old man, you know, same damn thing. Anyhow, he's gonna want a parade now."

"What?"

"A *parade*, for Chrissake! I guess he'll want a parade now, horns and sirens and floats."

"Oh."

Jud squinted and coughed and shook his head. He brought up a wad of phlegm from his throat, leaned forward and casually spat into the street. "Well, ahhhh, I guess you can tell your pa I'll get that parade arranged. I guess I can do that much."

"He's dead, Jud," Perry said carefully.

Jud squinted. "Thought he just got himself wounded in the eye?"

"No, my old man. *He's* dead."

Jud laughed. "Shit! You think I didn't know that?"

Perry grinned. He shifted the groceries again.

"Anyhow," said Jud, "you get the word to Harvey, okay?"

Jud coughed and spat a big bubble of mucus into the street. "Shit! Wolff says it's the first thing ol' Harvey asked about . . . a parade. Don't worry, I'll get it for him, ram it right through, no problem at all."

"There's no need for it, Jud."

"Just tell him, son." The old mayor sighed. "You better get on home then. Groceries there are leakin' all over you." He pushed the straw hat forward. "You say hey to your pa, now."

Perry grinned. "Okay, Jud."

Jud cackled. "Your pa's dead!"

"Yeah."

"I never said he was crazy, you know."

"I know, Jud."

"What about your ma?"

"She's dead, too, Jud."

"Jesus." Old Jud spat into the street. "Dropping like flies, aren't they? Well, what about Harvey?"

"Harvey's fine."

"Mother of Mercy."

"Right."

"Don't let your old man shove you around, you hear me?"

"Okay, Jud. Thanks."

"Not Harvey either."

"Okay."

"So long now, Reverend."

Perry grinned and saluted and started off, then stopped. "Jud?"

The old man was staring after him.

"Jud, you haven't seen Addie?"

Jud Harmor pulled off his hat to think. His skull was shiny.

"Addie. The girl who works in the library. You haven't seen her today?"

"Addie," Jud said, looking about. "Newcomer."

"A year or so. She works in the library. Just a kid. You call her Geronimo sometimes."

Jud grinned. "Shit, you mean ol' Geronimo. Some ass, right? Sure, I know her all right. You're talkin' about ol' Geronimo."

"You haven't seen her?"

"Wish so," Jud said. "Wish I had. Some ass, don't you think? No disrespect, Reverend. What you want ol' Geronimo for?"

"Nothing. Just looking for her. Thanks, Jud."

"Aren't thinkin' of converting her? That'd be some awful wasted hunk of redskin ass, I'll say that."

"Don't worry, Jud."

"No disrespect, Reverend."

"So long, Jud."

"Say hey to your pa, now."

Perry smiled and waved.

"He's *dead*!" Jud hollered.

"You're some politician, Jud."

"And you ain't exactly a reverend, neither." The old man waved. "Take care, son. Tell that brother Harvey I'll get his blasted parade for him, hear?"

"Okay."

"You tell him now. Get his medals patched on."

"I will."

"And listen. Hey! I wanted you to tell him this. Tell him that losing one eye never hurt a blind man. You tell him that for me. Perk him up."

"Okay, Jud."

"Tell him the town thinks he's a hero. Tell him we're all proud." Jud was grinning, waving his hat. "Tell him anything you want. A pack of lies, anyway. Okay? Hell, tell him he's lucky to be alive, that's what. Tell him I thought he was dead or something, that'll clear his head awhile. That Harvey. Some rascal, isn't he? You got to be careful now."

"Okay, Jud."

"Take her easy, son."

"Okay."

"Geronimo!" he wailed, and coughed, and spat in the street.

Perry decided to try the lake.

He swung off Route 18 and parked along the path leading to the beach. He walked fast, beginning to worry about the time.

At a small footbridge he slowed for breath, then kept on at an easier pace as the path gradually widened and the forest thinned out, finally ending in a sandy clearing that looked down on the lake.

He stopped there. He was out of shape and sweating. Addie's Olds was parked along the gravel lane that ran from the lake to the junk yard. He felt a little better. He found some shade and sat down to wait.

The lake was hard gray-blue, so calm it looked iced over, and there were no clouds, and it was mid-afternoon of summer with nothing to do. He put his hand down and squeezed the roll of fat under his ribs. Harvey'd never had that problem. Why not? Something to do with dominant and recessive genetics, most likely; or breeding, the old man's feeling at the time, or their separate moods, black bile and yellow, it was hard to say. The Bull, said the old man about Harvey, and that was that, and it was too bad. And like Jud said, maybe the old man wasn't crazy after all. Thinking about old Jud, Perry started grinning. Hard to tell if the old mayor was playing a great fool's game, darting in and out of time as if it didn't matter or exist, always confusing the living with the dead and Perry with Harvey and both of them with the old man. Every two years either Herb Wolff or Bishop Markham opposed Jud in the town elections, and every two years Jud got re-elected. Everything was always the same, Jud and the trees and the lake.

He sat in the shade and waited. He pitched stones down the embankment and watched them roll to the beach. He thought awhile about doing some exercises. Sweat off the fat rolls, turn lean, watch Grace's happy face, stir up some energy, get healthy, sit-up and push-up himself into bullhood and happiness. It was awfully hot.

The first movement was gentle. It was just a splash of light in the lake. He watched the splashes lap towards him like waves, moving in delicate arcs closer, and he stood up to watch.

She swam close to shore then turned and swam on her back.

Her arms reached from the water and dipped. He was too far away to hear the sound of her swimming.

After a time she waded ashore. She bent forward, her hands braced on her knees, her hair flopping forward in a wet black bunch.

She was very slender. She walked on her heels, and she was wet and her skin was walnut-coloured and shining.

Perry moved down the embankment for a better look. He was smiling. He found a log and sat down again, his hands folded nervously.

She wore a white swimsuit.

With her back to him, she walked on up the beach, stopping now and then to bend down, picking things up, throwing pebbles out into the lake, skipping rocks. She was slender and she walked and played like an athlete, bent forward and swinging her arms and walking on her heels. She walked a quarter mile up the beach. For a moment she disappeared in a stand of pines, then she was back and coming towards him.

She walked with her chin forward. Perry wanted to laugh. He was smiling and watching and sweating. Her hair lay over her shoulders in two black heaps, and she was lean and athletic, walked with long loping steps, on her heels, her arms swinging.

Perry watched her come down the beach. Her shoulders were brown.

Then, like a deer, she stopped. She seemed to look in his direction, her head turning up. Then she sprang for the water.

It startled him. He called out, but she dived headlong for the lake and white spray flashed and she was gone under and the lake bubbled ivory from the spot where she dived.

Finally emerging, she shook her head. Then she sprang high like a fish. She seemed to hover there, a strong golden arc suspended over the water, then she went under, her feet kicking at the last instant.

She emerged again further out.

Addie! he shouted. He stood up and waved.

She raised her hand. He couldn't be sure if it were a wave or another swimming stroke, for the hand poised for only a moment then it was gone and she was swimming again for the center of the lake. He grinned. She could be very quick. He could not make out her face. He waved hard.

She swam straight out, long arched strokes, and soon he saw only the wake of her swimming. He felt fine. He walked away slowly, for it was a hot day.

That July was quiet. The forest was being burnt out. People in town talked about forest fires, and the farmers talked about how the corn was already ruined, and Perry and Harvey walked and fished and played some tennis.

Except for the heat, it was not a bad time. Harvey was cheerful, always eager to get into the woods. He talked about building a house in Nassau, about taking a bike tour through Canada, about going to live in Montana or Oregon. While he never talked much about the war or losing his eye, he didn't seem bitter and even sometimes appeared to treat it all as a great adventure that, if opportunity came, he wouldn't mind repeating. At night they sometimes played Scrabble, sometimes watched television, sometimes drove in for a beer at Franz's Glen. It was not such a bad time. The newspaper sent out a reporter and Harvey was written up again, the lead story, and Grace clipped the piece and pasted it into a scrapbook. She had a scrapbook for Harvey and another for Perry. Harvey's was nearly full. She said she was keeping them for her old age and for her children when they came. In town, everyone asked about Harvey, raved about the newspaper article. There were pictures of Harvey and Perry and Grace and the old house.

"It's a pack of lies," said Harvey.

"It says you're a hero. See here?"

"True, true enough," he said. "But it's still a pack of lies. I'm gonna sue and retire to Tibet. I've always wanted to retire to Tibet. You two can visit me. How does that sound? I'll have you flown out. I'll sue them for every penny."

"It calls you a hero," Grace said. "Look at that. You're a hero."

"That's the only truth in the whole article."

"It says you're fondly remembered by everyone in town. Look, it's got Herb Wolff saying what a fine fellow you are. And Bishop Markham and the mayor. It says the mayor's going to give you a parade."

"Should hope so. My God. How many heroes does one town need before they fork over a few parades? I should hope so. Maybe I won't sue if they fork over a nice parade. Does it say the hero lost his eye?"

"No," Grace said. "It says you were badly wounded and that you served your community and country and everything."

Harvey had his stocking feet near the fire. He was lying on the floor, head on a pillow. "I don't know," he said. "This is some ticklish decision. I'll have to get myself a crooked lawyer. I don't know. Suing is always ticklish, you know. Maybe I'll just accept the parade and sordid apologies. A tough decision. What do you think? Tibet sounds awfully good, doesn't it? Or maybe Africa. A hundred thousand could take us a long way. A trip to Africa, small enough price for a pack of lies. Let's have a beer. Let's drink to Jud's parade, what do you say?"

Harvey's face was red by the fire. It was relaxing time, after-supper time, and they drank beer and played Scrabble.

In a while, Harvey got up and went outside. Perry knew where he was going. An hour later, Harvey was still in the bomb shelter.

Through July, they stayed close to the house. Harvey settled himself into the upstairs bedroom, sleeping late, sometimes walking alone into the woods.

There was no rain.

They stayed close to the house, but with Harvey there was a new sense of motion, energy that seemed to bundle and gather. At night Perry sometimes heard him through the old timbers, pacing upstairs, moving things, flushing the toilet, going out to sit in the bomb shelter. They stayed close to the house and surrounding woods. Perry would drive in to work, roll up the blinds, daydream, drive home. He didn't see anything of Addie. She was awfully young anyway.

Harvey talked about Africa and Nassau, talked on and on. He talked about fishing and the woods and the old days with their father. He talked about buying a sailboat and sailing the Mediterranean with a locker full of food and drink, getting a tan, getting healthy, enjoying things, having some adventures. He talked about buying a house in Alaska. Or Boston or Miami or Las Vegas or Berlin or Australia, jumbling them all together sometimes, getting red and eager.

"We've got to get out and really see these woods," he said one Saturday. "Seriously. Do you realize these woods are the best left in the entire country? Seriously. Lord knows how long they'll last. You've got to get deep into them. None of this piddling around on the outskirts, you've got to get right in. When you start to think about it, there just isn't a lot of forest left any-more. We ought to go, you and me."

"Not me, Harv. Mosquitoes and all that. You know how I hate mosquitoes."

Harvey made a face. "Some day it's going to be maggots. Think about old Jud. All he's got to look forward to is worms and maggots. Seriously. We could go deep into the woods. Bring backpacks and make a trip out of it. I can show you some of the places the old man took me." He picked up steam. "I mean, seriously. You can't believe how wild it is once you get a way in. Nothing but trees and lakes. Wild is the wrong word. What's the word?"

"Nasty."

"Wild."

"Bugs."

"Then we'll go this winter. How's that? You won't find mos-quitoes in the winter. I'll guarantee it."

"Snow."

"You don't like snow? What the devil's wrong with some snow? God's own stuff. Clean and pretty and white. Beautiful stuff. God's own stuff."

"Snow, cold, freeze. They go together. They give me the creeps. Why don't we go down to Iowa for a nice vacation? That sounds better. We can visit Grace's folks and have a fine time."

"Iowa," Harvey said with scorn. "Some adventure. What we need is a good adventure."

"I have an adventure," Perry said. "I'm a pioneer in this town. Scratching for a living, married, trying to help a bunch of crazy farmers grow corn in the woods, living in my father's house. That's an adventure."

"Curses to you."

"Ha."

"Damns and darns."

"Sorry."

"We'll go to Africa then," Harvey said. "Off to Africa. Do you have a problem with Africa?"

"I suppose not. More bugs. Tigers and lions and cannibals. Minor stuff. Do you know anything about Africa, Harv?"

"I'll learn. I learned about My Khe. I can learn about Africa."

"My Khe. Is that in Africa?"

"My Khe is a place in Asia," Harvey said. "Asia, Africa, Australia, Alaska. The big A's. Adventure, the big A."

"You'll forget yourself, Harv. Let's go see about Grace's supper."

"Grace is such a good sort."

"Come on."

"And the Arrowhead, another big A. You have to think about all this stuff. When you think about it, it's awfully interesting. You have to think about all the adventurous places that go back to the first letter of our alphabet. Think of Afghanistan. Think of Algiers and Atlantis and Allentown. Aruba and Athens. Athens, Lordy. I'd love to go to Athens. We ought to go. Just pull out of this burg and go."

Grace came to the porch.

"You're really an extraordinary sort," Harvey said. "You must be American."

"Through and through," she laughed. "Come have supper."

"Full-breasted American, I like that. You don't see many full-breasted Americans in Africa. Will you go to Africa with us?"

"Oh, yes. I'll start saving for it."

"You have to start talking my brother into it. Paul is very down on Africa. Paul is actually very down on the big A, you know. He didn't pay attention as a kid. Didn't listen to the old man, and look where it's got him. Doesn't respect the big A! Grace, you'll have to persuade him to join us. Otherwise, well, we'll run off together, how's that? We'll capture inchworms. Have 'em stuffed and mounted on the walls. Brother Paul loves stuffed inchworms and all other of God's bugs. Don't you? Sure. Brother Paul is actually quite religious. Learned it from the old man, right?"

"Sure."

"Just like you loved the old man, right?"

"Yeah."

"Let's eat," Grace said.

She guided them inside, lit candles and snapped out the lights. She served supper.

"Inchworms!" said Harvey. "My God, how did you know? My favorite."

Afterwards Harvey wanted to go into town. Grace stayed home, Perry drove. Harvey was already tight, drinking beer from an aluminium can. It was a clear night, and the sky was high and the headlights lit a narrow tunnel through the woods. Along the road there were crickets and mosquitoes.

"I'm home," Harvey said.

"Sure."

"I am. I'm really home."

The town was small, a few quiet campfires in the fog, and the forest grew everywhere, to the edge of town, into the vacant lots, on to lawns, brush and high pine. Perry drove around the sawmill hub and out to Franz's Glen. Cars and pickup trucks filled the parking lot. "I'm home, all right," Harvey said. "Make me behave."

"I will."

"What the hell do I say?"

"Tell them you're a hero."

"Perfect!" Harvey grinned and mashed the aluminium can in his hands. "Just like the old days."

"Sure."

"Everything's the same, right?"

"Exactly."

The tavern was crowded. Addie was there. She was with a group of young people, young to Perry. On the floors there was red sawdust and spilt beer.

Addie saw them and waved.

"Same place," said Harvey.

"Never changes."

A Hamms sign revolved behind the bar. In the corner a jukebox was playing loud music, and Addie was dancing with a stupid-looking boy. She was barefoot. Everyone was happy. The old men sat at the bar in brown cotton pants and flannel shirts buttoned at the wrists, and the kids were all at Addie's table, and others sat at the tables and booths, a middle group of married people, the in-betweens and stalwarts. The jukebox was very loud.

"It's the same," Harvey grinned. "This is a very lecherous place. Don't ever let your kids come here."

"Right." Perry watched Addie dance. She was a fine dancer. She smiled while she danced and he liked that. He didn't care much for the fellow she danced with. No matter, though. Addie waved again and Perry grinned and waved back, and a young waitress with a beehive hairdo brought them tall bottles of beer. Harvey took her hand and told her she had a lot of class.

"Perfectly exquisite," Harvey said when she left. "Very tight-assed and exquisite. Someday she'll be a virgin, I'm sure." His face was turning red.

"Awfully young, Harv."

"I'm young. Who says *I'm* not young?"

Addie was dancing with a new partner. The place was noisy, Saturday night. She held her sandals while she danced. Bishop Markham and Herb Wolff and another fellow were playing pinball machines under a giant walleye that hung on a wall.

Harvey asked the waitress to sit down.

"We're having a great homecoming party," he said, "and you have to join us. Really. You're a very classy girl, you know. Exquisite and quite classy."

She was very young. She had no expression. She was somebody's daughter. "I seen your picture in the papers," she said, staring at his bad eye.

"Ah, and very observant, too. Classy and observant."

"I seen your picture," she said. "Who are you anyhow?"

"A dentist," Harvey smiled. "This is my assistant Dr. Watson. We pull teeth. I might add that we do a very classy job of it, cut rate. Two for a buck. You might have seen our ads in the paper."

"Prob'ly," the waitress said.

"So," Harvey smiled. "Why don't you just sit with us awhile and tell us your life history. I'm sure it's classy."

"Can't," she said. She gave his bad eye a last look and wiggled towards the bar.

They sat and drank the beers and watched the groups move about. Perry cleaned his glasses. The jukebox kept playing and the place was loud with bottles and music.

"Hey, it's Harvey! Hey, Harvey, for Christ sake!"

It was Bishop Markham. Herb Wolff trailed after him, both of them grinning. They shook Harvey's hand, and Bishop beamed and ordered beers all around.

"Where the blazes you been hiding, boy?"

"Here and there and nowhere."

"Sonofagun! Well, let me say we're proud of you," said Bishop, holding up his glass. "Really proud. *Really*. You've heard it before and you'll hear it again, we're proud." Bishop wore a bow tie and crew cut. "You really made it, Harvey. And you look like a million bucks. Seriously. Doesn't he look good?"

Wolff nodded fiercely. "He looks terrific. You look absolutely terrific, Harv. By God, I'd say you look like a million bucks."

Addie was still dancing, a slow number. Her new partner had red hair. Her face was in his red hair.

"Crummy war," Bishop was saying, "but you did yourself proud, Harvey. I mean it. A goddamn war hero! I remember . . ." and he talked about Harvey's football days. Bishop was a classmate of Perry's. Now he sold life insurance and real estate and sat on the Chamber of Commerce and the draft board and chaired the Kiwanis Club. He loved to talk.

Perry went outside for air. When he returned, Bishop Markham and Wolff and the others were playing the pinball game. Harvey was with the young waitress. The place was frantic and loud. Addie was still with her crowd, they were all dancing. He stood alone until the music ended and Addie came up.

"Hey," she said. Her face was brown and wet. "Not awfully fond of dancing, are you?"

"No. Where did you get all those jolly young friends?"

"Oh, them. They're all right. The whole lot is from Silver Bay and they love to dance. Franz is going to play his accordion and we're all going to dance polkas."

"Wonderful."

"Sure."

"I saw you at the lake," he said.

"Ah," she smiled. "Yes. I waved. Did you see my wave?"

"I saw."

"You were playing a peeping tom, weren't you? You were out there spying."

"I happened along."

Addie took his arm.

"How's the dancing?"

"It's okay. You haven't been in the library. You're going to go illiterate. I've been saving all these books for you."

"I haven't felt much like reading. I don't know."

She leaned against him. "I've been drinking, Paul. I have to go to my friends. I'll make an excuse and come to your table." She turned, jerked a thumb towards Harvey. "Is that your brother the war hero? He looks like some fine war hero."

"That's him."

"He must be a pirate. He looks like a pirate."

"I guess he does."

"All right," she said. "You hang tight. I'll make my excuses and come to your table. But you can't feel my legs and you have to promise to dance the polkas. You promise?" She released his arm and it felt red where she'd been holding it. The tavern was thumping. "And you must stop spying," she said.

"Oh, it's not . . ."

"Promise?"

"Sure."

"I'll hurry over."

Harvey was wooing his young waitress. He was getting drunk and the girl watched him carefully.

"Hey, Paul! You met my classy friend, Linda?"

"Lorna."

"Lorna, Linda, no matter. Have I told anyone how classy you are? Imagine finding a classy person such as yourself in such an unclassy part of the world. Imagine that. I'm boggled by it. Paul, aren't you boggled by all the classy people you meet in unclassy places?"

"Always." Addie was still talking with her young friends. She had her hands on her hips, palms in. It was her odd way of standing, her pelvis forward and her eyes black and bright. Sometimes her eyes looked Indian, sometimes Asian, and she wore a white scarf on her hair. She wore sandals and white shorts.

"This is Linda," Harvey said. "Linda's going to get us more beer."

"Lorna," she whined. Her brown hair was strung in a great nest towards the rafters.

"Linda, Lorna. Something like that. Am I close?"

"Lorna."

"Yes, that's it. And this is my brother. Together we're a classy group, don't you think? My brother is my assistant, you know. He thinks I don't behave sometimes. He keeps me reined in, so to speak. Isn't that right, brother? I'm a quite famous and reputable dentist."

"I hate dentists," the girl said.

Her mouth snapped shut. She snuffed out a cigarette.

Harvey kept after her. "Don't take it wrong now. You're classy. It's just the teeth. Here, open up." He touched her lips with a finger. "Come on, honey, open up. That's it."

Tentatively, the girl's mouth opened. Harvey touched her front teeth. Her eyes rolled down. She held an unlit cigarette in one hand.

"Not so classy in here," said Harvey. "We'll need some time. Atta girl, hold still now. See here, Paul? Cap this baby. Build a bridge here."

"Stop it," Lorna grunted. She spoke between her teeth, holding them bared, but Harvey had her by the neck, craning over and pivoting.

"Easy does it," Harvey purred. "Ack! These things. Have to yank 'em, no question. Then drill a nice hole right . . . here . . . and do a canal job on the nerve, no problem. Open up now. What do you think, doctor?"

Harvey kept after the girl. She had a great red mouth.

"Infected," Harvey said solemnly. "Right here. Does this hurt?" The girl squealed and her cigarette rolled to the floor. "Ha! Infected, all right. No doubt about it. A very infectious young lady. Hoof and mouth, I suspect."

"Take it easy," Perry said.

"And these molars, my Lord! Look at 'em. All rotten and infected. Open up now."

"That's enough," Perry said.

"Ha." Harvey held her mouth open. "I must have a beer. Will you get me a beer, young lady?"

The girl fiercely nodded.

"All right then. And will you stop by on Tuesday? Make an appointment with my assistant here?"

The girl nodded.

"Very well then. Very well. Just bring me my beer." He released her and the girl went for the bar.

"She loves me," Harvey grinned.

"You were a little rough."

"She loves me. You see?" He waved and the girl waved back. "You see?"

"All right."

"You see?"

Someone unplugged the juke box.

"Franzie!" Harvey got up and clapped. "Nothing ever changes."

"Getting older."

Everyone started clapping. Franz came out in knickers and a hiking cap. A monstrous accordion was strapped around his neck. "What you wanna hear?" he called and everybody kept clapping, so he smiled and played a song and everybody got up to dance polkas. The crowd whooped and Perry leaned back, feeling swallowed in all the fun. Addie was there in the center of the crowd, dancing with one of the Silver Bay boys, and the wood floor and walls bounced and the crowd whooped and stomped and the room was brightly lighted. The young waitress took Harvey to the dance floor. Everyone cheered him and Harvey did a deep bow.

Perry stepped outside.

He stood very still. Music strained like lost Old World through the walls and rose to the forest and floated away in a single resonant chord that slowly swallowed itself. He could not get into it. He lit a cigarette. Old Addie, he thought. Addie could get into it.

He stood quietly. In the grass there were crickets and the air was warm and soggy. Down the road, out of sight, the lights of the town were eaten by fog. Old Addie. He smelled methane and ammonia. Mosquitoes, june bugs. He urinated against the foundation of the old tavern and Bishop Markham came out and peed beside him. "That Harvey is some rascal," Bishop said.

"That he is."

"He's having a helluva time. No bitterness there. Wolff was worried he'd be bitter."

"Not Harv."

"A hard charger."

"That he is."

Markham went inside and Perry smoked another cigarette, listened to the music. He flipped his butt into the gravel parking lot and went through the doors.

Addie waved. A Silver Bay buck had her tight, they were reeling, half polka and half two-step, *Du, Du, liebst mir im Herzen, Du, Du, liebst mir im Sinn, Du, Du* . . . the Black Forest, the Magic Forest, back and forth, the great campfire, tribal rhythms. Perry watched them all dance. Addie was hot and wet and brown. There were red callouses on her heels where the sandal straps rubbed.

"Come on," she called, "dance, dance."

He grinned, shook his head. He was a little drunk.

"Dance!" Harvey called.

Bishop Markham hollered something and waved. Herb Wolff, holding a big woman, also waved. Franz beamed and played the accordion.

When the song ended, everyone clapped and Addie's friends thumped the accordion player and bought him a beer.

Harvey sat down. It was too noisy to talk and they drank their beers and watched people.

In a while, Addie joined them. She could be very gay.

"You should dance more," she said, sitting down, "It makes everyone happy when they dance. Is this your hero brother?"

"This is the monster."

"You look something like a pirate. Do you know what the reason is?"

"Everyone says that."

"This is Addie."

"She looks like a bloody Indian."

"Everyone says that, too. Actually I'm from New Guinea."

"Really? No shit? I plan to go there someday."

"Look up my relatives," she said.

Perry found himself grinning. "Addie works in the library. She's a kind of assistant librarian or something. She saves all the good books for me." He wrapped his hands around the bottle and squeezed. It was a great blur.

"You look just like an Indian," Harvey said. "Sure you're not Indian? You could make a very classy Indian."

"Sure," she said.

"She is part Indian, Harv."

Addie was very gay. She talked about dancing and swimming and people. Harvey became quiet. Franz came out again with his accordion and Harvey asked her to dance and Perry sat alone and watched them, and when they came back he felt tired.

"You *must* learn to dance," she said. "A great picker-upper. All my friends have to dance." Addie moved beside him. "Here, I'll show you how. You can't be watching all the time, come on. I'll show you a tricky polka."

He put his glasses on the table. It was a long, exhausting dance. He was out of shape. Over her shoulder, he saw Harvey watching.

Afterwards he went outside to pee. It was a ritual that the men peed outside and the women peed in the women's room. He breathed some fresh air.

Inside again, Harvey and Addie were dancing. The Hamms beer sign was revolving. She was bright and fun and she danced on her heels. He got a beer and watched Harvey and Addie and Bishop Markham and the others.

Jud Harmor came in, took a stool at the end of the bar, refused a beer, and pulled his straw hat down. People gave him lots of room.

Harvey held Addie, whooping on the dance floor, and the old timbers were rocking.

When the dance ended, the young waitress took Harvey back to the floor.

Addie was wet and smiling.

"He's a real pirate," she said. "He can dance."

"I was watching."

She touched his arm. "Peeping Paul."

"Yeah. Ol' peeping Paul peeped a peck of pickled trouble."

"So clever."

"Would you like a beer?"

"Here, let's us sit down," she said.

They took a corner booth. Addie watched Harvey and the beehived waitress dance. "He *is* a fine dancer," she said.

"Sure."

"Tell me about your brother the pirate."

"There's nothing to tell. He's a nice guy. Everybody says that. He's a rascal and a scamp."

"A pirate!"

"I guess so."

Addie was barefoot. She put her sandals on the table.

"There's nothing like a pirate to brighten things up. Why isn't Grace here? You should have brought Grace. Then we would have been a group, and groups are always more fun. What happened to his eye?"

"He was wounded."

"Well, I know that. How did it happen?"

Perry shrugged. He had a tight fever. "The telegrams just said he'd been wounded, I don't know. He's all right now. He hasn't said anything about it."

"That's silly. I'll drag it out of him then. I'm good at that. I'll drag out the whole gruesome story and make him feel all better about it."

"You're the one to do it, Addie."

"Want to dance with me?"

"Not that. Not now, I'm pretty tipsy."

"Such a pirate."

"Yeah."

"Let's dance. That'll make it better." She got up and held his arm.

"Don't be so happy."

"I'm sorry."

"Everything gets better, you know."

"Let's dance then."

"I'll dance barefoot."

"Spectacular, Addie."

"Hmmm." She removed his glasses. "There, how's that?" Very slowly, she pulled him up. "Very tribal, don't you think? Firewater and campfires and wild rhubarb, all erotic."

"Stop that."

"Don't be silly. You should be barefoot, too."

She was lean and athletic.

"Isn't this a nice song? Very erotic, isn't it? Don't step on my bare feet."

"Jesus."

"Isn't this better now?"

"It's fine. I'm pretty hot."

"Dance closer. You don't have to be so stiff. That's better. See how? One, two, three. One, two, three. Isn't it nice? Think of campfires and firewater."

The accordion music was slow and swaying, deep forest. People were singing.

"Don't you like me?"

"Yes," he said.

"And isn't it nice to dance a little?"

He saw Jud Harmor watching. Jud smirked, raised his hat.

It was a long slow dance.

"We should all go for a swim. Is that your brother's girlfriend?"

"Are you looking at them? I thought you were dreaming with your eyes closed."

She laughed. "I was dreaming. Is that his girl friend?"

"Her name is Linda or Lorna or something. She's a patient of his."

"We should all go swimming."

She was light and the skin was tight across her shoulders.

"We really should go for a swim now," Addie said. "Wouldn't that be good?"

"I have to go home."

"Yes," she said. "There's always that, isn't there?"

In town, the dry spell was all they talked about. The air was crisp and inchworms were eating up the forest. At night, trying to sleep, Perry heard them munching with the sound of rainfall. But it did not rain. The days were hot and dry, and it did not rain.

It kept him busy. Meager to begin with, the corn crops were baked away. One by one, the farmers slipped into the office, shamed, filled out their loss statements and applied for loans. On the highway into town, the hands of the fire danger clock pointed to high noon: Forest Service firefighters checked into the U-Rest Motel, arriving in green trucks and jeeps. The town turned out to watch them arrive. People were excited. In the drugstore, they swapped stories about earlier fires. It was suspenseful and important. Heat killed the mosquitoes. It killed the grass on Perry's lawn. A dog dropped dead on the church steps. Everyone talked about it: the town was built of timber, white pine that had been cut and sawed and planed and notched and molded, hammered together and lifted up and painted bright. The paint was peeling. The forest crept up to the town and into the parks and on to the lawns and kept going, and if the forest burned, then the town burned, too. There was no distinguishing it.

Perry watched the excited faces through his office window. The twelve-man fire brigade was put on alert.

"You gotta sign up," Wolff insisted. "Your ass burns with the rest of us, you know."

"Not me, Herb. I'll watch it from the window."

"Harvey joined up."

'Harvey's good for that.'

"Geez," Wolff prodded, "you don't join anything around here. You ought to show a little more citizenship."

In late July a Forest Service agent stopped at the office. The skin was black and flaky in the hollows of his face. He wore a silver badge. He was solemn. He told Perry they were moving in another crew of firefighters. "Doesn't look good," he said. "One spark, that's all it'd take. I'm not kidding." He told Perry they worked for the same boss—"Good old Uncle Sam, the USDA.

We're going to have to use your office for a headquarters, just till this thing blows over."

Perry turned over the keys. He left quickly. He celebrated with a beer, drove home and went to bed.

Grace worked hard on the garden, watering the soil, protecting the tomatoes and green beans, fed them fertilizer, cooed to them. And she taught Sunday school.

Harvey prepared in other ways. He cleaned out the bomb shelter, throwing away all the rakes and hunks of hose and old furniture Perry had stored there. He swept the shelter down, hosed it out, repaired the air filter, filled the water tank, put in a new store of sheets and blankets and pillows.

That July was hot. There was small-town suspense.

Perry stayed away from the bomb shelter. He didn't say so to Harvey, but he thought the place dark and depressing and buried away.

"The old man wasn't so crazy after all," Harvey kept saying.

"Right," Perry said.

"You don't have to be so damn arrogant about it."

"I'm not."

"He wasn't dumb or crazy. You don't have to smirk."

"I'm not smirking, Harv. It's a solid bomb shelter."

The floor was laid in massive tumulary stones. The air was musty. Tepid air, a moldering preservation. The past and extended future. A stack of magazines lay in one corner. There were books and games, a typewriter, liquor and candies and soap. Boxes of canned food were stacked to the ceiling. There were cots and flashlights and folding chairs, candles and rope and wire, tools and cigarettes and matches, foul air, electric lights connected to a small generator, string and blankets, paper and silverware and pots and plates and survival gear.

Harvey's eye shined. "We could last it out in here."

"What?"

Harvey shrugged.

Gleaming, the streets were white metal.

Thursday, the last day of July.

There were jeeps and trucks and firefighters, the streets were fizzing with people, everyone was waiting.

It was Harvey's birthday. Grace held the party on the lawn.

When the sun faded, Perry turned on the spotlights and lit battery-powered lanterns in the trees. Then the guests arrived. Harvey received them in front of his bomb shelter. He drank beer from a paper cup. The sky was changing. Headlights flowed up the lane. Lantern shadows, sky shadows. The wind was changing. The party comers moved like electricity through the night, trooped in bearing gifts and loaves of bread, hot dishes, meat loaves. Old people and young people. Bishop Markham brought his wife and children. Reverend Stenberg brought candlesticks. Hot beans, hot corn, fruit salad, biscuits, burgers, ham and chops, baked potatoes, warm salted butter, pies, a birthday party. The ladies of Damascus Lutheran brought plates and tablecloths, their husbands carried ice. The sky was changing. The headlights kept coming up the lane, new voices. High above, in the highest depths, the sky budded new stars and the patterns developed. Herb Wolff brought his father, pushing him in a wheelchair. The forest was full. Jud Harmor came in his pickup and straw hat and talked about the war and garbage. Addie came alone. Grace was busy and happy. There was potato salad and talk about the dry spell. It was a birthday picnic, and the evening was dark and the lanterns played on the trees. Town shadows flowed about his yard. Addie was there. Now and then he saw her passing by a lantern. "Geronimo!" wailed Jud Harmor. Grace was happy. She served people's plates and cut the birthday cake. She fixed a smile on the festivities and held Perry's hand and bustled for paper cups. She was breathless and soft. She kissed him. "Isn't it nice? Everyone's here."

"You invited them. You're the attraction."

"It's so nice. Is Harvey enjoying it?"

"I think so," Perry said. Harvey was sitting on the bomb shelter with Addie.

There were forms and shadows and the sky was changing.

"Hey, Paul."

Perry walked to the shelter, head down.

"Addie says you have a secret."

Addie giggled. "Hop up here, Paul. It's a fine place to watch the party."

"Tell me the great secret," Harvey said.

"There's no secret. Tell him, Addie."

Addie giggled and took his arm. The party seemed far away. The townspeople were silhouettes and old shadows.

"What's this great and wonderful secret?" Harvey demanded.

"Nothing. I swear. Tell him it's nothing, Addie."

"If we told our secret, we would die and go to hell. That's what happens when people tell their secrets. People must always keep all their secrets secret, if you follow me."

"Tell me," Harvey said.

Addie giggled. She still held Perry's arm. "Okay," she said. "But first you tell us your secret, Harvey. Tell us how you hurt your eye, all the gory stuff."

Again the party poised.

"Nothing," Harvey said softly.

"Tell us all about the eye, Harvey. And tell us how you were a war hero."

"Nothing."

"Okay, then I'll just have to tell you the sad facts," Addie laughed. "You see, Paul and I are running away together. To the badlands of South Dakota."

Harvey stared at her. He was a bit drunk.

"Yes," she said. "We're going to Rapid City or Deadwood. I'll sell Indian carvings and Paul will . . . I don't know what Paul will do. Anyway, that's the secret. We've been planning it for ages."

"Rapid City," Harvey muttered.

"Isn't that a fine secret? Now you promised. Tell us about your eye."

"Crap."

"What? What's that? Harvey, now you promised."

"This is a bunch of crap."

"It's a fine secret," Addie teased.

"I'm going to Africa," he said.

Addie shrugged and giggled. "Don't be a silly. It wouldn't be the same at all. Who'll buy Indian carvings in Africa?" She giggled and there was new movement around them, in the air and woods. It stopped. It became quiet and for the first time Perry felt the transformation. The air was soggy.

"Wouldn't touch the badlands," Harvey muttered.

"It's actually quite clean in the badlands," said Addie. "Isn't it" She touched Perry's arm.

"Sterile," he said.

"See? Ha! Paul's taking me there."

"I don't believe it."

Addie moaned. "Tell him, Paul."

"Never."

"Oh, you will. Tell him you will."

"I won't. Let's go back to the party."

"You're both silly," Addie said. She turned to Harvey. "I swear he promised."

"Never."

"Betrayed," she giggled.

Perry left them. The new forest motion was back. And there was sound. The groups were mingling. Like compounds forming, electrons splitting and taking new orbits, shared spheres. From somewhere, music was coming on to the lawn, the lanterns were swaying. Bishop Markham was lecturing, Jud Harmor was squinting towards the sky. There was a hum in the forest. Perry wondered if old Jud felt it, or heard it.

He watched Grace move through the crowds. It was a fine big party, she was good at it. She listened to people. She wore dresses; it wasn't often she wasn't in a dress: in the garden, walking, combing her hair out. She wormed through the crowd and hooked his arm. "Hungry?" He shook his head. "You aren't drunk?"

"Nope. Don't always ask that."

'A nice party, isn't it?' She was whispering.

"Yeah. You did a nice job."

"Be nice then. Talk to people," she whispered.

"Okay."

"You aren't sick?"

"I'm fine, hon." He pulled free and held a paper plate that leaked potato salad. "I'm okay, really. How are all your lovely church friends? How's the Reverend Stenberg?"

"Stop that. He's a nice man."

"I know it. I'm sorry." He glanced over at the bomb shelter. Some luck, he thought. He rambled the yard and listened while people told him about things.

"A heat storm."

"What?"

It was Jud. His hat was pushed back. "A heat storm," he said. "Just a heat storm."

People began looking up.

"Rain," said Bishop Markham. "It's rain, all right." Bishop was GOP, Jud was Democratic-Farmer-Labor.

"Shit," Jud cackled. He shook his head and winked at Perry. "Guess I know a heat storm when I see it."

The first cool air came in one breath, and a dark splotch in the sky spread out, sliding down and out like a vast sheath or covering or mask. "Heat storm," said old Jud. He pulled his hat down to settle it. People stood with hands on hips to watch. Lars Nielson hustled his family to the car and drove away.

Others began to leave.

"It's a heat storm all right," said Jud Harmor. There was a single long wind and the lanterns blew horizontal. Jud's face was turned up. "I can see it," he said.

The wind died, turned warm, then turned cold, then turned warm again. Headlights were snapping on.

"Where's Harvey?" Grace was beside him. "People are leaving, he should be here."

The wind whipped the tablecloths.

People rushed for their cars. Jud Harmor stood alone, gazing at the sky with hands on hips. The wind was rushing to Lake Superior. Motors and headlights and opalescent beacons were flaring. Perry carried things inside, rushing, returned for armloads of bottles and cups and plastic forks, papers and bottle openers, party trash, wrappings and containers and leftover birthday cake.

"Where's Harvey?" someone hollered.

Perry folded up the chairs and carried them inside, stacked them on the porch. "Where the devil is Harvey?"

"Heat storm, heat storm," Jud Harmor chanted. He was now in a lawn chair, his straw hat gone. His bony face was sawed into a million upward-thrust planes. his eyes were pointed to the sky. "Lo," he chanted, "a heat storm. Watch the mother come."

Perry touched his shoulder. "Better be moving on, Jud. She's coming in fast."

The old man cackled. "Nothin' but a miserable heat storm. Can't see what all this fuss is. You won't see but a heat storm." Lightning flashed and the old man's skull shined like a jewel.

"Okay, Jud."

Grace came out wearing a sweater. She was hugging herself. "Where's Harvey?"

The old mayor cackled. "Takin' target practice. You two gotta watch that boy. Ha, ha!" He started to cough.

Perry went to the shelter. Some rotten luck. Rusty old jealousy. The emotion surprised him. He climbed the bomb shelter and stood on its roof. The wind was hard. Lightning showered in big fluffy puffs, and through the forest, looking out to Route 18, he saw the parade of retreating taillights winding towards Sawmill Landing. He called out and listened and heard a soft answer. Some rotten miserable awful luck, he thought.

Inside the concrete shelter, lanterns swung from the ceiling and the old generator was going.

"Ha! Not so crazy after all!" Harvey was grinning, rocking in the old man's discarded rocking chair. He faced a cement wall. Addie lay on a cot. The shelter was strangely warm and livable. "Beginning to worry for you," Harvey said. "I was just telling Addie how worried I was. Thought you got caught in it. Nuclear war, you know. You got to be careful. Got to be careful 'cause that fallout is powerful stuff. Rots your testicles off."

Addie chuckled.

"Just a heat storm, Jud says."

"Ha! Old Jud doesn't have to worry about his testicles."

Grace came in smiling, carrying the birthday cake. She handed out pieces on scallop-edged napkins.

"An end-of-the-world party," Harvey said happily. He was loud. "Can't think of a better place for it, can't imagine nicer people to end the world with. Too bad the old man's not here."

"It's quiet outside," said Grace.

"Ah," Harvey said. "The solemn silence. The silent solemnity." He stared at Perry. "Sure you want to stay, brother? Don't remember you giving me much help building this thing. Sure you want to stay?"

Perry shrugged. Grace cut more cake and the lanterns dangled from the ceiling.

"It's just a heat storm, Harv."

"Ha. Tell that to your testicles. Just ask the buggers. See what *they* say."

"Let's just all go outside."

"And be doomed?"

Gently, Grace bent over Harvey, felt his forehead. "You've a fever. Are you sick?" She inspected his face, frowning. The lanterns dangled from the ceiling.

"He's just a silly pirate," Addie said.

Harvey stood up. He was loud. "Right! Absolutely right. Addie, that Addie's something, isn't she? When all this blows over and the streets are safe again, then I'm taking Addie to the swamps of New Guinea. I've decided." He struck a pose that could have meant anything. Addie laughed. "Yes, I've decided. We'll begin a new life. Yes. Yes, we'll plant seed, new seeds, seeds that I've prudently set aside for just such catastrophes. I have many seeds. A bull, you know. Yes. Yes, we'll sail on a blighted sea for a new land, we'll arrive . . . arrive, so to speak and so on, arrive on a new and dawning day, again so to speak, and Addie will make Indian carvings, reminders to our hordes of forthcoming descendants, and I . . . yes, I'll search the jungles for food and shelter and primitive niceties, and we'll start afresh."

"You're drunk," Grace said.

"Or perhaps Africa," said Addie, who seemed to be enjoying it. "You haven't forgotten Africa?"

"Don't egg him on."

The bomb shelter was very warm, concrete hot, and the lanterns were swinging.

"Africa," Harvey stammered. "Ah, yes. Where are we going?"

"Outside," Perry said.

Harvey stared. "Think of your *testicles*, man."

Addie helped with him. They led him outside.

"The old man wasn't so crazy, you know. Not all that bloody crazy. Do we have a beer?"

"Gallons."

"Thank God for that."

"Can you walk?"

"Can I *walk*? Am I mad? What bloody nonsense. A time of national emergency and of course I can walk. I can walk, be damned! A beer." Harvey threw an arm around Addie's brown shoulder.

They came out of the bomb shelter.

Mammoth clouds had stiffened over the forest, very high and well to the southwest. Tumbling, flopping like earth under a spade, swirling in, coalescing and darkening and fusing into a single expansive element over the forest.

Harvey sniffed the air. "Mustard gas. Jesus of Mercy, who would've thought they still had *mustard* gas?"

The promise was great.

There was certain rhythm.

Jud Harmor still sat in his lawn chair. His eyes were closed.

"Poor old Jud," Harvey muttered. "Stuff got to him . . . We must all now buck up. The end is coming and we shall go with class. A little class never hurt. Buck up, chaps. Let us mourn old Jud, a finer man, parades and all."

The clouds swirled high, a breathing, soft respiration. Harvey filled a paper cup with beer. "A toast to Jud! A finer man we could not find, a finer man . . ." Odors rose from the forest tissue, compounds of chlorophyll and wastes. Great cavities opened, steam rose from the leaves, the clouds tumbled high, vapors filled the forest, obscene smells of salamanders and pine. "The end is with us," chanted Harvey. "And the old man was not crazy at all." The clouds stiffened and swelled. Old Jud lay in the lawn chair, eyes closed as the clouds rolled towards Lake Superior, huge and threatening but refusing to rain. "Let us . . . let us mourn old Jud," Harvey was saying. "A free spirit. A false prophet. A free spirit, thank God, free, free at last, old Jud."

"Hush," Grace whispered. "He's sleeping."

"Ha! Aha, you'll see. You'll see. The fallout's got him, sure as hell. Look at him. Let's examine the old gent's *testicles*. Ha, *that*'ll tell the old tale."

"Just relax."

Perry brought out four chairs. They watched the clouds roll towards the great lake.

Jud suddenly sat up. He started cackling, raised his fist up. "What did I say?"

The air was hot.

Energy charged out of the clouds. The sky went wild. Thunder created a wind of its own.

"Marvelous," Addie breathed.

The clouds moved fast.

"Heat storm," Jud cackled. "What did I say?"

The storm tumbled over on itself, and there was no rain. Grace pulled her sweater tight. Addie lay back in her chair. Harvey was shivering. A slice of electricity shot like white ribbon from the clouds. "Marvelous," Addie murmured. Her eyes were black. The clouds tumbled and flopped, rushing eastwards, the lightning exploding in fluffs, the whole forest stopped. Grace whispered something. Addie's eyes were black. She was barefoot. Her feet were under her, her legs were dark. The sky crashed. Grace was whispering. He watched Addie. Her cheek-bones were high and shining. Asiatic, Indian, primitive, shining, upward looking, and the lightning flashed again, and her hair was long and back over her shoulders without knots or bows or curls. "We should be going in," Grace was whispering, but the heat storm thrashed in the forest, all around them, and the wind swept in hot, and Addie's eyes were lighted, and Grace whispered, "We should go inside." She whispered, "I'm cold, hon."

"What?"

"I'm cold."

He heard her. He curled an arm around her. She could embarrass him.

Slowly the storm rolled overhead, high like a battle far off. It rolled towards the east and left a clean night sky behind it. There was no rain.

Jud Harmor stood up. "Show's over," he announced. He'd found his straw hat. "I'll be going."

Harvey did not get up. His eyes were wide open to the sky.

Perry helped the old man to his truck. Jud climbed in and slammed the door. He leaned his head out. "Just a lousy heat storm," he said. "You gotta watch your brother. I think he's insane."

He lay there. The storm was over.

Restless, he got out of bed and went to the window. A light was burning in the bomb shelter. He showered, lay down again. "Sleep," he said. He tried not to think. Addie. It didn't matter. Grace was awake. She whispered something.

He got up, went to the bathroom and shaved. Then he dressed. He roamed about, restless, tried to read, sat at the kitchen table. Then he went outside. The crickets were back. The lawn chairs were empty. The bomb shelter light was off and everything was quiet. He followed the path to Pliney's Pond.

The smell could be awful. All in the mind. He sat on a rock. Addie and Harvey, the names rattled back and forth. The water was deep and quiet. The creature he'd met as a child. Pincers and black eyes attached by cords to the ganglia. A body shaped like a barber's electric clippers. And the deep-down pond, he remembered. Addie and Harvey. No matter. The place could stink. It was algaed and full of primitive organisms.

No matter, he was older now, he wasn't a kid, he had a wife and his father's house. His father had taken him to the pond to learn to swim. His father. Harvey had come, too. That had been another July, and they'd gone the three of them to Pliney's Pond and his father had said, "This is where you'll learn to swim. No back talk, just jump in." Perry remembered undressing slowly. "It stinks," he'd cried, going in. Mosquito eggs, crayfish, larvae, slime and june bugs, frogs and newts and snakes and toads and lizards, Indian shit and rot, and Harvey had gone in, too. Harvey had gone to the middle of the pond. "No back talk," the old man ordered, and Perry waded in, waded in and fell headlong into the stinking water, eyes in terror and sobs choked in sewage. Ash and sewage, he remembered it. Then the creature, its pincers and dangling black eyes, an inch from his face, a quarter-inch, a real monster closing in, and he'd sobbed, sucking in more of the thick water, and the creature came.

The pond did stink. There was no question. Addie and Harvey.

Perry sat on the rock. It didn't matter. The place was quiet, the forest grew to the edge of the pond, and the pond was quiet. He relaxed. Things could be put in perspective. That was what had to be done. He dipped into the pond and took out a handful of water and let it straight through his fingers. Harvey and Addie, some luck. The water left a black residue. It was late. It was always getting late. He decided it was time for reformation. Begin exercising. Eat less. He would be kind to Grace; she deserved it. He would be kind to Harvey. He would get involved, paint the house, go into the woods, go deep. He heard a loon. It was far off. It wasn't such a bad night. It was getting cool. Harvey was fine. Addie was fine; she was something else again. The way she walked, heels down. Grace was fine, too. The loon called again and he got up.

Things were always better. He brushed himself off, followed the path to the house. There were no lights. The bomb shelter crouched low in the yard. There were no lights anywhere.

He folded up the lawn chairs, carried them to the porch and stacked them. He was careful to be quiet. He looked up and smiled. The sky was surprisingly light, and there was a moon and many stars.

"Feel better?" Grace whispered.

"Yes. I had a walk."

The sheets were cool now, and Perry held her.

"Tired?"

"Hmmm, I was sleeping. Storm over?"

"All quiet. Getting nice out there."

"Rain."

"No. No rain yet. It'll come."

She whispered. "Your face is burnt."

"It's all right. I feel better. I don't know what gets into me."

"Let's put some cream on your face." She gently touched his nose. Perry took her hand. "You are a woman," he said. "Gee," she whispered. She got the cream from the nightstand. They undressed and Perry lay face up on the bed. He closed his eyes. He breathed easy. He felt the lotion on his chest. He did feel better. He breathed slowly. "What are you doing?"

"Putting lotion on you," she whispered. "Hold still now."

But he wasn't thinking. He was tired. Wings clipped by the old man. No bulls here. Rushing from nowhere to nowhere and learning to swim. "Just lie still now," she whispered. But he wasn't listening because the thick waters were against his ears. "Shhhhhh," she whispered, "does that feel good now? Lie still, lie still," part of the pond, soft as water. He concentrated, finally opening his eyes, and she smiled at him. She reached in the dark for a tissue and wiped him. "Such a fountain," she whispered.

"Come here."

"Can we have a baby someday?"

"Come here."

Soft as water. He tightened his arms, squeezing, and he held her and squeezed, all his energy, squeezed until she said to stop.

Elements

They called it a dying town. People were always saying it: Sawmill Landing won't last another decade.
But for all the talk, Perry never saw the death, only the shabby circumstances of the movements around him. It was a melancholia,
seeded in the elements, but he had no idea where it started. It
might have started with the Ice Age. Four glaciers advancing and
receding over the course of a million years, freezing, stinging with
crystalline cold, digging out boulders, ice a mile deep, a permanent
stillness. Then the Stone Age. Indians. First the Sioux, later the
Chippewa. In the basement of the town library there was a mu-
seum that housed all the relics: broadheads, pottery, clay pipes,
hides and drawings. Then the French, taking what they could. Then
the Swedes. The Swedes built houses. Pine planks, dirt floors, hard-
rock fireplaces. The Swedes hacked at the forest, broke their backs
and ploughs trying to turn the Arrowhead into corn-bearing land.

In 1854, the Chippewa ceded their timber and fish and
game for a few hundred square miles of reservation.

In 1856, the Swedes named their hamlet Rabisholm. Fourteen houses, a blacksmith, twenty-six horses, a stable and a store. That same year Minnesota became a state.

In 1857, the Germans came. And a few Dutch and the Finns.

In 1858, an Indian boy was hanged for intention to rape. In 1859, an Indian family was found frozen in the snow, dead of starvation before freezing. In 1860, two full-grown Indian males were shot dead while stealing corn from Ole Borg. In 1862, while the southern Sioux were going crazy with revenge, three Chippewa renegades slipped into Ole Borg's house and cracked his skull with a hatchet. The renegades were later captured by a cavalry troop dispatched from Fort Snelling. They were hanged until dead.

In 1863, the town celebrated its first Ole Borg Day.

In ten easy years, the Indians were gone, pushed north and west.

Perry learned about the hardships. Hardship was something the old man stressed. He learned that the Swedes broke ploughs on base rock, got robbed on prices, seeded soil meant for spruce and not corn, wore silent hard faces. They were blond. He learned that they left Sweden in famine and, in perfect irony, came to Minnesota just in time for more of the same: locusts and drought, fierce winter and boulders; they left bad soil for worse soil, rock for rock, pine for pine. In some miserable genetic cycle, they did not leave at all and they did not arrive.

The Germans came later. The Germans came late enough to see that their future was not in the land. Instead they opened taverns and a hardware store and an implement shop, taking the Swedes' money, extending credit, turning the bundle of tiny farms into a hamlet. Within a few years it became a predominantly German village, both in numbers and power, but the

Swedes still remained vital to the tight circle of economics, because without them there was no need for German shops. Old World rivalries persisted, and Perry heard the story often: In 1863 a meeting was convened to choose the village's soldiers for the war against slavery. No one understood the war, but everyone wanted to fight it. They hadn't heard how many were dying. At the meeting it was decided that only a few could go, and after hours of haggling the number was fixed at fourteen, a quarter of the able-bodied men. The Germans, citing their new predominance, insisted on supplying ten of the fourteen. The Swedes wanted the war party split equally, arguing that they'd been the first to settle the forest, that they had eight more corpses in the cemetery, and that their farming sustained the small community. In short, Perry's father had explained with relish, in short they were arguing about the right to die. "Well," the old man said, telling the story, "the Germans threatened to foreclose on two mortgages. Herb Wolff's great-grandfather was one of the bastards. Anyhow, the Swedes told them to go to hell, threatening to take their corn and trade into Two Harbors. So the krauts threatened to close down their shops. And the Swedes threatened to boycott the shops. And the krauts threatened no more credit. On and on. Well, next thing you know there's a scuffle and somebody knocks over a lamp and the meeting hall catches fire, threatening a forest fire, threatening everything. And that, if you see the point, that was the final threat."

"Yes," Perry had said.

"And what's the point?"

"A big forest fire. The end of the whole village."

"Exactly," the old man had crowed, opening his Bible. "The end of everything. The end of the world." His voice rang like an old bell.

In the end, a single young Swede went to the war and fought

with the Minnesota First at Gettysburg. He was buried in the Swedish half of the cemetery, solidifying the Scandinavians' grasp on the land, another root sunk deep in. For reprisal, the Germans convened a secret meeting and voted to change the name of the place from Rabisholm to New Köln. The Swedes simply ignored the vote, and until 1887 the village had two names and the matter was taken quite for granted.

In 1887, the timber companies moved in.

They built their sawmill on Dunkle Creek and named the place Sawmill Landing.

It became a logging town—a town now and not a village. Simple frame houses went up, each identical to the next with their wide porches and crawl spaces and stone fireplaces and up-stairs bedrooms. It became a company town. Using the sawmill as a hub, the timber companies laid the streets like spokes into the forest, seven spokes that radiated into the timberlands, and as the forest was cut and gutted, the spokes were simply ex-tended and the town expanded. Each spoke was given a name: Acorn Street, Larry's Lane, Moose Street, Apple Street, Broken Axle Road, Sawmill Street and Mainstreet.

For nearly thirty years the logging companies ran the town, and the population climbed over a thousand. A school was built. And a jail and a town hall. The timber companies tarred Main-street and cut a highway out to North Shore Drive. An under-taker set up shop. A railroad spur was laid, a depot was built, new wells were dug, a water tower went up. The timber compa-nies built a pulp mill and a planing mill, changed Ole Borg Day to Paul Bunyan Day, and, indirectly through the labors of their wage earners, paid for the construction of Damascus Lutheran Church. "That," Perry's father had said with a customary spit at progress, "that was the only decent thing."

The timber companies also brought a second wave of Finns

into Sawmill Landing. They were gaunt families, blank-eyed and harsh and disciplined by tundra spirits, wide foreheads and black eyes and strong arms. Among the new Finns was Perry's own grandfather.

The facts of Pehr Peri's life were as bare and brittle as the scattered bones of some ancient reptile. All that was known came from the memory of Perry's father and from a tiny packet of papers buried in the attic. Up to a point the story was typical. Pehr Peri was born in a fishing community north of Helsinki. At sixteen, for reasons unknown, he boarded a boat for America, spent a year of near starvation in Baltimore, worked his way west to St. Louis, then boarded another boat that took him up the Mississippi as far as Red Wing.

For the next five years, young Pehr Peri was swallowed in a dark succession of lumber camps and pine forests, gradually moving north with the advancing timber companies, working first as a shanty boy, later as a swarmer hacking branches from felled trees, and finally as a fully-fledged lumberjack. While the specific events of that lustrum were murky, it was probably the story of thousands like him: immigrants homesick for the Old World, hard winters, danger, relentless work, fistfights, mosquitoes and loneliness and barracks yarns, campfires and boredom, northern hardships, frontier trials. Whatever the specifics, Pehr Peri emerged at the age of twenty-two in a camp outside Sawmill Landing—tall and strong, virtually illiterate, speaking a hybrid of Finnish and English and Norwegian, unmarried. And the father of a young son.

Sometime during those dark five years, in circumstances that could only be imagined, the young Pehr Peri had spent enough time out of the cold to sire a son, to see it through birth and to take the child with him. It was never explained. The identity of the mother, as well as the means by which Peri gained custody of the boy, was never told. The only clue—a minor one—was that the child was baptized Pehr Lindstrom Peri, and it was assumed that the mysterious woman, wife or mistress or lover, belonged to one of nearly three hundred Lindstrom families scattered between Red Wing and Sawmill Landing. But it was never known. In customary and callous disregard for reminiscence, Pehr Peri raised the child as though he alone were responsible for its propagation, refusing to talk about the mother, ignoring the very fact of motherhood, an asexual northern temperament that excluded and eventually scorned things female. "I didn't have a mother," Perry's father once explained, "because I didn't need one."

For more than a year, Pehr Peri continued working the forests outside Sawmill Landing, leaving the child in the daytime care of assorted shanty boys, camp cooks or idlers. Then, in August of 1901, his right arm was crushed in an incident that again went unexplained. In one of the few scraps of paper he left behind, Peri referred to the accident as a "thing which happened," accepting the crushed arm as a timber wolf might accept a broken leg, without bitterness or remorse, burning eyes, a natural thing of the north. Hardship was to be expected. At any rate, Perry's grandfather was out of a job, saddled with a motherless child, crippled, stranded in a town that offered nothing but hard work. So he became a preacher.

Despite the contradictions and ironies—semi-literate, not a trace of prior religious zeal, barely able to speak English—Pehr Peri became a successful stump preacher, shuttling from camp to camp, traveling by foot with his young son and a secondhand Bible and a store of winter tales, preaching a mixture of folklore and Christianity and Finnish mythology, relying as much on his native Kalevala as on Matthew, Mark, Luke or John. In time he became something of a hero in the outlying camps. He spoke their idiom, shanty talk that blended accents with nationalities and common experience. And he was also a born preacher. A preacher, not a minister. His sermons called for no acts of repentance, offered no hope of salvation, anointed nobody, elected nobody, promised nothing to the choppers and swarmers and barkers, ignored heaven and delineated only hell. His promise was that things would get worse, and his theme was apocalypse: forest fire, death in the snow, a new Ice Age. He was a preacher of the elements, more pagan than Christian, appealing to the only true emotion of his frontier congregations, which was fear. Looking through a few of the old sermons, Perry saw in his grandfather a simple glacial floe and a frozen spirit. The sermons called merely for heroism. *Urho*, in the Finnish. Practised endurance, silent suffering, fortitude. His symbols were snow and timber wolves, the forest afire, the world ending, the town collapsing. His hero was the bull. The Bull of Karelia, a moose with antlers gone and head down in the dead of winter. Pehr Peri left the lumber camps with the certainty that there was no alternative but to go on, which was what everyone was best at anyway. So, with a reputation anchored in realities, it was a natural course of events that culminated in his assuming the pulpit of a brandnew church called Damascus Lutheran. And even with a congregation of shop owners and farmers and wives, Pehr Peri never relented in his stern predictions of hardship and collapse. The more vivid his prophecies, the more popular he became, drawing audiences from as far down as Two Harbors and as far north as Grand Marais. Never exhorting, he merely laid down hard principles: the strong will not survive forever, but they may survive longer than the weak; things are bad now but in the winter they will be much worse, so take advantage of the present and prepare for the future. Since his ultimate prophecy of doom was always rooted in stories of present suffering, and since there were always ample cases of forest fire, hard winters, drownings or freezings or death, he could never be faulted for poor vision nor accused of promising too much. He saw no hope and offered none. Strokes of good fortune, he reminded the Damascus Lutherans, are forever followed by bad fortune; summer to winter; birth to death; construction to destruction; the elements. He was never wrong. He preached simple heroism. What cannot be escaped must be endured, and if it must be endured it might as well be confronted.

Pehr Peri taught his singular lesson with conviction. And he taught his son, who listened.

So in 1915, when the timber companies left Sawmill Landing, it was seen as something to be endured, a dying town, a minor collapse in a world of collapse, so inevitable that no effort was made to save the place. Rusting machinery, uncut weeds, unpainted buildings, unstopped forest. And in 1919, when Pehr Peri hanged himself from the rafters of Damascus Lutheran, his son was ready to endure, having listened. In a natural succession to the pulpit, Pehr Lindstrom Peri presided at his father's funeral, buried him in pine in the old cemetery, and the following Sunday preached that Sawmill Landing was a dying town, that there was no sense trying to escape it because the next town may already be dead and the next on the verge of death, that the Ice Age was returning, ice a mile thick, a glacier that would level the forest and fill the lakes, the sun would turn black and the moon red as blood. And as though to demonstrate the flux, Pehr Lindstrom Peri journeyed the next day to Silver Bay, where he changed the family name to Perry and eliminated his middle name, his mother's name, for he did not need it.

Perry's first memory of his father was neither striking nor unusual: a holiday, Thanksgiving or Christmas, snow on the ground, his mother only a pleasant shadow beside him as they huddled in the house to wait out a storm, his father nervously watching the snow through the kitchen window. His second memory, unconnected to the first except through later association, was of a long sobbing sound, the snow still blowing, a baby crying and his father wiping bloody hands. His third memory was of great loss. The house was stone cold. His father was holding a child, rocking before the fire, and the sobbing sound ran through the house like the wind.

The three memories might have been separated by years or seconds.

Later, as he recognized Harvey as a brother, he remembered other things: his father preaching the apocalypse, the word throbbing in four full-bodied syllables like the chiming of a bronze bell. The cold house. Harvey and the old man going off somewhere in the woods. The feeling of cold. Harvey playing football. The old man watching with blank eyes. Harvey fighting. The old man dying, ringing with a spoon in his spit bucket. Harvey digging a bomb shelter for the dying old man, pouring cement, stringing electric lights so as to work at night. Gaunt nightlong images, partly a combination of human beings and events, partly the town, partly the place, partly a genetic fix, an alchemy of circumstance. He could not find the start.

Perry carried the rucksack, Harvey plunged ahead. They passed Pliney's Pond and continued on. Hornwort and water moss grew along the path, in the shallow-cut parts of the forest. It had finally rained and the forest was soggy. Twice the path appeared to end in a tangle, but Harvey would push away the brush and the path was always there. They walked single file. The bushes leaned in from both sides, parting like water and Harvey pointed out the trees and gave their Latin names. He showed where mushrooms grew and explained how they should be eaten and how a man could survive for years in the woods if he knew what was what. The trail was black dirt. It twisted through alternating growths of birch and pine, slim white trunks with maroon leaves. The earth was springy from decay and rot. Harvey seemed very happy. They crossed a meadow, turned on to an old logging road that followed a creek into the thick forest. Perry walked fast. He'd lost nearly five pounds. It was a fresh day. Sometimes he could hear the creek rushing off to the left, bubbling against the rocks, and Harvey kept talking, explaining things, pushing on. He showed where poison ivy and poison oak and maidenhair grew. He was quite expert. The forest grew high and thick, big enough for harvesting, monster trees with gnarled roots that lay like fossils across the path.

Eventually the trail ended, facing dead into the woods.

"Nice, isn't it?" Harvey said.

"Fine."

"This is really it. I told you it was nice. What do you think?"

"I like it. Spectacular."

"I told you." Harvey pointed into the brunt of the forest. "Out there is the real stuff. That's the wilderness."

"Where do we swim?"

"Out there," Harvey grinned. "These trails we've been following are white-man made. Loggers mostly. But this is as far as they come, and out there you won't find anything. This is where the logging stopped." He pointed to where the trail widened. "See here? The wagons turned around here and went back. This is as far as they ever came. Isn't it something?"

"Real history."

"Right. No kidding." He waded into the brush, motioning for Perry to follow. "See this?" He picked up a rotted piece of leather. "Dad showed it to me. It's an old horse brace. See? You can imagine how it fitted over the horse's neck. The straps went here and were attached to a go-devil. All kinds of junk is lying around here if you can find it."

Harvey scrambled about the clearing, picking things up and explaining them. He held up a long pole. "See? This thing's called a peavey. They used it to manipulate the logs. See? The point's rusted off, but it used to have this sharp point on the end and they'd use it to pry logs."

"Where do we swim?"

It was hard going. Perry was sweating. His jeans ripped in the thigh. Harvey plunged ahead. The forest had been cut by glaciers, chunks of silicates and rock ripped up and carried forward by advancing ice, blistered and dried, holes and crevices and long strips of gully bulldozed southward. The good soil was skimmed off, carried south. And when the melting started and the glaciers receded, ice turned to water and the water filled the holes and crevices and strips of gully, becoming lakes and ponds and rivers and tributaries, a circulatory system, the land of ten thousand lakes. Only the tough things grew. Pine, birch, bristled brush, primitive kinds of fish, walleyes and pumpkinseed sunfish, bullheads and crayfish and northerns. Tough mammals, too: wolves and beaver and bear and moose, and the Indians and the Swedes and the Finns, all tough.

The country began to drop. It was a different kind of forest than he was used to. It was thick and blurred and impenetrable, going out and out.

Then he heard the water again. Then he was in it, up to his knees.

He followed Harvey up the creek. It was cold water. On each bank the trees grew like mutants, huge and old, and the water ran faster. He was in it. Harvey was moving fast and Perry lifted his knees high to keep up the pace, sweating, his glasses sliding down his nose. Bugs hovered just over the water. There were dragonflies and bugs Perry did not know.

Gradually the creek widened and flattened out and the water got deep.

Harvey stopped in a shaded part of the creek.

"A good spot," he said. "You like it?"

"It's fine. Water's freezing."

Harvey smiled. "Dad showed it to me. You'll get used to it. You want me to carry the pack awhile?"

"No. I guess I can handle it. Where the devil are we going?"

"Just a way farther. The creek empties into a small lake. We used to go there to fish. You'll like it."

"I'll bet."

"Nice, isn't it?"

"Spectacular. I hope to hell the creek doesn't get any deeper."

"Maybe you better let me carry the rucksack."

"No."

"All right," Harvey grinned. "We'll take her slow." He gazed up the stream. "Nice, isn't it? Even better when you get deeper in, but we'll go slow this time."

"That's the ticket."

"You'll love it."

"I'm freezing. Let's go."

Harvey waded up the creek. The water rose to his waist and then stayed even. The stream kept widening. Wishing he'd turned over the pack, Perry worked hard to keep up. He decided to stop smoking. He felt awkward and out of place.

Hooking in a last long sweep, the stream opened into a lake completely surrounded by pine. A beaver dam spanned the mouth of the creek. It was all quiet.

Harvey crawled on to the bank, waited for him, then they walked along the forest edge to a rocky beach. Harvey helped him out of the rucksack, pushed it underwater and weighted it with a rock.

"What do you think, brother? Didn't I say it was nice?"

"It's fine. It is. Didn't know there was a lake out here."

"Nobody knows. Farther out there are hundreds of them. This one's not even on the maps. Dad and I named it Lake Peri. With an *i*, the old way. What do you think?"

"Spectacular," Perry said.

"Come on. Let's swim then."

They swam until midday. The lake water was cold and clean. The sun got hot and the mosquitoes were back, breeding after the rain. Perry stayed close to shore, but Harvey twice swam to the far side, disappeared into the woods and came back. He drew up the rucksack and popped open two cans of beer.

"Not so bad, is it?"

"No. It's great. Really."

Harvey nodded. "I knew it. You only have to try it, that's all. You should have come when we were kids. You know?"

"Yeah."

"Dad would have liked it."

"I know."

"He was always a little . . . I don't know, a little sad when you didn't want to come. I don't know. You know how he was."

"Sure."

"Anyhow." Harvey smiled.

"Sure. It is fine. I like it."

"I knew you would." Harvey went out to swim again and Perry sat with his beer and watched. Later they ate cold meat and apples and had another beer. It was all right. Harvey seemed happy, tall and very lean and strong, and the air was good. Perry enjoyed it. For once, everything aside, he felt some sibling fusion. It was all right. It was a fine day and a fine lake.

They sat together with their beers and looked down on the beaver dam. Perry felt a little sleepy.

"What do you think of that Addie?" Harvey finally said. "She's some super wench, isn't she?"

"You like her."

"Yes. She doesn't have to say a word." Harvey lazily held up his can and the sun glittered off the wet aluminium.

"I know."

Harvey closed his eyes. For a while he was quiet, toying with the empty can. The sun was very hot. "You didn't have anything . . . You and Addie?"

"No." Too bad, he thought. Some rotten luck.

"I was just asking."

"No. She's pretty young."

"I know," Harvey said. "You can never be sure, though. She likes you. She's always talking about going off to the badlands with you."

"Dumb talk is all. Don't know where she gets that stuff."

"She's something, all right, isn't she?" Harvey said. He seemed relieved. "So maybe I'll take her to Africa with me."

"Sure."

"Is she truly Indian?"

"I've heard that," Perry said. "She's always giving a different story. I guess she could be a quarter or half blood. You can't get a straight answer out of her."

"Some fine half-breed," Harvey said.

"For sure."

Harvey smiled, his eyes still closed. "You're a good man, brother. Did I ever tell you that? Sometimes I forget we're brothers, you know? It's a strange thing."

"I know."

"We're a little different, aren't we?"

"A little. Not so much as I used to think."

"Right," Harvey said. "Exactly. Anyhow, I just wanted to ask because you can't ever be sure." He stretched in the sun. "I wonder if I can get her to go to Africa with me."

"Sure, no problem. Flash your funny eye at her."

"You're a good man." He got up. "Maybe you should come to Africa with us."

"Maybe so. We'll fish for alligators."

"Kill Zulus."

"Only in good cause. For truth and justice."

"Should we swim?"

"Why not?"

"Let's swim in the stream."

Harvey dived into the deep water behind the beaver dam. Perry waded in, feeling the way with his hands. The water was very cold and hard. The bottom was littered with the slime of the forest. He lay back and floated against the mud dam. Then he turned on to his belly and swam hard upstream, following Harvey, finally rolling on to his back and letting the current carry him back towards the dam. He opened his eyes and had the sensation of great speed, the grotesque pines sweeping overhead, a single blackbird splatting wings high.

The stream carried him down. He heard Harvey call. The sky was a blur and he was moving fast. Suddenly, as though it had been shot into veins by a needle, he felt fear. He fought the stream, righting himself, trying to stand. There was no bottom. The stream twisted him and he lost sense of proportion and distance, and he pushed towards the mud bed but it wasn't there, and suddenly in a lush blur he was thinking again, colored images, and he heard Harvey call, and lazily he called back and his lungs were as hot as white fire, filling like a balloon, and he was tumbling and thinking calmly that only a moment before the day had been fine, everything was calm and fine, then he felt arms surrounding him, straightening him, and sunlight flooded and blanched the images, and he was bobbing in the stream. Harvey holding him high, saying, "Drop-off, I called out to you."

Perry blinked, staring into Harvey's dull dead eye.

"I called out. It's a drop-off."

He felt no terror. Harvey's arms were strong and buoyed him high and the current raced all around.

"All right?" Harvey's marble eye rolled. A shark eye. "You're all right?"

He felt no terror but he was angry. He pushed away, and Harvey reluctantly released him, hovering close by. "You're okay? Take it easy."

Fighting back, Perry rolled on to his back. He was sick but he reached back and swam, kicked, thrashed for the bank. He smelled the hard water inside him.

He waded out, sat down, put on his glasses.

"You all right?"

Perry nodded, not looking up.

"You hear me call out? I did call out."

"I heard you. I'm all right. I would have been okay."

It was so fast he didn't remember it. He lay back. Harvey chuckled and shrugged.

"I can swim," Perry insisted. "I was all right."

"You're some great fish, all right."

They rested awhile. Then without talking they dressed and followed the creek to a footbridge, got on to a path that carried them to Pliney's Pond and from there to the house.

Harvey did not talk about the near-drowning, and Perry pretended it hadn't happened. He convinced himself it hadn't. That evening Harvey drove into town to see Addie and Perry stayed up late watching the driveway, and he fell asleep thinking colored thoughts: Addie, Grace, the beady-eyed creature and the cold water rushing through him.

He stuck to his rigors. He exercised. He ate cottage cheese and eggs. He went to bed early, arose early, worked enough to satisfy his conscience, took care to be kind to Grace.

In September school started and Grace resumed the teacher's routine: seven a.m. mornings, lipstick and makeup, talk of her new kids, bright talk that showed interest and concern and affection. He drove her in each morning, dropped her off, had coffee, then watched the leaves change through his Mainstreet window. He did not see much of Addie. Most evenings, Harvey would take the car and Perry felt no great desire to ask questions.

He began paying attention to things. He took short walks into the surrounding woods, sometimes alone and sometimes with Grace or Harvey. He looked for colors and connections. It was hard to tell where it started.

Unwinding towards the simple past, he was searching in a vague way for the first elements. Complexity to elementals, a backward tracing. It was not easy. He did not have the old man's extraordinary sense of the past or future. That had been one of the problems. He preferred warmth to cold, and from one of those early memories he recognized a lingering sense of great warmth loss, as if yanked sleeping from a bed, or as if something warm had been pulled from him. He did not know where it started. It may have started with the elements. He knew them from college, ninety-two chemical elements. He saw them around him, or imagined them. The elements of matter, the red tinge in the soil, the ore country periphery. Chlorophyll in the leaves being beaten away by September, revealing other pigments, autumn coming, and he tucked it away as knowledge to spring on Harvey. And the great alchemist's elements: fire, water, air and earth. And the great anatomical humors, the cardinal humors that flowed like north woods tides: cold blood, phlegm, yellow bile and melancholy sacs of black bile. Black bile struck him as important. He learned of it somewhere. He pricked open capsules of cellulose and inspected the pulp. He opened bulbs of honeysuckle and smelled the grease. Inside himself, he suspected, he would sometimes find a sac of black bile, and he would prick it open and smell it, too, rub his nose in it. He exercised, took the walks, listened to Harvey, kept his eyes open.

In a moment of openness, he told Grace about the sac of black bile he carried around in his belly.

"You mean *pus*?"

"Black bile. It's hard to explain. It could be responsible for all this."

"You're sweet," she said.

"Thanks."

"I won't tell the relatives."

"Thank God."

"But I want ice cream. Otherwise I'll squeal. I'll tell them all that you're loony and carry around black bile in your gut. Maybe the black bile causes your pot."

"What?" He stiffened. "I'm exercising. I'm looking pretty good. Look here, don't you think so?"

"Yes," she smiled.

"Really."

"Tarzan. You'll look like Tarzan someday, just keep it up."

"Seriously. Don't I look skinny?"

"Black bile," she whispered. "Pus gut."

"Okay for you."

"I won't tell the relatives if you take me in and buy me some ice cream. Is it a deal? Pus gut." She kissed him.

"You're a sleeper."

"That's another good idea," she whispered. "Smothered by ol' pus gut."

They drove in and ate ice cream in Wolff's drugstore. It was Friday night. Wolff was doing a good business. The stores were open along Mainstreet and the August shoppers were out.

Grace held his hand and they walked up the street, the streetlamps were on, Grace looked in the windows. She liked clothes. She tried on capes and sweaters in the J. C. Penney store. Perry stood with arms folded and watched the high-school girls.

She showed him a garment. "Do you like it?"

"I guess. What the hell is it?"

"A smock." Her lower lip dropped.

"I don't know. Try it on."

"If you don't like it . . ."

"I don't care, try it on. I'll tell you then."

It was tight on her. She was heavy in the chest. She stood before the mirrors, turning. The fabric was filled with printed apples. She put it back on the rack.

Outside, squat women stood with baskets on their arms.

Up and down Mainstreet, boys were driving their fathers' cars, an elbow out the window, radios on, sniffing the Friday night air. The high-school girls roamed the streets in tight frantic bands, heads together. Perry watched them. Their tiny asses and spangled jeans.

The movie was letting out.

Harvey and Addie were crossing the street. They looked good. Harvey was talking and they were together and holding hands and Addie's black hair bounced on her back. They both walked fast, taking long steps, and they crossed the street and Addie waved. Perry watched them come up.

"We're going swimming," Addie said. "It was an awful movie so now we're going swimming."

Grace smiled.

"What do you think?"

"You both ought to come," Harvey said loudly. "I can vouch that Paul is one great swimmer. He can be lifeguard. You both have to come."

Addie pried Grace's hand off Perry's arm. "We'll go out to the lake. I know the perfect spot. It'll be a perfect night."

Grace stuck to her smile.

"We were just in town for ice cream and shopping."

"A night swim," said Addie.

"That's all right."

"Okay then," she grinned. "Poop on you. Too bad for you."

Perry looked at her sandals.

"Have a good swim."

"Crumb," Addie smirked.

On the drive home, Grace sat apart.

"You didn't want to go did you?"

"Doesn't matter."

Her lower lip stuck out. "You could have gone if you wanted to. I didn't know."

He shrugged. "Doesn't matter."

"Well, you could have gone."

"But not you."

"Well."

"Yeah."

"Well. They were together and everything."

"True."

Grace sat still and he drove the car up the tar road.

"Addie's awfully pretty, isn't she?"

"Not all that pretty." He had to watch the road.

"You could have gone. I just don't enjoy that kind of thing, that's all."

"What do you enjoy?"

She was quiet. "Are you mad?"

"No, just forget it."

"Black bile?" she whispered.

"I guess that's it."

"Old pus gut."

"You put the finger on it." He glanced over at her. "Forget it. I didn't want to go."

"Really?"

"Nope."

He noticed, cleaning a walleye, that the fish's eyes were attached to the brain by a braided gray cord with hard little knots scattered along its length.

He noticed that Grace bathed and dried her hair and combed it and went to bed with a book and read until he joined her.

He continued his inspections, seeking the bottom of things. He noticed that Harvey sometimes drank beer for breakfast and hid the bottles in the trash.

He noticed that three families had moved away from Sawmill Landing over the past year and that no one had come to replace them.

The insights had to be separated from apparitions. Often he saw the old half-memories, patches of color, gleamings, and the illusions dissolved on a closer look. Once Grace appeared to resemble his mother, whom he knew only by photographs. But when he examined the pictures and puzzled over the problem, the differences jumped out, the mirrors reflected back and forth over time in a dazzling series of contradictions.

"The trees will be turning," he observed.

"Look closer," Addie said. "They *are* changing."

"Not much. In a week you'll see something."

"I already see it. Look close."

"Where the devil is Harvey?"

"He'll be along. Don't be silly, stop worrying about it."

"I just asked where he was."

"He'll be along soon. Do you see what I was saying about the leaves?"

"Yes, I see. I saw it before."

She was tall. He was glad they were lying on the beach. Long brown muscles ran up her thighs. The calves were long and all bone.

The trees above them were elm and sweet maple. Across the lake it was all pine.

"Are you taking Grace on a vacation this winter?"

"I guess so. I don't know. She's been talking about Iowa. I guess she wants to go down."

"Good God."

"Yeah. Not so good. She has her family there."

"Iowa, good God."

"She likes it," he said.

"Well, when do I get my vacation? You promised to take me on a vacation."

"What?"

Addie laughed. "South Dakota, the badlands. The badlands are actually quite spectacular. God's gift."

"It sounds terrible."

"You have to go there, just like Harvey says. We can find a nice motel and play stud poker. We can have a big shoot-out at high noon."

"You're always teasing, aren't you?"

"It requires a lot of imagination." She stretched out. "This is the last of the sun, I'll bet. Another week. I like it when the air is cool like this and the sun is still there. It's the best of everything."

"The fall is nice."

"Now Harvey. Harvey hasn't got imagination. He's a pirate and pirates don't have the imagination the rest of us have. Harvey never teases. He's silly, he's so blasted serious. He's always talking about Africa and wherever, and the bomb shelter—it's his favorite spot. It's all serious."

"I wonder where he is."

"He'll be coming." She got up and stood over him. "Now let's you and I swim."

"Not me."

"We'll race. But you can't touch my legs."

"Now you're teasing, Addie."

"Okay for you, crumb."

She stayed in a long while. When she came out, he pretended not to watch. She shook her hair and dried herself and draped her towel beside him.

"Wasn't that a swim!" she said. "Are you sleeping, Peeper? Wake up, I'm back, you can wake up, silly."

She knelt down. Her thighs flattened and spread out. Beads of lake water twinkled. She took his glasses from the sand and put them on his nose. "Peeping Paul."

"Stop that."

"Don't you like your pretty glasses?"

He pulled them off.

She was breathing up and down as if still swimming. Her skin was dark. She lay down. She was athletic and a great risk.

"You're pretty," he said.

"What we need is some food. I hope dumb Harvey doesn't forget the food. Did you say I was pretty? That's a compliment. That's nice. You're nice, aren't you?"

He deliberately closed his eyes.

"Did you say I was pretty?"

"Yes."

"Well, in that case you have to look at me. You used to look at me all the time."

"That's over, Addie. Be nice now."

"Peeping Paul. You have to stop looking at people. People will think you're obscene, you know. Smile now. You never smile, just pull the corners. See, like this. Everybody can learn. You aren't a silly mutant, are you?"

"You sound like Grace."

"Fine, Grace's on the beam." Her back arched and she stretched a mighty cat stretch. Perry imagined raw meat. "Ah," she groaned, then collapsed, her arms spread out on the sand. She was athletic looking. "You're getting wrinkle marks on your tummy," she said. "Now that's a sign of aging. It means you were fatter and now you're not so fat."

"I'm in good shape, don't you think?"

"You have wrinkle marks on your tummy, right here. What's the big word for tummy?"

"Stomach."

"No, the bigger word."

"Abdomen."

"Abdomen. That's it. You have wrinkle marks on your abdomen. That's a hard word to pronounce. I can't say it without hearing someone else say it first. Do you ever have that problem?"

"Only when I try to talk French."

"Have you been there?"

"Once, not for long. We were in Paris." He stumbled on the collective we, tried to slur over it.

She laughed. "A honeymoon, I'll bet. Am I wrong?"

"It was just a trip."

"Well, you'll have to take me on a trip, too. Nothing else will do. The badlands."

"Where do you get this badlands stuff? Harvey's thinking you're crazy."

"Imagination. You have to have it."

Cold rain drizzled down through supper and the summer seemed to end at 6 p.m. sharp. Harvey did not come.

"Scrabble?" Grace said brightly.

"No."

"You don't want a game of Scrabble?"

"No, I don't want a game of Scrabble."

She pouted.

"I'm sorry," he said. "Let's walk. How about a walk?"

"It's raining."

"Do you good to get wet."

"You're a clown."

"Aren't I? I wonder where the devil Harvey is."

"With Addie. You told me, remember? Don't they make a nice pair? I think so. I do. Karen Markham thinks so, too. She thinks they'll get married and she asked me what I thought and I said I didn't know. Addie's good for him. You know? She keeps him . . . You know."

"I know."

"She's nice, too. Addie. Don't you think so? I wish I could be that way sometimes. I don't know. Shall we just watch television?"

She washed the dishes and he dried them. The rain was cold, and he smelled the winter coming.

"Do you want to just watch television? Or we can listen to records."

"You're one for excitement."

"I was just . . ."

"I know." He pretended to smile.

"You're a kidder," she said. She looked relieved. Her teeth clicked together.

They finished the dishes and watched television, then Perry got up and put on his raincoat. She didn't say anything. Gently, he closed the screen door and stood on the porch. The yard light illuminated a narrow swath of the forest. Behind him, slightly muffled, he heard the sound of the television, Grace moving across the kitchen floor, hesitating then moving away. He zipped up the coat and put his hands in his pockets. He felt foolish, no longer restless, and for a moment he considered going back in. He heard Grace inside, running water, rinsing something. The rain let up, turning to mist and fog in a combination of great depth. He stepped off the porch and hurried blindly across the lawn, on to the path, and towards Pliney's Pond. The earth smelled of salamanders and pine, and it was cold and wet and deep, and the earth sank beneath him, and the fog transmitted faraway sound, and faraway stillness, and above him the pines were dripping, he heard water lapping somewhere, his shoes sucking on the forest floor. He came to the pond. It was dark, almost a part of the land. It was too cold to sit on the rocks. He stood with his arms folded and hugged himself and looked out on the pond. The summer stink was gone. The air was sharp. The pond was perfectly still. Sea of swamps, mother marsh, womb of man.

"So," he murmured at last. "So," he murmured, as if settling something.

So, he thought, a historic discord, linguistics and tone, a cataclysmic blindness, a pathless thicket of twisted meanings and intentions and desires, a guttural and inarticulate melancholy, passion without vision, simple elements.

Behind him there was a noise. A shadow came from the woods, dressed in fog. "I been lookin' for you," the shadow said.

"Who is it?"

"I been lookin' for you, all over."

"Who is it?" Perry said.

"Shit, you blind, son?"

"Who is it?"

"I been lookin' for you, son."

"Oh. Jud. What is it?"

Jud came hidden in fog, bent low.

"What you doing here?" Perry called.

"Ha!" the mayor said. "I could ask you the same thing, son. I could ask you the same question." He stopped and coughed and blew his nose like a trumpet. "I been lookin' . . . Goddamn cold. Gonna be one bitch of a winter, tell you that right now."

"Jud, what you doing out here?"

"Lookin' for you, son, just lookin' out for you." The mayor came to the rocks. The fog twisted about his face like a mask. He smelled of mothballs. He blew his nose, stuffed the handkerchief in a pocket, dropped his hands to his hips.

"Jud?"

"Just lookin' for you," he said. "Grace told me . . . One crazy place on such a night, expected to find you floatin' face down. Such a night. I had me a notion. Had a notion driving out. You gotta be careful, son. Here, you better swig on this. Helps y' see clearer, that's all. Seeing clear. Had a notion when I drove out, Paul Milton Perry floatin' face down. Take some of this, son, take it."

"Jud."

"Take a swig, son, take it. There. Ack, such a night, winter, winter. Phew. I had me a notion, all right, just in time." Jud coughed, spat into his handkerchief.

"Jud."

"Time's comin', son, it's comin'. Cold as shit, ain't it? Winter, winter. Here now, take some of this. There. Fuckin' winter."

"Jud?"

"Now," said the old man, "now what's this about sellin'?"

"Selling?"

"Ha!" the mayor cackled.

"Jud, you're sick, come on."

"Tell me about sellin', son, tell me. What's this about sellin' out?"

"Nothing, Jud. Come on. You've got it mixed up."

"You're sellin', I heard it, I know it. Had a notion drivin' out, you're sellin' and leaving, I know it."

"Jud."

"Here, take a swig of this, son, take it." Jud handed the flask through the dark.

"Jud, what's this about selling, tell me."

"Sellin'?" Jud turned to the pond. "Sellin', I don't know. Had a notion. You sellin'?"

"No."

Jud shivered.

"Come on."

"Jesus, son. What the shit you doin' here on such a night?"

"Come on, Jud."

"No need to sell," Jud said.

"I know. I know that. Now let's go get some coffee, what do you say?"

Jud pulled away. He backed off and slipped into the fog. For a moment it seemed he had gone. Then he cackled. "And, hey! Tell Harvey I got him his parade. You hear? Tell him I got his parade for him. Tell your pa, too. You hear? We're all heroes, you hear? Hee, hee. So long, now. We're all of us heroes, you hear, even you, down to the last man, hee, hee."

Shelter

It was an early snow, but Grace was ready for it. The firewood was stacked, the windowsills were puttied, the larder was full of canned tomatoes and peas and string beans from her garden. Burrowing in, she'd prepared the house for winter, spreading a new Hudson Bay blanket on the bed in time for the first snow. All summer she'd worked on it, quietly foreseeing winter, a blue and yellow blanket with the design of ripe orchids. There were warm clothes from the attic, rubber boots ready on mats by the door, a full tank of heating oil, potatoes in the cellar.

The snow started as a wind, then rain, then an expansive pale sky, then snow.

Perry watched it develop from his office window. It was Friday. Cheerfully detached, he watched the snow develop with the relief of knowing he would not have to anticipate winter any longer. He felt fine. The farms would be locked in, which meant that his work would end until spring, a dead-end job mercifully cut short, and the Swedes would lie low and hope for a better spring, better soil, another chance, good luck and fair weather, corn from boulders and water from granite. Sometimes he did not hate the town. Sometimes it didn't matter one way or the other. He whistled a little tune and watched the snow. It was always a new emergency, people scurrying before his window as if they'd never seen a snowfall before, as if they'd never seen winter, drawn faces pointing to the pale sky, anxiously conferring. There was nothing more to do. He swept down the office and when he saw that the snow would be permanent he pulled down the blinds and latched the door and left early. It was early winter.

The snow melted. For a week the skies were clear. Then it snowed and the snow hardened to ice, the pines turned stiff, then it snowed again.

Harvey began talking about winter camping. Ski racing, finding a job, leaving the town, leaving the state, becoming a mercenary in Africa, writing a book, rejoining the army, going to college. Some days he spent with Perry in the office, drinking coffee and elaborating on his plans, cajoling Perry into agreement or argument, persuading him. He talked of adventure. His bad eye would seem to roll. He talked about the cross-country ski races in Grand Marais. He talked about ice fishing, the hardships of cold weather, the exhilarations of the spirit. Perry listened and nodded. He had no better ideas. Evenings, Harvey would take the car to visit Addie, or Addie would come for supper and the four of them would sit at the fire and play cards or Scrabble, and Harvey would talk about adventures, always planning and always insisting that he be taken seriously, demanding that they all play together, drawing them all in. Perry would nod and Grace would quietly disagree, but only Addie could control him, teasing him out of plain nonsense, puncturing fictions, bridling him.

"Well," Harvey would mutter, "you can't live in your small worlds forever."

"What about Vietnam?" Addie would tease.

" What about it?"

"Some magnificent adventure."

"What about it?"

Pointing to his dead eye: "That," she would say, challenging him. "Tell us about that."

Startled, puzzled, Harvey would reach to it. "Oh. That's nothing. That's part of it. You see, I'd forgotten. Taking chances, that's all."

Addie would keep after him. "So tell us about it! Tell us how it happened. You haven't said a word about it. Tell us about your heroics."

"It's not important. It happened, that's all."

"Oh," she would grin, egging him on. "Did it hurt? Did you feel great adventure when it happened?"

"Hurt? Well, yes. Sure it hurt. What do you think?"

"Was it worth getting hurt? I mean, if it hurt, you must have thought something about it. You don't just lose your eye and forget it."

Harvey would glare at her. "I don't see what my eye has to do with anything. It's not the point. I don't want to talk about it."

"Just tell us how it happened," Addie would laugh. "Tell us about a great adventure where the hero loses his eye. I want to hear every last gruesome detail. How did it feel, what did you think, did you cry? Do heroes ever cry? How did it feel, what did you think? Did you think you were going to die, was it worth it? Tell us this great adventure story. Tell us everything!"

It would stop him. Addie knew how to pin his ears back. She could find his soft spot and sear it and stop the nonsense.

Perry envied her. She wasn't taken in. She was free and clear of his influence, able to ride him with ease, effortlessly swaying with him, guiding him like a matador, stopping him short, turning his plunges into wasted energy.

"Well," Harvey would say, "I still think we all ought to take a great ski trip. Anything crazy about that idea?"

"The cold," Perry would say.

"No spine. You don't really have spine, do you?" Harvey would sneer.

But Addie could smooth even those moments. She was good to have around. She was young and always teasing, and her skin stayed dark even without sun. The snows frosted on the ground. The days were crusted and cold. He continued his exercises, dieting, walking into the woods around the house. He felt stronger, but it was energy without much purpose. Preparing, searching for some use for his new leanness, he counted off the push-ups and sit-ups, listened to Harvey's talk, watched the town get ready for winter, watched Addie, dribbled from day to day in a sleepwalking, restless disgruntlement. Grace was quiet. One evening she suggested a vacation. He ignored her. She could be sweet and understanding and soft, almost infuriating, and he just ignored her. Harvey was harder to ignore. Sardonic and sententious, Harvey would lay his grand plans, playing on Perry's feckless preparations and invoking the teachings of the forest, their common history, their father, the town, the Arrowhead, adventure. At night, lying still with Grace, Perry heard his brother roaming the upstairs hallways, sometimes with the wind in the timbers, sometimes with Addie's voice, joint laughter. He felt alone. He felt sometimes, lying there, as if he were being hurtled headlong into a scrambled thicket, caught in Harvey's wind.

"Don't you like being warm?" Grace would say.

"Yes."

"Me, too," she whispered.

He turned, lay on his side, faced the wall. Her breath was on his neck. The wall looked like a sky. Sallying, dazzling white points of light.

"Are you sleeping?"

"No."

She was quiet. He turned again, involuntarily, wrapped around her. Now he smelled her hair. Her body seemed to sink away from him.

Harvey moved about in the upstairs bedroom. The ceiling squeaked. Perry listened and heard them talking. He heard Addie's laughter. He wanted to listen in, creep up the stairs like a cat and put his ear against the door and listen in, find a window to peer through beclouded. He was intrigued.

"Cuddle me," whispered Grace.

"I am."

"Brrr."

"I know, I know."

"Are you happy?" she whispered. She was happy, he could feel it. Bed was her place, the warm sheltered soft center of the bed, and she wanted a child.

He heard the toilet flush. He listened, fascinated, thinking of Harvey's blinded eye. The floor seemed to shiver. Then the house settled into quiet.

"I hate winter," Grace said.

"It's not winter."

"It is. It's here. I hate it. I think we should take a vacation. Don't you think so?"

He rolled again, restless, turned to the wall. He smelled her flannel nightgown. The house was finally silent.

"Wouldn't a vacation be nice?" she said. "Someplace warm. Wouldn't you like that?"

He murmured yes, it would be nice, and in a while he heard her soft breathing. He listened to her sleep. He listened to the house, brittle timbers, a man's house. He listened to the outside wind. It had been that way forever. He tried to reconstruct his mother's face. Imagination played its tricks. He did not know her but he still imagined a face, like Grace, a certain feel and sensation that was entirely separate from the old man's house. No notion of family, no blending of softness with the leaden tread of his father or the squatting bomb shelter in the backyard. Grace turned, curled to the bed center. The night thoughts crept on him. Disorganized. A new job maybe. He felt vulnerable. Grace was warm beside him. It was that water-like soft center that first attracted him. A ripe smell tantalizing his imagination, something known instinctively but never encountered, like a nerve numbed and blunted. His father hadn't liked her much. "Looks like somebody's mother," he'd once muttered, his only comment. Home from college, college boy with Iowa girl. He liked her bigness. It was nothing erotic, no Addie, but the big bones had flesh that seemed to sink to the touch, down and down. He wondered what the hell she thought about.

Harvey wore his dress greens. He looked trim. A silver bar twinkled on each shoulder. Five medals were linked in two neat rows on his chest.

"I'm so excited!" Addie cried. "Doesn't he look just like a war hero? This is a grand night. And I'm so glad I know a hero! Don't you think Harvey looks just like a genuine war hero? I think so. Smile, Harvey. There, you see? A hero. I'm trying to persuade him to walk with a limp. Don't you think a limp would add to the overall effect?"

"You look great, Harv," Perry said.

The kitchen was warm.

Grace put napkins on the table. She pulled goulash from the oven, then hot biscuits. They ate quickly and Addie chattered on, and Harvey was quiet and sober and trim. He'd had his hair cut.

Perry drove the eight miles into town. Over the forest, the white fuzz of the football field lights glowed. Perry drove up deserted Mainstreet, turned on to Acorn Street towards the field. Harvey sat in the back seat with Addie, straight and quiet and confident. The snow was steady.

The teams were already on the field warming up.

The bleachers were crowded. They had come from all over, Two Harbors and Silver Bay and Grand Marais.

The snow blew in drifts across the field. The high-school band marched on to the field and formed two rows, and the teams ran through the marching aisle to their dressing rooms and the crowd rose to cheer them.

Harvey was dignified and erect. A few teenagers whistled at his uniform. Harvey ignored them, and they took seats near the fifty-yard line. Bishop Markham waved. He was sitting with Herb Wolff and two members of the town council. They were the core of the Sawmill Landing Boosters. They all carried red and black pennants. Bishop wound down the bleachers to shake hands.

"This is your night," he said to Harvey. "You look great in that uniform."

Harvey nodded. He was solemn and dignified.

"A genuine hero," said Addie.

"I should say!" Bishop held both of Harvey's shoulders for a moment. "The town is proud. This is a fine moment."

Bishop went back to his friends and the band played the national anthem. The VFW honor guard carried the flag to the north end zone, hoisted it up into the snow. Then the crowd cheered again and the cheerleaders led more cheering, and on the opposite side of the field the Silver Bay rooters did the same, and the noise picked up.

Harvey stared resolutely at the snowed-in football field. The two teams returned to the field. They were jumping and exercising and the loudspeakers called out the starting lineups. Grace unfolded a blanket and draped it across everyone's knees. The bleachers were full of people. The whole town was there. The band played the Sawmill Landing fight song and everyone stood. Perry's glasses steamed over.

Spreading a white haze over the forest clearing, floodlights sparkled with the snow, and the teams lined up.

The Sawmill Landing boys were in red and black.

Silver Bay wore silver.

Grace passed along a Thermos of coffee, but Harvey kept his eye on the field, a grand marshal inspecting the troops, and the Sawmill Landing team booted the ball high and Silver Bay erupted, the snow drifted across the field with the sounds of sharp contact, silver and red and black and battle cries.

It was a bad first quarter, fumbles and intercepted passes, and neither team came close to a score. Harvey watched intently. Addie kept chattering but he paid no attention. In the second quarter, the snow began whipping the field, piled into drifts, and both teams abandoned their passing games and stuck to the ground. It was a battle of endurance. A big Silver Bay fullback plowed relentlessly into the left side of the Sawmill Landing line, battering and hitting for five yards a crack. The snow got fierce. Grace was shivering. The Silver Bay fullback continued slashing into the line. Leaning forward with each play, Harvey pressed back, never taking his eye from the game, and Perry watched the crowd and snow and cheerleaders and Addie.

With a minute left in the half, the Silver Bay fullback broke through and ran head down into the Sawmill Landing end zone. Harvey shook his head.

"Ha!" cried Addie. "Now there's a disaster. You would have stopped that brute," she said.

Harvey shrugged. "I like his style."

"But wouldn't you have stopped him?"

"Maybe," he nodded. "I guess I would have tried."

The half ended with another Sawmill Landing fumble. Familial blood was high and the crowd hooted.

A gun was shot off.

"Parade time!" Addie said.

Harvey climbed out of the bleachers and walked to the south end of the field.

After a time, the band marched on to the field with drums rolling and bugles and trombones. Addie leaned on the iron railing. She was grinning. Grace shivered in her blanket. The band fanned into a formation resembling an arrowhead. Seven baton twirlers then walked bare-legged into the snowstorm, flashing their silver instruments, all seven of them blonde and smiling, and the snow kept falling.

The band played marching songs and a microphone was carried to the center of the field.

Grace shivered and snuggled close to Perry. Addie leaned over the railing for a better view. "I hope he remembers to walk with a limp. I told him he had to pretend a limp, it would make him look so gallant."

Partly masked by the snow, Harvey's float emerged from under the goalposts. He sat on a crepe paper throne. The band broke into "Stars and Stripes Forever." Decorated to look like an American flag, the float flowed soundlessly through the snow, through the end zone and on to the field, into the white lights.

The crowd applauded. It was very cold and the snow was blowing and it was hard for Perry to see.

"I can't see his face," Addie moaned. "He has his own parade and, will you believe it, I can't even see his face."

The float rolled to midfield. There it stopped, the wind lashing at the crepe paper and colored streamers. For a time Harvey simply sat there as though abandoned, but then four men walked through the snow to the microphone, all in parkas with hoods drawn up. Harvey sat still, looking vaguely towards the bleachers.

One of the hooded men stepped to the microphone, Jud Harmor's old singsong voice. His formal political voice. The loudspeakers crackled and the storm picked up. Harvey sat very still on his float. ". . . honor and service . . . a hero in a war without . . . Sawmill Landing, where he . . . whose father for fifty-seven years served the town and the church, a man . . . a hero, badly wounded, yet coming . . ." The images were whipped like fluid in the snow, the words jumbled past with present, and old Jud mixed Perry with Harvey with their father, but Harvey sat still as Jud talked against the storm. The microphone gleamed in the floodlights. When Jud finished, Harvey climbed down from the float, back straight, and walked like a king to the microphone. The four hooded men shook his hand. Jud held up Harvey's arm. The wind lashed again, for a moment obscuring both of them in a blur of snow, and Perry strained to see.

"It's marvelous!" Addie said. "Don't you think so? Just look at him."

"Yes."

"Isn't he some hero?"

"He is," Perry said.

"I think it's silly," she said. "What do you think?"

"I guess it is."

"Aren't you jealous?"

"Maybe so. He did all right."

The loudspeakers crackled and Harvey was talking.

"What's he saying?"

"The wind, I can't hear."

"The pirate!"

Three cheerleaders ran to the field. One of them gave him a large glittering key and each of them kissed him.

"The cad! A typical pirate, rape and plunder."

Then the band played again. The air was frosted and the horns and drums played a martial tune.

"Just look at him," said Addie. "He's loving it, every silly second."

In slow motion, a grim forest mirage, Harvey marched to his float, mounted it, stood at the crepe throne with an arm hoisted high, spine straight, the band playing, the snow drifting across the field, the crowd's frosted breath, the coming winter. "Just look at him," said Addie.

The float maneuvered through a slow turn and circled the field. It departed through the north goalposts. Harvey waved.

"Touchdown!" Addie said.

Perry's glasses were steamed. A cold embarrassed blur. Instantly, the two teams dashed on to the playing field and the cheerleaders leapt towards the field lights and Harvey's float was fogged in the driving snow.

Grace was shivering. "I think we should go home," she murmured.

"What's the matter?"

"Can't we just go home?"

Perry looked at her. Her eyes were white.

"Are you sick?"

"No. It was awful. Let's just go home."

Perry wrapped her in the blanket. The wind picked up and the game resumed. Silver Bay took the kickoff and the big full-back charged into the belly of the Sawmill Landing line. There was no stopping him. He wrapped his arms around the ball, tucked his head in, and bulled ahead.

The odds twinkled by the billions in the winter sky.

Short days, and it was time for a change.

Harvey was sick. Grace called the doctor in, a young fellow with freckles and blue eyes, and he went to Harvey's room and spent a long time and came down smiling. "Mild," he said dreamily.

"Mild?" Grace said.

"Yes, mild."

"Mild what?"

"Oh," he said, closing his bag, putting on a nylon parka. "Mild whooping cough. Mild bronchitis. But it's mild enough, it doesn't matter. Bed and orange juice will do it. Natural stuff."

"Jesus," Perry said when he'd left.

"He seemed nice."

"Mild, my butt."

Harvey lapsed into a child's ways. Coughing himself to sleep, casting willowing searches for sympathy, moping about. Grace mothered him, but the sickness dragged on through two snowfalls and the rasping cough seemed to entrench in his lungs. He got sallow and thin. The doctor laughed it off. Harvey insisted he was seriously ill.

"Pneumonia for sure," he muttered. "I know pneumonia. The old man had it and now I have it. You remember? Remember when Dad caught it and almost died, it was the same as this. The old man told me it runs in the family and here's the proof, right here in my lungs."

"Whooping cough," Perry said.

"Know it all, don't you?" Harvey sneered.

It went on. Confined to the house, Harvey stalked the rooms like a wolf. He would stand at the windows without speaking and his bad eye would shine and he would peer out towards the woods. He refused to shave or bathe. He came to meals in his robe, sometimes refused to eat. When he spoke it was without inflection, tight little syllables. Some days he did not talk at all, choosing to spend his time alone in the upstairs bedroom. He insisted on keeping his room hot, and with the windows closed the sickroom assumed an odor of decay. The room began to stink and the odour spread like an infection. He would not let Grace change his bedclothes. The stink spilled into the hallways, seeping downstairs to infect the whole house like oil into timber. A cycle, Perry thought cynically, the same diseased smell in the air. He remembered it from the old man's last sickness. Infecting the spirit, a confrontation with the biology of doom. He had no compassion.

During Harvey's sickness, spurred by it, Perry continued his exercises. He was catching up. He liked creeping secretly into the bathroom, shutting the door, stripping down to weigh himself. He felt strong. He could do the push-ups without thinking. His weight was down to 142.

One evening he pulled out his skis and rubbed wax into them.

"You're all right?" Grace asked.

"I'm fine."

"I'm worried," she said. "You're always going to the bathroom."

"No, I'm fine."

"You should eat better, then. I hope you haven't caught Harvey's disease or something. Really, you should eat better."

In the morning he skied the eight miles into town. It was a

dull day and the pines were stiff along the road. Pushing with short jerky strides, he tried to keep the pace even, remembering vaguely how it was done, push and glide. It was exhausting work. Halfway into town he wished he hadn't tried it, but he kept going and eventually caught the right rhythm. The trick was in the glide, letting the skis flow with the land and not fighting them.

He was tired, but when the road descended past the junkyard and he was able simply to ride the skis, it felt good, and he pushed hard and came fast down Mainstreet. Two boys were shoveling snow and they stopped to watch him. He felt proud. He stacked the skis outside his office door, made coffee and spent a dreamy day, feet up, reading and pottering about, and in the late afternoon Grace picked him up to go home.

While Harvey sulked and recuperated, Perry got into the routine: ski the eight miles into town, exercise, remember the feel of the skis, preparing. He slept better. The night thoughts, if they were still there, were lost in thick good sleep. The northern way, it felt good. He stuck to his rigors: chopped wood, walked about the woods, practised skiing. The snows fell in layers, climbing the trunks of the birch and pine. The town was stockaded for winter. Red flags dangled from auto antennae, the basketball season, ice hockey, TV football, hot turkey, small-town pastimes, shovels and monochrome nights, the Big Dipper blazing in fireplaces.

In the bathroom mirror he looked strong. He liked weighing himself, seeing the needle stop short and shudder and rest just at 142. He was in training, working himself up.

He was learning.

"Brute," he smiled into the mirror.

Downstairs, Harvey was in his robe. He sat on the sofa, feet up. He cradled a beer on his belly. The television was on, Monday night football. Grace was ironing clothes with her back to the television.

"Hello, you bull," Perry said. He was in good humor. He sat in a rocking chair. "You're looking better, Harv."

Harvey gave a surly dispassionate shrug. His beard was growing out. He coughed and spat into a Kleenex.

"Good game?"

"Ten-ten," Harvey said.

"Sounds good. How you feeling?"

"Dog dung."

"That's nice."

At half time, Addie came. She brought a box of doughnuts. Grace made hot chocolate and they sat at the kitchen table.

"These are some rotten doughnuts," said Harvey.

"Cheerful, isn't he?" Addie was in good humor, too. She was wearing a large hat, a broad-brimmed felt hat that turned up at the back. She kept the hat on while she ate her doughnuts.

"I think we should all go into town tonight," she said.

"We can go to Franz's and dance. How would you all like that?" Nobody spoke. "It's settled then," said Addie. "We have to get Harvey into clean clothes and get that beard off and so on. Who's going to help me?"

The parking lot at Franz's was nearly empty. Inside, Harvey's young waitress took their orders, steering clear of them otherwise. The jukebox was silent. Nobody felt like dancing anyway. Perry felt they had all been together too long.

It was dead winter. Two men in overalls came in. They sat at the bar. The younger of them turned to stare at Addie. In her felt hat and dark skin she looked good. Perry stared at her, too. Under the table, Grace had his hand. The booths were hardwood. The tabletops were formica.

The conversation was clipped, eliding, drifting along the surface like snow, filling in the same old holes and crevices.

They finished their beers and Harvey had an extra, then they paid and left. Addie's Olds was cold. The starter turned and squeaked. Grace huddled against Perry in the back seat.

"Where to now?" Addie said. "Look at the lovebirds back there."

"Home," said Grace.

"What's home? There's nothing home. Let's go to the junk-yard and shine our headlights. Maybe we'll catch a bear."

"That's dangerous. Let's go home."

"Oh, it's not dangerous. Let's just see if we can catch a bear."

Addie drove up Mainstreet, honking at friends. She was well known. She drove fast past the pasteboard buildings, knowing the streets and turns, across the railroad tracks and up Route 18, swinging right on to the snowed-over gravel road to the junk-yard. It was a popular pastime, stopping just short of the heaps of trash, then holding quiet awhile, then blazing headlights into the piled-up garbage. Perry closed his eyes. They had all been to-gether too long. An old scene, nothing better to do. Shine head-lights into the trash? Catch a rat in forage? Watch his eyes sparkle at the inexplicable new sun? Catch a bear? Catch a starving moose in small-town garbage?

The car's heater was weak, blowing out musty, oil-smelling air, and Grace huddled against him. At the end of the road Addie stopped the car, turned off the engine, and they sat in silence. Everything was black. The junkyard was a great sprawling sil-houette. The smell was frozen. Addie laughed. "We have to wait now. Everybody be quiet." Perry always had the feeling she was talking directly at him.

Harvey lit a cigarette, cupping the red glow in his palm.

They sat quietly. A small-town junkyard. Perry grinned. It seemed fitting. Waiting in Addie's Olds, shivering, waiting for that moment when she would hit the headlights and the junk-yard and forest would blaze in fierce light. It was one of those things he would remember. He already remembered it.

They waited in perfect silence. *Shining*, it was called. It had a name. There was shining and ambushing, other games, too. Most of the games were played from cars. Little kids played forest games dangerously, on foot, stalking wild Indians. They'd done that, too. The insight lit up, Harvey on ambush. It was all more complicated than simple-minded adventure, that was sure. The red glow of Harvey's cigarette seemed to shake. Lying in wait, prey or hunter, the great beam of light erupting, star flash, the great beast caught in the sudden blaze, the great terror.

"I'm freezing," whispered Grace.

Perry put an arm around her, and they sat and waited. Harvey coughed and snuffed out his cigarette. Addie was perfectly still. There were noises in the junkyard. Perry couldn't be sure. Animals possibly. Or just winter sounds, ice forming on rusted typewriters, cracks in the frost.

They lay in ambush at the junkyard.

"How long do we wait?" Grace said.

"Shhhh," said Addie.

"Why don't we just go home?"

"Excitement," Addie hissed. "Now be quiet. Everybody be quiet. You have to play the game or it never works."

"I wish we had a beer," Harvey said. "A beer would make it better."

"Hush up. Everybody play the game."

"Can't we turn on the heater?"

"Shhhh."

"A beer would be enough for me," Harvey said.

Again they sat in silence. Perry watched Addie's breath steam against the windshield. It was very dark. He imagined the old days. Swedes dumping their rusted broken plows, then the Finns and Germans, layers of accumulated junk piled in a vertical graveyard like the strata of some ancient civilization, the town's history now being rummaged by night creatures sniffing at ghosts. It was an ambush, all right. Lanterns and midnight voices. He grinned at the thought. They'd all been together too long. Waiting in a small-town junkyard. He remembered carting truck loads of his father's trash to the junkyard after the October funeral. Open graves.

"I'm freezing," Grace whispered.

Harvey coughed and lit a fresh cigarette. Somewhere he'd learned the trick of cupping the glow in his palm. The old soldier, Perry thought with a grin.

"All right," Addie said.

"Now?"

"Everyone ready?"

Perry sat up for a good look. The junkyard was dark. He smelled Addie's hair.

"Is everyone ready?"

"I'm cold," Grace said.

"Shhhh! Here we go."

Addie reached for the dash and pulled the knob. In an instant, like a match igniting, the junkyard exploded under the headlights.

"Hooray!" Addie shouted.

Harvey coughed violently.

"No bears!" cried Addie. "What a bore."

A washing machine gleamed under the lights. Lumps of frozen snow, two automobiles rusting on their sides. The junkyard was shadowed and still. The headlights flowed through the trash like a white river.

"There," Grace said. "Now we can go home."

"See the rat?"

"Where?"

Perry saw only the eyes.

"There!" Addie said. "We got him!"

The eyes glittered under the white lights. Paralyzed and still, the rat crouched with its snout high.

"Success!" Addie said. "Isn't he ugly? Much, much better than a bear."

"Let's go home."

"A miserable rat. We should kill it."

"Addie!"

"A miserable rat," Addie said.

"This is awful. I want to go home."

"It's a game," Addie laughed. "We all love games, don't we? What a perfectly ugly creature."

The eyes glittered in the lights. Behind the rat was an old mattress and a sewing machine. The rat's teeth were bared but it did not move. The headlights were merciless.

"Paul, go out and kill that miserable thing. Hurry."

"No," Grace whispered.

"I'll kill it," said Harvey.

"No. I want Paul to kill it."

Addie laughed and partly turned. "It's exciting. Isn't it exciting?"

"I'll kill the damn thing," Harvey said.

The rat's eyes glittered red.

"Okay," Perry said. He slipped out of Grace's grasp. "Why not? I'll kill it." He watched the rat. The eyes turned back, still glittering. "I'll kill it."

"Excitement!" Addie squealed. "Hooray for Paul! Hip-hip! Everybody cheer for him."

"Are you afraid to kill it?" Harvey said softly. "I'll do it if you're afraid."

"No."

"Hurry!"

"I'll kill it," Perry said. "I'll kill it."

Like his father, in a mystical devolution, he opened his door and got out. Harvey was standing with him. "Very quiet now." Harvey said. The rat was paralyzed. Only the eyes moved. It was a medium-sized rat. The snout was long and came to a point below the whiskers. The tail was coiled. It crouched in profile. The headlights were merciless. Perry smelled the frozen junkyard.

"Go on then," Harvey ordered. "See if you can do it."

Perry took a step forward, staying in the light. His own shadow startled him. The rat watched but did not move. Perry pictured raw meat. Blood and tissue and lungs and what else. He was in the headlights. The eyes sparkled like black diamonds, and he took another long step, watching the shining eyes. Frightened, he was thinking for a moment about rabies, remembering horrid stories about people raving like animals with the disease. Harvey was breathing quietly behind him.

"Go on now," Harvey said softly.

"Won't it run?"

"Can't. Go on now. We've got it blinded. Smells us but it can't run. Be steady and just walk up on it."

"Jesus."

"Go ahead. You want me to do it?"

Perry stepped forward. The rat seemed to shift, just a hair, an instant breathless cocking motion, and he knew the rat smelled him or saw him or heard him coming.

"You've got it now," Harvey said softly.

"Got it?"

"Kill it."

The eyes glittered. The rat seemed to coil into a ball.

"Kill it?"

"Smash it. Here." Harvey handed him something, a long board. "Just bash the bastard on the head."

"This is insane."

"Just smash it."

"This is crazy."

"Here, Jesus Christ, then I'll do it. Give it to me and I'll do it."

The paralyzed rat shuddered. Perry lifted the board and held it over the rat and closed his eyes and crashed down. The sound was soft and sweet. The board sprang back and dropped again. Perry imagined crushed tomatoes.

The rat squirmed.

"Hit it!" Harvey yelled.

The rat's eyes were wide open. Slowly, Perry raised the board, hypnotized himself, paralyzed in the headlights as the rat squirmed and rushed at him, between his legs.

"Kill it, for Christ sake!" Harvey hollered.

"What do you think . . ."

"Smash it!"

"Jesus," Perry moaned.

The rat brushed against his ankle and Perry smashed down and the rat vanished under the mattress.

"Lord," he moaned. His eyes were closed tight. All around him the headlights were hot and dizzy.

"How the devil could you *miss*?"

"Miss?"

"By a bloody *mile*."

The headlights were blinking, and Addie was leaning on the horn.

"Smashed it to a greasy pulp," Perry grinned.

Harvey laughed bitterly. "Some killer. Eyes closed. A real killer, all right." Harvey went to the car and climbed in and slammed the door.

Perry stood still. The headlights were flashing. He dropped the board. He was grinning, and the grin tore at his face like a scar.

"Good show!" Addie cried. "Come on now. Gallant try!"

He went to the car and got in. He was still grinning.

"Good *show*," Addie said.

Grace huddled in a corner. She was deep in the back seat.

"Guess I missed," he said. He was dizzy. He tried to laugh. "Ha!"

"I want to go home," Grace whispered.

Perry slept well. He did not dream about the rat, and in the morning Grace did not mention it. Harvey and Addie were still upstairs. Grace was very quiet. She watched him muddle through breakfast. It was a sparkling winter morning.

"Okay," he finally said. "I'm sorry. It was stupid, wasn't it?"

She shrugged.

"All right? I'm sorry. Pretty dumb, wasn't it?" He smiled at her but she wasn't looking. She set up her ironing board and went to work on a pile of shirts. "At least I missed. Some great white hunter, right? At least I didn't kill the damn thing."

"You scared me."

"I said I'm sorry."

"You don't have to listen to them."

"What?"

"Harvey. And Addie."

"I'm sorry."

"You don't have to listen to them."

Perry kissed her cheek. "Back for lunch," he said gently.

"Fine. Have a wonderful time."

Outside, he held the skis while Addie stepped into them. He adjusted the toe binding and tied the safety straps around her ankles.

"Is that comfortable?"

"Not so tight. She doesn't mind then?"

"No. Why would she mind?" He pulled on his mittens and started off. At the end of the lane he stopped to wait for her. "Push and glide," he called. "Pretend you're skating." Soon she had the hang of it.

With the wind behind them, they skied along the road until it made its gradual loop into town. Then they left the road, skied off through a narrow channel that took them on to the ice of Elbow Lake. Four good-sized pined islands cut off the view of the far side.

"Shall we cross?" Perry said.

"Don't be silly, of course we'll cross. Let me catch a breath."

"You aren't tired? We have to go back, you know."

She grinned. "We can make a campfire on one of those islands. Build a snow fort snug and comfy."

When she was ready, they skied on to the lake and started across. It took twenty minutes of hard skiing to reach the first island. Distances were distorted. They rested against their poles then pushed off again, going slower. The exercising had paid off; he was strong, he could ski all day. He felt good. The air felt good. It was a fine day. Everything was fine.

Beyond the second island, they came on a gray-shingled ice-fishing house. Black smoke rose from the chimney and Perry stopped and rapped on the door with one of his poles. A young boy came out. He couldn't have been more than ten. He was bundled in an Eskimo parka and wore thick glasses that magnified his eyes. The ice-house smelled of kerosene. "Hi ya," Perry said. The boy raised his hand. "How's the fishing?" The boy shrugged and stepped inside and brought out a string of three large walleyes. "Pretty good," Perry said. The boy shrugged again. His thick glasses were steamed over. Addie skied up and inspected the fish and grinned at the boy, "Those are three good-looking fish," she said.

"I've caught a lot of bigger ones."

"I'll bet you have."

The boy took off his glasses and put them in his pocket. "You want to come in?"

"Sure," Addie said.

They stacked their skis against the house and went inside. Perry was surprised at the warmth. The boy had three lines going, each tied to his wrist. The hole was very small, four or five inches in diameter, bored through a half foot of solid lake ice. The water was oil colored.

"You want to sit down?" the boy said. He gave Addie his stool. Perry took her mittens and laid them with his on the stove.

"This is my pa's house," the boy said. "I helped make it."

"Well, I say it's a pretty good house," Addie said. "Keeps the cold out, I guess."

"You can take your coats off."

"That's all right. We'll just warm up."

Perry recognized the boy from somewhere. Probably one of Grace's students.

When they were warm, they went outside and put their skis on. The boy watched carefully. "You know where you're goin'?" he finally said.

"We're not going anywhere," smiled Addie. She leaned down and kissed the boy's cheek. "Don't fall in that hole," she said.

"Reckon it's too small for falling into."

"Be careful."

They skied away and stopped and looked back, saw the black kerosene smoke moving to the sky like the first early fires. "That's a nice kid," Addie said.

It was fine flat skiing and they moved fast. Addie learned to lean forward to get body weight over the ski tips. They passed the third island without stopping. When it was behind them,

Perry pushed in and skied very hard. He reached the last island and kicked off his skis and sat to watch Addie come up. She might have been a photograph. She moved slowly, taking her time. Sunglasses covered the top half of her face. She could be nice looking, all right, the high cheekbones and brown skin. Watching her, he felt a little lonely.

"Had enough?" she laughed. She shook her hair out.

"Enough for today."

She stepped out of her skis, left them on the lake and sat with him. "It's awfully nice, isn't it?"

"Yes."

The day was bright but he couldn't find the sun. It would be at a low angle beyond the trees. He remembered Grace at her ironing board. It was a bad thing to think about.

Addie took off her sunglasses.

"Paul?"

"Yes, ma'am."

"I was terrible last night."

"Sort of." He grinned without looking at her. She was looking at him and he liked it.

"I knew it all along but I couldn't stop. You know how I am, don't you?"

"Sure."

"I'm just a silly . . . I don't know what. Poor Grace. Poor me. Really, I can't blame her a bit. I'm obnoxious." She laughed in a high voice. "Anyhow." She was still looking at him.

"You must have minded terribly when I took up with Harvey."

"No."

"Very well," she smiled. "In that case . . . I have to stop teasing."

"What do you want to do?"

"Do? Do. Yes, do. I want to do." She laughed. Sometimes, Paul, you can be absolutely loony, can't you? I don't know what I want to do. What to do with you? Do. Isn't it a funny song? Do, do."

"I mean, what about school or something?"

"You mean career!" she said, sounding the word out slowly: ca-reeeer.

"No. Not that exactly." He tried to think of a better word.

"You mean life! What do I *do* with my *life*?"

"You're teasing."

She clapped her mouth, then giggled. "I *can't* help it. Pauly, Paul, Paul-Paul, I *can't*. I don't know. Write Indian poems, I guess. And, gee. I don't know. I draw. Books and movies and dancing and sex. I got an A in sixth-grade math. My aunt said I might make a fine poker player. I got a C in effort, a B-minus in health, a D in hygiene, an A in human relations."

"All right," Perry said.

"You want more?"

"That's enough."

"Is that all?"

"That's it, Addie."

"I've failed," she sighed.

"Let's go."

"Listen," she said suddenly, stopping him. "I have a theory. Are you interested?"

"No."

"Just listen." She sat cross-legged, Indian fashion in the snow. "Are you listening? Good. Now, you know how we're always going into postures? Do you like my posture? Of course you like it, don't be silly. We're all competing for you, and do you know why? Let me tell you my theory. Harvey. Now there's a pirate for you. Do you think he's really a pirate? Really? No. He's not a pirate. It's his crazy posture. You see? Grace has her way, and I have mine. Indian, do you think I'm some loony Indian? You see? It's terribly difficult to say, but do you see? Do you like my theory? It doesn't sound so wonderful when I say it. I have to be witty now. What are you staring at?"

"Nothing, Addie."

"Ha!" She took an elastic band from her hair and twirled it around her index finger. Then quickly she stretched it to its full length and shot it at him.

"Addie . . ."

"Don't you see? You're the wishy-washy man in the middle, and we're all vying for you, winner takes all, you see? Grace offers you supper, I offer the badlands and Indian adventure and my lovely personality, quite a lot actually." She took another elastic band from her hair. "So you see that it's actually quite a fine theory. Harvey told me you wanted to be a minister. He says that you're . . . I don't know if he said it exactly that way. No, he didn't. I deduced that. *Deduced*! You see, I know some big words. Anyhow, he says you wanted to be a minister, so I deduced that this minister business is awfully important, so now you have to tell me all about it. Bare your breast, so to speak."

"It's nothing."

"Ah." She fingered the elastic band. "Harvey says you used to dress up in minister clothes." She smiled a little, examining the elastic.

"He's crazy."

"He swears to it. Fits rather neatly into the theory, actually. I deduced . . . See? I deduced that you're basically a moral transvestite, dressing up in minister clothes and so on. Got defrocked before you got frocked. There's a nice sound to that, in fact. I rather like it. Musical, don't you think-defrocked before frocked. I told Harvey, I said, the best thing would be a good frock for ol' Peeping-Paul, that's what I said. Get frocked."

"Addie."

"Don't tell me I'm teasing. I'm not. I can't help grinning, I grin all the time. Part of my pose—remember the theory now. It's a great theory. What do you think?"

"It's wrong," he said slowly.

She shrugged. "Well, then. I had my say, didn't I?"

He put on his skis. Lightheaded, he started back across the lake. She shot the elastic band at him. "Pow!" she shouted.

Jud Harmor hustled down Mainstreet. Hands thrust far into his hip pockets, the old mayor was in a hurry, passing the drugstore without a nod, crossing the street diagonally, his chin pointed straight at Perry's window. The old man seemed alarmed. His mouth was opening and closing, talking either to himself or some unseen companion, rushing across the street without looking for traffic. Watching him come, Perry saw something unnatural and erratic in the old man's stride. Jud threw open the door and crashed in: "Ha! And what the hell do you think you're doing? Selling!"

"Hey, Jud."

"Hey, yourself. Stop that grinnin'. Don't hey me."

"What's wrong?"

"Wrong?" The old man spat. "You tell *me* what's wrong, son." He cocked at the waist in some personal condemnation, leaning forward and still breathing hard: "I'd like to *know* what's wrong. Selling! Shit! Thought I knew you better, son. Who's mayor here? That's what. Selling that old house like it ain't been yours ever. Not tellin' me. Think you can just run out? Shit." Jud jabbed a finger at him.

"Jud, we've been through this before. What . . . ?"

"Don't what me. Just tell me."

The old man's eyes were fierce red. He was angry and trembling.

"Jud, go slow. Selling? What is this?"

"Selling!" the old man bellowed. "What happens when everybody sells? Tell me that? The fuckin' trees come in, the whole town goes under. Think you're a tourist? You think that? You think you can't stick it out?"

"Jud, take it easy. There. Sit down. I'm not selling a thing, believe me. Where'd you hear it?"

"Sources," the old man said sullenly. "A notion." Jud shook his head. For the first time, Perry noticed the sickness. Jud's throat bobbed. He trembled. Then with an oracular shudder, he quickly straightened and put a hand on Perry's shoulder: "Think about it, son."

"Jud. I'm not selling. You got me mixed up with somebody. Think about it. You got me mixed up again."

"This here's a good town," the old mayor said. His mouth quivered, opening and closing.

"Jud. You better sit down."

"Selling," the old man cackled. He wheeled and crashed out of the office.

"Jud's sick," said Perry, leaning into the stove with a flashlight.

"What was he saying about selling?"

"I don't know. Hand me the pliers. Top drawer under the sink. I don't know. He went crazy. He came banging in like a crazy man, screaming about selling. The house, I guess. I don't know where the devil he got it, but he was bananas. He's sick. You should have seen him. You know how the old man got? Same way, shouting about selling the house. I don't know . . . He thought I was somebody else. Ranting like a crazy man."

"He's just old. Is it the pilot light? Yesterday it was fine. Poor Jud."

"Ought to retire, that's what. Selling. Can you believe that?" Perry leaned into the stove. "Gas connection . . . I don't know where he got all that crap about selling. You don't think Harvey's talking about it?"

"What?"

"Selling."

"No. Harvey's barely been out of the house. He's talked some about getting a job, that's all. And I don't believe that."

"What job?"

Grace was whimsical. "Oh. A job. He was just talking. You know how Harvey talks. Something silly—running for city council or something. I don't know what, something dumb like Harvey. You know how he is. But I hope he does find something. Don't you? I told him maybe he'd have to go down to Duluth. I mean, if he wants a job . . ."

Perry twisted the gas connection tight. He pulled out of the stove and blinked. "There." He tested the flame.

"Paul?"

"Yeah."

"Paul, do you think maybe Harvey should go down to Duluth for a job?"

"Tired of him?"

"Paul! Of course not. I was just thinking."

"Oh."

"I was thinking that . . . . Oh, I don't know." Deftly, she took the pliers and kissed him. "I love you," she said.

"I love you, too."

"I know it."

"We ought to take a ski trip," said Harvey. "I've been thinking, and I think that would be good. I'm getting better. See?"

"You need rest."

"Just you and me. What do you say?"

"I say you're still looking sick."

Christmas decorations were already on the lampposts. They walked up the lighted street. A sputtering tractor, chained tires and lost, came down Broken Axle Road and turned past them, leaving a trail of black smoke. It was almost dark. The snow was hard and permanent. A loudspeaker was playing Christmas music.

"What do you think?" Harvey said.

"About what?"

"What? About taking a ski trip. We could get out together, you and me. I was thinking we could all go up to Grand Marais for the races—you and me and Addie and Grace—then we, just you and me, we could come back by ski."

"You're nuts."

"No. Look. I'm fine now. See? It'd be good for us, both of us. What do you think?"

The town was dreary. The tractor, a car and two pickups were the only vehicles moving. There were no people. The car went by with its chained tires biting desperately for traction. Banks of crusted snow blocked the curbs.

"What do you think?" Harvey said. "Doesn't it sound good?"

"It's something nice to think about," Perry said.

The winter days were nights. Outside his office window, the days were neither portentous nor dismal. Merely the same. He had nothing to do. To make it bearable he told himself he could bear it: "I guess I can bear it," he would murmur. He hung a red Christmas wreath in the window, plugged in the electric candle and admired his handiwork. His sober, slow cast of mind was numbed to a standstill. The window was a kind of magic theatre of holiday bustlings, hailed greetings, and he was a captive one-man audience, listening to the bells of Damascus Lutheran and the music playing from loudspeakers over the bank, a dull and constant saturation of Christmas spirit. He saw on the streets a savage and resolute celebration. "Hark the herald angels sing," sang the loudspeakers in defiant repetition, and he found himself whistling along, caught up in the hypnotic spell of each note and clang of the bells. "Got to get out of here," he told himself aloud, sitting still, unable to move. Some days he did not go to work at all. Other days he came in, watched the window shadows and listened to the monotonous peal of his own uneasiness. Other days Harvey or Addie would stop by and they would sit together. And one day before Christmas: Harvey hurried in, slamming the door, pounding his boots on the floor, spreading snow, excited.

"Well!" he said. "I got 'em! Four reservations. Last two rooms they had, so you can bet we were plenty lucky." Harvey was healthy. "Are you ready for this? Perk up, brother. Now listen: the races actually start on New Year's Day, but we should be there the night before. Don't you think? I wouldn't put it past that hotel creep to give our rooms to somebody else and take a fiver under the counter. Now. I've got us into the first-flight races, that's all they had open. Doesn't matter. If somebody scratches then I'll go for the championship flight." Overnight, in the space of a single sleep, Harvey was recovered and clear-eyed and erect again. "Now, it'll cost us twenty bucks each, not including rooms or meals or anything. I guess we can swing that, can't we? Cost us just as much for a weekend here, darn close anyway. Now . . . they'll give us starting times the day of the race. The hotel creep said they've got a lot of people entering, all the way down past Duluth, but most of 'em are clowns, so anyway it looks like they'll have to do the races in heats, you know, six or seven at a time and they'll time us with stopwatches and then have the fastest times compete in the final race." Harvey paused for a fast breath. "So. We can all get out of this burg and have a good time. Right? Addie and Grace can watch the races and ski if they want, or ice skate or whatever, and they have some sort of a fashion show, winter fashions, for the women, they can do that, and at night they have parties and movies, it's all part of the deal. After the races, we can just take our skis back here. You know? We can ski back. Addie and Grace can drive the car down and we'll come back on our skis. We can take our time and see the forest. How does that sound? It's wild as the dickens between here and there, but it's not all that far really, fifty or sixty miles maybe, something like that. Probably take us three days going slow. Bring the sleeping bags and the nylon tarp, that's all we'd really need. Races, a good time, then come back on our skis. What do you think, brother?"

Jud Harmor was waiting outside his office, holding the mail out for him.

"Was lying here in the snow," Jud said. "I'm gonna have to have myself a sit-down talk with that mailman, what's his name?"

"Elroy Stjern."

"Yep, him. Leavin' the mail out here like this."

"Thanks, Jud." Perry stacked his skis against the door. Jud handed him the mail.

"I'll talk to that mailman Stjern."

Grace listened softly. "I half expected it," Perry explained, "and I don't feel all that bad about it. It was there in the mail.

Xeroxed, not even signed by anyone. I guess they have them ready in the back room someplace in St Paul. I half expected it for a long time."

"What exactly does it mean?" Grace was listening and reading the neatly typed and Xeroxed letter. She could take bad news as though it were someone else's, making the adjustments and calculating the changes.

"I guess it means pretty much what it says. In a way I'm relieved, hon. Honestly. I thought it was pretty bad at first but not now."

She nodded. "But it says you still have your job. Right here."

"Yes. That's right. They're being polite. You see? I mean, nobody was fooling anyone about the situation around here. Seventeen farms in the whole blessed county, the whole county, and half of them not more than ninety-five acres and the other half going plain broke."

"That's what all these numbers are?"

"That's right. They're not stupid. So plain and simple it means what it says—they're merging my office with the one in St. Louis County and the whole operation will be run out of Duluth. What it says, politely, is that the office here is inefficient and a waste of taxpayers' money and plain crazy, and they're absolutely right. They're getting rid of it."

"What about this part about finding you new employment and working in Duluth if you want? Right here."

Perry smiled.

"Well, doesn't it say that?"

"Yes," he smiled. "It says that."

"Well, then?"

"Well, I'll finally be out of it, won't I?"

She frowned and bit her lip. Big wrinkle marks formed on her forehead.

"I'm happy, hon," said Perry. "It's a good thing. Honestly. We have to celebrate."

Grace studied the piece of paper as though searching for something just out of reach. "All right then," she smiled. "I'm sure you know what it's all about. I'm glad I'm not so smart."

"You're brilliant," he said.

"What you're saying," said Bishop Markham as they drove home, two Christmas trees in the boot, "what you're really telling me is that the Federal Government, the nation's most unsophisticated and gratuitous employer, you're telling me that they fired you. Is that what you're telling me?"

"That's hitting it on the nose, Bishop."

"You must have been some real stink bomb, kid."

"I guess so," Perry smiled. He heard the Christmas trees jostling in the boot. Bishop drove with both hands on the wheel, slowing for each turn, hitting his turn signal, checking the rearview mirror, the perfect driver. It was a year-old Buick. The tire chains ground the snow into fine powder and sent it flying into the ditches.

"So what will you do when all this happens?"

"I'll guess I'll start a farm."

Bishop shot a red-eyed look at him. "You kidding, buddy?"

"Yes."

Bishop looked again. "Seriously. Are you kidding?"

"I'm kidding. Sure. I don't know though. That's about all I was ever trained for, ag science, and it'd be kind of nice to give it a real try. Just dreaming though. Why, you have a job for me?"

Bishop paused too long to be real. "Tell you what, I'll look around. I guess if anybody can find you something it's me, buddy. I'll have a snoop here and there."

"That's good of you."

"Can't promise anything," Bishop said. "But I'll snoop around. Here we are, kid," He turned the big car into the lane, circled in front of the house. Perry pulled out the Christmas tree and stood it in a bank of snow where it might have been growing on its own. Bishop flashed his taillights driving away.

"I love you," said Grace in their bed.

"I thought you were asleep."

"You don't know everything then."

"I guess not."

"Are you glad we're taking a vacation? I am. It'll be nice up there."

"I guess it will be."

"Listen. Harvey's moving around upstairs."

"I hear it every night."

"Poor boy."

They listened. Grace finally sighed. "Oh, it'll be a nice vacation, I know it. I like holidays. Did you like decorating the Christmas tree? We really should do those things together all the time, don't you think?" The ceiling creaked as Harvey moved. "Poor boy. Maybe he'll get a job in Minneapolis. I hope so. He was talking about it again tonight. I hope so. Do you want a rub?"

He rolled on to his stomach, kicked away the sheets.

"There," she whispered. "Isn't that better." She sat up to rub him. "Poor boy. I hope you don't worry about that stupid job. You won't, will you? Really, I don't think it's so terrible, now that I've thought about it. And if . . . I don't know. It's not so terrible, is it?" Everything was whispered interrogatory, gently probing. "Stupid job, anyway. There, there. And going on the trip up to the Winter Carnival, we'll get to be alone for a while and maybe take some walks, won't we? Don't you think?"

"Mmmmm," he said.

"Harvey's moving again. I wish . . . He told me he's thinking, I shouldn't say. I promised I wouldn't. He said he's thinking about marrying Addie. Wouldn't that be nice?" She stopped rubbing him, poising for response, letting it linger. Then she probed at his neck muscles. "You can't tell when he's serious, of course. I think he should find a decent job first, don't you? I suppose he has money saved from the army, though. That's what he says. He seems to have enough money, I suppose. He talked tonight about maybe going to Minneapolis for a job. Does that feel good? Good. Am I talking too much?"

"No. Rub a little lower."

"Anyway. It would be nice to have the house alone, wouldn't it? I was just thinking. I liked it while we were all alone. Wasn't it nice that way? She moved down, rubbing his butt and then his thighs and then his calves. "I suppose that's being spoiled, isn't it? It's Harvey's house as much as ours, yours. But I still liked it being alone. I don't know. I guess I'm spoiled. But I liked it tonight putting the decorations on the Christmas tree. I can't help it, but I do enjoy that, don't you? Harvey's feelings can get hurt, too. He isn't so . . . such a great hero as he pretends. I don't think for a minute he fools Addie, do you? I think she's good for him and I know, I know he likes her a lot because he told me. He talks to me more than you think. Sometimes he surprises me. I think it would be very good for him. Marrying Addie or someone, and it would be good to have this house alone. I was just thinking, we ought to paint it next summer. The wood needs a good paint, don't you think? And . . . I've been thinking. I don't mind about the closing down of the office, not anymore. At first it kind of bothered me, mainly because I thought it would make you unhappy, more unhappy, I mean. But now I think it's all right because . . . because, well, you don't seem to mind and it would be something new, wouldn't it? So don't worry about it, and I'll keep on teaching, of course. I like teaching, I like kids. I was just thinking. Someday, I don't mean right away or anything, someday don't you think it would be nice to have kids? I guess it's just the mothering instinct, but I can't help that, but it would be kind of nice, don't you think? Certainly, certainly there's plenty enough room for one or two kids in this big old house and I think it would be kind of neat and all. Addie told me she wants to have kids too someday, but not right away. I asked her how many and she said a litter, can you believe that? A litter! She was joking, I'll bet. Isn't she always joking? Does that feel good? Oh . . . the tree looked good. I thought we did a good job on it. To-morrow after school I'm going to buy some new bulbs for it, I know just what I want, just what that tree needs. I saw them at Woolworth's, great big giant green ones. I wish Harvey would have helped us decorate. The way he just sat and watched like he wanted to help but was embarrassed or something. And I still wish he'd go to a doctor about his eye, it's looking so bad. Any-way. Oh, did I tell you? Paul? At the church they're having the Christmas pageant early this year, next Tuesday. I forgot to tell you. You don't have to go. I know you don't like going, but al-most all the children, all except for the little baby they've got to be Jesus, all the rest are in my class this year and I really ought to go. You don't have to go if you don't want. It would be nice. It would be nice, wouldn't it? If you don't go it's all right. Don't worry about it. It just would be kind of nice. Maybe after our va-cation to Grand Marais you'll feel better. I hope so. Does that feel good? My hands are getting a little tired. We never get to just talk to each other, do we? I mean, nobody around here just talks and says everything they think, do they? Have you noticed that? We all ought to just talk and say exactly what we think, that's what I think. You'll hate me, but I think Harvey ought to move out of this house and leave us be. Sometimes he just gives me the willies, I can't help it. I can't help feeling the way I do. Sometimes he can be very nice. I know that. But I don't for a minute . . . Oh, did you know that Bishop Markham's little boy's going to be Joseph in the pageant? It's true! And his name is Joseph, I mean that's his real name. I like it when we talk, Paul. Do you remember . . . when Joey Markham was just a toddler, he couldn't have been more than five years old, and we were at the church picnic and he came up to me, I guess he thought I was his mother, I don't know why, and he wrapped around my leg and just held it and bawled and bawled. That was so sweet. I felt so good. He thought I was his mother. Can you imagine that? He was . . . really, he thought that. He was crying mommy, mommy and holding on to my leg. I tell you, I think Karen Markham was upset by it. She never said anything, she's sweet herself, but I think so, I think so. I remember that. It was like the time down in Ames, in college, when you thought I was somebody else, I can't remember who, and you were calling for me and I answered the phone, remember, and you said is Grace there and I said no, but my name is Rhonda and you started talking, all different, such charm you were putting on. You were so embarrassed when you found out. I don't know . . . wouldn't it be nice? I don't want a litter like Addie—I'm sure she's only joking anyway—but I think it would be neat to have a child. Really, there's plenty enough room here, we could paint the room Harvey's staying in, of course he'll have to move out first, and we could use some of the old furniture you stored away. Well. It's something nice that I think about. You don't know everything I think about, you know. Sometimes I'm thinking about things and you don't even know I'm thinking at all. But I like Addie. I do like her. She talks to me sometimes, too. She's very different, an entirely different person when you talk to her without lots of people around, she's kind and isn't always joking. Sometimes. She talks to me more than you think . . . Of course I'll keep Harvey's secret about Addie, getting married to her. I hope it works out, you can never tell, can you? Oh, Addie is nice. She talks to me more than . . . She told me something. You know how pretty she is, don't you? She's certainly very pretty, but she told me, she told me she's always been upset because she didn't have bigger boobs . . . breasts. I don't know why she said that, and she might have been joking. She said she used to cry about it, can you believe that? I didn't know *what* to say. I told her I used to feel funny having such large breasts, and she thought that was very funny. I didn't tell her everything, of course. She never asks about you so I guess she knows some things are private. I told her that in college everybody used to call me Boob because of . . . and she thought that was very funny, but I told her that at the time it made me upset, thinking I was a mutant or something. I hope she doesn't tell Harvey. Harvey will start calling me Boob again, I'm sure of it. I'm glad you never called me Boob. It sounds like a dummy's name, doesn't it? Boob-Head or something. I don't know. My arms are tired. Is that enough? Does that feel good? I hope you can sleep now. Everything's so changing. When you hit that poor rat I was so mad. It really wasn't like you, Paul. I don't know why you did it. Why did you do it? It was just a poor little rat and I've never known you before to . . . But I guess it's all right. I shouldn't say anything because I set traps in the basement and catch mice and don't think a thing about it. I love you. I'm sure our vacation to Grand Marais will be such fun and we'll be alone together and have some time. Next year I hope we can go down to Iowa, though. I know you don't like to go but I think it would be okay. My family is really pretty nice if you get to know them. But . . . I hope you don't take that dumb ski trip back to Sawmill Landing. Can't it be dangerous? Harvey sometimes plans the most stupid and dangerous things. And Addie! They can both be so nice sometimes and other times they can be . . . I guess they're made for each other. I talked to Jud Harmor after school last week and he was saying that they're made for each other, then he laughed like he knew something special I didn't know, but he said to be careful of Harvey and then just laughed again. I guess Harvey's war . . . experiences . . . you know, he never talks about them. Yesterday he was talking about his training but he never talked about the war. I think it would be good for him to just talk about it. Don't you ever wonder if he *killed* anyone? Does that feel good there? I wonder about that. But I'm sure if he did kill somebody then he just had to do it. I wish he'd see a doctor about that eye, it sometimes looks awful. He never talks about that either. Nobody ever talks about anything really. I can never talk about anything either. Oh. I've got to stop now, I'm tired. I'll put some Ben-Gay on your neck but then I have to stop. Doesn't that smell good? I love the smell of it. I wonder what they put in it. It feels so warm and tingly. Hmmm. It seems so good, I wonder if it really does anything for the muscles, I don't know. I guess it's psychological mostly because it smells like it should feel good and help the muscles relax. Are you tired now? I've got to stop. There, is that good? Are you asleep? I love you."

Black Sun

They pulled into Grand Marais in the early evening. A snowstorm had made the driving treacherous and they'd each taken turns at the wheel, peering into the storm and trying to follow the narrow track of Route 61 along Lake Superior. Even so, it was a nice drive. The last twenty miles, Harvey sat with Addie in the back seat, drinking wine and singing Christmas carols and teaching everyone army marching songs. The storm let up a few miles outside Grand Marais.

It wasn't a big town. A lighted banner welcomed them to the Winter Carnival. Most of the shops were closed.

"Awfully quiet," Addie said.

Harvey laughed. "Here maybe. Wait'll you see the hotel. They go crazy. It's all at the hotel anyway."

"It's a lovely town, isn't it?" Grace said. "Doesn't it remind you of something in Europe? I don't know what."

"France," Harvey said.

"I think that's it."

The hotel was set off in the forest two miles from town. Seeing it again reminded Perry of the times they'd come with the old man for the races. It was a fine old monstrosity that grew on itself like a cancer, gabled and tiered and decadent from the days of the timber barons, red wreaths in the windows and a dozen chimneys perched on layered roofs. The windows were all lighted and the parking lot was full. Happy music played from loudspeakers.

Perry parked alongside the road and two boys came to help with the baggage. Harvey carried the skis inside, then went off to check on starting times for the morning races. The lobby was full of music and people and colored sweaters. Everyone seemed young.

"I love it," Addie said. They found a place to sit near the fireplace. "Makes me feel rich. Really. Doesn't it make you feel stinking rich?" Watching as she smiled at the crowds, Perry recalled how young she was. "Love it, love it," she said.

Harvey came back with keys for the rooms.

"All set," he said. "We're up on the second floor. I vote we have a fast supper then join one of these parties. How's that?"

The crowds were very loud. Somewhere off the lobby a rock band was playing and the drums thumped like cannon through the hotel. Harvey led them through a wide corridor and up a flight of stairs. The rock music seemed to follow.

In its way, the hotel was rather elegant. Originally it had been owned by a prominent St. Paul lumber family, and the fact showed in the fine timber work and beamed ceilings and the shadowing smells of old wood. Native fish hung on the walls with huge eyes and silver bellies. Except for the lounge and first-floor restaurant, which were carpeted, the floors were all polished oak, and the guest rooms were large and livable.

"Ten minutes," Harvey said, handing him a key. "First supper, then we do some hard partying."

"All right. Knock when you're ready."

"Ten minutes." Harvey followed Addie into the adjoining room. Perry listened for a moment, heard them laugh about something, told himself to wise up and forget it. He opened the door and watched while Grace tested the taps and bed.

"Like it?"

Grace smiled.

"Better hurry then. Harvey says he's giving us ten minutes."

Grace bathed in the cramped porcelain tub, then Perry showered and they got dressed and listened to the radio until Addie came by with a bottle of wine.

"Got waylaid," she grinned. "Rather, got laid on the way. Harvey's still dressing." She held out the bottle. "You want some of this?" She wore a white band in her hair.

"No."

"Don't be a sore loser. Here, drink up." She poured some into two glasses.

When Harvey came they went downstairs for a late supper. The restaurant was full of music and young people and noise. Harvey and Addie were eager to get through supper, and afterwards they hurried off towards the sound of drums. Grace seemed glad they were gone. Perry noticed she'd developed the nervous habit of playing with her wedding ring, all the while smiling and nodding and agreeing. He told himself to be kind.

They spent a long time over coffee, then took a stroll through the hotel, then went up to bed. Grace wore a new nightgown she'd bought for the trip, and Perry told her it was sexy, and they listened to the radio until she fell asleep. For a time he felt fine, lying still, listening to the muffled drums and Grace's breathing, not thinking about anything. Then he started thinking. He got dressed and went downstairs.

The bar was crowded and loud. Feeling guilty and lonely and

a little foolish, he stood in the doorway until a man said he would either have to pay a dollar or find another place to stand, and Perry gave the fellow a dollar and went in. It was a mistake. Except for the dance floor and a section of the bar, the room was dark as a cave, bristling with ski sweaters and tight pants and blond hair, frantic noisy boisterous crazy sex.

He moved towards the bar. It was always the safest place. Three cash registers were busy and he waited in line, keeping his head down, scolding himself for not having the sense to stay away. He felt old. Bars always did it for him. Eventually he got a beer and retreated to one of the dark tables. He promised to drink the beer and get the hell out.

Harvey and Addie were dancing in the center of the crowd, and he couldn't help watching. They looked happy. He felt rotten, but he couldn't help watching. Some luck, he thought. A yellow-sweatered girl passed by, smiling at him, and he felt a little better, and in a few minutes she passed by again, then stopped and came back. He couldn't see much but the yellow sweater.

"What do they do with an amputated leg?" she said.

"What?"

"This guy I was just dancing with asked me that," she said. "I didn't know the answer. Amputated legs. What in the world do they do with them?"

"I don't know. I give up."

"Don't you know?"

"No. Is it a riddle?"

"Oh, no," she said. "This guy I was dancing with . . . Do they bury them? Or maybe they just burn them. You aren't a doctor, I guess."

He said he wasn't. He saw Addie and Harvey were still on the dance floor.

"Oh, I thought maybe you were a doctor," said the girl. The yellow sweater seemed to swallow her. "You kind of look like a doctor, you know."

"I'm unemployed," Perry said. He had to shout.

The girl nodded sympathetically. "I know. Times are bad. This guy I was dancing with, he had the same problem almost." She looked about the room and pointed at a blue and gold sweater. "That's him," she said. "I suppose you don't know his name."

"No." He tried to think of something else to say. It wasn't necessary. She sat down. A moustached waiter brought over two mugs of beer, and the girl said she worked in Duluth for the port authority, and Perry nodded, and the girl told him how she'd been coming to the winter games for years and years and years, but that actually she'd never tried skiing herself, and that her home was originally in Chicago, but that she hated the place and never went back except for holidays, and that she was here with a darling friend who never got in the way, and that she loved meeting new people and that this was the perfect place for it, and that she wore her wedding ring only for nostalgia because the divorce had been more than a year ago and she'd forgotten all about him. The yellow sweater swallowed her up.

"You want to dance?" Perry said.

"No." As though hearing a dinner bell, the girl checked her watch.

"What do you want to do?"

"Oh, you know." Vaguely, she turned her finger in the smoky air. "Meet people, that sort of thing." She looked about the room, saw someone and waved. It was the blue and gold sweater. He came over smiling. She got up to dance with him. "Thanks for the nice talk," she said. "You're a nice man."

"Bye," Perry said. It happened all the time.

He got up to go, but Addie and Harvey were already at the table.

"Wow," Addie said. "We thought you scored, what happened?" She was a little drunk. She seemed even younger when she was drunk. She took off her shoes and put them on the table. "Tell us what happened."

"Nothing. I came down for a drink. How's the party?"

"Spectacular. You had me furious," she grinned. "Give me your beer. You had me furious with . . . I don't know what. Tell him, Harvey."

"Jealous," Harvey said.

"That's it!"

"I'm going to bed."

"No. It's a party."

"Okay. Tell me all about it in the morning."

"But it is . . . it is morning. We have to dance. You had me furious." She pulled him up, and they went out and danced, then they drank a pitcher of beer and he went up to bed.

Grace was awake. She didn't say anything but he could feel it. Some luck, he thought. He kissed her and lay back and listened to the drums pounding downstairs, wondering how it would have felt to have danced with the yellow-sweatered girl, remembering how it felt to dance with Addie, the way she danced with her pelvis out, barefoot and saying how furious she was, the band playing louder until it stopped and just the drummer played, how everyone stopped dancing and clapped in time to his drumming, then how the guitar joined in and then the electric piano, then how everyone began dancing again, the way Addie danced.

Much later, Harvey woke him. "Come on, come on. We're partying in our room. Big frigging party, must have you there. Addie's kidnapped a genuine Olympic cross-country skier and we're holding him for ransom. It's a big frigging party. A sad spectacle."

"Are you drunk? What time is it?"

Harvey threw on the light. Grace rolled over and pushed her face into the blankets.

"No, you have to come. It's a fine spectacle of a party."

Reluctantly, Perry dressed and followed into the adjoining room. A radio was playing loud music.

'This is Danny or Dan or Daniel, one of those names.' Harvey pointed out a handsome boy asleep on their bed. Addie was wiping his brow with a cloth.

"He's a little sick," Addie said. "Hi, sleepy. You've missed a fine party. Did Harvey tell you? We've missed you. I think we're all raving drunk now. Harvey, see if there's wine for your brother. Look in the bathroom."

"I thought you people went to bed. What time is it anyway?"

"Oh, we went to bed and then got up, you know very well how those things go, up and down, in and out, all that. Anyway, this is Daniel. He's going to be skiing in the Olympics, did Harvey tell you? He is. I wish I could wake him up. Isn't he some handsome Olympic skier? He got a little sick and threw up in the bathtub but now he's all right. Did you find your brother some wine?"

Harvey handed him a full glass. "This . . . wine is slightly used but it's vouched for as very good wine."

"Oh, Harvey. Harvey, you're a boor. Behave. Get your brother something respectable to sit on, that chair. And behave yourself."

The boy awakened and got up and went into the bathroom.

"I think he's sick or something," Harvey said. "Just a kid, you know. Some Olympic champion he'll be."

"Had his picture in a ski magazine," said Addie.

"Salute him." Harvey lifted his glass and spilled some. "Salute. Addie's been fawning all over him. She gets that way."

"Behave yourself," she said. "Paul, do sit down. We can keep the party going."

"I'm going back to bed."

"Never! No." Addie sat on a blanket cross-legged, struggling to pull the cork from a fresh wine bottle.

"Victory for Daniel!"

"Behave."

The boy came out of the bathroom. He looked a little better.

"Daniel, this is another of my great friends. Now, you just sit still, you can't have any more of this."

"Victory for Daniel!" shouted Harvey.

"Hush up, you. Daniel, this is Paul. Daniel's going to be skiing in the Olympics, aren't you? Daniel's all the way from St. Paul. Everybody sit down now."

The boy was white-faced. Addie took his dirty sweater and wrung it out and hung it over the radiator. The boy sat on the bed then he lay back. "I believe Daniel's very drunk," said Harvey. "I do believe so. Got to have more stamina. Stamina and wine. Wine and stamina. Isn't this a great party? Just me and you and Daniel and stamina and wine. Make a fine group. And Addie, too. Addie, aren't you going to tuck Daniel in? Addie's found an Olympic skier. A sad spectacle."

"Harvey, behave yourself. I think we should all be quiet."

"Stellar human being," Harvey said. He was drunk. "Everybody's stellar. Why aren't we asleep? Bad races tomorrow. Wonder what time it is."

"It's dawn," Perry said. "I'm going to bed, so you all have a nice party."

"No!" Addie said. "Here, I have to get Daniel back to his room. Somebody has to help me."

"Not me."

"Victory for Daniel!" muttered Harvey. He was sitting on

the floor. The radio was still going. Addie got the boy up. "Come on now, we'll get you to a bed. Be a good boy. Isn't he a fine-looking lad, Olympic material all the way?" She led him to the door. Perry held it open for her, and Addie guided the boy down the hall.

Harvey was slumped on the floor.

"Better get into bed," Perry said.

"Think I'll sleep here. I'm fine. A fine party. A stellar lad, that Daniel. Olympic material in his blond hair, don't you think? Stellar. Wine and stamina."

Perry helped his brother undress.

"Yes, that Daniel is a fine lad. He's a fine, fine, fine . . . boy. Daniel is his name. Did you meet him?"

"Yes," Perry said.

"Stellar lad."

"Take off your shirt, Harv."

"Addie's fallen for him. Poor fella. You got my shoes? Can't find them anywhere."

"They're under the bed. Lie down now, Harv."

"What time is it?"

"Dawn and you have to race tomorrow."

"Dawn. Good God. Gotta brush my teeth."

"Just lie down. I'm going back into bed now."

"Bed, my God. Gotta brush my teeth. Breath'll stink in the morning if I don't brush 'em." Harvey went into the bathroom and closed the door. Perry heard him vomit, then the water ran in the sink and he listened to Harvey brush his teeth.

"Much better now," Harvey said. He sat on the bed. "Stellar human being. Why can't everyone be so stellar?"

"I don't know," Perry said. "You all right now?"

"Good God, yes. Do you have my shoes?"

"Under the bed. Good night."

"Dawn. Night. Addie fell for the stellar chap."

"I know it. You'll be better."

"She falls and falls. She falls for everyone. Why can't I be stellar?"

"You're a one-eyed stellar fellow."

"War hero. I'm a bloody war hero. You know that?"

"I know it."

"Scary. Did you know I lost an eye over there? Do you know how it happened?"

"No."

"Me neither. Turn the bloody light off. Can't even remember. Everything was so dark, cow shit and mildew. Addie and that stellar . . . Some holiday."

Perry woke up with a toothache. He pushed his tongue against the raw tooth. Warmed it. He dressed, took two aspirin, and washed his face. There was a note from Grace; she was having breakfast. He shaved and pulled on a sweater and hurried downstairs. It was nearly noon. A blackboard stood in the center of the lobby, posting times for the first heats. Harvey was listed for an afternoon heat, and his own name was down for the last race of the day.

He went to the starting table and scratched his name from the races. He was too tired. The starter gave him a ten-dollar refund, and Perry walked up to the restaurant and found Grace and Addie having breakfast. Addie looked fresh.

"Some party last night," she said. "I was just telling Grace about it. Do you want some coffee? I think they've stopped serving by now."

Perry called the waiter over and ordered a fresh pot. His tooth was still aching.

Later they walked outside. After the night snow, the day was bright. Grace took his arm and they walked the half-mile to the racecourse. Addie went off to wish good luck to her new friend Daniel.

Balloons were tied to spruce boughs and the crowd was young and happy. The racecourse ran along an eleven-mile stretch of the Gunflint Trail, emptying on to the flat snow of a small lake. Iron poles were sunk into the ice and between them was stretched a cord with red and green banners dangling, the finish line. A heat was in progress on the trail and a loudspeaker blared out the positions and numbers of the racers. The crowd cheered and moaned and clapped for the unseen skiers, watching for when they would break on to the lake for the final half-mile. The day was brilliant. Children were building a snow fort behind the finish line, and further back were two large warming houses that sold beer and hot coffee and sandwiches, and when the loudspeakers weren't announcing races they played happy music. Perry caught a glimpse of Addie and the boy, then they disappeared in the crowd. It was a bright day. He smelled hot popcorn. Soon the heat of skiers broke out of the woods and on to the lake. By the naked eye, they did not appear to be moving at all, spots of color crouched low, so slow in progress that to someone not looking for them they would have been missed entirely, tiny patches of color that instead of moving appeared rather to expand and grow, the sun behind them giving the scene a fluid unsteadiness. Perry stood and watched them come. The loudspeaker announced the leader as Number Nine, heat four of the championship flight. A few people cheered, likely Number Nine's family or friends. Gradually the skiers came into focus. Then quickly. Then the sound of their skiing. Number Nine held a great lead. He skied with long professional strides, good rhythm.

When Number Nine cut through the bannered finish line, the rest of the pack was so far back that Perry could not make out their numbers.

Grace found a bench and they sat to watch three more heats finish, then they walked back up towards the hotel, Grace holding his hand and chatting, and they had a long lunch alone. Afterwards she went up for a nap and Perry looked in on Harvey. The shades were drawn but Harvey was awake and waxing his skis. The room was littered with bottles and glasses. It had a peculiar odor.

"Hard night," Harvey said matter-of-factly. "I swear that's the last ounce of booze I touch, forever and ever. Truly a remade man."

"Well, you look all right."

"I slept. Clean living, too. Say, have you seen Addie?"

"No." Perry decided to lie. He didn't decide, he simply lied. "No, but you'd better put a hurry to it. You're scheduled for three o'clock. You feel up to it?"

"Clean living. How about helping with that other ski? Be a good brother."

Perry found a sock and began waxing one of the long skis.

"What time do you ski?"

"I scratched," Perry said.

"Scratched?"

"Too tired. I'll just relax and watch you win a big trophy."

"Too bad. You were in the money, I'll bet. All that practice and everything." He started to smile, but the smile jerked like a tic.

After a time Harvey went to the bathroom and brought out a half-empty bottle of wine and drank without a glass. He was wearing a T-shirt and blue jeans. Even after his sickness, he looked strong. He was lean. He lit a cigarette and rested it on a bed-stand. "That Addie." He wiped another coat of wax on his skis and shaved the edges with a razor blade. "I've carried on too much. Have to stop carrying on."

"You'll win her, Harv. It'll turn into a good vacation. Grace is loving it. She likes vacations no matter what."

"Got to stop carrying on so," said Harvey.

"Right."

"Came home from . . . feeling like a bum. War and all. Wasn't so good, you know. I told you something about it last night, didn't I?"

"Just a little. You were drunk. I forget."

"Forget, remember, forget, remember. No matter, I was a goddamn baby anyway. Is that ski done? What time is it? Just forget everything I say." Harvey took a swig on his wine bottle. He went to the windows and looked out towards the west. Then he came back. He put a hand on Perry's shoulder, slight at first and then harder. "You're a good man, brother," he said. He looked at Perry through his good eye. "I'm serious, you're really my goddamn *brother*, aren't you?"

"Right," Perry said.

"Impossible, you'd think."

"I guess so."

"I mean, what's a brother?"

"Yeah. I don't know." They were quiet awhile. "I don't know, Harv."

"Don't ever listen to me."

"I don't, Harv."

"That's good. Don't ever start listening."

"You'd better put a step to it. Quarter to three already."

"I mean, what are we? We're bloody *adults* now, have you ever stopped to think about that?"

"Now and again."

"So you know it's true. Bloody adults, I can't get over it. You understand what I'm driving at?"

"More or less, Harv."

Harvey smiled. "Good. You want some of this wine? Awful

stuff. Don't know where I got it." He stood up and slipped on his sweater. He put on sunglasses and a fuzzed-tipped stocking cap. "Did I tell you? I was thinking. I shouldn't say, I guess. But what the hell. I was thinking maybe about asking Addie to get married, the whole schmeer. What do you think? After last night, I don't know. I was just thinking about it."

"Good idea," Perry said.

Harvey grinned. "Good idea if it works."

"Right. Don't forget your leggings. Can't be a winner without those leggings."

"I'm a winner, all right," Harvey said. "And you are a brother, aren't you?"

"Stellar," Perry smiled.

"Stellar. Right. Stellar, now that's a good word."

Perry carried his brother's skis from the hotel and down towards the starting area.

"I'm betting on you," he said. "Give it hell."

It was the last championship heat. The day was already coming on towards dusk. Perry watched as six ski-mobiles took the racers down the trail to where the heat would begin. When they were out of sight, he walked to the finish line and had a cup of coffee and watched several heats come in. One turned into a good race, a wild and desperate finish that had the crowd yelling, won by a fifteen-year-old boy. The boy was a native and the crowd's favorite. Perry cheered along with everyone else. The boy's father was drunk and happy, hugging the boy and dancing about, holding a can of beer that spilled everywhere. The crowd was happy. Everyone jostled the winning boy and Perry went over to shake his hand. The boy's father was jumping and dancing. While everyone celebrated Addie came through the crowd. Perry watched her. Eventually she saw him and smiled and waved and came over.

"Don't be so nasty. I hope you aren't going to start, too."

"Some sweetie."

"Peeping Paul. Here, let me have a sip of that. It's actually colder out here than you'd think with all the sun."

"So where's your new friend Daniel?"

"Racing. Don't be nasty now. I'm terrible, I'm a witch. Where's a good spot to watch them finish?"

They found a bench overlooking the lake.

Addie had a pair of binoculars and she scanned each group of racers. As the heats finished, the crowd got smaller and less boisterous. The dusk was rapidly coming on, and with it the cold. Addie went off for more coffee, and as she returned a group of skiers broke from the forest. The snow had formed a dark crust. On the far side of the lake, the skiers seemed to advance just on the edge of dusk.

A brace of spotlights was turned on, illuminating the finish line and part of the lake, but beyond the slice of light it was night.

"Can't see a thing," Addie said. "Wouldn't you know it?"

She handed Perry the binoculars. Through them, he could just make out the forms of the skiers. They were hunched low and did not look much like people.

"What number is your friend Daniel?"

"Six. Sixteen. Sixteen, I think. He's wearing that maroon and gold college sweater."

"Can't see color." He searched for Harvey in the coming forms. The binoculars were useless.

The forms were knotted together. They came in a pack. He heard them before he saw them. He heard their skis gouging the snow, then he heard them howling. He heard their breath in the back of his thoughts.

He gave Addie her binoculars.

"Here they come!" she said. "Here they come."

Perry pulled his glasses tight and peered out. It was cold and he was shivering.

They were howling. The pack was tight together. Dark, hunched shapes. In the dusk, they had the forest weight behind them and they came hurtling in their pack, howling and banded together and merging into a single shadow as they crossed the lake towards the bannered cord and spotlights, the harsh sounds of their flight and chase coming closer. Their heads were low out and deformed over the snow. Their tongues and teeth. One of them fell and toppled and the fallen was left abandoned, and the others came on, crossing the lighted fringe and into the spotlights. The skis snapped against the snow, a quick crisp cutting sound, and in the spotlights the ski poles gleamed silver and Perry saw the racers' breath frosting in a single cloud that was swept behind them, and the racers were braced in the spotlights. Perry leaned forward. Their faces were red. One of them shrieked and the others took up the howl. Red faces, shining, nostrils flared, they were separate from their skis. Twenty yards from the finish line, another skier fell and rolled.

It was over in a moment, the pack had a leader. Low and poles under his arms, the leader's mouth was pulled in a long fierce grin, and he crossed the line and held his poles high and howled. The others came across like gazelles on a faraway plain, then a herd, the harsh grating noises as they braked.

"It was Daniel!" cried Addie from somewhere.

"What?"

"He won! I knew it, I knew all along."

Addie got up and gave him the binoculars to hold and rushed off to the finish area.

The winner was surrounded.

Perry waited awhile then went down to the finish line. Daniel was being congratulated. The loudspeaker gave his winning time. The boy did not look tired. The other racers were sitting or lying still, breathing hard, but the boy was standing and leaning against his poles while people shook his hand. His time was marked up on a blackboard.

Perry shook the boy's hand and said it was a good race, and the boy nodded but he was looking at the blackboard, then at Addie, and he did not seem excited.

Then Harvey crossed the line. He was alone and his leggings and sweater were snow-clotted.

"Harvey!" Perry called, and watched as his brother slowed to an awkward silence under the lights. Harvey raised his head and his throat bulged, his skin cream white and old, and he howled. He quivered, his throat bulged again, and he turned to howl at the black sky, then his skis slipped from under him and in slow motion he sat on the lake, then lay back, face up.

Perry knelt down. Harvey was grinning. "Just a stupid country race," he said.

"I know it."

"Help me up, for God's sake."

"What happened?"

"Nothing. I fell."

"How could you fall?"

"I just fell. I got tired. Help me up."

Perry unbuckled the skis and clapped the snow from them.

"I suppose the Olympic champ won."

"It was a good race. You all right?"

"I guess. Just a country race."

"Yeah, come on."

Harvey brushed the snow off. As he stood, the spotlights were turned off and the lake went dark. The remaining crowd was leading Daniel up towards the hotel. "There they go," said Harvey. "It was just a crummy country race." He bracketed his skis together and flung them over his shoulder.

"Where's Addie?"

"She's around. Let's go up and get Grace and have some supper."

They had a quiet meal. A small band played in one corner of the restaurant. Grace was golden and consoling. They had creamed chicken and fresh spinach and wine. Grace wore a long dress and she looked good and Perry was proud of her. Towards the end of dinner, Addie and Daniel came in, and Addie waved but she did not come over. They sat at a table near the band.

"That girl is a goner," Harvey said.

"Forget it."

The band played quiet music and a few people got up to dance. Harvey took out a packet of cigars and they had brandy and watched the dancers and drank their coffee from pewter cups. Later they went into the lobby, sat in stuffed chairs, then Harvey went up to bed and Perry took Grace upstairs to dance.

He went to the window. It was morning, and a crowd of skiers and brightly dressed people were milling in the snow. He touched the window, steamed cold. Outside, a platform had been erected in the snow and decorated with colorful pennants and streamers. Perry dressed and hurried outside. His tooth was hurting again.

The six championship-flight finalists were being introduced by a man in a giant Eskimo parka. Daniel was on the stage along with the fifteen-year-old and the others. The crowd was dressed in sweaters and nylon ski jackets and stocking caps. They clapped loud for the fifteen-year-old.

Perry found Grace and Addie sitting on a bench. They stopped talking when he came up.

The man in the Eskimo parka made the introductions and

the six finalists trooped off the stage. Everyone applauded and waved scarves.

"Just a minute," Addie said. "Don't have breakfast without me, I'll be right back." She hurried over to Daniel and walked with him partway to the starting area, then she kissed him and came back. "Okay," she grinned, "now we eat. He'll win."

"Bless your Olympian."

"You said it."

"I think it stinks."

"Maybe over breakfast it'll smell better." She smiled straight at him.

Later Harvey joined them. He was sour, refusing to look at Addie. As soon as possible Perry took Grace's arm and led her out of the hotel. They took a van into Grand Marais and spent the morning looking in the shops. Grace found a set of carving knives she liked, and Perry bought them, then they decided to hike back to the hotel. It was a sunny, deceptive sort of day.

"Sorry it's not coming to a better time," he said.

She took his hand and they walked quietly for a while.

"That Addie should be spanked."

"It's all right," she said. "It's a vacation anyway." A big truck went by and they moved off on to the shoulder of the road. "I like it when we're alone like this. And it was nice of you to dance with me last night. Wasn't it fun?"

"Yes."

"Good. I'm glad. It was nice of you. Sometimes you do nice things and I like it."

"It would all have been better if Addie behaved herself."

"Well, I like being here with you. Can we come back in the summer? I'd like to be here in the summer. We could spend a whole week here, couldn't we? I'd like that. Can we do it? I was looking at some brochures in the hotel and they have all sorts of things going on. We can come alone then, all right?"

"Maybe. Maybe so."

When they got back, the championship race was over and Daniel had won easily. The times were posted on the hotel blackboard.

Perry sat with a newspaper in the lobby, content to be alone. He read about events in Washington and Paris and Minneapolis, forgetting the details as he read. The twilight crowds were coming in, some heading for the bar and others to prepare for dinner, and people were laughing. Perry put the paper down. For a time he simply sat alone, watching the people move through the lobby and listened to them. He saw the yellow-sweatered girl and she said hello and passed on towards the stairs. A fire was going. The lobby had high ceilings and crisscrossing beams and leather chairs.

Reclining, absorbed into the lobby as if he were an odor or physical object, Perry sat alone. The winter evening restlessness. Too bad about Addie, too bad for Harvey, too bad in general. Everything was too bad. He did not want to go upstairs. And he did not want to go to the bar, or sleep, or wander, or be still. He lit a cigarette and snuffed it out, then thought what the hell and relit it, crossing his legs. When the cigarette was smoked, he took a walk around the hotel, stopped to watch some children skating on a large artificial pond, then he went inside and took a chair nearer the fireplace. Too bad about Addie, too bad about Harvey, too bad in general. He untied his shoes, slipped them off, let the fire bake the smell of his socks into the air. The yellow-sweatered girl came by again. She waved and said hello and continued into the bar. Too bad in general. Later the tiny elevator deposited a group of young skiers into the lobby, the doors creaked, the elevator climbed again and came back with Addie and her new friend Daniel.

She was playful. She wore a long dress with gloves. The boy was careful not to touch her.

"Do you know Daniel? Daniel, this is my very good friend and confidant and trainer, Paul Milton Perry. Paul is a special friend and you have to be nice to each other. And Daniel, Daniel is the cross-country champion, you know. Daniel is my new friend, Paul, and you have to be kind to him, you must promise."

Perry promised and shook hands with the boy.

He seemed nice enough. The boy had nothing to do with it. Sitting with his chin slightly tilted, he looked a bit of an aristocrat. He wore a maroon sweater trimmed in gold. Perry asked him about the Olympics and the boy blushed and said it was something he was aiming at, nothing certain.

"Oh, you can't listen to Daniel," said Addie. "Daniel *never* says the truth. The truth is always too good to be the truth. Daniel, Daniel has already qualified and he's in training. He just won't say that. Isn't that right, Daniel?"

The boy nodded and smiled at the floor.

"And Daniel is also a student at the university and he's majoring in . . . What is it? Premed. That's it, he's going to be an Olympic champion and then a doctor, isn't that right?"

"Yes," the boy said, smiling at Perry. Perry smiled back at him.

"The skiing doctor," said Addie, "can't you see it? Skiing out to the farms with his black bag, arriving just in the nick of time, saving the pregnant mother, the baby dies but it isn't Daniel's fault, and the woman cries but he consoles her and tells her there will be other babies, other pregnancies, other dreams, other . . . I don't know what. It's a great story and I can't wait to watch it on television."

"Shut up," the boy said suddenly. He didn't appear angry, but he meant it.

"You see, you *see*?" said Addie. "Doesn't he have an Olympian doctor's presence of mind? He's so positively certain about everything. It drives me wild. He's not at all wishy-washy. Now, watch me ask him to get us all a drink and watch him refuse. Daniel?"

The boy shrugged and sauntered off towards the bar.

"He *is* a good lad," she said, watching him go.

"You're a sweetie, Addie."

"Thank you," she grinned. "And where's your lovely wife Grace?" Then she stopped. "I *am* sorry. I'm being nasty and I hate myself. I'm in a mood. It isn't so easy as you think, you know."

"I know."

"You don't know. You think you know. You don't know at all. You don't know this—Harvey wants us to get married. There's something I'll wager you don't know. He asked just yesterday, can you believe that? Even with Daniel and everything, he asked even then. Now there's something Peeping Paul doesn't know. How's that? How do you think that feels, smarty-know-everything? Think it over awhile. You don't know everything, you see?" She looked at him as though he'd hurt her, glaring. "There's something you don't know," she ended softly.

"You're such a sweetie," he said. "Some sweetie to ruin it all."

Then she grinned again. "Yes. Yes, that's one of the world's great truths. I'm such a sweetie." She sighed, and her grin relaxed and she just looked at him. "I love you anyway."

The boy came back and said the hotel didn't allow drinks in the lobby. He was polite, winking at Perry as if there were knowledge between them.

"Well, we must go inside then," said Addie. The boy stood aside, waiting for her to stand. He was careful again not to touch

her. "Aren't you coming? Daniel will be upset if you don't celebrate with him."

"Please come along," the boy said.

"I'll just sit. Thank you."

"Very well, very well," Addie laughed. "You have only yourself to blame when you die of thirst."

"Have a nice celebration."

The boy nodded and smiled, and they went off. Addie
walked fast ahead of him.

Perry spent another hour in the lobby then went upstairs.
Harvey was not in his room. Grace had finished her postcards
and they went down together to post them. They took a walk
outside, down towards the lake and back up and around the hotel, then to their room. Harvey was still not in.

"Poor Harvey," said Grace.

"He'll be all right." It was just too bad. They ordered sandwiches from room service. Grace wrapped up her new carving
knives. Perry finally turned on the color television.

Such a small place, Perry thought. He had experienced the
sensation before—inconsequence and smallness. The hotel restaurant was deserted. Red and blue tableclothes were draped in random readiness and the hotel had collapsed around the emptiness.
Already the smell was musty. It overwhelmed him: an enormous
lassitude that pressed down like low gravity, anchoring him to
each slow-moving unfolding, each conversation like an echo, unspoken currents, each concern a well-traveled maze with each
step plodding in the tracks of that previous. He waited a long
while before a woman opened the kitchen door and took his order. When she was gone, Grace began talking, a waiter brought
coffee, the morning unfolded as if begging for corroboration, and

Grace was talking. "And I don't see why you should go, it doesn't make sense. It's another of Harvey's ideas and it's worse than most of them, so it must be pretty awful. I just wish you wouldn't."

"I promised I'd go along. You know that."

"I know . . ." she trailed off.

"It won't be so bad," Perry said slowly. "Harvey's got things arranged, maps and about a billion dollars worth of gear, the best stuff, and he's . . . After all this, maybe it's what he needs, I don't know. And it's only for a few days and all. You should stop worrying about it."

"I'm not exactly worried," she repeated. "I just don't know."

"You're acting like it."

"I'm sorry then."

"Don't be sorry. If you're worried, say so. There's nothing to worry over. Three days, four days. It's not like we're going whoring. That's how you're acting."

"Paul."

"All right."

Nothing was settled. She ate her breakfast in a puckered, hurt way which he tried to ignore, knowing that in the end she had no real choice in the matter and would accept it as she accepted everything. Finally, when they finished coffee, she asked if they could take a walk. The invitation was a cripple. Pathetic except for the porous affection. So they walked out of the hotel and down to the lake and watched the ski-mobile races. Grace hugged his arm.

Afterwards they hiked down the road to the parking lot, and Perry got out the two orange rucksacks and threw them over his shoulder and they returned to the hotel. He went back alone for his skis. The sky was frosted gray.

Waxing his skis, he held quiet against her sulking. She sat on the bed and read travel brochures. "Maybe Harvey will call it off," he finally said as a gesture. She didn't look up. He shrugged and went next door and knocked and went in. Harvey was drinking red wine.

"You get the rucksacks?"

"In my room. Where's Addie?"

"I've put her out of my head."

"I see."

"Yeah, out of sight out of mind and so on. She's well out of sight. Having a good-bye with her Olympic champion. What's his name?"

"Daniel."

"Right, Daniel. The giant slayer. No, is that Daniel? Daniel, David. I don't know. Lion slayer? Anyway they're off having their good-byes and we're here. Did you catch any of the ski-mobile races?"

"A few minutes. Stinking boring. What you doing there?"

"Just encasing this map in plastic. It's always a good thing to do," said Harvey. Here, take some of this.' He handed Perry the bottle and Perry drank some and gave it back. "I suppose Grace is still putzing and moaning?"

"She's accepted it. She's that way."

"A stellar woman. Truly. Has a lot of sense and a good head on her shoulders and all that."

Harvey's face was sliced into two planes, sallow and bright red. The bones seemed to want to push out through the skin. He was in his shorts. His beard was full now and dark against the rest of him. It looked to Perry like a fungus, some sort of fuzzy parasite that had taken Harvey in his sickness and was not yet defeated. "So," Harvey was saying, "I'll take a run into town and get the things we'll need. I've got a list ready. I'm glad we're going. I'm glad. Plenty of chocolate and peanut butter. Did you know how many calories peanut butter has? Guess. Just take a stab."

"I don't know, Harv."

"A hundred! A hundred calories for each tablespoon, can you believe that? Each *tablespoon*! And it has protein, too. Anyhow, I'll pick up a couple of big jars and some instant coffee and matches and chili and canned stew and that sort of thing. It's all down on the list." Perry took the list and scanned it. It looked complete.

"Okay, Harv." Perry tried to think. He wasn't a woodsman. "You called the weather bureau?"

Harvey stared at him. Then he grinned. "Sure. Hunky-dory. Just don't forget your sleeping bag."

"All right then. I'm going to take Grace down for some lunch. Want to come along?"

Harvey shook his head. He was intent on rubbing the gold wax into his skis. "Say a beautiful good morning to Addie if you see her."

"I will, Harv. Take a nap if you can."

"Righto."

Perry went downstairs for cigarettes. Addie and her new friend were sitting by the fire. They didn't notice him and Perry turned his back and went outside and smoked a cigarette, walked once around the hotel for air, and they were no longer in the lobby when he went in.

He went to his room. Water was running in the bathroom. He kicked the snow off his boots, unlaced them and put them before the radiator. The room was cold. He lay on the bed. A pack of Grace's menthol cigarettes was on the night stand, and he took one and listlessly smoked it down to the filter. He thought of Harvey for a while, then of Addie, then of Grace, then quickly of Daniel. Then of himself. It was too bad. He smiled. He went to his suitcase and took out the thermal underwear and put it on. He looked at himself in the mirror. The underwear made him look fat. Amazing changes. He got into his jeans and shirt and had another cigarette, and when Grace came out of the bathroom they went to the restaurant for lunch. It was nearly empty. The parties were over. A resonant hollowness followed everywhere. Three young girls were sitting at one table, quietly having their lunch. They were not very pretty. Perry guessed that it had not been a very good weekend for them. In a while Addie came in. She did not have much to say. She looked tired. She ordered a Coke and asprins.

"Suppose Daniel's gone," said Perry.

"I suppose."

It was a slow anesthetic lunch. Perry found himself happy in Addie's new pensiveness. And Grace was quiet, and the hotel seemed to cry with tinny echoes, and Perry for once felt they were all in it together, the same mood as on a dying January day.

It seemed to Perry that they rushed too blindly to the forest. Too quickly and without proper preparation and forewarning.

Harvey was in a hurry.

They dressed in high wool socks, cotton anoraks and parkas.

Harvey was all business, taking charge. He packed the new-bought rations into the rucksacks, rolled the sleeping bags and tied them and stashed them inside the packs.

The momentum of departure was taking hold, an inertia that seemed to have started years before, slowly growing until it was a locomotive that wailed down an incline uncontrolled, and Perry held on, following Harvey's lead.

They helped Grace and Addie carry the baggage to the car. No one talked much. Grace seemed far away. As if viewing her through a badly remembered dream, physically out of joint. He gave her a short kiss and she held his arm a moment, then she whispered something he couldn't hear and got into the car.

Without looking at anyone, Addie grinned and waved and got behind the wheel. Perry wanted to say something. Instead he waved at Grace and stepped back. Addie drove the car over the icy parking lot, honked and turned on to the road leading south. "That's that," Harvey said. Perry shook his head as though trying to clear it of apprehension. "That's that," Harvey said again. He smiled ghoulishly, letting his dead eye float upward. The iris disappeared behind the bone of his forehead.

In the lobby they gave their skis a last coat of wax. Everything was still. Harvey studied the map again, jotting notes in the margin, then he gave the map to Perry and went into the kitchen to fill his Thermos with coffee. Perry sat with the map. The lobby fireplace was sputtering and all was warm and quiet and still. When Harvey returned, they had a cigarette, threw their butts into the fireplace and helped each other into their packs, breathed in the warm hotel air, then went outside.

Perry was lost.

He stepped into his skis, pulled up the woollen leggings.

Down the road, hanging from evergreens, were batches of half-deflated balloons and scraps of crepe paper. A man in earmuffs was dismantling the loudspeaker platform, using a hammer to knock the wooden struts out of place, and the man's breath hung in the air.

"Saddle up," Harvey said.

"Which way?"

"After me, after me." He stooped and tied his safety straps. "We'll take it nice and easy. Ready now?"

Harvey skied down the slope leading to the lake. Without pausing, he swept across the road and on to the lake, the orange rucksack bobbing on his back. Perry hurried to catch up.

Two

Blizzard

Sobbing sounds: coffee into a cup, leaves into a bushel basket, feathers into a pillow, air into a vacuum. He listened. No certain sounds, vague and muffled and indistinct. No rustles or movements. A sobbing sound, many sobbing sounds. Inanimate and elemental, into him and out of him, some distant time, very distant. Perry snuggled deep in the bag. He was warm enough. Goose down—the best insulation, Harvey said. He was warm enough but he could not sleep. He disliked the slick feel of the bag's nylon lining. And the bag seemed to anchor him, pinning him down, and he tossed about and fought for some accommodation with it. He poked his nose free. The night air was cold and almost sweet, and he pulled it into his lungs and warmed it and released it as steam into the forest. He listened: the sobbing sounds. He tried to place them. He listened carefully, holding his breath to let the sounds come through pure. There was no wind, no motion. The night was solid and still. The sobbing sounds continued. He peered ahead, looking for the source, but he was blind. Harvey had promised his eyes would adjust to the winter dark, but he was blind. The fire was dead. Not even an ember left. There was no colour or form or motion. Inside the bag it was warm. But it was artificial and tenuous warmth, absolutely dependent on the sustained well-being of his own body. He thought about it. The sobbing sounds: indefinite, gradually compressing air, the sound of frost going deep. He couldn't tell. It was all too demanding. Too wild and too lonely. Harvey began to snore. The snoring seemed far away, as though overheard in another room, or in a hospital ward where the patients lie separated by curtains, each suffering alone. He couldn't tell. Eventually the snoring merged with the other sounds. Turning on to his side, he faced the black brunt of the west forest. There was nothing to see. He moved deeper into the bag and lay still and tried not to think and he began thinking. He thought about having to find another job, about Grace, then about Addie and Harvey, then about himself. He thought for a time about his father, nothing specific, letting the colored memories flop like television advertisements, the bomb shelter, the pond, growing up, growing down, getting married, wandering, letting go, thinking forward and backward with futile aimlessness. He decided to pray. He thought about Damascus Lutheran. Desperation mixed with guilt, and he prayed for Grace and for finding a new job and for Harvey and for himself. He prayed the Lord's Prayer, then he prayed for another vacation soon. He stopped praying and listened to the sobbing sounds, then he remembered Jud Harmor. He prayed that Jud Harmor didn't have cancer, then he prayed that, if it were cancer, the old man could be saved, then he prayed that, if he couldn't be saved, the old man would die fast and not feel pain, then he lay wide awake and listened to the forest's sobbing sounds. He was surprised at how warm the bag was. Harvey knew how to do it right. Goose down. Dig a trench in the snow, lay the bag in, cover it with a foot of snow. Insulation, Harvey explained. A snow nest. A snow den. Like the bears, Harvey explained. He concentrated on the sounds of the forest: like rainfall, all around, high and low, pouring everywhere. He turned on to his back. For a while he was able to lie still, thinking about nothing but the sounds. A good woodsman would identify them. Harvey could name them, give their source and place and exact distance. Harvey was sleeping. The fire was dead. A hard day. Leaving, the anticipation, Grace. All told, they hadn't gone very far, barely ten miles. But it was nothing easy. When Harvey left the trail, plunging dead west into the woods, they'd gone slow, picking the way, Harvey's orange rucksack bobbing ahead, weaving and flanking the impenetrable thickets of pine. No more paths, nothing but the lay of the forest the way it had always been. Nothing easy. Harvey's orange rucksack always moving. Perry turned and thought out the day and listened to the sobbing sounds and tried to sleep. He heard Harvey move. He thought he heard it. He wasn't sure.

"You awake, Harv?"

He listened but it was nothing.

In the morning a natural alarm punctured his sleep, a slight change of temperature and the sun's light. Harvey was standing at the fire.

"Fine day," he said, without turning. He was wearing a sweater and blue jeans. His parka hung on a birch branch.

"Damn cold day."

"That's no way to talk. Get out and help me with breakfast. We'll eat a nice big breakfast, you'll be surprised. Come on."

"Get the fire hotter. I'm staying here till it's hotter."

Harvey laughed and pushed a new log into the fire. Perry watched him boil water and make coffee and put two cans of chili on the fire. It was a sunny morning. Harvey brought him coffee in a tin cup and Perry lay in his bag to drink it. The sun bathed a jungle of green pine. The shadows stretched across the camp clearing and into another, deeper growth of trees.

"Not so bad, is it?" Harvey said.

"Cold."

"Cold," Harvey laughed. He looked much better. He smiled and his teeth were white through the beard. He looked recovered. "Get out and move around and you'll see how cold it is."

Perry hooked his glasses with his toes, brought them to the head of the bag and slipped them on. Things looked better. Reluctantly he pulled his clothes on and left the bag. He did not need his parka.

"Not so bad, is it?" Harvey said.

They ate the chili and had more coffee, then began packing the rucksacks. By the time the sun cleared the pines, everything seemed fine. Perry kicked snow into the fire.

"A good skiing day," said Harvey. "Just look at it. We'll make twenty miles."

And it was a fine day.

Harvey's orange rucksack flashed ahead of him and Perry followed, feeling strong and comfortable, stabbing the snow with his poles, rushing on. The motion was swift and unconnected to anything solid. He gained confidence. The morning skiing was easy as the forest descended and the trees grew far enough apart not to worry about quick stops. They crossed two medium-sized lakes, neither of which were on the map, something new and undiscovered, and the land continued its descent in a gentle downward flow. When they crossed the second lake, Harvey found a small frozen creek and they followed it deep in. On both banks evergreens grew tall, their branches intertwined to form a wall. The sky became a narrow slit.

Perry did not notice the clouds coming in. When the clouds

covered the sun, he did not notice. He followed Harvey's orange rucksack.

Twice Harvey stopped to consult his compass. On the second stop, they took off their packs and skis and stood together and urinated under a pine. Harvey unwrapped a bar of chocolate. "Nice country, isn't it? I told you. We can rest awhile if you're tired."

Perry waved him off and they continued up the creek. Eventually it emptied on to a large lake and on the far side they had to carry their skis through a tangle of brush and pines. The country got rocky. The slope of land began turning up. Skiing was impossible. They climbed a pine bluff, then another, and the country kept angling up and up. Perry noticed then that the sun was gone. When finally they stopped climbing, the sky was a sickly gray color. Harvey grunted and unzipped his trousers.

His urine made a yellow patch in the snow.

"What time is it?" Perry asked.

"About three thirty, judging by the sun."

Perry laughed. "Okay, woodsman. There isn't any sun. How about judging by your watch?"

"Ha. Okay. Judging by my watch it's four. Not bad?"

"Nice trick. Where to now?"

They sat on their rucksacks and Harvey took out the map. "An hour and a half of good light left. All right." He placed his compass on the map. "Parent Lake is dead west of here, half an hour." He pointed to a place on the map.

Perry studied it. A thousand lakes looked back at him. "Where are we now?"

"Here. Right about here. I can tell better when we get out of this thick stuff. But right about here."

"All right," Perry nodded. "And this river? Have we passed this river yet? I didn't notice it if we did."

Harvey folded the map up and shrugged. "Who knows? The

way everything's frozen over. Snowed under. Could have crossed a hundred rivers. Damn river doesn't even have a name. See?"

"Yeah, Harv. Rugged country, right?"

"Absolutely. Let's go. We'll have a fire blazing in half an hour."

They strapped on their skis. The bluffs fell to a natural valley that burrowed southwest and then opened on to a meadow surrounded by more trees. The trees were very old, mostly pine but some birch. The birch were slim and tall, and the white bark stretched in large sheets around the trunks, crinkling at the black seams. There was nothing moving. Perry looked once at the closing sky then decided to ignore it and followed Harvey's orange rucksack. A palpable, bitter air kept him going.

For a time it was easy skiing again, but then again the forest thickened and they were forced to walk. Harvey followed a chain of moraines that gradually flattened and gave way on the rim of an ancient gully. It was getting dark. They didn't talk. Harvey took out the map and compass, spending a long time over them, and finally he grinned and said they should make camp. He pointed into the gully: "Down there, I guess. It'll keep the wind out."

"You know what's what," said Perry, and he threw his skis into the depression.

Without being told, Perry began the search for wood.

"Made fifteen miles today," Harvey was saying. "Not at all bad considering all the walking. From here on it'll get a lot easier, once we get to the string of lakes."

"Right."

"Nothing to it."

"A nice crackling fire," Harvey was saying, confident and cheerful, dumping an armload of wood into the gully. "What we need now are some logs. About a dozen good-sized logs."

"You sure that's enough?"

"Sure I'm sure."

The forest light was gone. Calcified, frozen, the forest was quiet except for the light wind.

"That'll do it," Harvey said.

They dropped their wood into the gully, then Harvey held Perry's wrist and lowered him down. For a moment he was free of the earth, dangling. It sucked his breath away. He gasped, and felt the strain on his shoulder, and he was suddenly afraid, not of falling but of falling nowhere. Harvey released the grip. Perry fell to his knees, his hands sinking into the snow.

"That'll do it, that'll do it," Harvey said. "You all right?"

Perry nodded in the dark.

They gathered the wood into a pile and Harvey separated the twigs from the branches from the big stuff. It was dark. Perry could see only his brother's form squatting in the snow. The wind seemed wet.

Crouched down, Harvey dug out a hollow in the snow. "Easy does it," he purred. He took a sheet of newspaper from his pack, crinkled it and laid it in the hollow, then he added the twigs, then branches. He braced the pile with two logs. "Easy does it," he purred. The wind was picking up. "Here she goes, here she goes," said Harvey, striking a match, touching the newspaper.

The fire burned away the newspaper, then the twigs, then took hold of the pine branches.

Slowly at first, then quickly, the fire's light spread across the snow and climbed the banks of the gully, and Perry saw it was snowing.

It was snowing, and the wind was coming down the gully from the north in a low whine. It was snowing, and the fire climbed the banks of the gully and the snow crackled in the heat. Harvey's face was bright red, his eyes were red, his brown beard sparkled, he was grinning, and the fire leapt up into the coming snow.

"There she is," he purred.

"Harvey?"

"Look at that nice baby, will you?"

"Harvey, it's snowing for Christ sake."

Beyond the ring of light there was nothing. The wind and snow seemed captured in the fire. There was not a sound, just the fire and the settling gravity of the snowfall.

The fire sputtered and shifted from the branches to the logs.

"For Christ sake, Harvey, can't you see it's snowing?"

Perry moved close to the fire. Harvey was crouched low, building the flames up.

"Harvey."

"Shhhh," said Harvey. He hovered over the fire and continued to feed the wood.

"Harvey, it's a goddamn *snowstorm*."

Perry was cold. He unzipped his parka and thrust his hands into his armpits and let them thaw. He stood still and watched Harvey and watched the snow slant across the flames. He was tired. He wanted to sit down but there was nothing but the snow.

"There she is," Harvey purred. "Some fire, isn't she? She'll keep us well all night." At last he stood up.

"Harvey. For Christ sake, can't you see it's snowing?"

"Hmmm. Yes, I see it, I see." His eye was fast on the fire. "Isn't that some beaut of a fire? Proud of it. Sure, a little snow. Winter, isn't it? What do you expect in winter. Come on, let's get the tarp up and have some coffee and supper. Nothing we can't handle, brother, let's get a move on."

Harvey slung the rucksacks over his shoulder and took them to the fire and dumped their gear close in, then he climbed the gully and in a few minutes came back with pine boughs. "You see? No problem. The old man taught me all about this stuff. Dig around and find a couple big branches to hold the tarp. Let's get a move on, brother." Glazed and angry, Perry wandered up the gully looking for branches. When he got back, Harvey had the sleeping bags unrolled on the boughs and water was boiling and the snow had stopped, leaving just a light bitter wind. "See?" Harvey said.

Perry watched while Harvey pushed the branches down and erected a taut lean-to over the bags. "Nothing to it if you know how," Harvey said. "You paying attention?"

"This is crazy, Harv."

"It's not crazy. Not at all. This is just how it's done. Let's have some supper now."

He watched while Harvey heated cans of beans and Spam, prepared coffee and tended the fire and cut squares of chocolate on to plastic plates. Perry watched with the sensation of great blocks of time passing by, a long cold suspension in which he was outside looking in, seeing his brother in some distorted and disjointed trick of history, going backward too fast to care. Perry watched with his hands folded under his armpits.

The snowfall had ended.

He was embarrassed. He sat on a rucksack and accepted a cup of coffee and drank it down and held it out for Harvey to refill. Fear and longing had combined during the dusk, but it was over, and he was left with a kind of intellectual wonder, watching Harvey perform his woodsman's tricks.

"Not so bad, is it?"

"I guess not. That snow."

"Nothing to worry about, believe me. Eat up now."

Afterward, Harvey cleaned the plates and cups and stashed them in the packs, then he took off his parka and got into his sleeping bag and tinkered with the fire. The wind died. Harvey curled into the bag.

"You going to sleep?" asked Perry.

Harvey mumbled something.

"You aren't going to sleep, are you?"

"Why not?"

"I don't know." Perry thought about it. "We've got enough wood, I suppose?"

"Plenty."

"Maybe. I don't know. Maybe one of us ought to stay up while the other sleeps. What do you think? To keep the fire going and all."

"Shit," Harvey laughed.

Perry pulled his pack closer to the fire and sat still. Harvey was buried in his bag. He'd been afraid. Outside the fire's light, the night was there. The fire was nice. It made his face and chest and belly warm, and it left his back cold. He closed his eyes. Later he had a cigarette then crawled into his bag and watched the fire. With Harvey's lean-to and the sleeping bag and the pine boughs, he felt comfortable and warm. A few tiny snowflakes still drifted across the fire. He put out his hand and caught a few and licked at them.

His mind wandered. Then for a while he was asleep.

When he awakened the fire was still going, Harvey was snoring, it was all peaceful and a winter night.

He removed his glasses and pushed them to the bottom of the bag. He lay still and listened to the fire and Harvey's snoring. Sound asleep. A bull, all right. He knew what he was doing. The Bull of Karelia. No question about it. They were different. Scratch everything else, no matter, they were different. Harvey knew what he was doing. Calm, building that fire, unafraid, a full-fledged undaunted hero, absolutely no question. A little snow. A flutter of snow, a minuscule flurry. He watched the fire draw down. There was a different sense of time, all right. By civilization's time, it was probably still early. Eight o'clock, nine o'-clock. Scrabble time.

The fire drew into a ball and Perry watched it.

A billion, a billion billion separate details, piled and lumped together, a billion sparkling facets, angles, faces, lightings, memories, distances, square and round and jagged and triangular and pointed and sharp and full and flat and dull, rugged and even, a thicket. He felt grafted to the forest floor. A vast cold froze it all together. The black forest was fused to the black sky, the black sky to the clouds, the clouds to the snow, the snow to the fire, all to one.

He pushed his thumb and forefinger to the bridge of his nose. He rubbed his eyes and blinked. The forest was colorless. In the morning it would have color. In the morning Harvey would rebuild the fire, he would make coffee, he would roll up the sleeping bags and take the lead and they would go on, Harvey was a woodsman, no question about it. The way be could sleep and snore. The way he could build a fire, make coffee, make supper, curl into his sleeping bag and sleep and sleep, the snoring sounds mingling with the forest's sobbing sounds. Old Harvey. And the times. . . .

"Paul?"

"You scared me. I thought you were asleep."

"I woke up. Can you reach out and put one of those logs on the fire? It's ready to die."

"Yeah. There."

"How you sleeping?"

"Not at all. Not yet. It's all right, I'm warm enough."

"Try counting out loud."

"What?"

"It's a trick . . . it's one of those things I learned from the old man. Just give it a try, can't hurt."

Harvey turned softly. Fire shadows played on the lean-to ceiling and the flames caught hold of the new log. Harvey's voice was slow with sleep, smooth and calming in the woods. In a while he turned again. "Nice, isn't it?"

"Fine."

"Did you try counting?"

"Yes."

"You have to do it out loud. Like this: one, two, three, four, five. Until you're asleep."

"How do you know when to stop?"

"You just stop. That's the good part. Hey. You want a beer? I've got four of them hidden away in my pack. Special occasions and all. You want one?"

In the dark Harvey hooked his rucksack and dragged it under the lean-to and Perry listened to the tops pop off the cans. "Good," said Harvey with a satisfied smacking. "Try that, isn't that something special?"

Chunks of ice floated in the beer. It was sweet and good.

"You see? There are some pleasures, real pleasures out here. All it takes is to try it." Harvey was quiet for a while and Perry heard him sipping at the beer. "The only problem is taking a pee after drinking beer," Harvey said. "Getting out of the sleeping bag and everything. No fun at all. I heard a story once about Admiral Perry running across a guy who had to pee in the Antarctic and the guy was frozen right into the ice like a snowman. Poor Admiral Perry kicked at the guy and got all the snow off him. What do you think he found? Well, he found the frozen bugger had peed himself right to death, that's what. A three-foot arc of golden ice going from the poor guy's weenie to the snow, frozen stiff. Some rainbow, don't you think? Story goes that Admiral

Perry accidentally kicked away the frozen arc of pee and the frozen bugger toppled and shattered. A true saga of adventure, don't you think? A slice of life, as they say. I don't know. Personally I don't believe it for a minute."

"That's an epic story."

"Yes. Don't you think so? I'm thinking of writing it up." He giggled. He looked happy. "We ought to do this more often. Don't you think? All that Addie nonsense. Don't know what gets into me. She's something, isn't she? Keeps calling me her bloody pirate. Don't know where she gets that pirate business, it's absolutely crazy. She thinks my Admiral Perry story is true. She didn't believe me when I told her it was a lie. I don't know. You have to be with her all the time, I guess, because when you're with her she's terrific, she really is terrific, but when you're not with her and she's off somewhere, well, then she doesn't even know you. Isn't she something? And that Daniel. I don't want to talk about it . . . She keeps asking strange questions. She wanted to know what it felt like when I lost my eye. What it *felt* like! Jesus. Can you believe that? Then she gets all teasing and makes you feel like a crazy for not wanting to talk about it, as if . . . I don't know what. Jesus. She wouldn't believe me when I told her I didn't even remember what happened. Now isn't that something, not even believing me? The way she's always grinning and teasing. Really, she's just a kid . . . I don't know. Sometimes I don't think she's part Indian at all; I think it's one of her teasing stories. Think about it, sometimes she doesn't even look Indian, does she? I mean, I guess it's true. Sometimes she does look Indian."

"Yeah."

"Shall we have the other two beers? No. We'll save them."

"Save them," Perry said. "That's a good idea."

"I'm glad you came out here with me. You didn't have to.

I'm glad you came though. You should have come before. I don't know, but I think Dad would have been happy. Never said anything, of course. I don't know. Sorry. Maybe we should have those other beers now."

"Maybe so."

"What do you think?"

"Yeah. Let's have them right now."

"Good man! Good man. That's what I think."

The pop-tops cracked open. The can was cold in his hand, and there was nothing to think about. The bag was warm and the beer was cold and the night was dark and the fire was different colors. There was nothing to think about. "Anyhow," Harvey was saying beside him, talking on, "anyhow, I've pretty much decided to get a job and get on with it. I don't know what yet. That's something I'll have to think about. I know I'm dreaming but I'd give a million bucks for a job out here. I don't know doing what, something. Too bad they don't need lumberjacks anymore. That's what I'd be good for. Anyhow, pretty soon I'll be getting a job. I was thinking maybe we could start some kind of business together, you know? What do you think of that? I'm not sure doing what. We could start an army or something. They always need armies. Anyhow. Anyhow. I had it all planned out. It was all planned."

"It's a crime."

"She's all right though."

"Forget it."

"I'm going to sleep."

"Good night, Harv."

"Night. We're always saying good night."

Deceptively, the morning snowfall fluttered down. It wasn't much. Flakes and swirls. The snow came and went, a bit at a time, very quiet.

They cooked breakfast in cans. Harvey was happy and eager. He took charge, rounding up firewood and striking the fire, opening cans, hustling.

The snowfall was light and loose and constant. At first, Perry did not hear it. Then the sound was clear, the sobbing sound. It was that light hum, a respiration that was all around, and the snow fell like a gauze curtain. On either side of the gully, the evergreens sagged with the snow and the sky was gray. For breakfast they had soup and Spam and coffee. They opened a sack of cookies and ate them all, drank more coffee, then Harvey unfolded the map and laid it on his rucksack.

"We're here," he said.

"Where?"

"Here. See? The gully must have been a river or creek or something when they made this map. That means we're right here. If we follow the gully it should take us straight into Parent Lake. Half an hour maybe. Then turn south."

Perry nodded. The map was reassuring. It was very green. Blue lines and lake splotches were drawn in certain detail. He looked at the names of the familiar towns. They seemed close, inches away. Silver Bay, Lutsen, Finland, Two Harbors, Sawmill Landing. He felt much better looking at the map. He clapped Harvey's shoulder.

Harvey grinned. "Glad you came? Not so bad, is it?"

"It's all right, Harv."

"One more day. We'll be home for lunch on Thursday." Harvey spread his palms out, let the snow flutter into his bare hands. "Terrific," he said. "There's something very virtuous and terrific about it, isn't there? I think so, I think so."

They packed the tarp and sleeping bags. Harvey dug a hole to bury the empty cans. Then they started up the gully.

The new powder made the skiing smooth, cushioning the hard jolts of the day before, and the light snowfall continued.

Perry enjoyed it. The cold snapped all around, but they kept moving. Harvey's orange rucksack leading through the gully, and all he had to do was follow. He felt strong. He heard Harvey singing ahead of him. The air was clean and gustatory with delicate pine smells and the hard oxygen. Harvey's orange rucksack bobbed merrily and his singing drifted back and Perry felt good.

On both sides of the gully, the evergreens grew high and close together. They skied on. At times the snowfall seemed to stop, hesitating, and the sky would open up and the day would try to brighten, but then the snows would start again and the day would get listless.

Snaking gradually north then twisting back sharply, the channel carried them ahead and the skiing was easy. Perry's thighs began to tingle. It was a pleasant healthy ache. It was easy, following the orange rucksack, following the simple channel of the gully. It was easy. There was nothing to think about. Once they stopped to carry their skis over a pile of fallen boulders. Otherwise it was easy. Perry wondered about the gully's origin. Once a river perhaps, or a rivulet, or a cold creek. Dried up, left in the earth like an unmended wound. He skied and listened to Harvey's singing, and the gully began slowly to dig deeper and the banks climbed higher. It got dark and the gully continued burrowing deep down. Harvey finally stopped to consult his compass.

"Fifteen minutes," he said. "The lake's coming up. We'll ski right on to it."

They pushed off again. The incline was gradual. Mulberry bushes grew in patches along the gully banks.

In an hour they stopped again. Harvey took out the compass and map. They were deep in the gully and the sky was only a sliver.

Harvey kicked out of his skis and climbed the left bank and

stood with his hands over his eyes. He held the compass and map at belt level, looking first at the sky, then ahead into the forest, then at the map, then at the compass. He slid down the bank and buckled on his skis.

"See the lake?"

"No lake yet. Too many trees."

"It's all right then?"

"Awhile more. No problem."

Perry looked at him. "You aren't lost, are you?" It sounded almost trivial.

"Fifteen more minutes. Damn map is just scaled wrong. It's pretty old."

"Okay."

"You want a rest?"

"I'm all right. I just want to get to that damned lake."

"You look pale."

"I'm fine."

In twenty minutes they came to a lake, Harvey smiled but did not say anything. It was just a tiny lake surrounded by birch and evergreens and blue spruce, more a pond than a lake.

"Okay?" Harvey said.

Perry looked about.

"I guess we can rest now," Harvey said. "How does peanut butter and crackers sound?"

"Fine. The lake doesn't seem as big as the one on the map."

"Bad scale. You know how it is. Come on, I'm hungry."

They sat on their rucksacks. Perry finally saw the sky and it was gray, a single mammoth cloud hanging low. Snow rippled across the lake in drift waves, and the light snow kept falling, and there was more of a wind.

"Do we head south now?"

"Eat some of this peanut butter?"

"Okay. Let's hurry."

"There's time."

"I know. I just want to hurry. Let's just hurry."

Harvey laughed and the cough started.

"You're all right?"

"Perfect. Everything's perfect. Eat up."

He laughed and the cough followed.

"Let's just hurry."

"We're on the way, buddy."

They skied to the center of the lake. They exercised a sweeping turn and skied into the forest.

For a time Harvey kept a fairly straight course and the trees filtered out the falling snow and the day was dismal gray. Weaving and picking the way, Harvey led him through a stand of old pine, then through a natural clearing and into dense birch, then into more pine. The country was flat. It was all the same, and Perry followed the orange rucksack. There was no distinguishing it. Harvey was no longer singing. Perry was not thinking. He shuffled after his brother, not thinking, pushing with the poles and hearing only the sound of his skis and his breathing and the gentle constant snowfall. He was afraid. It was not a thought, just a feeling that seemed to well somewhere behind his eyes, and he did not recognize it as fear. It was a deep sting behind his eyes. It was a redness, a kind of growing red welt that made his eyes begin to water. The forest was all the same. It was flat and the snow was falling and there were no birds or sounds and Harvey's orange rucksack was far ahead, sometimes disappearing in the evergreens. His eyes were watering and he felt the sting expanding in his head.

Smooth motions, bent at the waist and leaning slightly forward, letting the skis carry him, routine, thoughtless, inertia and gravity, the smooth skating motion, the sound in the snow. His eyes stung. It was a kind of acid behind the eyes, a dizzying and blinding kind of pressure that made them water. The trees were everywhere. He brushed against one and it rustled and sprinkled snow. He tried to think of a song to sing. Each step, one at a time, it was easy. The country was flat and the snow was all fresh powder and the skis were well waxed. He had prepared. He was strong, and the red sting persisted, he couldn't place it. He blinked and his eyes watered. Harvey was moving fast, getting too far ahead. Perry pushed hard with the poles, brushing through the pines, hearing them ripple behind him, hearing the skis cut the snow. Harvey's orange rucksack bobbed and dropped down an incline and disappeared. The wind was whipping the snow. He tried to think of a friendly song. A nice cheerful skiing song. He pushed in and skied hard, the sting growing behind his eyes. It was cold. A nice friendly yodelling song. He tried to think and ski and follow Harvey's orange flaming rucksack. The wind came from behind him and pushed him along, and he felt his skis slipping downwards, down the incline, and Harvey's orange rucksack darted behind a rill and Perry followed. Old Harvey, he thought. A good wind. They were moving fast. He pushed with his poles and the wind carried him down. Such a bull. The red sting was pressing against his eyes, flooding the membranes, and he blinked away tears, chasing Harvey. It was snowing. Now it was snowing. It was white sleek powdered snow. His eyes burned. The harder he skied, the harder he pushed, the more his eyes burned, the faster Harvey's orange flaming rucksack receded. He chased and chased and the orange rucksack receded. Now it was snowing. It was thick soft powdered fine snow, and he saw it for the first time, more and more of it, and Harvey's rucksack glittered orange far ahead through the snow. He started to call out. Then the red sting seemed to rupture. He stumbled and his eyes flooded. In a great painless collapse, the pressure blew off and it gushed out and his eyes flooded, and he called for Harvey and stopped pushing and skiing and held his hands to his face and let the skis carry him to a long slow stop.

Then he knew he was afraid. It was all over him. It was behind his eyes and flowing out, and he was truly afraid.

He stood alone in the falling snow, bent over his skis. He rubbed his eyes and tried to think. He was afraid. He knew what it was. He understood it with perfect clarity. He was afraid. It came to him simply, stupidly, with perfect and absolute clarity, flooding out all over his face. His belly was light and fluttering. He leaned forward, breathing hard, leaning on his poles stock still, watching his skis settle in the snow. A great broken membrane. It was in his belly, too, the ruptured membrane, that punctured sac of black bile. It was simple and he understood, and he leaned forward and breathed.

When he caught up with Harvey, he felt empty and relieved. He dropped his rucksack and sat on it and removed his skis. Harvey was studying the compass. There was no reason to talk. Resting, closing his eyes, he waited for Harvey. "We're lost," he finally said. "Now we're lost. Aren't we lost?"

"It's under control," Harvey said. He sounded calm and reasonable and far away.

"We're lost."

"Compass," Harvey murmured.

"What?"

"The compass. I've been watching the goddamn compass. It has to be the stupid compass."

"It's not the compass, Harv."

"It's the goddamn compass. Incredible."

"Harvey. The compass is brand new. You told me that."

"No, it's the compass. All the iron in the ground. Something, I don't know. It's okay, though. We're under control. Maybe the goddamn map, I don't know. The goddamn map must be a million years old."

"What happened?"

"What do you mean what happened?" Harvey looked at him, partly closing his bad eye.

"I mean how the hell did we get lost? How long have we been lost?"

Harvey shrugged. "Doesn't matter much, does it? Compass, map. I don't know. We've got ourselves a challenge so let's just sit back and think about it, all right?"

"A challenge? What's this challenge stuff? It's *snowing* for Christ sake. It wasn't supposed to snow."

Harvey shook his head and grinned.

"Well?"

"Relax. It's winter. Sometimes it snows in winter."

"It wasn't supposed to snow, was it?"

Harvey grinned at him, then he turned to the map and was silent. His face was obscured. He rocked back and forth on his rucksack and peered at the map. He was flushed and red. In a while he got up and strode off alone. He stood under a pine and gazed off and did not move. The snow was up to his knees. His hands hung by his sides, one holding the map and the other the silver compass. It was snowing and Perry couldn't see his face. The pine dwarfed him.

When he came back they built a fire.

They dragged boughs from the forest and dropped them beside the flames, then Harvey set up the lean-to and rolled out the sleeping bags. They did not talk. Harvey used some of the boughs to form a makeshift windbreak, stacking the branches against the low limb of a spruce tree. The wind seemed to die, but the snow kept falling and they sat and fed the fire and waited while the sun fell. Later they ate sardines and chili and drank coffee.

"Feel better?" Harvey said.

"No."

"You will." Harvey pulled out the map again. Together, they went over it section by section, tracing their planned route out of Grand Marais. Harvey guessed that they'd gone wrong on the second day, and Perry nodded. He wasn't sure, but he nodded anyway.

"So we're probably pretty deep into the woods," Harvey said. "Look here. We didn't hit any one of these big lakes today. We can't be far north. We would have been bound to hit at least one of them or at least seen one." With his mitten he drew a circle in the flat center of the Arrowhead, an inch in diameter. "Somewhere in here. It has to be. See here? All fairly thick forest, all flat, only a couple of small lakes. Almost has to be."

"What do we do?"

"Very easy. Too easy to even worry about. No matter how far we're off—and I don't think it's very much, I think we're in this circle somewhere—but no matter how far we're off we can't be more than twenty, twenty-five miles from Lake Superior and the highway. We go southeast."

"All right."

"Not even a bloody challenge really."

"Forget the challenges, Harvey."

"No problem. Trust the old soldier. I figured out what went wrong. I'm sure of it. The bloody ground. Absolutely filled with iron ore. Tons of it. It's all over, and it probably nudged the compass off just enough to get us lost. If it's off even a hair for two or three days, a couple of degrees or so, well that's enough to get you pretty darn lost. I'm sure of it. Tomorrow we'll just, we'll just watch the sun and head southeast."

"Where's the sun? What if there's no sun tomorrow?"

"What if the goddamn world ends?" Harvey said cheerfully. "What if the world collapses and the fucking Russians shoot off their bombs?"

"Cut it out, Harvey."

"What if the world cracks in half, you know? Consider that. What if the moon blows up?"

"Be serious."

"The old man wasn't that loony, you know."

"All right. I know it, Harv."

Harvey began coughing. They drank coffee and kept the fire going.

"It could be a blizzard," Perry finally said. "It could be."

"Then we'll hole up. People used to live like this."

"It wasn't supposed to blizzard."

Harvey grunted. He stood up and walked away from the fire. The wind was gone and the snow fell in silent clouds.

Harvey returned to the fire. "Being lost isn't the worst thing in the world, you know. At least you find out what it's like to be lost. If you're found, well, then you're found, or you get out, and you've had something interesting happen. I can think of worse things."

They sat on opposite sides of the fire.

It was not a cold night, but the snow fell and did not let up.

It was steady and monotonous and came to seem a natural element of the air.

The sound was monophonic, a single repetitive sobbing sound without dimension.

Late in the night, Perry woke up. Harvey's bag was covered with snow. The whole forest was covered with snow, and it was still snowing. He was afraid again. The fire was dead. As he lay awake, he remembered the bursting feeling of being afraid and he was afraid all over again. His feet were cold. Then he was cold all over. There was no excitement or exuberance.

He hadn't been dreaming but he had been thinking. He'd been thinking in his sleep. Like a cat, the thought had crept out and smelled the first dark of sleep, sniffed around to be sure. He could not remember it. He'd awakened too slowly. The cat thought jumped away, disappeared, and he was awake and cold and afraid again. He began thinking and decided to buy Grace flowers for Valentine's Day. He hadn't done that. He began to think about everything he would do. He would take his time about finding a job. Find something right and decent and concentrate on it and do it well. He thought about his father in the pulpit at Damascus Lutheran and suddenly felt some sympathy for the old man, and he started to pray and strung vows together as they came to him, praying fearfully *hallowed be thy name . . . kingdom come, will be done . . . I will . . . practise Lutheranism like Luther, I will treat Addie as a friend . . . on earth as it is in heaven . . . I will accumulate money to retire on and draw up a decent will . . . I will . . . on earth as in heaven . . .* He beaded vows on to the prayer, a whole string of promises and remedies, to take Grace to the movies, to treat Harvey well, to be happy, to be smiling and extra happy and not complain and be virtuous, to continue his exercises, to never smoke or drink in excess, to be happy, to follow Grace into the church where his old man preached and not complain and not have self-pity and listen carefully and obey. To love the old man.

He fell asleep and woke up again. His muscles were stiff. His back hurt and it was still snowing. Inside the bag, the smells were bad. His tooth hurt, the pain stretching across his jaw to his right ear. Slowly, he moved a finger to the ear and pressed against it, creating a quick vacuum to relieve the pressure. The bag stunk. He put his head outside. Still snowing and dark, and Harvey's bag was a gently rolling lump under the snow.

He scratched his head. His hair was straggled and tied in fine knots. He touched his jaw. The beard was raw, and the skin was tight and drawn. His elbows, the cartilage and tendons and bone sockets, everything was rusted shut and creaking like frozen weaponry.

"Harvey? You awake over there?"

"Affirmative. Now I'm awake."

"It's cold out there."

"It's a bitch. Go to sleep."

All night, Perry had been cold. Now, unzipping his bag and stepping out, he was seized by great warmth.

He helped Harvey rekindle the fire.

They moved slowly, each motion separate and distinct and labored over, and it took a long time. They ate the last two cans of chili.

Whining, the snowfall was nearly over. But the clouds remained full and gusted in desultory snaps. They did not talk while packing up the tarp and sleeping bags. Perry felt lazy. He did not want to move. Sitting still, he was amazed at Harvey's calm way of waxing his skis, deliberately spreading the paste on and rubbing it into each blade, taking care and time. He sat still while Harvey studied the map and the sky and the compass. He was warm and lazy. The forest was all the same. Without thinking, he got up and slipped into his skis and followed Harvey's tracks into the woods.

It was a sense of interlude, a secret waiting. He was not much afraid. Lazily, he gazed into Harvey's orange rucksack and followed. He considered it a kind of riding, a train trip through the forest, warmth within the coach. The trees and snow passed by through a secret window. It was simple movement, and he skated and pushed only when necessary. He felt strong, gaining confidence by not thinking. He kept his head slightly forward, and when his glasses fogged he did not bother to wipe them. No exercise of will and no deliberations.

The morning was monotonous and flat, flat through the planed country, and gradually he fell into a rhythm that synchronized motion and thought in an even, unruffled pattern of crystal images. He might have been dreaming: the bomb shelter, the sound of the old man's spoon clanging in the spit bucket, the television telling of A-bombs in the Caribbean. It was a memory he could trace over and over, wondering what he might have done differently, what he might have said to ease the old man's death or what he might have done to help with the digging, the pouring of cement. Then the image would slide away, join another image as the snow country went on in its monotonous eliding flow.

Once he saw a deer. He did not exactly see it. He saw through it and beyond it, the form registered, and he passed by. Then he saw it. He stopped and turned, and it was a white-tailed doe. The forelegs were splayed, delicate as though of brittle bamboo. It stood deep in snow, twenty yards away, its nose pressed against a birch trunk. He was startled to see it. He stood very still. The doe was brown and speckled white and the nose was black and the ears perked and large, as big as the snout, and the eyes were watchful, and the belly and tail and legs were cream white. It was unexpected. Without thinking, he called to it as if calling a dog for petting. The doe looked at him oddly. Then she arched her back, raising her head to reach higher bark, all the while watching him. She was frail and hungry-looking. In greeting, Perry called again and raised one of his poles. He was struck by the desire to hail the beast, and he called once again and the doe continued to watch. Her eyes were cautious but not unfriendly. Then the wind changed. The doe's head jerked and held for a moment in a sharp, electric pose of perfect alertness, and then it bolted, and Perry realized they'd never met, and the doe was gone. He reminded himself to tell Grace of the fine doe.

When half the dull day ended, they stopped and made a small fire and had coffee. He told Harvey about the deer.

Harvey nodded. "That's how it can be."

"Then the wind changed."

"That's how it goes," Harvey said. "You know that deer are close to being blind?"

"Is that right?"

"It's in the nose and ears. Those big ears and that long nose."

"I swear it was watching me."

Harvey shook his head.

"I swear it."

Harvey kicked out the fire. Perry drained his coffee cup and stashed it in his rucksack and got ready. "How are we doing?"

"Fine. Made seven miles maybe. Maybe more. At least we're moving and that's the big thing. With luck we can maybe make it to the shore highway before dark. I'm pretty sure. Are you worried?"

"Aren't you?"

"I don't know."

"Well, I guess I am. Yes."

Harvey laughed. "Smart man, then. But really I think we're all right. I was awake before dawn and watched where the first light came from, so I know we're headed southeast. Mostly east. For all I know we're headed right back into Grand Marais. Don't worry."

"I guess it won't help to worry."

"That's the ticket," Harvey said. "In the war . . . some very sensitive guys. They were good guys but they worried and they were bad soldiers. They were smart to worry. Had the good sense to worry. But they were awful bad soldiers."

"Did you worry, Harv?"

"About what?"

"That answers it."

"No, about what?"

"Did you worry about . . . having your eye ruined. I don't know. About getting shot in the nose or something. Whatever. Ghastly things."

"Did I worry? Yes, I worried." Harvey buckled on his skis. "Sure. Like when you cut open a fish and you're kind of scared about seeing the insides. It's because the fish never thought about them but they were there all along. It was the same. Hard to say. It wasn't the pain I was scared of. I think it was that I wanted to . . . react right when my legs got blown off or my chest got shot open or something, you understand, seeing the stuff inside and not going crazy bananas. I used to worry some about that, but not a lot. I didn't want to bawl like a baby."

"What about your eye?"

"My eye, yes. Yes, I don't remember that much."

"It must have hurt."

"I suppose. That's what I don't remember. If I don't remember, I guess that means it didn't hurt much. You care about this, don't you?"

"Sure."

"Yeah, I see that." His palm passed to his nose in a precise gesture of dismissal. "You're a good brother anyway. I'm not much of a fine brother, am I? I do certain things and you do certain things and here we are together at last. Not much. It's actually too bad we weren't better brothers before."

"Well, we were different ages."

"Yeah."

"Different friends and everything."

"Right."

"I guess we know each other better now."

"I guess. It's still a crime," said Harvey. "Talking about it and so on."

"It should have been more like me and the deer."

Harvey smiled as if into a flash camera. "Yes," he smiled. He clapped Perry on the back. "That's it," he said smiling, "right on the button." He clapped Perry's shoulder. "Let's get going before we have a fight and ruin it. Someday we'll get on a train for Africa. Would you like to go to Africa?"

"Not much, Harv."

"Where then? Name it."

"Paris maybe."

"What the devil is in Paris?"

"Nothing, I guess. Some cafés and people and Notre Dame and things."

"Okay," Harvey nodded, reserving the black judgment in his eyes. "I'll buy that. Paris. After that, then we'll go to Africa." Again he smiled with sympathy. Perry wondered where he'd gone wrong.

It was an afternoon of communication by hand signals. Harvey stopping him with a fist raised.

Starting him with a sweeping overhand motion, a wagon master seeing the way and leading.

Rest, a certain delicate signal.

Traverse, carry through the flat pine country, skirting danger, flanking the tangles that went nowhere. "Up to you, buddy," said his father way back, not even looking at him, as if knowing beforehand he would not go. "You can sit home here, or you can come with us and we'll have a fine time, but it's up to you, buddy." A communication of spirits. Language an artifact. Language a way to ask for the garbage to be taken out. A communication of tacit compatibility of spirit. "That's all right, buddy," no explanations, no sharing of insight, abandoning him as his son the none-elect. And Harvey guided with the same ease. If you saw into the forest, then you saw. If you did not, then you did not. "There's vision on the one hand and there's blindness on the other," was the Kalevalian paraphrase used by his father to organize the Pentateuch sermons of 1962.

Not so perfectly crazy, after all. Effortlessly, Harvey took him deep in. They crossed a lake and it was snowing again. It was snowing in earnest. The lake wind was up, and dunes of snow tumbled along. That tension. It was that long far-back tension, a kind of tugging, a feeling of vast bewilderment and eventual melancholy at not seeing so clearly. The wind of his father, the southern calm of Grace, and all it stood for, not a matter of choice and less a matter of pure inclination, entirely a matter of circumstance, genetic fix, history, events, a long-standing ambivalence or uncertainty, pure open-mindedness. The magnet was in the North Pole, the magnetic pole. Revelation. Some sort of great and magnificent epiphany was what was needed. Some luck. The magnet was in the North Pole and there was shelter in the south. There was a warm deep soft algaed spot somewhere, a stewing brewing simmering place of contentment. Revelation was what was needed. Some rotten luck. He had a hard time moving. The lake wind was dead against him. Harvey's orange rucksack sometimes disappeared in the eliding, slipping, skip-beat dunes of snow. Perry's skis no longer slid along so easily. He pushed hard with his poles, kept his face down and out of the direct force of the blowing falling snow, the drifting dunes.

Harvey guided him on. They got off the lake and into some trees, where Perry stopped.

He leaned against his poles, watching Harvey continue into the forest. Perry searched, squinted and peered in another effort to find something warm in the woods, such as a sight or bundle of colors or sounds that would spark dazzling streamers of color and light in the sky, light the forest, an electric dazzling array of lights. He rubbed his mittens over the frozen lenses of his glasses, cleared the steam and looked about.

He looked back at the tumbling duned lake. It was behind him now. He could not see to the far shore. He turned and followed after Harvey.

After a time the trees thinned dramatically and the land was ripped into rugged slopes and bluffs.

The snowfall was a snowstorm. The closed, nearsighted feeling of tall timber relaxed, and the snowstorm came in. Harvey stopped and pointed at shriveled old fungus growing on the bole of a birch, nodded meaningfully, and Perry nodded back wondering, and they continued skiing. The clouds were like ordinary viscous glue. Perry ignored them. He followed the patch of orange like religion.

Beyond the slopes and bluffs was more forest.

Perry thought of a cheerful song to sing.

> Frosty, the snowman,
> Da-da da-da da da-da da

It eluded him.

The forest was older. The trees were giants with mangled thick trunks, clawing boughs and roots that erupted from out of the ground and twisted like serpents under the snow, making the skiing treacherous.

Another cheerful song.

> Oh, my name is Kalota
> I'm from Minnesota
> I rip up the soil with my teeth
> I'm big as a bear and I'll give one a scare
> And I ain't never been touched in my sleep.

Harvey climbed a lonely bluff. He reported lakes ahead, hollering like a crow's nest sailor. They came to the first of the lakes and crossed through the storm, followed a channel to the second lake, crossed the second unnamed lake, portaged through thick forest, eye-deep in the falling snow, and the earth inclined steadily upwards, peaked and descended towards still a third lake, which they crossed without comment, drifting with the drifts.

There on the far edge of the lake they found a broken dock, six posts frozen solid in the ice, a few broken slats.

"Well!" shouted Harvey against the storm. "Well, now we've arrived somewhere."

Perry looked for smoke.

"We've come to someplace," shouted Harvey again. "Where there's a dock, there's a cabin or a house."

A trail led from the dock into the woods. The trail widened and climbed with the upwardgoing land. The road opened into a clearing in the forest. Perry, for the first time, pushed hard and passed Harvey and led the way into the open space.

He saw the broken stone chimney. He knew as he saw it that he'd seen it before, in one of the night dreams, in preparation, in a light-headed push-up. It was a broken old chimney fallen from some invisible earlier height. A broken stone chimney that jutted from the snow as the mast of a sunken fish-eaten schooner, a broken stone monument. A tombstone, reverend and presiding. Blinded and fooled. A broken stone chimney. Snow stuffed and snow surrounded. A clearing in the woods occupied by the broken stump of a chimney that had once, maybe never, but perhaps once had released hot black smoke and covered a burning fire and grown hot, the stones growing hot and glowing: just a spindly sawed-off pocked old chimney. Blinded and fooled.

"I think we've found our place," shouted Harvey. The wind was hard.

"What place?"

"Some homesteader's cabin. Dumb bastard, coming way in here."

"Yeah."

"A dumb Finn, I guess," Harvey shouted against the wind.

"Didn't last long."

"Bloody dumb Finn."

"Let's stop here. I want to rest here."

"There's still some light."

"I just want to stop and rest here."

Harvey nodded sympathetically. "All right, buddy."

"I'm not tired. I just want to stop here. Awhile."

"Sure thing. It's a good spot."

It was comfortable. He had the feeling of civilized content: a chimney, the timbers of the old house comfortably under the snow, the beams and broken panels, the clearing spreading out into the forest. Harvey was busy scrambling for wood, clearing the hearth for a fire, tunneling into the drifts, but Perry was comfortable. It was an old homestead. A meadow hacked from the trees. Maybe farmed for a year and lived on. The dock meant fresh fish in flour. Bleak and comfortable. The warm hearth. He sat on a cleared-off timber. The snow was jagged around the chimney, rolling up and down where the cabin had collapsed. Buried were pots and the stone foundation and a hundred different things of shelter.

Another song. Sung with the snow. Sung by the old man with the snow.

"We've got some sardines left," said Harvey. "What do you think?"

"You know these things."

"No sense saving them," he said. "May as well eat them now. We'll eat them now and have a good rest and see what there is tomorrow."

"I don't know much about it, Harv."

"That's what we should do."

"All right."

"We can fish if we have to."

"Good idea. What about the ice?"

"There'll be a way," he said, beginning to cough. "We'll see what there is tomorrow."

A warm hearth, fire merry in the old homesteader's fireplace with smoke creeping as in olden times up the broken chimney.

The moon was high and curved and bright above the storm, and Perry knew it and saw it, the dock mended and well on an August night, loons swimming underneath and Grace calling for supper from the door.

They woke to the blizzard. Before it had been a snowfall, and then a snowstorm. But it was different. Perry saw it immediately. He even spoke the word as he was waking. A latticework. "Blizzard," he said.

They huddled against the stone foundation.

After a time Harvey stood against the blizzard and tried kindling the fire in the homesteader's fireplace. He worked at it a long while then gave up without saying a word. He waded to what would have been a cosy corner of the broken cabin, dug into the snow, stuffed his sleeping bag inside and covered it partly with more snow, then climbed inside and zipped himself shut.

Perry stayed at the chimney. He was warm enough and unafraid. He took a nap, slept hard, and when he woke the blizzard was about the same, a bit tamer, but it was still bad and he slept again.

He woke, his glasses were hopelessly fogged. The torpid soggy memories. The blizzard was very loud and deep. He took off the glasses and slipped them to the bottom of his bag and stared ahead, seeing only a cold hole.

He slept again and then Harvey was shaking him, insisting they get up and walk. Perry closed his eyes but Harvey kept it up, unzipped his bag and pulled him out, and they walked and stamped their feet and waved their arms like hawks. They marched in a circle around the homesteader's cabin, and Harvey sang marching songs and Perry sang whatever came into mind, his father's songs. *Them Gopher girls are gamey, them Buckeye girls are gay, but them Hawkeye girls with them Hawkeye curls, them's the juicy kind of lay*, and they tramped a path around the broken cabin. Perry's head was hanging and Harvey was singing marching songs, singing *If I die before I wake, pray to God my soul to take; and if I die on the Russian front, bury me with a Russian cunt; and if I die in a combat zone, box me up and ship me home; and if I die before I'm rich, bury me with a British bitch; and if I die locked up in jail, free me quick before I stale; and if I die and turn to mold, smother me in broads and gold; g'left, g'left, g'left-right-left*, round and round the broken tombstone chimney, right, left, wading with fullback high strides. Harvey was singing, then coughing, then singing, and Perry's legs were heavy and the snow was thick. His legs were heavy. His thighs hurt. He was cold, wide open and vulnerable. His tooth hurt, him. He opened his mouth to speak and the wind was drawn in, blowing his cheecks out, forcing back his own stinking breath.

"I'm hungry," Perry said.

"Just relax."

"Where are my glasses? Put them down in the bag and they're gone."

"You're better off without them."

"I need them. Get out and help me look. Harvey."

"Better off staying inside the bag."

"I *can't*. I have to have them."

Perry's throat hurt. Shouting, it had become a natural means of fighting the blizzard. Calmly as possible, thinking it out, he began the search for his glasses. First the bag. He groped methodically through the folds, down deep. Then, removing his mittens and carefully storing them in the bag, he got to his knees and searched the snow immediately surrounding the sleeping bag, working slowly in a circle, moving further out with each sweep. The blizzard had gone mute. It whipped and swirled but had pitched somewhere too high or low or fierce for him to hear. Instead he heard Harvey's coughing and a later growl as he pulled phlegm from his lungs and spat it out, then a long whining breathing. Perry's wrists iced. He plunged after his glasses, closing his eyes so that without sight and sound the blizzard was gone and only his wrists and hands were cold.

It seemed to be a nap, or verging on it, but he found his eyes were open. He was propped in his bag against the white chimney. And he was hungry. He sat still, wishing he'd found his glasses. More rotten luck. It was dark enough to be night. It was night.

He got himself up and leaned against the chimney.

The frothing sensation bubbled him all over, a boiling without heat or any sound or light. Harvey's coughing again. More rotten luck.

Perry leaned forward. Nearsighted, he moved away from the chimney and uncovered Harvey's bag. He got him up and held him and walked him around the fallen cabin. It was night, Perry was sure of it. They walked without singing. They stopped for Harvey to lean over and cough and spit. Then Perry helped his brother into the bag and covered it with snow, then he climbed into his own bag and forced the zipper to the top and propped himself against the broken stone chimney.

He was certain he was awake, and he blinked to be sure. Inside the bag he smelled himself. Dark and even warm. A cold winter's morning with oatmeal in the kitchen and his father at the stove in slippers and flannel, Sunday before church. What month was it? Winter. Winter month. It was not 1962, it was winter. It was not October. What time was it? Wintertime. Sunday before church in wintertime was the old man's quiet time, cooking his own breakfast and letting Paul sleep late, then waking him, the only gentle time, and a very fine time. He was sure the blizzard had passed, for there was not a sound. The old man in flannel and slippers, cracking the door quietly, looking in. It was *his* time. The old man came in and his eyes were never cold-white on Sunday wintertime mornings, sitting sometimes reading, thinking maybe Paul was asleep. A quiet morning time. He was certain it had passed. That Sunday morning wintertime feeling, wrapped and warm with the Hudson Bay blanket all around him, deep in the bed, the old man reading or getting a yellow-paged sermon ready, checking things, a calm rested look when Paul peeked, peeking in on the old man's quiet time. The old man's face ageless and kind at those times. A slipper dangling from a rocking foot, hooked boyish on the toe. Those had been *his* times.

He tried Harvey's counting trick. He kept his head deep in the bag. He counted slowly until he was bored and still not asleep. He got to eighty-one and decided it was a bad trick that never worked because it was not supposed to work, making the staying awake boring and fruitless and not helping anyway.

He considered putting his head out to test the blizzard. He could not hear it but he knew it was there. Once in the night he had looked and it had frightened him and he'd decided not to look again until daylight.

Then he wondered if it were day.

He considered taking a look, then decided to give it more time. He tried remembering some fresh songs to sing. If they'd only talked. He could think of a million things to say now. He would say things about Grace. That would be one subject. He could talk about Grace for a year or even two, describing parts of her waking dreams and talk and talk. And ask about his mother. That would be something magnificent to talk about. He would just listen and drink coffee politely and hear his father talk on and on about his mother. Then they would reminisce about the scrapes together. Maybe taking an hour apiece, each could say what he was thinking when they'd argued about this and that; the old man could say: I got angry because you did this, and I was thinking that, and I wish this, and I wished that, and we agree on this, the time was mid-afternoon, it was July, no . . . October, the bomb shelter was being built, I thought we should have it, you thought it was crazy, Harvey was out there working, you were watching television, I finally died, the shelter was finished, though. He would pay close attention. He would change that. He'd never really paid attention, always hoping the old man would change when instead he ought to have paid better attention to why he hadn't changed and wouldn't and didn't.

He twisted, lay on his belly and cradled his head. He was hungry. He tried counting again and gave it up at sixty.

He considered again taking a look at the blizzard. For all he knew, down deep in his goose-down bag, for all he knew the blizzard was over and it was daylight and all was in a thaw. It was a nice possibility. Nice idea, he thought. Everything was such a damned nice idea when it was an idea.

The air inside the bag was bad.

Time stretched, then dissipated and took on excruciating importance and then disappeared entirely, less than important, non-existence and false.

Except for his toes he was warm enough.

His tooth was all right.

His legs ached but it was from immobility and not the cold.

The important things were all right. He was dry, the most important thing. He'd kept the snow out. His chest and back and legs were all warm.

He had to pee. It had been a long while. Stretching, contracting, tricky time.

He knew he had to leave the bag. Knowing it, he waited, letting his bladder percolate with the anticipation and concentrating on the coming pleasure.

He played a guessing game, guessing if the blizzard had ended, guessing if it were day or night or one of the transition times, guessing how many hours or days had passed since various points in the past, all warped now.

He waited and let the fluid push like gravity. Almost as a ritual, he thought for a moment each about Addie, then Grace, then Harvey, and jumbled together his father and old Jud, stopping suddenly in the quick realization that, taken together, they were the only names he knew, just a clutter of other junk faces.

The bag air was rotten. He smelled himself. When the blizzard ended, he decided firmly, he would have Harvey build a fire and they would boil water and wash themselves. Rinse away all the frozen sweat. Then, if any instant coffee were left, then they would drink hot coffee and things would be much better. It made a nice thought. Clean and hot coffee and a nice fire and some sunshine. It was another nice idea.

He heard a gurgle somewhere, and he listened, thinking maybe it was a sound of melting and thaw, or a change in the blizzard, or daylight. He listened closer and heard it again. It was fluid. A sobbing sound. He listened and it grew louder and changed into the sound of Harvey's cough.

Perry crawled out of the bag. He was surprised at the daylight, a bright white blizzard, beautiful with white boiling snow that was perfectly lighted.

He zipped his bag shut, waded a decent distance away from the crumpled cabin, stood with his legs apart and anchored, and urinated with long pleasure. As if tidying up after him, the blizzard whipped clean snow into the steaming hole. He removed his mittens in order to force up his zipper. He felt better. He steadied himself and muttered consoling helpful sounds and waded back to the chimney and thought about what to do next. He did some exercises, talking to himself about staying dry and taking care, easy does it. Jumped like a jumping jack, flapping his arms high and clapping his mittens together, side-straddle-hop. He hopped to Harvey's sleeping mound: "Up and at 'em!" he shouted. "Up and at 'em!" He had to bellow. He stopped and listened: the wind, the wind . . . "Harvey! Gotta get up! Buddy!

Old buddy buddy! Up and at 'em as they say! Get that old blood circulating, up, up, up! Come on, Harv! Toro! Toro! Up and at 'em, Toro! Hi ya, hi ya!" It was spectacular boiling white daylight. "Up, up, Toro!" he called, getting Harvey out of his bag and walking him round and round the homesteader's tombstone chimney. "Easy, easy," he consoled. He walked Harvey around the broken chimney. Later, he thought, he would build a fine fire and they'd warm up and rest on the hearth. Get to someplace warm, get to where he could think. A dazzling, dazing lightness, illumination as if the snow itself were a source of inexhaustible light. Harvey clung to his arm and Perry led him around the stone chimney. Harvey held tight and Perry led him. Perry led him. Round and round. Harvey's grasp was tight, and his head was low, and round they went.

"What time is it?" Harvey asked from his hollow.

"Don't know. You all right?"

"Sick." Harvey's voice came muffled by his bag and the covering snow and phlegm. "Bronchitis, I don't know. Pneumonia."

"Just lie still, Harv."

"I know what it is."

"It's not what you think. If you lie still and sleep you'll be fine."

"I know exactly what it is."

"Be still."

"It's bloody pneumonia, that's exactly what it is."

"Go to sleep then."

Indecently low, through sheets of snow and beyond the wind, he saw the moon. Propped against the chimney, his eyes and ears and nose out of the bag, he was looking at the storm, but he saw the moon. Inside the bag it stunk but outside there was the clean smell of the moon.

"Hey, Harv!" He shook Harvey's bag. "The moon! You can see the moon."

He giggled.

"Harv, just take a look at this."

Amazing. Science was confounded, for the moon was its own source of light. Reflecting and illuminating nothing, an internally fired, softly silver globe. Indecently low, below the clouds, below the tips of the trees and below the storm. Even without his glasses, Perry saw it clearly. He tried to wake Harvey to show him, but Harvey was sick and sleeping and lost.

Perry remembered.

"I want a bomb shelter built," the old man said from his bed. "About standard size, serviceable and square and nothing very fancy. I want it for you and Harvey as much as for me. People will talk but they've talked on and on anyway, and more talk will just keep them lubricated, don't worry about it. Put it right on the lawn, right in front if you want." The old man's eyes had that blank red glow of prophecy. Failed prophecies mostly. Perry himself, a failed prophecy. He remembered.

"We've got to do it," Harvey said.

"Not me."

"The old man's dying and you won't help build a crummy bomb shelter?"

"No."

Harvey paled.

"It's gone too far," Perry tried to say. "He's . . . okay, he's not crazy. I'm not saying that, Harv. But just *look* at it. He's dying and he wants us to build him a bomb shelter. Now is that *right*? Does that make *sense*?"

Harvey was just a kid. He looked away. "The old man's dying."

"I know."

In the morning Harvey started digging. October, and the earth was already tight. Perry watched from inside. The deathwatch was on. He watched from the kitchen window, watching through gauzed curtains that had hung for years. Some rotten luck. Harvey used a spade and wheelbarrow, just a kid, patiently digging as the day got late and the old man lay upstairs ringing a spoon in his spit bucket. An old signal. The chiming rattled down the stairs to the kitchen, persisting until Perry left the window and reluctantly pursued the chime to its source. Crazy and sad. The old man did not look as if he were dying.

"Goddamn Russians!" he hollered.

"You all right?"

"Goddamn Russians. I was saying it years ago." He dropped his spoon into the spit bucket and waited for the final shrill chord to ring to its end, inspecting Perry top to bottom.

It was October, and the radio was playing.

Perry shrugged and grinned. The old man did not look as if he were dying. Burnt outdoor health covered him like a cosmetic. "You hear that?" He pushed up in bed. His hair was full and bushy and still speckled partly black. "It's coming," he said loudly, "and I been saying it for years. The world's going in the big Russian blowout, you *hear* that?" He reached down for his silver spoon and pointed it at Perry. "You think I'm crazy now?"

"I never said that, never."

"You believe me now?"

Perry shrugged and grinned. The old man did not look like death. Clean shaven and strong in his undershorts and bare chest, lying with the window wide open and no blanket.

"You think I'm mean and crazy?" Oddly, the old man smiled.

Perry grinned again and shrugged. It was hard to believe the old man was dying. He straightened a pillow and partly closed the window. Harvey's digging sounds came through clearly.

The old man lay back. "Well. Guess this'll show them."

"What?"

"This," and the old man gestured towards the radio.

"Oh."

The old man inspected him gravely. Then he shook his head. "You aren't out there digging, are you?" he said.

"No." Perry couldn't stop from grinning.

"You think . . . No."

"Comfortable enough?"

"Did I ever teach you anything?"

"Yes," Perry said.

"I tried to teach you about things."

"I know it. I know."

"I tried to teach you everything I know."

"I know."

The old man shook his head. "And you aren't helping with my bomb shelter."

Perry grinned. He could not shed the ghastly mistaken grin. Tragic and distorted and unmeant.

He wanted to hear the old man's thoughts, but the old man was talking about the world blowing up. A bomb shelter.

Perry remembered.

"I'll bring up some supper soon."

He went to the living room, turned on television and let it blare out afternoon quiz gaming and spot bulletins. He turned the volume high to dull the old man's chime. Beat the bucket, old man. Perry grinned sadly. Kick it, old man.

Harvey came in at dusk. Perry made sandwiches and they

ate without speaking. The house was cold and womanless with its dark-stained pine timbers and hardwood floors and yellow-gauzed curtains without origin, no origin except what was locked in the old man's brain, unspoken origins and locked-up secrets and thermostats kept to sixty on January mornings.

"How's it going?" Perry said.

"You want to help?"

Perry grinned. He didn't mean it and he couldn't help it.

Harvey went upstairs to look in on the old man. Silently, Perry listened. There were those secrets between them. He wanted to hear, listening and cleaning the sandwich plates. The kitchen was lighted white. It was empty. The floor tiles glistened. The refrigerator was white. There were murmurs up the stairs, Harvey was moving around in the old man's sickroom, the timbers creaked. He imagined they were talking about fishing. An apt subject for them. Not really talking, he grinned. No one ever talked, not in the rugged house. Fishing. The time they saw the wolves, a whole pack of them together, all caught in the deep snows behind Pliney's Pond. Smiling in their knowing ways for many years. Perry started on the dishes. Comfortable work. At last Harvey came down the stairs and took out two extension cords without a word, thereby accusing, and Perry suffered with his head bent fixed over the dishpan.

Perry remembered, one of those lasting nightlong images.

Cold October, and Harvey's hole was shadowed by four bare electric lights dangling from birch trees. The forest all around him, such a cold night, and the already grieving boy digging a monumental bomb shelter.

Clucking, Perry wandered the house. He stayed awake and away from the old man's sickroom, kept the television loud, wondered if the old man could hear, thinking: another distortion, for he cared. Harvey out digging the old man's bomb shelter and instead they should be together, reading at the foot of the sleeping man's bed, whispering over him and talking with him whenever he awoke, tying up conversational ribbons that had been fraying for years, finishing thoughts while there was time, learning titbits of the old man's life that hadn't before come out, plumbing the old man's last reservoirs for whatever was left, tertiary recovery, learning about the stack of photographs in the attic, learning who the bright-pictured faces were, learning about the old man's photographed gray navy battleship, learning about the pictured woman's face, listening in on the man's last dreams and forging brotherly communion out of the deathwatch. Instead of a bomb shelter.

Simultaneously, Harvey's spade struck a rock and the old man's bucket chimed. The chord carried Perry outside. Harvey steadfastly dug into the yard.

"How's it going?" Perry asked.

The spade struck and lifted and deposited hard soil into the wheelbarrow.

"How's it going there?" Perry asked again, and again the spade thumped into the yard.

"I can bring out hot chocolate. How would you like that?" The spade hit a rock. Sparks in the hole, a fire in the hole. The four dangling electric lights swung with leaf-empty branch shadows, the forest all around them, how long had it been going on? Blanched, grieving Harvey struck and lifted and struck again. "Hot chocolate. I'll go get it then. You just stay here, all right? I'll get it and bring it out."

Perry hunched over the stove, blending sweet milk with syrup, clucking at his warm work. Fall was always a nice season. The Arrowhead forests and the clean air. He carefully poured the hot chocolate from pan to mug, put a napkin on a saucer, put the mug on the napkin, put cookies on the saucer, put everything on a tray, carried it out to Harvey's night dig. "Some hot chocolate for you. I'll just put it here till you're ready for it." Perry put it down far enough from the hole to be free of dust and dirt. "All right?" he said. He watched the spade rise and fall, then he turned and took a few steps, then turned again. "Don't forget and let it go cold." He turned again, stopped again. "We can talk when you come inside. How will that be, then?" He turned once again, seeing them imagining the rise of the spade, its downwards electric arc, sparks of the breaking splintering shattering mug, the full-expected explosion of hot chocolate and glass and tray and saucer. And he turned and saw Harvey's aggrieved spade wet with sweet milk. "Yes," Perry said, "then we'll just talk when you come in. It's all right."

It went on that way while the old man died. Perry remembered.

Jets scrambling over Miami Beach, trawlers in the Caribbean, an address by the President that began: *Good evening, my fellow citizens* and the old man rang with his spoon in the spit bucket, as though celebrating his insight. *This Government, as promised, has maintained the closest surveillance of the Soviet military buildup on the island of Cuba* chiming in doom like a vindicated and vilified prophet while Harvey's spade thumped in the October soil. *Within the past week unmistakable evidence has established the fact that a series of offensive missile sites is now in preparation on that imprisoned island. The purposes of these bases can be none other than to provide a nuclear strike capability against the Western Hemisphere* although the old man insisted it was the whole world coming to ruin as he banged his silver spoon in the spit bucket, calling out.

The bomb shelter arose from its hole. The walls were standard two feet thick. The great body of the shelter hulked underground and only its flat top actually emerged, the roof coming just to Harvey's breast. A stainless-steel air filter climbed like a chimney from the center of the roof. In the sunlight, the shelter was bright white and in the shade it turned gray. It was a center of gravity in the yard, with the grass sloping towards it from all directions.

"I see Harvey's got it done," the old man said sternly.

Perry shrugged and grinned. "Pretty much. Has to cement seams or something. And put in the door bars and steps."

"Just in time," said the old man. He was propped against three firm pillows. Bare-chested, covered to the knees with a sheet, he spoke harshly: "You think it's crazy, don't you? You never listened."

"I listened," Perry said. The old man did not look as if he would die.

"Harvey knows."

"I guess so."

"Why are you grinning?"

"I can't help it," Perry said.

"Happy about something?"

"No," Perry said.

The old man became silent. It was as if they hadn't spoken at all.

"Get some rest," Perry said softly. He closed the door.

"Love you," he whispered.

The old man didn't really look like death.

Grinning so that his eyes watered and his glasses steamed and his nose hurt dreadfully, Perry moved down the stairs.

He turned on the television. Another bulletin, which was unreal and hapless as anything spouted from the old man's pulpit.

It was impossible, of course.

The old man was ringing again in the spit bucket but Perry stayed away. And Harvey's spade was clanging outside.

The house was very cold.

It was impossible, of course.

"Love you," he whispered, grateful that the old man couldn't hear.

On the television, a reporter was reading the text of a White House statement, smiling slightly as though both disbelieving and reassuring, and Perry had sympathy for the fellow. Nobody believed but they imagined, and Harvey's spade clanked against the concrete bomb shelter as the reporter said, *In summary, there is no evidence to date indicating that there is any intention to dismantle or discontinue work on these missile sites. On the contrary, the Soviets are rapidly continuing their construction of missile support and launch facilities* . . . the language of the old man's religion: facilities and missile support systems. Perry listened with a grin and without watching, listened as another reporter interviewed nailbiting breathholding flushfaced citizen prophets. Incredible. Disbelieved. Incredible that the old man's craziest prophecy was not crazy at all, therefore perfectly crazy, completing a grand cycle. Perry sat and listened, primogeniture in a Finnish man-family of October doom and swamps at sea, while the truly sad thing was that the old man was dying, and nobody cared, least of all the old man, while ships moved to sea, alerts and re-alerts and civil defense, and the craziest thing of all was that the old man's craziest prophecy was not really crazy. Nobody believed. It drove the old man crazy.

The old house was cold.

It got late and the old man slept for a while, but Harvey continued his work.

Perry wandered the house. Once he looked in on the old man. His chest was fuzzed with black hair and the window was wide open.

Around midnight the old man woke up and began clanging for attention.

Perry remembered:

The echo in the house.

The banging of Harvey's hammer at midnight in the mostly finished bomb shelter.

Then the ringing in the bucket. The chiming, clattering demonic ringing of the old man's spoon in the bucket.

The thermostats turned to freezing for the old man's dying comfort.

The chill in the house.

The persistent hammering and bucket ringing, while the radio went berserk with midnight Action Line call-in oracles: "And no one ever listened and now it's too late, because I was warning of this twenty years ago when I lived in Mankato, twenty years ago. I warned about the Chinese slinking on the sidelines while we fought it out with the Russians, and who'll be left? You guessed it. Just lucky we caught them, that's all. Quemoy-Matsu. It's the Chinese that's behind it. When we had the chance, then we should've let them have it with both barrels at Quemoy-Matsu. Now all we can do is pray. Pray we win, that's all. But, anyhow . . ."

The house was cold.

He built a fire.

The television was all news and desperation, and the clanging and hammering rang like bulletins from the meat-hungry Caribes.

Once, for relief from the incessant bucket thumping, Perry stepped outside and took a long walk around the yard. It was late enough for the moon to be on the descent. Its color was harvest red. There was no sun at all. The lights in the old man's upstairs bedroom shined out and partly lit the crouching bomb shelter. Harvey was somewhere inside. Filling water jugs or something. For the moment he was quiet. But upstairs behind the lighted windows the old man still rattled in his spit bucket, and the mostly finished bomb shelter cowered like a concrete-scaled fossil.

Perry went inside. An electric light dangled from the ceiling and Harvey was rocking in a rocking chair.

"Looks pretty solid," Perry said gently.

Harvey kept rocking.

"I say, it does look strong," said Perry. "You've done a good job on it."

Harvey got up, keeping his face in the dark. "It'll take anything," he said. "I made it that way. I guess it will take just about anything that comes."

"Are you going to come inside now?"

"Nope."

"You can't . . ."

"Don't tell me."

"Look. There's no sense moping out here. It'd be better now if you come inside and look in on him. He'd like that. You've got it done now. He said so himself. He looked out and saw it was all done. You got it built."

"Just don't tell me. You can stop telling me."

"What should I tell him then? Tell him you don't want to look in? You got better things to do? Shall I tell him that?"

"He knows."

"How does he know? What?"

"*You* don't know. Just don't tell me anything. He knows. I don't have to sit with him for him to know. You sit with him. You need to sit with him. Don't try to tell me."

Harvey picked a hammer off the cement floor. He sat in the rocking chair. Slowly rocking, he banged the hammer against a thick wall, shooting sparks, tiny chips scattering.

"You want to help?" he said.

"Help what?"

"If you don't want, just hop along inside and sit some more by the television, see what good that does."

Outside, the ground had frosted. Perry stood alone. The old man's bucket clanging had stopped. The window lights were on, falling full across the bomb shelter.

Harvey's hammering followed him inside, up the stairs, totally alone now except for Harvey's cement hammering.

There was immense vision in the old man's eyes.

Later Perry went to the bomb shelter and told Harvey. Then he asked: "Is there anything I can do?"

"The work's done," Harvey said.

"Let me do something."

"It happened, didn't it? The old man was right."

"Yes."

"Finished it just in time."

"Just in the nick of time," Perry said quietly.

Harvey shrugged and gave Perry his hammer. "Just hammer at that there wall." Then he left to go upstairs.

In the morning they drove into town. Harvey went first to the church. Perry went to the drugstore, where everyone was. The place was arattle with frightened talk. A radio was playing behind the counter. Herb Wolff's cash register sang as the town congregated for their coffee and hushed talk, and Perry let his dime clatter on the counter so that people looked up to see him grinning as he ordered his coffee, nothing outlandish but sufficient grinning to show them that the old man wasn't so crazy after all. Old Jud Harmor came in carrying his straw hat, and they sat together. Bishop Markham was reading aloud the *Tribune*'s thick black front page. Others were listening. And Herb Wolff was shuffling between cash register and counter, counting coins up to the very end of the world, and nobody was joking about the old man being crazy. Perry could have burst he was so proud. He could have laughed.

"Talked with Harvey up at the church," said Jud at last.

"Yeah. The old man's dead."

They were quiet awhile. Herb Wolff turned up the radio volume. Everyone was very quiet as the radio reported that the U.S. Navy was at that moment intercepting the Russian Navy somewhere in the Caribbean.

"Funny, ain't it?" old Jud said softly and without malice. "Your old man was a . . ."

"He wasn't so crazy after all," Perry said.

"That's it," Jud said. He paused. "Harvey sure loved him."

"He sure did," Perry said.

"Never saw anything like it."

"Yes," Perry grinned. "Harvey sure loved him, all right. He sure did, didn't he?"

Crystalline sounds.

Ice cracking, the frozen air, hard oxygen.

The blizzard had ended. Towards dawn, it simply ended.

Then long silence. A vacuum, nothing. Not even cold.

Perry was part of that. Hunched against the broken chimney, blood still, he'd been sculpted into a great drift of snow. It wasn't at all bad. He couldn't think and he didn't feel the cold. Like the elements. Like the earth and glazed lakes and silence and winter he was frozen in his tracks, stopped cold.

The stillness lasted through dawn and into first light. He huddled at the foot of the old stone chimney. Daylight came and he was in the Ice Age. Frozen fast ahead, he was sightless with blue shiny eyes unrooted to memory or desire, and the image of the old man and the bomb shelter and Harvey and the great sadness was frozen fast. There was stillness and winter sun, and the sunlight charged the cold with complex tensions: ice cracking, the frozen air, hard oxygen.

Crystalline sounds. And he blinked. Snapping sounds, and again he blinked.

Heat Storm

He blinked but he did not move. The sun cleared the pines.

Crystalline sounds, cracking ice beneath the drifts. A bough snapped and again he blinked. He waited for a great nuclear explosion. It seemed to him he'd been waiting a long time, and the chancre was growing and filled with black bile that puffed to explode. But he was not cold.

He had no real thoughts. The image of the old man and the bomb shelter and Harvey had frozen stiff and mostly clogged his thinking. He would have to do something, he knew, but he was not sure what, and he was too tired and too lazy and too numb to move from the drift.

Crystalline sounds, snapping crusts of snow. Again he blinked.

Then his eyes closed. For a time he seemed to sleep, but it was not quite sleep. He was back in the blizzard again, and the light had no color or warmth but rather a kind of primitive pho-

tochemistry, and with all the cracking and snapping and breaking sounds, the sun rose higher, and the snapping sounds gradually sweetened and there was no great nuclear explosion, the
world survived in a calm diathermy, and the new sounds seemed
promising. Then he truly slept. He slept as the sun arched north-
east to northwest and paused from the white pine at the far edge
of the clearing to a stand of birch at the near edge. The deformed
forest began its thaw. Clumps of snow dropped like paste from
the trees, and the great drifts fashioned by the storm began to
sag and buckle, and the crystalline sounds changed into soft
sounds: feathers into a pillow, air into lungs, coffee into a cup,
silent respiration, and the world would survive.

He emerged from his drift at dusk.

He was single-minded. He moved mechanically. He pulled
his sleeping bag from the snow and draped it over the broken
chimney. He took each thing at a time.

Bending stiffly and still not thinking properly, he burrowed
in the great drift, searching, finally finding the orange rucksack.
The image of the squatting gray bomb shelter still clogged his
thinking. He kicked at the snow and uncovered his pile of wood.
Picking up each log separately, he clapped the wood against the
chimney, shaking off chunks of ice and then stacking it in a dark
pile. It was hard to think beyond the separate motions. He was
not hungry. He was not hungry and it was hard to think, but he
imagined a fire, and he opened the rucksack and found the
matches and dropped to his knees. Then he dug into the drift.
Dusk ended and dark began but he did not notice. He burrowed
into the drift, carving out a firehollow at the foot of the chimney.

He cleared the hearth, cleared the flue and the stack.

Rubble of the old homesteader's house lay around him,
stones and frozen timber, but the broken chimney still stood, the
fireplace was there, and he whisked it clean.

He placed the logs in the fireplace. He took great care. He piled the wood neatly, forming a box into which he dropped his store of twigs. Without his glasses he was nearly blind, and he squinted as he worked, taking care.

Behind him the snow sobbed. He stopped, listened, tried to remember. He could not think. There was a white winter moon.

He removed his mittens and struck the first match.

Cupping it in his hands, he leaned forward and took heavy drafts of heat and sulphur. He held the flame to his eyes. Then like a woman bending for potatoes, he reached down and touched the flame to a single twig. The flame shriveled. It held its beaded shape but shrank away, dwindling like a Doppler and carrying Perry after it, chasing the flame into the darkness. When the flame was gone, he held the match for its warmth.

He struck the second match. Again he cupped the flame and breathed deep, then touched it to the twig. The moon was white. He watched the flame, his fingers, his fingers dangling like Christmas tinsel. He envisioned raw heat. The elements. It was impulse and he could not remember. The old recollections . . . his own church, the high apse, reading as his father from the pulpit of Damascus Lutheran. Defrocked by the mockery of child's play, pretending, practising, play-acting. "Take that robe off," his father had said. "You're just pretending and it's a mockery." And Perry: "I was *practising*." And his father: "Go on outside and play with your brother." And Perry over supper: "I'm not goin' to church no more." And Perry, sitting on his tricycle: "Pooooo-oooooor me." Not understanding. Anything. The boastful old thoughts had been stiffened to stone by the blizzard. Storm fury defeated thought fury. He could not remember. He squatted down. He held the match to the twig and hovered close and coaxed the flame. He wanted to speak, and he tried to think of the words. He watched the flame burn down its stem, shrinking away, and when the flame died, he could not think of the words, and he quickly struck a third match and held it to the twig. Behind him the snow sobbed. He listened but he could not remember. He held more matches to the twig, drying it and raising its temperature, and on the ninth try the twig took. It smoldered, then for a moment flowed red like lava, then burned. Again the snow sobbed, somewhere behind him in the drifts of blizzard snow, buried somewhere, and he stopped and listened but he could not remember. He turned to the flame. The twig burned white, turned gray, ash, and Perry guarded it. He wanted to speak. He made clucking sounds instead. The flame shuddered then burned steady. He held the match tight against the twig, afraid to remove it. The match burned red and blue, the twig burned yellow and blue. He breathed slowly. When the match flame died away, the twig continued to burn. It burned from the center out, breaking into separate twin flames.

Perry wanted to speak, but instead he clucked to the fire. He took out a pile of matches and stacked them against the twig, watched the flames creep towards the poised sulphur, and he grinned—grinned when the matches took in three fast explosions, flaring and cracking open, grinning when another twig went afire.

He wanted to speak. Behind him, the snow sobbed again and again with soft respiring sounds.

He had plenty of matches. It was the one thing Harvey had done right, insisting on carrying hundreds of stiff kitchen matches. Harvey, *that* was it, old Harvey. Behind him, the snow sobbed, the pouring sound, the delicate respiration.

He wanted to speak, but instead he stacked a handful of matches against the promising part of the fire and watched them burst in a tight fist of fire. He arranged the twigs around the ball of flame, placing each twig with exact care, watching as the fist of fire clenched white and hot and began to grow. He let the fire eat at its own pace. He was careful. He wasn't a woodsman, but he knew a little about fires and he was careful. Fires have to breathe: Harvey's teaching. Old Harvey, the woodsman.

Gradually he added larger branches. He moved slowly. He watched the fire. He leaned close. His eyes were now hot, but he peered steadily into the flame, greedy, clucking and guarding it and waiting for it to grab hold of the larger logs. Snow melted from the chimney and slowly trickled down the stack, sliding and melting and sputtering like grease, forming a pool of water at his feet.

At last it was done. The fire filled the old homesteader's hearth, and Perry stood up and watched to be sure, his arms hanging low.

It was done.

He looked up, saw the moon, and tried to remember. He wasn't hungry. Harvey, he was thinking, trying to form the word on his lips. The Bull. "Sure loved your old man," old Jud had said. *I loved him, too, goddammit.* That was it, old Harvey. *Could have been a minister, could have done acts of mercy and acts of love.* Performing acts of mercy and acts of love. Saving souls, ministerial balm, unction. It could have been, all right. It was Harvey's fault, old Harvey.

He turned his mittens inside out and laid them on the hearth, then he spread his sleeping bag to dry. He moved woodenly.

His feet hurt. Harvey said aching feet are a good sign, no frostbite. Old Harvey.

Perry bent once and reached for his ankles. He felt brittle. His spine would not give.

Stamping his feet, flexing and bending, he exercised, stopped to add wood to the fire, then marched in a circle around the chimney until his feet were tingling. He fed the fire and waited. His face was raw. The skin was drawn tight around his nose and cheekbones. He was weak but he exercised, marched around the fireplace. The moon was out. He thought he should be hungry. That had been one of the old thoughts. Before the blizzard—food and hunger and self-pity. Angry. Starving and being angry, angry and self-pity, sadness and hunger, anger and hunger and melancholy, fear and hunger. The nightlong images had lumbered. But, now, nothing more to do. The hunger was gone. It had been beyond anything, a cadaverous emptiness that had moved from belly to brain and became its own great giant thought, a great beast that stalked and ravaged and gobbled all the other frantic thoughts, foraging and kicking and thrashing and shrieking, ravenous, attacking. He could not remember much about it. The blizzard iced it and stopped it cold. Another numbness, a bad sign, but he was grateful.

He leaned against the chimney and rested. The stones were warm now. The hunger was gone. The passion was gone. Another bad sign. Old Harvey had the passion.

He tried to think. It was a good fire. The moon was white. He knew no fine tricks for escape. Except for the cold and blizzard and fire and elements, he knew little. He could not think.

Behind him the snow sobbed.

He was empty. He was weak and dizzy, his brain was slow, and the stones were warm and he heard the pouring sounds, the snow sobbing, the fire. He tried to speak. It was that clucking sound, a mixture of strange sounds.

He returned to the fire and methodically warmed himself. He removed his parka and hung it to dry.

Behind him, the sobbing sound, the snow buckled. The sobbing sound. Harvey. *That* was it, old Harvey. That dry sobbing sound. He listened, partly remembering, then remembering. It was Harvey, that sound.

"Harvey," he said.

He found the drift, and while the moon shifted angles, he began digging. "Harvey," he said. That was it, Harvey the Bull. He spoke his brother's name and dug into the night snow. He was thinking and finally remembering. He attacked the tumular drift, digging fast.

"Well, look at this, look at this, look at yourself now."

He dug into the drift, and the sound flowed out. "Look at yourself now, Harv. Harvey the pirate, Harvey the great bloody pirate."

He found the bag. The cloth was frozen stiff.

He tugged at the zipper. "Some great pirate. Some great woodsman." Perry worked the zipper down. The sobbing sound came out, mixed with a thick smell. "Look at this, you bull. Look at this stink bag. Some stink bag."

"A bloody disaster, you bull." He felt his brother's flesh. The bag was very warm. Goose down and snow insulation, body heat, decay and excrement. "This is where it ends, Harv. The old stink bag. Harvey in his stink bag."

He forced the zipper further down, gutting his bag like animal hide. "A disaster. Right from the start. Some hero."

Perry pulled at him. "Come on out, Harvey. Come on now, out of your stink bag."

Harvey wheezed, the sobbing sound. The great wild. The great elements. Perry gripped the bag and pulled it from the drift. The rasping sobbing sound swelled. He dragged the bag to the hearth. "The hero in his stinking stink bag. Think about *that*." He rolled his brother out of the bag and on to the hearth. He was dizzy. He put his head down and rested.

Later he sat up. The moon had become yellow. He stoked the fire and added new wood. He felt better.

Working slowly, he propped Harvey's head on the rucksack, covered him, heaped snow into a pot and hung it over the fire.

He inspected his brother's face. The breathing was bad. The neck was arched and stiff, and the raspy breathing would not stop.

When the water was hot, he washed Harvey's face and neck, then held his head and forced hot water into him. He dipped a cloth in the hot water, wrung it out and laid it over his brother's nose.

Then he rested. He sat with his back against the warm stones. He tried to plan. If the blizzard did not return, then they would leave in the morning, there was nothing else to do. If Harvey could move. If the breathing could be eased. *If I die before I wake*. His brain was starved. If he could manage. If he could keep the fire going. Then the morning. It was hard to think. In the morning they would leave on skis. They would try the skis. Or maybe rest. He was glad the awful hunger was gone. The hunger had stopped him from thinking. No bloody thinking. That was the problem from the beginning, no thinking. No bloody thinking. That was Harvey's word, bloody. No bloody thinking and he'd gone along with it, no thinking from start to sorry finish, and now they were lost and in the morning they would have to try the skis. Or they could rest. They could stay at the old homesteader's fireplace. They could stay at the chimney. The old homesteader had built a solid chimney, and the fire was good. Perry was proud of the fire. He was no woodsman but he'd built the fire and Harvey . . . Harvey in his stink bag. They would leave on skis. The complications baffled him. Harvey's magnificent adventures: "It's a bloody cinch, brother." Harvey could bubble with it.

Perry sipped hot water. If he could eat.

He thought about numbers. He counted moments and sounds. He counted his store of logs, eight of them. Two logs for each hour, four hours of fire. He would have to go to the pines for more wood. He would go when the moon moved. When the moon moved a foot in the sky, then he would go after the wood, but first he had to rest.

He watched Harvey sleep. The bronchial rasp seemed almost natural, with a rhythm that rose and fell like winter.

The bag did stink. He could not get over it. Even with the burning wood and open air, he could not get the smell out of his head. He watched the moon and counted and waited. For a time he drifted along the borderland of sleep. He could not think and he could not dream. There was no great insight. He wished he had his glasses. They were buried somewhere in the drifts. He should have had better sense.

He tinkered with his fire. He was proud of it. Built it from scratch and without any help or smug advice from Harvey.

He crouched and hugged himself and huddled by the fire.

He watched a million stars. He recognized the Big Dipper and the Little Dipper and the North Star, but the others he didn't know. Harvey would know them. The Latin names or Greek names or whatever, the constellations, the orbits, the Sioux names and the Chippewa names and all the gods and myths and stories.

It was dark. They would be searching. Perhaps the search was over. He imagined a thousand Boy Scouts, a thousand searching flashlights closing in, a ring of Boy Scouts drawing closer.

He wanted sleep. The fire was sleepy. Harvey was sleeping.

The moon slipped across the clearing and disappeared behind the birch trees. He wished he had his glasses. It did not matter, because there was nothing much to see.

Dawn came up in slivers.

Bits of light streamed through the trees, slowly expanding

and broadening, and the day got bright and the sky grew blue like summer.

Perry lay with his head and shoulders inside the fireplace, where a tiny flame still burned. He waited for the fire to die. He listened to his own breathing, then to Harvey's breathing, the mistaken sounds of atrophy.

He blinked. He watched the embers, then the ash. He was comfortable.

The snow was clean. The snow rolled out and out. He kept his sights low, there was no sense looking further.

"Harvey?"

Perry pulled himself up. He balanced in the snow, holding a hand against the chimney.

He wondered if he had slept. He couldn't be sure. The elusive thoughts or dreams had not stopped. He was tired.

"Harvey?"

The snow was deep. It was a fine high sky.

Harvey's neck bulged, contracted, and the sobbing sound came out and his Adam's apple lurched. Perry shook him. "Harvey, have to get up now." He helped him sit against the chimney. Harvey's face was drawn.

"Have to move, Harv."

Harvey lay against the stones. His eyes opened, surprising Perry. The bad eye was like marble.

"We'll have to leave now, Harv."

Harvey peered ahead, resting against the stones.

"Just rest then I'll find the skis and we'll leave."

Perry shaded his eyes. The day got bright. Perry rested, then waded through the snow. He wished he had his glasses, but they would be buried deep and there was no sense looking for them. He found the skis and poles and carried them to the chimney. The equipment was brittle and shiny. The skis needed a wax job.

He clapped the snow from the toe bindings, leaned them against the chimney and went out after Harvey's rucksack. He poked through the snow with one of the poles. It was a long search. He stumbled on rubble of the homesteader's collapsed house, timbers and beams and granite stone, poking with his pole. He found the rucksack, slung it over his shoulder and waded back to the chimney. Harvey was sleeping. Perry shook him again. Harvey nodded, closed his eyes and lay back.

"Leaving soon," Perry said. It was hard to talk.

Harvey nodded, eyes closed.

"Do you hear me?"

"I'm sick, brother."

"I know it. Doesn't matter. We're leaving."

Harvey rasped, then chuckled. His eyes were still closed.

"Do you hear me?"

"I hear," Harvey said.

"We're leaving."

"You don't understand, do you?"

"I understand that we're leaving."

Perry rolled up the sleeping bags and stuffed them into his rucksack. He folded the map, studied it blindly, then put it in his pocket. The forest was all the same. He packed the water pot and matches. He got to his knees and reached through the snow, searching for his glasses. When his hands began to numb he gave it up. He warmed himself, exercised, then dumped snow into the fireplace. Smoke jumped from the broken chimney, hovered and finally dissipated.

The forest was bright and white and still. He looked once more about the homesteader's clearing.

He looked for a sign or a direction. He let his eyes turn across the plot, across the snowed-under foundation of the old house, to the fireplace, and chimney, to the stand of birch and beyond to the old dock and the frozen lake. There were no roads.

He turned and faced the brunt of the forest. It was opaque. It was spruce and birch and white pine.

He reached down for Harvey. "Leaving now."

He pulled him up. Harvey wobbled. He blinked.

Perry helped him into his skis and clamped the toe bindings and tested them.

Awkward, heady with departure, he rolled the nylon tarpaulin into a ball, tied it to his rucksack and slipped the straps over his shoulders. For a moment he was pleased with himself. Harvey stood like a fresh-born colt, head drooping. The forest was straight ahead.

Perry stepped into his skis and flexed his shoulders to shift the rucksack higher, then he pushed off and he felt strong at last.

They skied slowly. The land sloped down from the chimney, into the woods. There were no paths and Perry wound his way ahead, letting the skis take a natural course downwards. He steered southeast. Sooner or later the ski course would bisect North Shore Drive, the highway and the great lake.

It was a gleaming cold day, and the skis bit the snow crust and the forest was still and brittle, and Perry pushed without thinking, and he did not worry. The pines were tall and thick. The forest descended.

At intervals he rested and waited for Harvey.

They did not speak. The skis crunched and bit the snow, and Harvey's dry breathing followed him both driving and pursuing.

Perry felt lean.

Though blind and groping from tree to tree, he still had a sense of great new clearheadedness. He skied erect, thinking he might be watched, photographed for some epic motion picture spinning on sparse themes of survival and manhood, and he counted moments and pines. A dozen simple tasks, step and glide, push and glide.

Harvey moved slowly, head down, dragging his poles like

outriggers. Perry waited and watched. The gallant pirate. He felt some shame, even a pinch of embarrassment. He knew so much about his brother, the memory of his climbing out the school window, perching on the ledge, then plunging to the school yard, hollering Geronimooooo. And other such memories. Nothing false about the bravado, and certainly nothing make-believe.

"One glide one, two glide two, three glide three," Perry murmured. He felt lean. The old fat was gone. To be a great bull.

"Twelve glide twelve," he murmured, and the land swept down. He skied erect. He'd lasted it out. He was leading now. He felt good and he felt strong. "Twenty glide twenty," and the snow squeaked like chalk on a blackboard. Harvey's breathing followed him, the harsh bronchial sound.

"Fifty-nine glide fifty-nine, sixty glide sixty," he chanted.

He came to a stand of dense pine. Sidestepping, he jabbed at the trees with his pole, testing it. He felt the branches buckle and pushed through. He stood alone. The woods were very high and thick. Behind him, he heard Harvey's breathing. He unbuckled his skis and walked back for Harvey.

"Well . . . the trees are too close. We'll have to walk awhile. We're going to walk awhile. You hear?" He knelt in the snow and helped Harvey out of his skis. "Take my shoulder now. We're going to push through." Harvey was tall. There was a slight shadow. He cradled the skis and led Harvey into the dense trees. "Stop here." His voice was stiff. It was all right. There was some authority.

They walked a long mile. The country began to rise and they rested often, then the forest thinned out and fell sharply, and again they skied.

The forest finally fell to a frozen river. Like a hook, it curved away from them. Perry studied it. What he could see of it, the river bent almost directly south. If it continued south, they would get deeper lost. If it straightened out somewhere ahead, a generous twist, it might lead to the southeast and the highway and the yellow end. He took out the map. There were a thousand small rivers. Ten thousand, twenty thousand lakes. It looked simple. Lake Oslo. Whitefish Lake. Caribou Lake. Beaver Lake. There in the corner, a small black dot, was the town, Sawmill Landing, stenciled in black. The Arrowhead engulfed it. And all the rivers; blue lines running into blue patches, surrounded by green, raw forest.

He looked for a river with a big hook. They all had hooks. He did not know much about maps. Ought to have gone out with his father, he might have learned something. But there was no sense asking Harvey now. All the blundering. Perry folded the map and returned it to his pocket. He helped Harvey on to the river.

"No," Harvey murmured.

"What?"

"Nope. No more." Harvey shook his head, his eyes down. His bad eye was hard. "I'm sick. This is far enough. This is enough, brother." He planted his poles and leaned on them. Slowly at first, then fast, his skis slid backward and he fell face forward and lay still.

"Get up," Perry said.

"This is enough."

Perry hooked his arms around his brother, lifting him. "Up," he said.

"You don't understand. This is . . ." Harvey coughed and Perry pulled him forward and they moved down the river, rounding the bend, and they skied south.

The pines were high on both banks. Icicles dangled from the branches.

The white river sparkled ahead. "Eighty glide eighty, eighty-one glide eighty-one, eighty-two glide eighty-two, eighty-three glide eighty-three."

Far ahead, over the forest, a mammoth cloud hovered. It was the backside of the blizzard.

The river flowed south and Perry worried. They would have to leave it if it did not soon bend southeast.

The skiing was flat and easy. He glided along the frozen river, letting inertia carry him. Numbers flopped in his head. He counted aloud, counting for each skating motion, each breath. The mammoth cloud looked natural over the forest. It shifted, regenerated like an ameba. It was familiar. He'd seen it coming. Harvey had laughed. He counted numbers, hard numbers. Ninety glide ninety. He counted faults in the river crust, keeping his head down, a way to keep limbs functioning, methodically step by step, ninety-one glide ninety-one. He counted Harvey's respiration behind him, turning the disease into dry numbers, counting the days they'd been lost. He concentrated, searching for something unique in each of the lost days. He counted to nineteen, juggling numbers, but finally losing track as the blizzard blended the days into an indistinguishable force, extinguished day and night and time and even number. At last the river turned. It was a slow arcing bend, and they rounded it and came to a bridge. The bridge was old, plank flooring and silver-iron railings, high enough to ski under without stooping. Perry stopped. He leaned on his poles and waited for Harvey. "Bridge," he said. Harvey sat on the river. "There's a road up there, Harv." Perry unbuckled his skis. It was a steep, long climb up the river-bank, a sheer bluff that was iced and deliberately imposing. "I'm going up." He tackled it without thinking, digging with his fingers and pushing against the bank for adhesion. Roots of old trees bulged from the bank and he used them as a ladder. He did not stop climbing until he'd scaled it. He rolled on to his back and spread his arms and lay still.

He was dizzy. He'd been dreaming. Not dreaming, thinking. And not thinking, a combination of dream and thought.

He could not remember. He may have slept, he did not know.

The sky was darker now. He was cold.

He pushed up, leaning on an elbow. He was very cold. He saw the bridge. "Gawwd," he moaned, remembered, then quickly scrambled along the bank and got to the bridge. It carried a narrow trail across the river and into the far pines. Probably a logging trail, he thought; Harvey would know. It was a plain dirt road that emerged, crossed the river and submerged again.

He walked on to the bridge. The planks shivered. The frozen bolts creaked. He was very cold. He looked each way, hugging himself. He looked up to where the trail tunneled out of the forest and down to where it disappeared again in a mountain of pine. A crust of night grey was coming down the river. He was cold.

He leaned against the iron railing. He was hypnotized and cold.

Harvey lay on the river below.

Perry stared down. Harvey's arms were splayed, disjointed, his skis jutted at two obtuse angles. His yellow parka shined. Snow spread out and out to the banks of river, climbing the banks, spreading out and out into the forest.

Perry gazed down.

Harvey's brown beard had frosted. The gray crust came sliding up the river. The yellow parka shined. Making angels in the snow: Harvey as a kid, making angels in the snow, arms and legs splashing. The forest was closing up, all right. Perry gazed down. Harvey was still, frozen in the river, cemented in the frost. His bad eye was open, wide open, bulging out. "Hey, Harv!" he called. "Hey, Harvey. What you doing down there?"

The forest was closing up fast as the gray nightcrust came

sliding in. "Harvey!" he called, a war game or something, just a tattered remnant of childhood, there lay Harvey shot dead, tumbling dead to the river, freezing in fun. "Hey, Harv!" he called. Harvey looked young, even with the frosted beard and red skin and play-dead pose.

He was tired. He sat down. The day was brittle and the shadows were still coming. Had he slept? They needed a fire. He turned, saw that the river bent sharply, twisted once more, then continued south. They could not stay on the river. He got out the map. He unfolded it and spread it against the railing and began searching it for a bridge and a river and a road. He was tired and cold. Squinting and bending over the map, he searched it top to bottom. He stopped once to look down at Harvey. The bad eye was still open, dull. "It's all right, Harv. Old Harv."

The map was yellow, encased in plastic. It had belonged to their father. Scribblings and cryptic X's and dotted lines had been traced on it. In red letters, stencilled across the western width of the map, it said: *World's Greatest and Only Exclusive-Canoe Country*. Canoe country. Ski country. Indian country. Camping country, lake country, pine country, old forest, lost country. It confused him. His eyes hurt, he needed his glasses. It was too simple and easy. On the map, everything was unmistakable and clear, nothing dangled and no height or depth. The great forests were reduced to a pale green sheen. From bottom left to top right ran the sharp coastline of Lake Superior, a sheaf of blue that formed the Arrowhead's cutting edge. At its tip was Grand Portage, stopping place for the voyagers, the Indian reservation. Fucking greasy Indians, the old Swedes said. A sliver of land, the tip of the Arrowhead stabbed into Superior at a place called Pigeon Point. Perry had once been there. With his father and Harvey. It was all rock and pine and still wild, and his father had pointed out at the lake and called it the cleanest lake in the world. He'd taken them along the portage trail, lecturing, explaining that La Vérendrye landed there in August of 1731, that the French used the place as a launching pad for the great Northwest Passage quest, that later it became a bustling English fur outpost, stockaded, growing, doing big business in beaver hides and bear and moose. And they'd walked along the portage trail and his father had lectured and Harvey's eyes gleamed and dreamed, and they came to the Pigeon River and the pathway west into rainy river country, saw old Fort Charlotte, the site anyway, and it was all history, the Glacial Age, the Stone Age, the French and British and the coming Swedes and Finns and Norwegians and Yankees, opening it up. Perry stared at the map. He was cold. Harvey lay on the river below, his yellow parka still shining. The map was a maze. The country was thick with lakes. He tried to count the blue splotches, forgetting himself, forgetting Harvey frosted below, and he counted until losing his way in a tangle of channels and unnamed lakes and long blue stretches of lakes merging with other lakes. The whole history was there, printed on the map, all the moraines and blazed boulders, the sweep of the giant glaciers. And the names, some Indian, Lake Kawishiur and Lake Gabimichigami. French names, like Caribou and Brule, and English names and Swedish names and half-breed names, and when all the names ran out and still other lakes were discovered, the lakes were called by number, Lake Number Three, Lake Number Four. A pity, Perry thought.

Entranced, he stared down at Lake Number Four, hypnotized. He darted back and forth in memory, and Lake Number Four intrigued him: not at all a small and unimportant lake, rather a very large and interesting chunk of blue on the map, shaped like an upside-down deer with small islands where the heart and kidneys would be. The name, Lake Number Four, thumped mechanically through his head, solid, a solid name, countable. Number Four in the land of ten thousand lakes. An injustice. Deer Lake would be better. Peri Lake. No, deer-shaped, Deer Lake. He looked closer and found a dozen other Deer lakes; then Elk lakes and Moose lakes and Reindeer lakes and Beaver lakes and Bear lakes and White Bear lakes.

He was cold. The map shivered. Harvey was still down there, still on the frozen river.

It was so big. He looked to the cutting edge of the broadhead, the string of towns along the coast—Tofte, Lutsen, Silver Bay, Hovland, Grand Marais. And the starting point, Sawmill Landing, a black dot, inland slightly, a dot representing all those wooden buildings, the tar strip of Mainstreet, Route 18. He touched the dot. He traced his finger north, through the heart of the Arrowhead, up to the northern edge where a chain of lakes and rivers and portages formed the intricate border with Canada. Somewhere in the broadhead, between the cutting edges, somewhere along a river where there was a bridge and an old logging trail. He looked carefully, squinting, bending over the map. The wind began and the gray nightcrust swept down the river, across Harvey and then under the bridge.

"Harvey!" he called.

Hugging him like a doll, Perry pulled his brother up, removed his skis and made him walk.

The river ice snapped and the day was late and crystal sharp and cold. The snow cracked into sheets. They walked in a circle. Perry had no hope. Twice he stopped to massage his brother's thighs.

Harvey's arms dangled.

"Come on, Harv, come on," Perry clucked. "One step one, two step two, three step three, easy, easy." Morphia, each step.

Harvey began to cough. He held a choking grip on Perry's throat.

"Harvey?" Perry at last stopped.

"I'm sick."

Perry waited for the coughing to stop.

"I was sleeping. I'm sick."

"We have to get off the river. We're going up to the bridge."

Harvey coughed. "I don't . . . No, I don't think so." His voice had an icy, nasal tinkle. It was his old voice hollowed out.

"We have to climb the bank."

"Shit."

"I'll help. Can't stay on the river. Can you hear me? The river goes the wrong way. There's a road up there. We'll go up and make a fire and tomorrow we'll take the road."

"I'm hot."

Perry kneeled and rubbed Harvey's thighs and ankles. His own hands were getting numb. The winter moon was already up.

"Bloody hot," Harvey coughed. "I'll take the coat off."

"No, you won't."

"I'm hot."

"It's the fever. You're keeping the coat on. Later I'll build us a fire. Take hold now."

"I'm sick."

"Yes. You're climbing the bank. You're leaving the coat on. Take hold."

"I don't want to."

"Doesn't matter. Take hold."

Harvey pulled an arm from his parka. "I'm . . . let me get this coat off. I was sleeping, you know."

"You were freezing."

They stood facing each other. Harvey suddenly smiled. He started to laugh and the cough caught hold, a dry hack. "You . . .

You don't know what you're doing." The bad eye shined. "You don't know *what* you're doing."

"Take hold then."

"You . . . You don't know a hell of what you're doing, do you?"

"You're climbing that bank."

"All right then. But you don't know."

Harvey climbed recklessly. It was Harvey, his old carelessness and certainty, climbing as though daring the bluff to cast him off. He climbed to the top and smiled down at Perry, then, grinning and coughing, he curled in the snow while Perry scaled the bank for the final time, bringing up the skis and poles.

Perry used the last light to gather wood. He shaved splinters from a rotted bridge plank and used it for kindling to build a fire.

He tied the nylon tarp to an iron railing, unrolled the sleeping bags. Harvey lay by the fire. His eyes were listless and wide open and he did not move.

As the night went on, Harvey's breathing settled into the forest background, replacing the wind. From time to time Perry fed him hot water, holding the pot while Harvey breathed the steam.

Perry slept well. He woke once, rebuilt the fire, then slept again.

At dawn, he doused the fire and packed their gear. He was nervous. He would look for food during the day. Squirrels maybe. Harvey sat with his back against the bridge railing.

"Get up," Perry said.

"This is the end."

"What?"

"You aren't facing it," Harvey said.

"Get up."

Harvey kept grinning. "You don't even know the end. This is

the end, brother. I'm not going on, I'm sick." Perry stood back. He watched and did not go close.

He watched until Harvey slumped against the railing.

"Get up."

"You don't even . . . don't understand," Harvey muttered. "This is, just look into it. For Christ sake, this is the whole purpose of it, don't you see that? We did all right. This is forest here. This is wild stuff, don't you see that?"

Perry blinked. "No."

Harvey shrugged and grinned. "Well, I'm staying behind. I'm through."

Perry put on his rucksack. "You're not," he said. "You're coming."

Harvey grinned like a wolf.

"You are coming," Perry repeated.

"Don't have to be so afraid."

"What?"

"You can stop fearing it. You're always so goddamned afraid."

"Get up."

Harvey began his cough and Perry took the chance to get him up and into the skis.

"You're coming," he said.

"You're afraid of everything."

"That's right."

"You're lazy and you never learned a thing. You're afraid, you're afraid of everything," then he coughed again and Perry strapped him into a rucksack.

"Don't you like to talk?"

"No."

"I want to talk," Harvey said.

"Then you talk. Let's go."

"I want to talk about being brave and doing things."

"We've done that before." Perry started across the bridge.

"Let's talk about you then," Harvey grinned. "Let's talk about brother Paul Milton Perry, how's that? How's that?" he crowed. "How's that?"

Perry waited for Harvey to push off, then he skied off the bridge and on to the road and into the woods, checking to be sure Harvey followed.

"Yeah," Harvey crowed behind him, then coughed, then crowed: "Let's talk about you, brother. See? See here, brother. You came with me. Came along free and clear, you hear?"

Perry now led the way.

"Free and clear! You hear? You could have stayed home. Didn't have to come, nobody forced you. Came free and clear. You hear me? Let's talk about your shining moments in the great history of things. You hear? You hear me? Let's talk about *you* awhile. Let's talk . . . Let's talk about your great shining love for your father. You hear me? You want to talk? Nobody forced you out here. You just came, you hear? Let's talk about our father awhile. Let's sit down and talk about how you treated him, your great love for him. Let's just stop and talk about that . . . No-body made you come out here. You think I feel sorry? Wrong! You're wrong, buddy. You hear?"

Perry skied straight ahead. Harvey was far behind him. The trees were growing everywhere, full pine and spruce, and the land sloped down.

He led the way.

The trees went on and on. He tried counting them.

At midday he stopped and motioned for Harvey to sit down. They rested on their rucksacks. Harvey had thin blue veins marking his forehead. His face was wet.

"I'm taking off this coat," Harvey said.

"You're not." Perry did not look up.

"I'm sick."

"I know that. You're keeping the coat on."

Perry sat and looked up the trail and tried to think it out. He was hungry but he felt all right. He admired the trees. They were green as summer, long and short needled spruce. Further ahead, up the trail, they turned to birch but beyond they turned to pine again. All over, the snow sparkled. It was a fine bright day and he saw everything clearly. The brightness made him close his eyes.

"I'm taking this coat off," said Harvey.

Perry got up and slung the rucksack behind him.

"Did you hear me? I'm taking this coat off."

Perry buckled on his skis, leaned on his poles and watched Harvey until he got up.

He waited, then without a nod he pushed off down the trail. He couldn't get over how bright and clean a day it was, as though the blizzard had scrubbed everything like steel wool. On each side of the trail, the trees grew in neat rows. He was hungry again. It struck in strange places. The hunger had moved from his belly to the back of his brain, in some primitive transferal of sensation. The hunger would strike for a moment, throbbing as if it had been plucked like a guitar string, then it would shimmy and make him dizzy, then slowly give out and he would be clearheaded again and in control. He was leading. Lean at last, and clearheaded and cleareyed.

They skied up the center of the trail. Perry leading. He skied with his eyes closed. He wondered if a man could sleep and still go on, eyes closed, maybe even snoring, while the skis simply carried. Each time he opened his eyes, the snow was brighter.

The road was hypnotic in its stretches of long forest and snow and bright blue sky. All quite beautiful. The trail sometimes was very wide in places where the loggers had stopped to cut, and other times it was impassable, grown over with saplings and coppice. Except for the sound of their skiing and the undertone of cracking in the snow, the forest was still, and the old trail swept through the woods like a river.

For a time they were followed by a hawk that dipped down on them, wings fluttering in a slow graceful breaking motion, then jerking suddenly upwards and disappearing high over the forest, then later returning to screech low over the trail, winding over their heads and jerking up and away again. But except for the lonely hawk and the sound of their skis and the sound of the cracking snow, the day was dumb and empty, a long track of light and snow along the trail. Perry played his counting game: trees, strides, breaths, memories, saplings, spurts of hard hunger, minutes, hours, backward, forward. He ran out of things to count, or they stretched on so far that he grew restless with the prospect of never reaching the end.

The forest kept coming and it was always there. The birch trees gave out to acres of evergreens. He could close his eyes and ski and imagine himself finally stopping and freezing and fossilizing and sprouting needled branches and joining the pines in a perfect communion. One of millions. Each the same. No cold, no hunger, no memories and no fear. An element among elements in the elements. He thought about it and followed the trail, sometimes not thinking at all, other times thinking: the road had no ditches. No rest stops. No fuel stations or scenic overlooks or picnic tables. No refracting road signs, no speed limits, no limits at all. Limitless. The trail was its own perfect logic, for it went from one place to another place, starting and ending, and they were following it so that sooner or later it would empty them either at the starting place or ending place. It was perfect, hypnotic logic. Then he began to think he was an adventurer. He would have some fine story to tell. He could tell it to the son Grace wanted. He could tell it in the drugstore, and people would listen, the whole place would go quiet and Herb Wolff would ring his cash register while people listened and drank coffee, and he would have a great thing to remember and ponder. He could tell about this very moment. The very moment: the trail there before him, the big scary-looking pines walking in from both sides, the sound of Harvey's cough behind him, the hawk now and again swooping down with its screech and talons, now, the hunger at the back of his brain, he could tell them all that. He could tell them he was, at that moment, just at that particular moment in that adventure, he could tell them he was absolutely and undeniably unafraid, fearless, simply acting, thinking of the things he would tell them. He was thinking. He was not sure about Harvey. Old Harvey, such a bull. He was not sure. The cough was bad. It was genuine sickness, all right. He would tell about Harvey's sickness, how the cough always started with the fluid sound deep in the lungs and then came out in a flood of mucus and then ended in a whooping wheeze, and how they would stop for Harvey to catch his breath, and how Perry would then turn and begin to ski and how Harvey would finally follow, now following. The trees went on and on, and the trail wound on and on.

When they stopped for rest, Perry consulted the map, looking again for some correspondence between the lay of the land and what was printed under the plastic. A few county roads cut into the Arrowhead, none of them seeming to go anywhere in particular, winding into the forest from the cutting edge of Lake Superior, roaming about, then either ending entirely or twisting in a circle back towards the lake.

Harvey started coughing and Perry had to stand him up. When the coughing got bad, Perry leaned him over and clapped his back, clucking to him gently like a mother at bedside. The coughing eased off and Harvey sat down on his rucksack, his head in his hands, and Perry went back to the map. Surprising himself, he realized he was developing a new and not entirely desirable capacity for treating suffering with clinical dispatch, solving a crisis, moving himself to do what had to be done and nothing more or less, then moving on to the next thing. The next thing was the map, finding a way out. He'd stared at it so often that it somehow seemed an inscrutable but still friendly companion, as if offering something in a language Perry did not understand. The map seemed to stare back at him. Saying: look closer. Look at the elevations. This chain of lakes here, this river connecting them. He peered at the map and the green and brown map peered back at him, and at last he slowly folded it and returned it to his parka pocket.

"Are you ready now?" he asked Harvey. He stated the question.

Harvey coughed again. Perry stood him up and clapped him and helped him into his skis.

"Awhile more," he said, "just awhile more and we'll stop and I'll boil you water."

He had nothing more to say. Speaking seemed out of place, almost unnatural. Stammered, implied meanings. He realized it and did not like it, but still he could think of nothing to say.

"We'll go," he said.

Harvey did not look up. He stood with his skis wide apart.

He could have been standing at a urinal, looking down, his face composed and unstrained and content.

"Harv. We'll go now."

With a slow gesture of languor, Harvey nodded and moved forward, and Perry pushed off. Almost as they started, Perry was tired. He could feel it in his thighs and calves and in the bones themselves. He wanted to stop, build a hot fire, bring out the sleeping bags and then sleep and sleep. He came close to stopping. He hesitated with his poles, relaxing his grip and feeling his arms float away from him, his knees start to cave as if cut like giant spruce to begin the long slow creaking fall to repose. He could have stopped and slept. Nothing to stop him. Easy. His body would have crumpled and his brain would have never known, and Harvey would have come beside him and they would have slept. The tiredness came just like the hunger. It simply came. As uncomplicated and elemental as water or lightning. And the trail wound into the forest in the same indifferent way. Perry pushed with his poles and kept skiing.

The day lasted summer bright, lasted and lasted, and the north was filled with white light.

Soon the trail began ascending. They moved slowly. Harvey had a hard time of it, sometimes seeming not to move at all.

At the trail's summit they rested. Then they skied down. They moved fast, riding the downward-sloping trail, riding their skis and the downward-going forest. Perry did not need to push with his poles. He let the shining poles hang behind him. The speed blended with his tiredness. Sleep-speeding, the evergreens spilled by, then the straggly branches of birch trees, and the colors sped by in greens and silver and white light, and through an ice cocoon, a fast moving downward-going ice capsule, he slept-sped down, branches and snow glittering, and when he closed his eyes he could still see the brightness.

Harvey's face was wet and red at the fire. Sweat dribbled from his forehead to his cheeks and into his beard, but he did not seem bothered by it. Rather, he lay against his rucksack with the air of wise content, and even when he coughed he did not move a hand to his mouth nor bend forward to ease the coughing. He sat still, letting the coughing shake him like some electrical current, not moving or changing expression. He did not wipe away the sweat, or close his eyes, or try to sleep, or talk. At times he suffered blankly, at times not at all, at times appearing to be deep into thought and at times as hardened as a glacier, neither breathing nor moving. His bad eye seemed to be the active eye. While the rest of his face was tranquil, the dead eye rolled askew, untethered by nerve or muscle to its socket, aggressive and dominant. The eye was attracted to the fire as though by magnetism. And when he coughed, the bad eye remained open while the other closed and while his body tightened in a spasm, the bad eye peering out at the fire perfectly indifferent to the sickness.

Perry melted snow and boiled water and gave it to Harvey to drink. Perry held the tin cup, watching the water wet his brother's beard, watching his brother's eyes, holding the cup until he saw Harvey's throat bob.

And it was snowing. There was still some fire, and the snow was sweeping before the fire. He awoke and saw it was snowing. The sky was black and clear, the northern stars, the dippers, everything shining, and still it was snowing. He held out his hand. It was fine dry snow. Then he saw it was snowing from a pine tree. A pine tree was snowing on him, snowing on the fire. A pine tree pregnant and sagged with snow, buckled almost sideways with the weight, snowing on him.

He was looking for airplanes. Sometime while he was trying to sleep and not sleeping, he had thought that they would have airplanes looking for them. Important to keep the fire going. At night an airplane would see the fire. He got it going high, then lay back and carefully scanned the sky for airplanes. He searched

the sky section to section. He searched each of the constellations, and the moon, and the huge sprawling spaces of open
black. He scanned each horizon. Then he divided the sky into
quadrants and did it again, systematically searching for an airplane.

He heard Harvey move.

"Sleeping?" he said softly.

Harvey moved again. His breathing was wet and deep down.

"Sleeping?"

"I'm sick."

"Here, let me heat up some water for you."

"I don't think . . ."

"Hot water'll cut through the crap. Hold still and rest."

Perry heaped snow into the pot and put it on the fire.

He lay back and continued his search for airplanes. Harvey
was mumbling, but Perry gazed upwards, looking for lights.

Harvey's fluid talking was background music: "I'm sick, I
guess . . . I guess I was right about that, wasn't I?"

"You'll be all right."

"People have always told me that. Harvey, they always say,
Harvey, you'll be all right."

"Lie still."

The sky had no airplanes. Perry continued his search, thinking about the form and shadowed wings and red and green
lights, looking from horizon to horizon.

"Anyhow," Harvey said. "Anyhow, here we are. I didn't force
you to come. You can never say I forced you."

"I didn't say that. Relax. I'll give you some water when it's
hot."

"Anyhow. Here we are. You and me. I don't mind it. Really, I
don't mind it at all. I'm sick but I feel all right anyway. I don't
mind it . . . I wish Addie was here. That's what I wish. That Addie, she'd be teasing me and telling me I'm not sick. Really. She'd

be teasing me and saying pirates don't get sick. She calls me her pirate, did you know that? She does. Her pirate. I'm not really a pirate. She'd say pirates can't get sick. Who ever saw a sick pirate? she'd say. Do you know . . . do you know this, that when I asked her to get married, I asked her polite and straightforward, but when I asked her to get married, Addie said, just like that, she said pirates don't get married. Who ever heard of a married pirate? she said. Can you believe she'd say that? Who ever heard of a married pirate? I can't believe that . . . I don't know. I don't like those sorts of names. The old man, he liked to call me a bull. I never said anything about it to him, though. Never told him I didn't like being called a bull. Or anything else. You probably think I always liked being called that. People always think they know what people think and everything, but they don't. There's a lot you think you know you don't know . . . I'm not criticizing. You know a lot, you know more than me, I guess, and you're always sensible and there's nothing wrong with that, so I'm not criticizing . . . And I'm sorry I was hollering at you back there. I get that way. I don't know why but I sometimes get that way. You probably think I'm always thinking about going to Africa and remembering the war and doing all those strange things, but that's not true. People always think they know what people are thinking about. Anyhow. Anyhow, I'm sorry I hollered at you, I just get that way. I been thinking about getting a job, maybe you didn't know that. I was telling Grace about it, and I told her not to tell. Grace is nice. She is. I'm sorry about that, too. You must think . . . I don't know. I remember things, too. Sometimes I got scared going out with the old man. Not later on, I wasn't scared then, but the first times going out for a long time, when we went way deep and I was just a little kid, I couldn't have been more than eight or nine. Do you remember that? Do you remember?"

"No."

"I was just a kid. You probably don't remember. The old man got me a new rifle. You remember that?"

"Sort of."

"He got it for me for Christmas. I remember it. It was behind the tree and I knew it was there all the time, for a week or something, but I never let on because I knew he wanted me to be surprised and happy on the morning when we went down and opened up the presents, so I didn't let on I knew about it. But I was scared of it. I remember crying upstairs, knowing in the morning I had to go down and open up the gun and look happy, and then knowing I had to go out and shoot it, scared silly. Jesus, that was funny. That was something funny. But I was scared. You don't know that, I'll bet. But I was scared and I never let on to him, 'cause I knew he'd think I was ungrateful or didn't . . . didn't love him or something, so I kept quiet. And in the morning, sure enough, it was a rifle. Just a measly rifle, a twenty-two. Don't you remember that rifle?"

"No."

"Well, it was a twenty-two. I guess you never got one, but anyhow there it was, and sure enough the old man took me outside with it and we went walking in the snow and out into the woods, Jesus, you can't believe how scared I was of that fucking gun . . . This cough . . . and he showed me how to load it, sticking the bullets into this rod that was under the barrel, the magazine, and he shot it a couple of times to show me how to do it, putting holes in this birch tree. Then it was my turn and he gave it to me, and I just stood there smiling and smiling till I felt like crying, and the old man smiled and seemed to think I was happy, and he told me to shoot it, so I put it up and shot it. I don't remember hitting anything, but I shot it and pretty soon got used to it so I wasn't so scared, but all I remember about the whole thing was being scared and shooting it anyhow. Anyhow. So I told Addie about it and she started laughing and told me to buy a sword or something. Sometimes I do think she's Indian. I can't ever decide. What do you think? I think . . . I think we oughta take her into some hospital and have blood tests made, what do you think? I like her. I told her we ought to get married and she told me pirates are never married. I don't even know if she thought I was serious. I was serious all right. Sometimes I think you never think I'm ever serious, but I am. You can't ever know for sure what people are thinking. And sometimes, sometimes people are thinking just the opposite of what they pretend they're thinking. When the old man died I was pretty sad, but I know you were sad, too, because you were always having run-ins with him, but you were sad. Weren't you? Don't have to say. You can't tell. But that Addie . . . You see anything? What are you looking for there?"

"Airplanes."

Harvey laughed and coughed again. "You're some sensible brother, aren't you? You are. I guess we're really brothers, aren't we? Don't know what that means, except it means that some of the same things we remember. You don't remember the rifle I got?"

"No."

"Well . . . You really don't remember it? Guess you just never noticed."

"Do you remember the time that the old man took us to learn to swim?"

"Sure . . . Well, no. Sort of. No, I guess I don't."

"We remember different things."

"We both remember the bomb shelter, though."

"Yes."

"And I guess we'll remember this, too."

"Want some of this hot water?"

"I better have some. I feel okay, though. I don't mind a bit. I don't care what."

The trail slowly bent and they pushed around the bend. More road opened in a long snowflow. The land kept descending. The forest thinned out, and they came to a crossroad. Perry pushed the pole through the snow and it clanked sharply against the road.

"Tar," he said.

He waited for Harvey. Then again he thrust his pole down and listened to the civilized sharp thud. "It's tar," he said.

They rested there, sitting on their rucksacks at the center of the crossroads. It was a real road this time, and Perry studied the map. From the sun, he judged the road to be running northwest-southeast. From the map, he guessed the tar road was one of two, both of which emptied eventually on to the shore of Superior. And he was hungry.

"All right?" he said. He put the map away.

"I'm pretty sick. Can we rest?"

"We can rest. You're going to get sicker, though."

"Just awhile. Not long. We're going to die, I guess. You know that?"

"Yes," Perry said, thinking it would be just as difficult later on. He was lightheaded himself. Cleareyed and lightheaded. The day was bright as damask steel, tough and swordlike and shining, and he rested against his pack until it was a choice between sleeping or moving on, and he got up and helped Harvey into his skis and pushed off.

Even as he started down the new road, he was hungry and very tired. He tried then not to think about it. He thought about the new tar road. He concentrated on it. The new road was not much different from the logging trail, slightly wider and straighter and more even. It seemed to have a destination. Alongside it, the trees were cut in a sharp and beveled way, as though the builders of the road had surveyed the path precisely and without thought of frills or beauty, cutting it out of the forest in the easiest and straightest and simplest fashion. He thought about it, imagining the road being bulldozed in the summer months, imagined the slow progress, the swath of cut timber, the mashing roar of yellow-painted construction machines and the quick dash of frightened deer, the hunger, he was hungry. It was not a stab any more. He was hungry but he did not feel it. He did not ache from the hunger. There was no pain. His belly felt full, even swollen. The dark place at the base of his brain was numb. He was hungry in a lethargic, purely empty way, fatigued, spent, drained, hollow, weak, ballooned, oxygen-light, emptyheaded, lightheaded, sleepy, sleepy. He tried not to think about it. It was impulsive hunger without sensation, as a baby at birth, hungry from the beginning, and he tried not to think of it. Vaguely, he recalled warnings of extreme hunger. Famine, warning from the pulpit. He tried not to think of it, concentrating on his breathing and the steps and motions of skiing. It was a bright good road. Suffocating. It was a kind of suffocation, the hunger, suffocation without pain or even knowledge, sleep-suffocation far beyond knowledge or feeling. He tried the counting game. Counting days again. The days blended with the trees, each identical to the next, and he lost count and could not remember, and he tried counting only numbers, seeing how long and how far he could go on. He was glad the sensation of hunger was gone. A bad sign, he knew, but he was glad not to have to withstand it. The dull emptiness was better for thinking. He had his wits. He could count. He counted on, the numbers flopping in his head as he counted, physical objects. Some of the numbers seemed to stick, looming in huge black numerals, and he counted the stuck numbers over and over until they snapped away to be replaced by the next numbers, and he counted to a thousand and kept going, counting on, perfectly in control, his wits intact, beginning to believe he could reach the very end of the numbers, the last number, 1201, 1202, 1203, 1204, 1205, 1205, 1205, 1206, 1207, 1208, 1209, 1210, 1211, 1212, 1212, 1212, 1212, 1213, some of the numbers having a symmetry that made them stick in his brain, and he counted in the growing conviction that one of the numbers would pop before him as the final number, beyond which there would be no further numbers, the red limit, the very edge of the universe beyond which the past started, and he would only have to turn backwards, flowing evenly into the past which was not any longer past, turn to begin counting in the other direction, going backwards until it became a countdown for a great red explosion to send him hurtling head over heels in numbers back towards the edge. He was glad the hunger ache was gone. He had his wits. The trail was now a road, and the road was straight and level, flat and solid as the numbers he counted, flat on the green globular forest.

He came to a minor bend in the road. On the right, a pine bluff was high. On the left, the land sloped sharply down. Partly chiseled into the bluff's face, the road executed a slow graceful turn, and Perry followed it. Then he realized he was gazing into a black arrow that traced the curve of the road. A black arrow on a yellow sheet of metal. The arrow pointed the way. It seemed a kind of form in his head, along with the numbers, a black arrow on yellow metal that was so compatible with the numbers that he merely nodded at it, as if counting it with all the rest.

Then he stopped.

It was a road sign, a black arrow on yellow metal that

showed the curve of the road, a warning posted for those who came that way.

It was hammered to a shiny silver stake.

He heard Harvey brake behind him.

Perry felt a deep spark, and he was happy and wanted to say something. "Well," he said.

He looked at the wordless bent arrow.

"It's a road, all right."

The sun hovered just over the western trees. As he turned, it settled into the clutches of the topmost branches.

"What do you think?"

"Poachers," Harvey said.

"What."

Harvey motioned towards the snow, a few yards beyond the shiny stake. He began coughing and leaned on his poles. "There. Poachers." It was the carcass of some dead animal. Most of it lay buried. "A deer," Harvey said. Perry skied to it and brushed the snow off. The hindquarters were completely gone. The carcass was frozen and there was no odor or blood. Without the hindquarters the animal looked tiny, not much bigger than a house dog. The eyes of the deer were like rock.

"Poachers," Harvey said again, repeating himself in a glazed way. He sounded like an old man. "They got the antlers, too, if there were any. Leave it be."

Perry kicked at the carcass. He was hungry, but the animal, what was left of it, did not tempt him. He thought of the deer he'd greeted, then thought of his hunger again. "Can't eat it, I guess."

"If you want."

"I'm not hungry."

"You don't think you are. You are."

Perry covered the carcass with fresh snow.

"Poachers," muttered Harvey. His voice was eaten out.

"Yeah. You all right?"

"I'm sick. Poachers. They take the hindquarters for venison. And the antlers. Use a knife with a dropped point so as not to cut the gutsack while they butcher. Poachers. Then dump kerosene over everything. Keeps the wolves away, kills the scent. I'm sick. I want to take off my coat. I think I'd better take it off, brother."

"You know better."

"I've got to. This time I've got to. Poachers, Jesus."

"Are you hungry?"

"Jesus."

"I think we'd better eat some of it."

"I'm sick."

"We better eat some of it."

"Jesus. Fucking wolves."

"Can you go on awhile?"

"Poachers and wolves. Can you beat that? I'm sick, I am."

Fine, thin winter light came through in patches. It was high cold light. Perry looked at the buried carcass and the black bent arrow.

"All right then. We'll go on. All right? I think that's the right thing. Either that or eat some of this deer. We can find something on it to eat. It's been frozen. What do you think? It's not spoiled. Either eat some of the deer or go on."

"Wolves."

"Harvey! Leave that coat on."

"I'm sick. I'm hot."

"You're cold. You don't know it."

"Don't know anything. You know everything."

"Just leave the coat on."

Harvey's skis slipped from under him. He fell backwards,

sitting with his knees bent. Perry got him up again. A patch of filtered light caught the yellow metal sign. "All right then," Perry
said. "We're going to go on now. This is a real road, it goes somewhere. We're all right now."

"You don't know, do you?"

"I know we're going on."

Harvey started to grin, then say something, then he
coughed. Then they followed the road and the black printed arrow. Perry had something to think about, something new in the
carcass of the dead deer, and he skied and thought about how he
would have used his knife to cut the carcass, how he would have
tied the tarp to their skis, made a lean-to, gone out for wood,
built a fire, thawed out the frozen hunk of carcass, roasted it, sat
at the fire and eaten full, rested, started fresh. He skied and
thought about it, slowly realizing he'd made a great mistake, that
he wasn't thinking at all, that he was moving and losing strength
and getting stupid, thinking about the carcass and the deer he'd
greeted, thinking how stupid he was, moving along the road,
thinking they should turn back and then thinking turning back
was worse than not eating. He marveled at how much he could
see. Even in the pale winter lighting, even with the light coming
through the trees as through a billion smoky prisms. Even without glasses. They should have stopped and eaten the remains of
the deer. He skied on, wanting to go back. It was the numbness,
the stupidity. The hunger had been numbed, the sensation of
hunger, and it had made him stupid. He skied on and still marveled. How stupid, how clearly he could see. There were squares
and triangles in the forest, the angles of branches that he could
trace with his hands and follow round and round, corner to corner. He could see clearly, how stupid, he could see with his eyes,
the bright pale light behind the branches, he could see with his
nose and ears, and he could hear the very sound of distance—

muffled and quiet, a hiss originating with the very birth of himself, part pure length and part separation by time.

Behind him, he heard Harvey still talking, mumbling in the voice of an old man.

The road kept going.

At sunset they stopped for a short rest. Perry took the chance to dig through the snow. The road was tar, black and hard.

The moon came up and he decided to keep moving. The road was snow-covered and clear, running in a white streak through the woods.

The moon rose fast. It was white. Clear as a light bulb.

They moved down the road. He was lightheaded. Everything was beautiful and still. The road, the night. He could see clearly. He wasn't hungry. He felt fine. Everything alternated. He was hungry, then he was fine. He followed the road like a white sleep, a long twisting beautiful white sleep. The moon went higher. It was winter. The stars did not twinkle. The stars glowed steady through the thin atmosphere, the sky was black.

Everything was beautiful. The old man was right. Harvey was right. And it was easy. He felt fine. He skied along on the white strip of sleep through the woods.

The road went on in gentle turns. It was beautiful and fine and easy.

His skis whooshed on the powdered snow.

The moon crept even higher. It was three-quarters full. He was lightheaded and seeing clearly. Even without his glasses, he saw the white winter light of the moon.

Later, as the night went on, his skis made biting sounds on the snow. The powder became brittle. A yellow light sparkled ahead, and when he came to it he saw it was another twisting arrow and he went faster. He was cleareyed and clearheaded and he could see to the end of the road, and he pushed with his poles and skated, feeling the wind, feeling raw and clearheaded and light as helium. He skied fast. He leaned forward, crouched low, banked along the arrow-pointed curve, went down, pushed with the poles.

Another shining road sign went by, another arrow and another downwards curve of the road, and he crouched low and spiraled down. All the fat was gone. He could fly, and he gained speed and curved along the white sleepribbon. He coasted down. When the road flattened and turned up again, he could no longer ski. He slowed and slowed, the fine lightness leaving him, turning to gravity, and he slowed and slowed to a stop, standing still with his head down.

Finally, he removed his skis and speared them into a drift beside the road.

He removed his rucksack and dropped it under the skis.

He sat on the rucksack, looked up the road and waited for Harvey. It was a long black wait. He was in a grove of some sort. The trees hung over the road, darkening the road and snow. The forest grew up to the edge of the road.

Still waiting for Harvey, he got up and began gathering scrap wood. He was alone.

He piled the wood in the center of the road.

Using the last of the paper in his rucksack, he took care, piling the wood into a pyramid, finally striking the fire. As the fire caught, everything else stopped. He stopped thinking and he stopped being tired. He watched the fire and forgot everything else.

Harvey skied up without making noise.

He stopped and stood over the fire in his skis. Then still without removing the skis, he sat down. The tips of the skis were in the fire. He sat with his face red and wet, watching the fire lick at the skis. They both sat and watched. The tips of the skis glowed. At last Perry got up and unbuckled them from Harvey's boots, lifted them and speared the glowing tips into the snow.

He zipped their bags together. He helped Harvey in, then he added wood to the fire, then he climbed into the bag. He lay back and stared straight up at the white moon and the rest of the sky.

He lay still a long time. At last he said, "We'll eat tomorrow."

Harvey was asleep.

"We'll eat tomorrow," Perry said.

Then he lay still and looked at the sky and felt the warmth in the bag and listened to Harvey breathing. The bag was hot. He could not see his brother. He could feel him and sense the warmth and smell his body.

Later he heard Harvey moaning or sobbing, something in between.

Later still he heard the sound of air flowing through an open window, a July afternoon, Grace in the garden, young girls playing games in the yard.

He slept then and heard himself breathing.

Later he awoke. He thought about the carcass of the deer. He wished they had eaten it.

He listened to Harvey's breathing, listened to his own breathing, and soon he was warm and sleeping again and not listening or thinking.

Elements

Harvey's cough got worse. The fever had him bad. The sun cleared the eastern pines and the day became white and almost warm, and there was nothing to do but wait at the fire and wait. The cough came in a rhythm. Prefaced by wheezing, then the deep fluid sound in his lungs, then the cough, then more wheezing as Harvey leaned forward and strained into the cough as though pushing against a locked door. His hands were wet and cold and his forehead was wet and hot, sweat dribbled into his beard. There was nothing to do but wait. Neither of them spoke. Perry kept water boiling, dipping a rag into the water and wringing it and spreading it over Harvey's nose and mouth, regularly changing the rag to keep it steaming. The morning went slow. Perry was restless. Stretching ahead in open invitation, the road enticed him and he was eager to move. He found it hard to pity his brother. He thought about finding food, and finding shelter, and finding the end of the road. The sun was brilliant white. There was no wind. With the hot rag on his face, Harvey had the look of a strange old man, abandoned in a corner of a sickroom and caught up in some grand and final suffering. He was perfectly still as in a kind of summer repose. He only moved when the coughing grabbed him and shook him and jolted him upright. Otherwise he was calm and quiet, his eyes almost smiling in secret wisdom. The bad eye sometimes seemed unfocused and other times appeared to have clear hold of a great faraway vision.

"We can't sit all day," Perry finally said. He waited another half hour, letting the fire die naturally. Then he said again:

"We can't wait."

He rolled up the sleeping bags.

One of the ski poles was missing and he spent a long time searching for it, groping on hands and knees through the snow. When he found it Harvey was asleep. The lid of his dead eye was half-open and the eye itself was focused and bright and awake.

"We're going," Perry said.

"You don't remember me getting that rifle?" said Harvey. "I can't . . . That, I can't understand. Thought sure you remembered it. You were laughing at me. You saw how scared I was. The old man . . . he never saw it. You saw it. You remember? And I . . . don't you remember? I went upstairs and put the rifle under my bed. I was scared to take the bullets out. Don't know why. You remember now? That damn rifle. You came up and saw me lying on the bed. You started laughing. You asked to see my new rifle. You don't remember?" He grinned and began to laugh and the laugh choked, broke and sobbed, and he was coughing, and Perry got him to his feet and leaned him over and clapped his back, then got him into his skis. "I don't . . . I asked what was so funny and you just laughed and asked to see my new rifle. You don't remember that? I'm sick. You don't remember? You had all those shiny bullets lined up in a row on the floor. Then father came in and told you you hadn't finished the dishes, and he gave you a swat and sent you down to finish them, then he sat down and showed me how to oil the rifle and how to keep it on safe, and I sat there scared, and he never knew it. You don't remember that? It was just at Christmas. Just the day after Christmas. I don't remember what you got. You . . . You ought to remember that. I thought sure you remembered it. Ever after that, I thought you remembered it whenever you looked at me. You . . ." He coughed and wheezed, and Perry pulled up the zipper on Harvey's parka, put the ski poles into his hands. "It was the same. Jesus, I'm sick. I'm hot. Can I take . . . . No. I can't. Even after I was sure you remembered. Every time something happened, I was sure you remembered that. You don't remember? You don't? I don't believe you. That Christmas. Not that Christmas, but the Christmas when I went off to boot camp and you drove me into town, and you were so quiet and I was so quiet, and I know you were remembering it, thinking I'd go off and get killed . . . I know you were remembering it and thinking I'd get killed . . . I'm sick . . . And, I know, you were sad. You tried not to be, you pretended and I pretended, but I know you were thinking I'd get myself killed. I was scared. The bloody things we always remember. You don't? You always stood up to the old man. He liked it and I could never stand up and say what I thought. Jesus. Do you know how sick I am? I'm going to die, you know. You're pretending I'm not. I'm pretending, too. We're pretending, aren't we? I'm sick. I've got it and it's got me good. Jesus. I'm hot. You remember all the times I got sick? You never got sick. The old man left you alone and he liked it when you said you weren't going to listen to him preach anymore. You just told him. You told him and he never said a word. I remember you telling him. He asked if you were sick, and you said nope. You never did get sick, did you? I can't understand why it was always me that got sick. But you said nope, you weren't sick, and you just said you decided not to go listen to him preach anymore. And that was that. I remember. You looked down to eat, calm as could be. You remember? Jesus. And he smiled. Did you see him smile and wink at you? Then he winked at me. I felt . . . I'm hot. I'm taking this coat off. Don't move so fast, I can't . . . I felt like bloody rotten crap, that's what. Hold up. I'm sick. Do you remember all that stuff? I been thinking about it. Wait up and I'll tell you more."

The trail was a road, and the road was flat, and the country was all pines and sky and snow and sunlight. Perry remembered. He'd planned it. Frightened, a way to strike back, settle the score against both of them. *I decided, that's why. No, I'm not sick. I decided, that's all. I'm not going to hear you preach anymore.* The version of the same story, remembered a hundred different ways: himself, Harvey, the old man in the cold of Sunday mornings, coming into his room, thinking he was asleep, reading in the chair by his bed, reading, his slipper dangling from a hooked toe. He felt himself grinning. He touched his face with a mitten. He had a beard. Grace would make him shave it off. Addie would tease about it. He wished he had a mirror. He would take a good long look at it and admire it, then maybe, if Grace was nice and Addie didn't tease, then maybe he'd go ahead and shave it off. Maybe he'd keep it. Maybe he'd move to Minneapolis and find a new job. Maybe he'd move to Chicago. He'd never been to Chicago. He'd been to Ames and Iowa City and Kansas City. Maybe he'd move to Kansas City. The trail was a road, tar beneath the snow, and he followed it and listened to Harvey skiing behind him, still trying to talk. He would have to find them food. He was still grinning. He could feel it under his beard, that great wide grin. *I'm just not going, that's all. I decided, that's why. No, I'm not sick. I decided, that's all. I'm not going to hear you preach anymore. I'm not listening anymore to your preaching.* He grinned and thought about finding them food. Grace would hate the beard. She'd puff up and pout, tell him to take a long bath and shave it off and come to supper, all is well. Maybe he'd shave it for her. Maybe not. Maybe he'd leave it on. He could tell everyone in the drugstore about the adventures, he had a lot to tell, and they'd all listen and admire his new beard. He was lightheaded and cleareyed. He'd keep the beard and not buy new glasses. *You aren't sick?* the old man had said. His face had been ruddy, his hair curly and speckled black and white, and he'd left the table silently, and Perry remembered feeling sad and wanting to take the old man's head in his arms and curl around it and warm it and him and them all. *No, I'm not sick. I've decided, that's all.* Perry skied and grinned, thinking backward and forward, thinking he would have to find them something to eat.

The road twisted once, and Perry slowed and followed the curve, and on both sides of the road the forest was pushed back to form a pine glen. Beside the road, in the shadowed center of the glen, there was a shed.

There was a shed. Its roof sagged. The slats were gray, and the whole sad structure trembled as he tried the door. The latch held tight. Perry stepped out of his skis, grabbed the handle with both hands, pulled, and the latch gave way.

He unbuckled Harvey's skis.

"You don't remember that blasted rifle?" said Harvey clearly.

Perry took him inside.

It was a timberman's shanty. There were no windows. It smelled no different from the rest of the forest. Wood, a drifting sense of silence and cold. He helped Harvey sit down, then he braced the door open and inspected the shed, moving quietly from corner to corner. There was a stove. There were four chairs, four bunks, a pine table, a trunk, a pile of yellow newspapers, shelves holding tins of coffee and flour and tea and salt and cornmeal, a Bible, more shelves holding a coffee pot and two iron kettles and a rusted ladle and a blue-smoked jar of matches, a red and black flannel jacket hanging from a wall, a spider web over the door. He circled the shanty again and found an axe and four saw blades and a screwdriver. The shed was dark and clean. Leisurely, he opened the jar of flour and saw it had molded and turned green. The crawled with small insects. The cornmeal had a strange smell but he put it on the table, then he helped Harvey into a bunk, then he rested, sitting with his back against the cold stove, watching the walls, realizing that under his breath he was still counting.

He rested there until noticing that the rising moon was framed in the open door.

Then he went outside. He gathered wood and built a small fire in the stove. He found a candle, lit it and placed it on the table.

Harvey slept soundly, sometimes mumbling and turning, sometimes just breathing with the heavy fluid sound. Perry covered him with a sleeping bag.

Sheltered, he stood by the stove, arms folded across his chest. He thought about Grace, then about Pliney's Pond, then for a long long time about Grace.

The water boiled to a froth. The bubbles steamed from the kettle, broke open, scattered, then bubbled up again.

He dipped a rag in the boiling water, wrang it out, and draped it over the coffeepot, holding it firm with one hand.

He scooped coffee grounds on to the cloth.

Then with his free hand he ladled boiling water into the coffee.

The grounds blossomed and broke open and water bubbled up against his hand and burned it, but he held it steady and watched the brown-stained water trickle through the cloth and into the pot.

Still holding the cloth, he put his nose down and smelled the exploding coffee.

He rinsed out two mugs and filled them with drink.

He opened the jar of cornmeal and sprinkled some into each cup, then he woke Harvey and fed the brew to him, clucking gently and smiling and watching Harvey's throat bob.

"There," he murmured, "there, there now."

When Harvey was fed, Perry took his own cup outside and drank standing up, leaning lazily against the shed and looking up the road, seeing that it was close to dawn.

He had a hard time finishing the drink. Two sips filled him.

At first the brew had no taste at all, merely a kind of nutritious warmth, but as he forced himself to drink more of it the taste became intriguing. He had tasted or smelled it before. It was not a coffee taste, nor a corn taste. He couldn't place it. But it was warm and it filled him.

Inside, he brewed two more cups. He used the last of the cornmeal. He woke Harvey and fed him.

Then he chose one of the old newspapers and sat at the table.

He drank the hot coffee and read the old news and felt the morning sun rise. The old news was about a 1928 St. Paul fire. It was about a new water tower being built. It was about people being born who were now dead.

So he sat at the table, drank the brew, read the paper and felt the sun rising. Everything, including the old news, seemed quite fresh.

———————

In the morning he took Harvey's knife and went out to find food.

It was a powdered fine morning and he had hot coffee in his belly.

Following instinct or whim, he set out without second thoughts into the forest behind the shed. He wasn't sure what he was hunting, but he was hunting, and he was certain that when he saw it he would know it and kill it on the spot.

It was a new feeling. He was walking now rather than going by ski, lifting his knees high and using new muscles.

He held the knife before him, blade down, remembering the deer he'd greeted, hoping to meet it again so as to kill and eat it. He would greet it with another wave, then he would kill it with Harvey's knife.

He walked straight into the forest.

The snow came to his knees and sometimes higher. The top snow was fresh and light, but below it became hard and packed. He tried to walk with stealth.

He considered the kind of thing he would kill.

There were deer. Deer would be good. He'd been stupid not to eat the frozen carcass. There were deer, but a deer would be hard to kill with the knife, harder yet to catch to kill.

And there were a few wolves. He had never seen a wolf, not even a dead one, but he had heard his father and Harvey talking about the day they saw a whole pack of them trapped in the deep snow behind Pliney's Pond. If he came on a wolf, he decided, he would try to kill it. A pack of wolves he would leave alone. He was feeling brave.

There were no animals and the only noise was his own breathing. He thought some more about wolves and begun to hope he would not meet one. In a contest between himself and a wolf, the wolf would be better at killing and probably the hungrier. But he was feeling brave, holding the knife before him with the blade inclined towards the ground and pointed slightly forward, walking with high steps, stopping now and then to see what could be seen. He hoped he would not meet a wolf. He could not think of many other animals—squirrels, birds. There were bear and moose and elk, but he'd never seen one alive and could not imagine trying to kill one.

The feeling of hunger was back. The coffee and cornmeal brew had revived it.

The knife felt solid. It had a long straight blade and a wooden handle that fit neatly in his hand. It looked built for a purpose. It was heavy and solid. It belonged to Harvey and Perry imagined that before that it had belonged to the old man. It did not matter.

He walked until he was far enough from the road to be in animal country. Then he began searching for a place to kill from.

He was not sure how it was done. The woods were friendly and still. He imagined himself in hiding, waiting, perhaps setting some sort of lure and then killing whatever came to feed. He wished he'd saved some of the cornmeal.

He walked until he was tired.

He found a clump of small and closely grown pines, pushed them aside and went into hiding. The branches closed around him.

At first he was able to stand and practise hunter's silence. Holding the knife at his waist, he peered through the needles and watched the forest before him. The snow crested in a small clearing. Everything was bright and friendly and composed, and it was hard to imagine trying to kill in the friendly looking clearing.

He practiced quiet, turning the knife in his hands, holding it slightly cocked, trying to think of it as an extension of his wrist, testing the feel and weight.

He was tired. Hunching his shoulders, he backed into one of the trees, letting the tiny needles run over his shoulders and spray out in front of him, and he rested against the pine's trunk, nestled in a bough. Hidden and braced, he concentrated on the act of hunting. He remembered his father explaining to Harvey that the chief element of hunting was neither surprise nor stealth nor good fortune, but instead the capacity to cast oneself completely and without motive in the role of the hunter. It was typical, the circular and almost mystical logic: you are a hunter if you are a hunter. He burrowed deep into the pine tree and concentrated, but soon he grew tired again, and he moved away from the tree and knelt in the snow to rest.

Crouching down, he began to think about the hailed deer. He tried to imagine it coming into the small snow clearing before him, imagined it stopping with its neck arched and eyes wide and straight, the huge ears perked, then slowly turning to feed on the bark of one of the spruce, then its eyes fastening on his own eyes, watching one another, the deer feeding and watching him, and he imagined creeping close to the deer, imagined waving to the beast in another friendly greeting, hailing, beckoning, meeting as strangers on the street and knowing they'd met once before, imagined the other hand behind his back with the knife, creeping on the deer closer and closer until finally . . . He was cold. He was cold and hungry. He had not been hungry for a long while—not in the same way, not with the sensation of hunger—and he wondered whether a hunter became a better hunter when he was hungry, and while he was wondering the hunger grew worse. The hunger was a kind of stream that ran from the base of his brain down to his belly, reversed course and ran back again. He thought about it, deciding it would have been better not to have eaten the cornmeal and coffee.

A hunter was a hunter. He concentrated again, squinting his eyes in concentration, concentrating on the sound a hunter would make while hunting.

The forest was snowy and brilliant and still. He moved back into the branches and breathed softly. He wanted to kill something. He had the desire to do it. He had the desire to kill an animal and then eat what he had killed. He had neither desire separately. He did not want merely to kill, nor to eat merely to eat. He had a great and world-wide appetite, realizing it as he felt it, knowing as he crouched in the pine trees that he had the appetite and that his father knew it all along, darkhaired and stealing quietly into the brush behind Pliney's Pond, preaching about the way it should and would be done, and how it would taste afterwards, once killed and cooked, and how Perry would at last huddle with the old man and eat with him and hold him and warm him beside the waxing fire, hold the old man and tell him, tell him . . . Hold him and warm him and not speak, knowing without language the way the old man knew everything without language and spoke without language. He had the great appetite. The knife was cold. Through his mittens he could feel it. There was frost on the blade. He wiped it on his parka.

"Slowly, slowly," he said aloud, moving once again out of the pines, finding a new position from which to make a kill. The woods were brilliant white and still. He shifted the knife to his left hand. Crouching to a squat, he peered into the woods from under the bough of a new tree. He was poised and ready to use the knife, but nothing came. Thinking about killing and eating, he thought about being hungry, then he felt the hunger even stronger and it made him forget his concentration, making him instead afraid. He held the knife with both hands and squeezed it until the hunger was gone. "This is a bad spot," he said then, suddenly, deciding as he spoke that it was a bad spot to kill from, and he moved out of the clump of pines and into the clearing.

He waded to an exposed fallen tree. He sat on it and told himself to think of a plan. The important thing, he decided, was first to find an animal to kill. Once the animal was found he could begin figuring ways to kill it. He put the knife in his pocket. Then he got up and waded deeper into the forest, again focusing his thoughts on the act of hunting, casting himself as a hunter and thinking only that he would find an animal and then kill it with the blue-bladed knife and then eat it.

"Easy, easy," he said aloud.

The forest sloped upwards, turning much thicker. He was careful to keep close to the trees, now and then stopping to listen and look, watching the snow for tracks.

He wished he had a better weapon. Harvey's rifle would have been better, he thought, the rifle he could not remember but now wished he had. The knife was heavy in his pocket. With a rifle he would have a chance. But he couldn't remember it and he did not have it and there was nothing in the sterile forest to shoot with it.

He walked up the incline and stopped at the top of a bluff.

He turned and looked back.

Smoke from the shanty stove was climbing over the trees and coming towards him.

He thought of Harvey sleeping. He would be sleeping while the fire burned and made the smoke, sleeping on the bottom bunk near the stove, covered with the sleeping bag, still warm and full from the hot brew. Old Harvey, he grinned. "Slow and easy," he grinned, moving along the bluff and looking west. He felt silly. He took out the knife and held it again.

Coming to the edge of the bluff, he looked down and saw the road below.

He held the knife and felt foolish.

Turning quickly, he maneuvered back along the bluff and followed his tracks downwards through the thick part of the forest, down to the flat country. He was blushing. He felt a fool and he hurried to get back to the shed. Embarrassed and blushing, he hurried along his tracks, almost running. "Jesus, Jesus," he moaned, and he was grinning and blushing as though caught by the old man acting the part. Playacting and practising. He hurried back through his tracks in the snow.

He came to the fallen tree, then to the clump of pines where he'd crouched in silent hunt, fondling the blue-bladed knife. He felt silly and stupid and embarrassed, and he hurried to get back to the road. The knife was still in his hands. He was holding it by the handle, both hands squeezing. The blade was pointed upwards. He pocketed it and continued towards the road.

Gradually he slowed down.

He came upon a gorge, followed his hunting tracks down the slope and up again.

He was breathing slow, still feeling silly, when he saw straight ahead of him the head and quick movement of a brown animal.

He stopped even as his next step was starting, poising like a motion-picture reel gone dead. He stopped with his knees flexed, his back heel partly lifted. He saw it and then was not sure he saw it at all. If it hadn't moved he would have never seen it.

But he saw it, and he stood still. For a long while the animal did not move and Perry did not move. The animal was buried deep in the snow, and Perry watched it, thinking it might have been the branch of dead pine, anything but what it was.

He took a breath, deciding to move as he moved, and he stepped forward, finishing the step he'd started and watching the clump of brown fur. He had no plan but to get close enough to kill it. The image of a rabbit was in his head but he knew it was not a rabbit. He took another step and slowly took out the knife and held it at his side.

He was able to take a dozen more steps before the animal moved. When it moved, Perry saw the eyes. They were the rat's eyes, only it was not a rat but a woodchuck, and its eyes were glittering and the snout was close to the ground. It was deep in the snow, nestled in one of Perry's hunting steps, the body buried and only the head and eyes and tail showing.

He had done it before. The woodchuck did not move, only the eyes which followed him in. The eyes were deep black. He knew what to do. He held the knife.

He did not want to kill it with the knife. Backing away and still watching the animal, he retreated to the gorge and picked up a thick bough nearly twice his own height and walked back to the animal. He pocketed the knife and grasped the bough in both hands and lifted it and smashed down, hitting the animal's hindquarters with a lush thump, again raising the bough and striking, hitting the animal's thick back, watching as he again raised the long bough and again struck down. The animal squirmed and its mouth opened and showed him its fangs, but Perry cracked the bough down and the mouth came shut. Perry stopped and watched the animal. There was no blood. He moved closer, bending over the body. It did not move but he doubted it was dead. The eyes were open. He stood back and raised the bough high and brought it down on the animal's skull and then there was blood. The animal came part way out of the snow with its mouth wide open and fangs chomping, the eyes glittering in a way Perry had never seen before, except for the junkyard rat, but he had closed his eyes as he missed killing the rat, and this time his eyes were open and he raised the bough and crashed it down solidly, hitting the animal square on the head, feeling the impact through his arms to his spine.

He waited awhile. Then he prodded the corpse with the bough to be sure.

Then he took up the dead woodchuck by the tail. It was dead and heavy. It surprised him. It was thick and heavy and entirely dead.

He laid it out on the snow and rested. When he was ready, he covered the blood with some snow and took the animal by the tail and walked to the shed.

Harvey was still sleeping.

Perry added wood to the fire, then laid the animal on the floor, then used the knife to slit it down the middle. He tried not to think about what he was doing.

Mechanically, he cleaned out the guts and scooped them up and carried them outside. Then he went to work on the hide, slipping the knife under the fur and pressing down and pulling with his other hand, stripping the hide upwards as though pulling off a nightshirt, the animal going naked and the eyes wide open and glaring. The flesh underneath was red. There was not much of it. When he had the skin over the animal's front haunches, he closed his eyes and sawed off the head. Harvey woke up and asked what the awful smell was. Perry told him he'd killed the woodchuck, his eyes still tightly shut, grasping the knife with both hands as he sawed off the head. When it was done, he scooped the hide and head on to a newspaper, wrapped it up and buried it in the snow.

"A woodchuck?" Harvey said.

"I killed it."

"A woodchuck?"

"Yes. What's wrong?"

Harvey laughed.

"What's wrong?"

"You're going to *eat* it?"

Perry shrugged. He cleaned the knife on newspaper and cut the meat into quarters. The animal's blood had already seeped into the floorboards. The meat was warm. There was not much of it.

"You're going to *eat* it?"

"I guess I am." Perry looked up and grinned.

Harvey laughed and coughed. "Do you . . . do you know a woodchuck is a fucking big *rat*, that's all? Did you know that? Just a rodent."

Perry grinned. "No. I didn't know that. You better be still. How's the fever?"

"Better. I think it's better. How the devil did you do it?"

"I went hunting," Perry said.

"What?"

"I went hunting and killed a woodchuck."

"You went hunting for woodchucks?"

"For anything."

Harvey rolled up and laughed until the cough started, and then he coughed and the bunk creaked. Perry gave him water to drink.

"Well, how did you do it? How did you . . . kill it?"

"It was just there. I was on the way back and there it was in the snow. Guess it was tired or something. It was pretty deep in the snow and it couldn't move, I guess. I just clubbed it."

Harvey laughed into another fit of coughing. "You killed a bloody woodchuck! Some gourmet hunter. Personally, personally I *hate* woodchuck. Don't touch the stuff."

"I guess you'll eat some though."

"Thought woodchucks hibernated or something."

"Not this one."

Perry got the fire high, then let it draw down to a tight flame, then he put the meat on. He made coffee and watched the meat fry. He was content. He wanted a cigarette and some music. He whistled one of his favorite pop tunes, watching the meat fry, feeling good. Mostly luck, he thought. Purely lucky to find it. Then he thought awhile longer and decided it was part luck and part something else. He wasn't sure what. Something else. He'd gone out to hunt. He'd gone out and had some luck and the meat was frying. When the animal was brown, he pulled the pan out and washed off their tin plates. He was content and whistling, and the room smelled of roast chicken. He woke Harvey and helped him to the table and they ate the meat and drank the coffee and afterwards Harvey went to sleep while Perry cleaned the dishes and had more coffee and sat the rest of the day in the dusty sunlight. He was exhilarated, proud, content and warm. He sat and watched the sunlight fade through the open door.

Later as he lay in the bunk above Harvey, he tasted the meat for the first time. It was a strong and wild aftertaste, making him hungry all over again, and he lay in the dark remembering the woodchuck, wondering how much wood . . . how much wood would a woodchuck chuck . . . how much would the woodchuck chuck if the woodchuck could chuck wood, or how much wood would the woodchuck chuck if the woodchuck could chuck wood, then saying it aloud as a kind of game, over and over, tumbling the rhyme out fast and without a stutter. "How much?"

He was up with dawn, boiling water and making coffee and seeing after Harvey. He spent the day inside, going out only once to gather wood and urinate and fill the two kettles with snow. That evening he heated water and washed himself. He stood naked before the stove. Sloshing water over his face, he scrubbed hard. He washed his beard and hair and then the rest of him, taking a lot of time and enjoying it. He did not like the white look of his skin, but all the old fat was gone and he was proud of himself, pleased at the idea of being positively skinny for the first time he could remember. He washed his legs and feet, then brought the kettle up and let his genitals float free in the warm water. Then he let the fire dry him.

He rinsed out a cloth and mopped Harvey's face. The fever was steady. Perry unbuttoned his brother's shirt and got it off. It had a wet foul smell.

He clucked, washing his neck and chest. "This feel a little better now?"

"Hello."

"Hi. You feeling any better?"

"I guess so."

"That's it. Sit up and I'll wash down your back."

Harvey got up on his elbows and rolled over. "Why aren't we dead, brother?"

"There. There, how's that feel now?"

"Why aren't we dead?"

"I don't know, Harv. I really don't know."

Harvey coughed and laughed. "We're heroes! We're heroes, that's why!"

"There. You'll be all right now."

"What time is it?"

"Night. You've been sleeping and sleeping. You'll be better now."

"I'm sick. I guess I'm pretty sick."

"Well, we'll get you washed up and you'll feel better. You want to sit by the fire awhile?"

Harvey nodded. Perry gave him a hand, got him into a chair and covered him with a sleeping bag. "How's that now? Isn't that better?" He pulled off Harvey's socks and threw them into a corner. "You really stink, you know that? Phew. Here, now put your feet in this water. Kind of hot so be careful."

Sitting by the fire with Harvey, he had the bloated feeling of contentment again. The shanty seemed familiar, a personal shelter that he'd found and made his own. Except for Harvey's fluid breathing the only sound was the fire.

After a time, he helped Harvey back into his bunk, then spent the rest of the evening in a chair, his feet propped on the stove, resting, reading some of the old newspapers. It seemed much like home and he fell asleep in the chair. Then he dreamed. He dreamed first about Addie. It was a vague, strange dream without motion or sound. She was drowning. Far out in the lake, she was drowning and grinning at him while he stood ashore unable to move. Later he dreamed about a blackbird. The bird's wings were spread and splatting the air, attacking with a jagged beak, screeching and attacking, and again he was unable to move.

Then he dreamed of a wailing sound, a wailing screeching sucking sound.

He woke up. The fire was dead and the wailing sound continued. It came to him slowly. It drifted from the dream and into the dark shed and surrounded him, then he was fully awake and listening. He was weak. The shed was dark and the sucking sound persisted. "Harvey?" As if in answer, the sound stopped, leaving a tinny echo. "Harvey?" Then there was silence, a long silence in which he tried to get up. It came again: the wailing and sucking, deep in one of the dreams, gasping sounds, then suddenly he was awake, recognizing it as the sound of drowning.

He sat up. The shed was dark. It was full of the wailing sound, the sound of drowning from his dream.

He yelled Harvey's name and the room seemed to tumble around him. Yelling, he moved out of the chair, stumbled and scratched himself—a nail or hook or splinter. He yelled Harvey's name again. He thrust out his hands, groped towards the bunk, feeling his way. Everything was black. The drowning, sucking wailing sound swelled up and the room floundered. "Harvey!" he bellowed. His hands touched the stove. He grabbed the hot iron and held on until it burned him. "Harvey!" he yelled, and the sucking drowning sound came like a flood, and he pushed away from the stove, disorientated, plunging towards the source of the sound. "Harvey, for God's sake!" He reached out, suddenly realized his eyes were closed, squeezed shut. The sucking sound went even higher. He shivered. He found the bunk. The sucking sound was everywhere, close and far and deafening. He had his arms on Harvey's shoulders, pulled him up, shook him, and the wailing sound crescendoed.

Still blind, he dug Harvey out of the bag, hauled him off the bunk and laid him on the floor. "Harvey!" he was still yelling, his face down low. Harvey was partly entangled in the bag. Perry ripped it open and reached in. He leaned close and searched his brother's face. Everything was black and tumbling and the wailing drowning sound was a reverse wind that pulled everything far away. Harvey's chest sloped in like a valley. "Harvey!" He tried to think. The thinking stopped. He grabbed Harvey's arms, yanked him towards the stove. "For Jesus sake!" he was yelling, yanking his brother across the floor, pulling him like a rope and getting him to the stove. "Jesus, think," he was hollering, trying to think. He stopped, dropped Harvey dead on the floor. He found the stove. Still hearing himself bellow, he opened the stove door, reached in with his hands and wrists and arms to stir the ashes for light. Then abruptly he stopped. He dropped to the floor. He learned over his brother like a lover and put his ear to Harvey's mouth and listened.

"Harvey?" he said, not yelling, a question.

He tried to compose himself. His brain was tumbling. "Harvey?" he said again, still leaning close and listening.

A light froth boiled to Harvey's lips. His eyes were open. The bad eye glistened; the iris had dissolved in the fluid of the white tissue.

"Harvey?"

The good eye was rolled away and completely gone.

"Harvey, Harvey," he chanted.

The sucking sound was gone, and the wind was gone.

"Harvey! Jesus sake, Harvey."

He touched his brother's chest. It was sunken and shaped like a bowl. It was hard and stiff. He touched Harvey's throat and it was like steel pipe.

"Harvey! You bull. Jesus sake, Harvey."

He stopped, peered into his brother's dead eye.

Then he bellowed again, shuddering and losing sense. He hauled Harvey upright, dragged him by the arms, got him to his feet and held him in a great bear hug. Then he squeezed. He closed his eyes and squeezed, locking his wrists together and squeezing and squeezing and turning dizzy and pressing his brother in a great bear hug, holding him upright and squeezing. He squeezed himself dizzy.

Distantly, disgusted, he heard himself moan. Then he lost strength and Harvey slipped from his arms and fell heavily. "Jesus sake," he moaned. "Jesus sake, Harvey." Such a fool, he was thinking, such a foolish fool. Everything was too dark and quiet. "Harvey, Harvey," he was moaning, grasping his brother's shoulders and partly lifting him, then losing strength again like a leaking tire, feeling Harvey slip away, "Harvey, Jesus sake," hearing the sound as Harvey hit the floor. He was dizzy. He crouched down: "Dear God," he was saying or thinking, "help me now, help me now."

He found the mouth and reached in, frightened at what he would touch.

He pulled Harvey's tongue up and out. Contracting, sliding away like a morning dream, the tongue was wet and slippery and elusive, going away, a piece of wet flesh, but he grabbed it hard and pulled and held it out.

Bacon, he was thinking, almost grinning. Bull's bacon. He pinched the nostrils and put his mouth to Harvey's mouth and blew and listened to the wail, a two-note tune that went

He blew and listened to the wail, a two-note tune that went high and higher. He was dizzy. He blew and listened. Huff and puff, he was thinking, you Bull, you poor poor poor bull, breathe Bull. He was sick. He wanted to vomit and sleep, but he covered Harvey's mouth and blew deep. He did not care. It did not matter. He blew and listened, blew and listened, rising and falling in a dizzy sick rhythm. Harvey's chest seemed to quiver, and he blew again.

The breast rose up, and he blew again, and Harvey's chest snapped like a bone breaking.

Perry stopped, rested, waited for the chest to sink again, then he descended and blew hard. He was sick.

"Harvey?" he murmured.

He waited as the breast ballooned up and quivered and slowly sank.

"Harvey. Harvey?" He waited again and the chest did not move, and he leaned down and blew again, forcing respiration and suddenly feeling strong and gaining something from the exchange. Such a bull, he thought, poor thing. Too bad. Harvey's chest twitched and snapped again. A bubbling sound came from Harvey's lungs, a breathing sound, erratic and dumb and startling as misfiring machinery. "Harvey?" he whispered, listening as the sound smoothed and the breathing became languid as through a drunken sleep.

"Harvey?"

Perry lay with an arm around his brother. His face was buried in Harvey's flannel shirt. He was warm. He had urges to sleep and to vomit, the sleepiness making him sick and the sickness pressing him down towards sleep. He snuggled around Harvey's warm body. He lay still. The wind was outside. He lay still and listened and cuddled around his brother and listened to the outside wind and Harvey's breathing and his own breathing, a respiring postlude in three high pitches like a lullaby. He was warm and sick and sleepy. "Harvey, Harvey," he murmured.

He might have slept. He lay still a long while. But at last he got up and rebuilt the fire and boiled water. Smoothing his brother's hair, clucking, he washed the red face and beard, got him into the bunk, laid a warm cloth on his brow.

With the last of the coffee grounds, he brewed coffee and held Harvey's head and helped him drink. "Harvey, Harvey," he murmured. "Love you, Harvey. I do. You know?" He wiped brown spittle from his brother's mouth. "You bull, I do love you, you know. There, there."

Later he drank his own coffee and went outdoors and looked at the sky.

The wind was gentle. Not such a bad night.

He would have to leave soon.

He would have to make Harvey comfortable and then set off on his own, and he thought about it, feeling neither guilt nor pride.

He looked at the sky and knew it as a fact. They would die

separately or together, or one would die and the other would live, or they would both survive. The possibilities seemed infinite. In the morning he would leave.

He went inside and put a fresh cloth on Harvey's brow. Then he spread his sleeping bag on the floor and spent the night in nervous brilliant sleep, hearing his own blood rush with dreams and half-awakenings, and in the morning he remembered only the sound of drowning.

He bathed Harvey's face and chest. Then, avoiding talk, he went outside and gathered a large store of wood. He had no idea how long he would be gone, though it seemed likely he would be gone forever, and he spent the entire white morning bringing in the wood, stacking it behind the stove. He felt Harvey's gaze but he kept working. He heaped snow into the two kettles, boiled it down to water, then poured the water into jars and pots. Harvey lay quietly in the bunk with a cloth on his brow. There was nothing they could say. Harvey's face was blood red and raw, and the dead eye was glazed as though it had already given up, and behind Harvey's beard there was no expression, just the glazed and lazy eye that followed him as he stoked up the fire, grabbed the bunk and moved it wholesale nearer the fire.

"You're going," Harvey finally said.

"Have to."

Harvey nodded, either settling it or accepting it, then closing his eyes.

"Otherwise . . ."

"I know," Harvey said. "Bum deal. Sorry."

Perry ignored the acid building behind his eyes. He turned and sat on the floor and waxed his skis. When he was ready, he took the skis outside and stacked them against the shanty. His eyes were stinging.

He went inside and shook Harvey gently. "All right," he said in his cheerful stinging voice. "Harvey, are you awake? Listen. While I'm gone you're going to have to do some things. Are you listening?" He waited for Harvey to nod. "All right then. Listen up. First, I want you to keep that fire going. You know? No matter what, you've got to keep that fire going. Okay? There's plenty of wood there and all you've got to do is put some on now and then. All right? Okay. Listen. I've got to go. After last night, you know what's going to happen if I don't go. Sooner or later, right? Okay. Now I want you to promise to keep that fire going and to always keep the water heating. You hear me? Okay then. When you think you're having trouble, when you can't breathe or start coughing bad, you just get to that hot water, and start breathing the steam. It'll cut through all that crap. Just keep the fire going, keep the water hot. There's plenty of water here. All right?" He gently shook Harvey. "You got me? The fire and the water, those two things."

"I guess you're going."

Perry nodded. "You got it. Don't worry. I'm going to go until I find some people or the highway or something, so don't worry. Now listen. The other thing is this. You've got to stay awake more. You know? All the time, you've got to think about staying awake. The cough comes worst while you're sleeping. You know? Okay. And you can't keep the fire going if you're asleep. All right then. Try to read, walk around if you can manage. If you keep awake and keep the fire going and keep the water hot, then you're all right, we're both all right. You're not going to give it up. You hear? Just do those things."

Harvey smiled and Perry smiled.

"I guess. I guess maybe you think I'm pretty stupid," Harvey said.

"You're improving."

"Sure. I hear you."

"You're going to do what I tell you."

"Cross my heart. I'm not all that stupid."

"I know it."

"This is the best way," Harvey said. He smiled again.

"Just keep that fire going. Keep the water hot. Don't let it all boil away, just keep it hot."

"You're a good fellow. You are. You don't remember that rifle, do you? That's strange but it's good. I always thought you remembered it but you don't."

"I don't."

Perry put his mittens on the stove to warm. He pottered about, wondering what to do. He rigged a string to the door so Harvey could open or close from his bunk.

"Okay. Okay now?"

"It wasn't supposed to snow," Harvey said loudly.

"I know. I know it."

"It wasn't supposed to. Those things just happen sometimes in winter."

"Okay. Take it easy. I believe you."

"It wasn't planned to snow."

"Just rest."

Perry got the fire high and put fresh water on. He put on his parka, and shook Harvey's hand, and they hugged and separated, and they laughed. Harvey's beard was full and soft as baby fuzz. "Remember everything. Stay awake." He closed the door. He carried his skis to the road and snapped them on. He pushed off and skied fast up the road, turning out of the sun, slowing down when the shed was far behind him.

The road was flat. There were birds in the sky and in the trees along the road, sparrows and blackbirds mostly.

He skied stiffly, adjusting again to the feel of the skis and poles and motions.

The day was as flat as the road. It was a day so like all the other days that for a time Perry believed it was one of the others—Harvey behind him, the certain feeling of there being more than one person in the forest, the feeling he could stop and turn and talk if the urge came.

His arms gave out fast. It worried him. He let gravity carry him. Somehow, his knees would not flex properly. Each bump in the road jarred to the base of the brain, but he held on and let the road and gravity and skis carry him down.

He let the road carry him down and tried counting the days. More than a week for sure. Ten, eleven. More than that. Fifteen, at least. More than that. Twenty seemed closer. Three weeks. He couldn't be sure.

The road pulled him down and gradually he fell into the proper balance and motions, bending for the turns, using the ski edges to slow the steep descent, leaning forward and crouching to absorb the bumps.

Sometimes the road leveled off but it never climbed. He moved fast. Around midday the sun came out and the snow got mushy. The trees were full of blackbirds and sparrows.

He skied and did not worry about the map or sun. He had a road and that was enough to think about, and the road kept descending. Towards the middle of the afternoon the road dipped and rounded a bluff and he was able to look off far over the forest. The road twisted along the face of the bluff, turning fast down, and he leaned hard left and felt the skis bite, and for a moment he was parallel to the road, hanging free, then he straightened and the skis touched again and he was descending. The road was down and down. He thought about Harvey, imagining him in the shanty alone. It was not a good thing to think about. He concentrated on the skiing. The road dropped before him into a funnel of trees. White pines grew to the edge of the road, arching over it in a great canopy, and he skied down, raising his arms as though flying. He leaned far forward. The road swept him down, into the pine funnel, a dizzy circus chute. The speed snapped at his ears. Then the road dropped from under him. He could see the speed. Something seemed to fling him downward, and for a moment he was terrified, then his skis touched down and the road snatched the left pole from him, tugging it up, and it was gone, glittering for an instant over his shoulder, then it was gone far behind him and the road swept downward. He heard the lost pole splatter in the snow behind him, a tinkling sound, and the road swerved, still falling, and he leaned hard to his right, and let the right pole drag for support.

The road dipped and straightened and still descended. Below was a vast gorge of pine. He held on, dragging the right pole for balance, and in an instant he was in the gorge and still flying downward and downward. The road at last dipped and ascended, and he took the small hill without effort, carried up by simple momentum. He stopped there. He removed the skis and fell back in the snow. He spread his arms and closed his eyes. The sun was tropical.

He was on his back. Basking. Some warm salted ocean.

He slept for a time. It might have been a long time. It was long enough so that when he awoke the sunlight had turned hard gray.

He was tired. He sat up and looked back the way he'd come, down the small hill, into the pine depression, then up the steep hill towards the place he had lost the pole. He was tired. Pushing up and brushing away the caked snow, he buckled on his skis, stood still a moment, then removed them. He was angry at himself. Angry for losing the pole, angry for almost killing himself, breaking a leg, ending it for himself and for Harvey. He considered going back for the lost pole, but the fatigue was too much, and at last he walked into the woods and after a long search found a branch the right size. Breaking off its twigs, he tested it and decided it would work as a substitute. The branch was much heavier than his pole, but it was the right length and it seemed strong enough.

For at least an hour he skied steadily and carefully, forcing himself to ski and not think. Then he had to stop. Bending over the branch, he began to vomit, his stomach contracting in empty shivers, and he was sick. He was hearing bells. Music of a distant sort. He swayed with the dusk wind, caught himself with the branch, then he heard it again, thinking it was a chime inside him, in his head or belly or memories, and again he shuddered and retched, and again he heard the faraway music of bells. "Sleep," he said, "now I lay me, now I lay me."

He was in a glen. The forest rose steeply on each side, and the road burrowed ahead into the edge of dusk. The sky was dull and crowded with clouds. He leaned on the branch until the sickness passed. He decided he would not stop again. He would not think about another night in the forest. He pushed down the road, head down, passing through the glen and into an open meadow and then back into the trees.

The sound of the winter bells. At times the chime seemed to sound just up the road, at times behind him, at times deep in his skull. He was sick. His nose dripped with thin syrupy snot without substance, dribbling into his lips so that he could taste it, then into his beard. He was alone and he felt the full loneliness of the wintertime. Steadily, the road climbed. Perry sensed it was climbing for a reason, and he followed it up, shuffling the skis and pushing with his branch and pole. The sound of winter bells surrounded him. The branch tore a gash in his mitten. He was sweating. His nose dripped with the sweet tasting winter snot, and he reached the road's summit where the bells were again ringing and he came down, followed the road as it twisted left and flattened and began climbing again.

It was night. The sweat froze under his parka. He skied with his eyes down, watching the few yards stretching immediately ahead.

He heard the bells.

Then he heard a dog. It was a big dog, he could tell from the bark. It was excited, too. He pushed harder. The barking was somewhere ahead of him, not far away, perhaps at the top of the hill or just below, not far. A little to the right.

It was a big dog, all right. A town dog.

He made the hill. He stopped and listened, wiping his nose. The barking was gone but the sound of bells seemed even louder. He glided down the hill and followed the road in a long slow arc, and on the far end of the curve, just as the road straightened, he came upon a yellow litter bin and picnic table. The table was brown pine, turned upside down. It was civilization. He could smell it now. Smell its complexities. It sobered him. He stopped, rested against the litter bin, and tried to clear his head to think it all out. It had been a dog, all right. He was sure of it. And the bells were still chiming, not so loud now but still there, somewhere to the right and in the woods. When he was rested, he started off again, trying to ski smoothly so as not to wear himself out. The road climbed and hit another apex and began falling. It was a long, gentle slope. When he came to the end of it, the night was complete, nothing but woods and dark and the strip of white road, and he listened, but the bells were gone and the dog, if it was ever there at all, was silent. There were no stars and no moonlight. "Wish I may, wish I might," he murmured.

It was very cold. He hadn't felt it before.

He let his mind clear. He wiped his nose and a blind dizziness settled in his stomach. "Star light, star bright," he said, "have the sight I might tonight." He held his mittens under an armpit. He blew into his hands and waited and listened for the bells.

An hour of darkness passed. The road was smooth and flat. Skiing steadily, not stretching himself and not stopping, he grew warm and the sickness eased off and left a taste in his mouth that no longer frightened him. It was a quiet cold winter night. He thought of Christmas, then of particular Christmases. Then he thought of summer, summer in general, summer with sun and mosquitoes and short cool nights. Then he thought of Christmas again.

The smell of civilization was gone. Without his glasses, he might have passed a town without noticing, a town or a house, something, the bells and the big dog. He considered turning back, calculating the time he would spend retracing the road towards the sound of the barking dog. Without deciding on one course or the other, he skied straight on, thinking about the dog, picturing it in warm greeting, thinking next about the bells, then thinking about a flurry of things.

In the night he heard an airplane.

He sat up. He hadn't been asleep. He'd found another picnic area and sat down for rest, and sometime during the night he'd drifted back and looked at the sky. He'd been thinking. His mind was out in the woods, roaming by itself in and out of the trees, rambling about, trying corners here and shadows there, lazily exploring.

Then he heard the plane.

It made perfect sense. Without having to look for it, he saw it. It was high and far away. He saw the red and green wing lights. He did not have to move. He watched it come, aimed right at him. He saw the dark hole of the cockpit. The cabin lights. He thought he saw faces and hats. He imagined cocktails being served. And toasted almonds and smiles. As the plane passed overhead, he stood and waved, and the trees seemed to waver with the jet's wind.

He was part of a thaw. The morning glowed and water came dripping from a tall evergreen.

For a while the country rolled as it always had. Then it straightened. Perry heard a high voice calling. The road wound through pines and into a stand of birch, through the birch and into more pine, and then into a clearing where a young child was pulling a sled.

Although her back was to him and she was trudging away, Perry knew the child was female. He was skiing in the slim tracks of her sled. All morning he'd followed the tracks, knowing it was a child and even knowing it was a young girl. She called out again, a high commanding voice, but she did not appear to notice him and he had to hurry to catch her.

Then the child must have heard him coming, for she stopped and turned and watched him without surprise but with clear disappointment, as though she'd been expecting someone else. She wore a stocking cap and snowsuit and blue mittens. When he got close, she turned again and began walking with no effort to conceal her indifference. Perry fell in alongside her. They went together, the child first, then Perry, then the sled. They followed the road through a grove of sugar maples and then through small pines, over an iron bridge, past another picnic area with the upside-down table and yellow litter bin, and neither of them spoke. Now and then the child called out in a high fierce voice that showed both command and desperation, a single syllable that he did not try to understand, and he simply followed her. She asked no questions and he asked none. Except for her slow trudging pace, it made no difference to him that he'd found a child at the end of the road.

"I ain't lost," she said at last, shaking her head and refusing to look at him. A while later, crossing the bridge, she stopped and examined the snow, and Perry obediently stopped and waited until she was through with whatever she had to do. When they started off again she demanded his name.

"Paul," he said and said no more, though there were many things he wanted to say. The child knew precisely where she was and what she was doing.

"You comin' to see my ma? Pa ain't home, you know. He ain't home till tonight, Ma said. Then Ma said he can start lookin', too. What's that thing on your back for?"

"A rucksack. A pack to carry things in."

"What's in it then?"

"Nothing," he said.

She nodded as if the answer were known before spoken.

The child kept on steadily, stopping only to call out the deafening syllable, waiting for whatever was supposed to follow, then continuing down the road with Perry and her sled.

"I bet my ma's lookin', too," she said when they passed through the picnic area. "She said she wasn't gonna look but I bet anything she's lookin' same as me. She said she wasn't gonna look no more, 'cause it was my fault and I'd have to look and not her anymore, 'cause I did it and not her. But I'll bet she's lookin'. Pa ain't lookin' 'cause he ain't here, but Ma said he'd help look when he got back, and he's comin' back tonight or tomorrow."

She stopped again and screamed: "Muggs!" She listened then. "Shit!" she said.

"I been lookin' and I'll find him," she said in a hard high voice, jerking the sled and starting off again. "And I bet Ma's lookin', too, even if she said it was my fault and I got to look an' not her. Since yesterday. You bet I had him tied up good. Ma said it's my fault but it ain't 'cause you should've seen how I had him tied up, right to the tree an' I went out an' he wasn't there, just the rope. Was

Pa's fault, not my fault. It was Pa's rope and it was this rotten rope, that's what, an' I told Ma and she said Pa'd have to look then if it was his fault. I had him tied up good. Ma said Pa'd go lookin' when he gets home tonight or tomorrow, and I'll bet Pa finds him fast. Ma says he's prob'bly got hisself caught in a trap, so I got my sled out and everything in case, but I don't think he'd get hisself caught in no trap, 'cause he's smart and knows all the traps anyhow."

She stopped again and Perry stopped. "Muggs!" she screamed. He shivered and felt sick and waited for her, "Muggs!" she screamed fiercely. Then she continued walking.

"Anyhow," she said, "he ain't the first dog ever run away. Pa says it don't matter what kinda dog it is, they all run away, an' Ma says he wouldn'a run away this time if I'd got him tied right, an' I says to her I did tie him tight, an' I did all right. The rope broke, an' Ma says I should've used some other rope, an' I says it was the only rope I had an' Pa gave it to me, anyhow, an' she says she's got other stuff to do except look for a dog, an' I says, well, I'll do it, an' just in case he's in some trap I got my sled out. You ever seen a lost dog? You try to catch him an' he just don't want to be caught at all, like he thinks he's not even lost an' doesn't know it."

"Muggs!" she screamed. "*Goddamn* dog!"

In a while, Perry sat the girl on her sled. He slipped the rope around his chest and skied down the road, which slowly curved left and crossed another road, this one plowed clean, and, the girl told him to turn on to the new road, and he turned and pulled the sled down into the ditch, and in a half hour they came to a white house with a stone chimney and an old Ford station wagon standing bumper-deep in snow.

"I guess you just have to stay or else go on," said the woman who looked too young to be a mother. "Arild'll be back either tonight or tomorrow dependin' on the weather. The car don't start, like I said, and Arild's got the pickup in town so I'm stuck and that means pretty much you're stuck, too. I told him, well, I said to him we oughta get the station wagon started 'cause sometime I'd be needing it, an' sure enough, now I need it and I ain't got it. I feel awful bad, 'cause I know you're wanting to get out of here, but that damn station wagon ain't had a good thing for it all winter. Don't know what I'd do if somethin' happened and we had to get into town or somethin'—somebody gets sick or somethin'—and I don't know what I'd do, like now. And then that damn *dog*. I been goin' crazy tryin' to keep up with that dog of hers, and Arild he ain't been any help at all. Now you got maybe five miles into town, or six I guess, in there somewhere, an' you come this far so I guess you ain't gonna have any trouble the rest of the way, just rest up some first, I guess. What you oughta have is a bath."

The young brown-haired woman put on her coat and went to the car and got a map and showed Perry where he was.

"Now, you see here? You got a choice. You can go into either Lutsen or back up towards Carl Larson's place, except Larson's don't have no phone neither, but they got a car. Or I guess you can go into Tofte, too. It don't make no difference. They're all about the same distance, I guess, except maybe Tofte is a mile closer. Up to you, though. What you ought to do is get in there and take a good bath, that's what I'd say. I ain't one to say, though, 'cause I got the same problem tryin' to get Arild into the tub after work. He always says it can wait till after he gets some-thing to eat and I tell him it'll taste a sight better if he smells it in-stead of himself, but it don't matter none to me. Now you can walk if you want over to Larson's place, it don't take long and I go in the summers an' it takes me, oh, half an hour, forty minutes, but that's in summer. Or sometimes I just get on the school bus an' ride it into Lutsen and then do my shopping an' either take the school bus back in the afternoon or catch a ride. When Arild's here he'll take me an' drop me off, but that way I gotta hurry 'cause he's forever in a hurry. I don't know. I reckon you're about ready for this supper, though. It'll wait till then. Arild'll maybe be back tonight an' he can just drive you in and that'll save you some work, all right, but if you're in a hurry then I guess you can just go, and if he comes I'll just tell him to go out an' get you and drive you the rest of the way, but it don't make no difference one way or 'nother. That damn dog'll drive you bananas, though. He was here then gone, just like that. Altogether, I spent half the winter lookin' for him and the other half feedin' him and the other half tellin' Carla to tie him up good, an' what's the use? Can't keep no dog like that tied up, but if he ain't tied up you see what happens, just gets hisself lost. You chase him, chasing that bell, an' you think you got him good an' he's gone again, just like that. You can just count yourself lucky not to be out there still chasin' that scoundrel of a dog. Carla! You just sit down till Mr. Perry gets through eatin'. And yesterday I told her she wasn't goin' to get me out lookin' for that scoundrel dog, not no more. Anyhow, it's gettin' to be night an' if I was you I'd just count myself lucky enough and stay here till Arild gets in, or wait till morning and then you can go if you got to, but you're awful sick lookin' to me, and I know how that is, believe you me, I know what it feels like, I had it this winter, too."

The little girl climbed back on the table and the woman shushed her away and stacked Perry's dishes in the sink. The food held him fast to his chair.

"I told Arild, too, a hundred times, I said to him we oughta get the phone company to get a line out here. You know what? They won't do it. It's nothing to do with money for us if we got to call somebody and we can't do it. You don't look so good, Mr.

Perry. Carla! You either stop that or get into bed, you got your choice. You all right, Mr. Perry? You better get into the tub or lie down, one or the other. You all right?"

She held her wrist, standing well away from him. She was very young and slender. And she was always moving, touching things to be sure they were there, patting her brown hair, pulling her sweater over her hips, holding her wrists, first one then the other. "You really sure you're all right?" she was saying from a fog by the sink. "You best rest awhile. You ask me, you got no sense going back out there tonight. If I was you, Mr. Perry, I'd just get myself a hot bath and start good'n fresh tomorrow, that's what. And you're looking awful white and scratchy. You always wear that there beard of yours?"

"Do they have a doctor in town?"

"Which town? Lutsen or Tofte?"

"Either one. Where's the closest doctor?"

"Tofte, I reckon. I ain't never been. Except to have Carla and then that was in Silver Bay. Don't know his name, though, 'cause I haven't ever been to him, but he's there."

"It's not for me. Look—" Perry started to get up but the food had seemed to clot in his belly like cement. "Look, my brother's still out there in the woods and he's pretty sick."

"Can't be a sight sicker than you."

"Worse. I've, we've got to get somebody out there for him."

"You're looking awful sick," she said from far away. "Carla! How many times . . . There, now that's better. Get some hot water going for Mr. Perry. Right now, Carla, and none of that back talk, we'll get your dog for you. Mr. Perry? Get up now, you'll be a lot better. Carla! Carla, you hear me in there? Get Mr. Perry's shoes . . . There, you better now? You just get in the tub now. You're just a might sick . . . Carla! You clean up that mess and stop your bawlin' for that damn dog. Mr. Perry said he'd seen him, heard him back up the road a piece, clean up that mess there, there's some rags under the sink . . . There, you feel better now, Mr. Perry? We got some hot water in the tub. No, don't worry about that mess. Mr. Perry? Hey now! Carla, get over here. . . . . Now get them socks an' put them in the sink an' run some hot water over them, you hear? Mr. Perry? There, now you're looking a sight better, I should say. Awful sick there for a while, I should say so. Oughta told me you was feeling so bad. What you oughta been doin' is lying down, you know that? There, it's better now. Carla! You get some hot water back in the tub, it's gotten all cold. There. You reckon you can take a good bath now? I should say. You hustle on in there now and take a good bath and we'll see what's what."

Lying in the tub, he had the sensation of perfect detachment. Once he opened his eyes and saw the water was stale green. It was an old-fashioned enamel tub, so small he lay with his knees bent, his head resting against the tiled wall. The smell of the water embarrassed him. He pulled the plug, drained the tub and rinsed the scum out, then filled it again with fresh hot water and lay back. Vaguely, he heard the young woman and child talking in the next room. Then he slept. He awoke with the door banging. The water was room temperature. He got out, dried himself and put on a robe she'd left for him.

"Had me plenty scared for a minute," she said. "Swear to God, you was in there I don't know how long."

"I fell asleep."

"Well, I should hope so. I got some hot cocoa and whip cream out here." She beckoned him by turning and going to the kitchen area. The dishes were washed and stacked. His socks were soaking in an enamel basin on the floor. Somewhere in the small house there was the smell of burning kerosene. The little girl was sleeping on the floor in a corner of the living room area, wrapped up in a thick quilt.

"Anyhow, I guess you need a warm bed tonight," the young

woman was saying, "so I got clean sheets on it, and me and Carla will be sleepin' over there, I guess we can take the floor for one night, an' you just take the bed. Can't really call it a bedroom, but Arild's got a curtain up round it and you get a little privacy that way. Carla always sleeps with Arild and me, anyway. We only been here now about four months, no, five months, and so he says that when we get settled in and he saves up some money, then we'll have a carpenter put up a wall over there and make it a real bedroom like we was going to do in the first place. And . . . There's your cocoa. You just squirt your own whip cream on. I always let Carla do it herself, 'cause she gets a kick out of seeing it come out of the can. Anyhow, you can just sleep in the bed tonight an' me'n Carla will take the floor."

"What day is this?"

"I reckon it's Friday. Arild, you know Arild, he works down in Silver Bay like I was telling you, and he comes home Friday nights or Saturday mornings, most time Saturday morning, so. . . ."

"No," Perry said slowly, "I mean what day of the month is it?"

The young woman stared at him. She could have been in high school. He knew the cool assured look. "It's the twenty-ninth of January, I guess."

He nodded. He drank the cocoa then followed her to the curtained-off bed. He lay back without covering himself. He closed his eyes and heard her closing the curtains, heard her move off towards the kitchen. He did not immediately fall asleep. Later he heard a child crying, and a woman's calm young voice.

Shelter

Next it was dark.

The curtain was thick green. Lights were playing somewhere behind and beyond it.

He was cold. Dimly, without sound or cause, the curtain moved like foliage brushed by wind. A fire was going in the next room, the same room really, and it glowed against the veil of a curtain. Something clattered. A pot or kettle. Nearby, the little girl was whimpering. He felt uncomfortable, too warm and too cold, a stranger in the house. He was no longer tired. For a few long moments he watched the bright firespot on the curtain, then he got up, looked for his clothes. Everything was very dark except for the veiled fire. Finally he tied on the robe.

The child was still on the floor. She seemed asleep.

Wide awake and fresh, Perry went to the kitchen.

He heard the young woman singing in the bathroom. He found the refrigerator, took out a can of beer and drank it down. He was greedy and hungry. He found a package of sliced bologna. He opened it and ate two slices and slipped the package deep towards the back of the refrigerator. Then he opened another can of beer.

Outside, his skis were propped neatly against the front steps. His rucksack lay where he'd dropped it, now covered with a coat of frost. He stood on the porch in his bare feet, sipping the beer and looking out on to the lawn and towards the road. He figured it was not far from dawn.

When he went inside, the young woman was at the table, her hair wrapped in a towel.

"What the dickens you doin' out there?"

"Hi," he said, smiling at her. He held up the can of beer. "I woke up. I'll pay you for this, I was just thirsty. I had some of that bologna, too."

She laughed. "Well, what the dickens? What you doin' out of bed?"

"I woke up."

"Woke up! I should say. You only been sleepin' a half hour or so. Twenty minutes. I was thinkin' you'd sleep till forever or something."

"Really? Felt like it *was* forever. What time is it?"

"Close on to midnight maybe. You went to bed round eleven. An hour's all you was in there at most. I thought you'd be sleepin' till Sunday at least." She lit a cigarette and offered the pack to him. "Guess you oughta be hungry. Here, when I get my hair dried I'll fix you a sandwich. The way you was throwin' up I thought sure you'd be sleeping till . . . Anyhow, I guess you're feelin' some better now."

"A lot." He finished the beer and watched her dry her hair. The house had no luxuries. It was washed clean and the furniture was old and polished and sturdy. On one wall was the fireplace. A photograph of the child hung over the mantel.

The young woman made him a bologna sandwich. Freshly washed and dried, her hair was very long and straight, cut neatly across her forehead. She had the pale skin of her child. She wore a clean white robe pulled tight across her shoulders and waist, and as she washed and rinsed and stacked the dishes the robe folded around her legs. She wore fluffy white slippers. The light was bad. A single kerosene lamp stood on the table as a center-piece. The water splashed gently. She dried her hands, knowing he was watching, and slowly she turned, her eyes down. "'Nother sandwich, Mr. Perry? Reckon you could stand some food. How the dickens you get yourself lost anyhow?"

"There was a blizzard."

"You seen yourself in a mirror?"

"No."

"Y'oughta look. You was a mess when you come in here, I'll tell you that much right now. Still look awful sick and skinny and all."

"That's fine with me. Look, you don't have to make another sandwich, I've had plenty."

"No problem."

"Really."

"Okay then, you're the boss. I reckon when Arild gets here—he'll be here tomorrow for sure—when he gets here he'll drive y'on in to Tofte or Lutsen, whichever you want. He'll be glad to know you found, I mean, glad that you heard the dog barkin'. He likes that dog, too. Both of 'em like that dog, though I can't think of one good thing to say about him, except he's big, that's the only thing. Arild's big, too, though." She finally looked at him, forming a circle with her hands. "Got muscles like this."

"Sounds strong."

"You bet he is. I don't know what he's gonna say when . . .

Anyhow, he's somebody to be careful of if you know what I mean, Mr. Perry."

"I know."

"Okay then. Just wanted . . . Okay. He's older'n me, too. Graduated year before me. We both graduated. He's over twenty-five now."

"He sounds good."

"He's gonna laugh when I tell him you got lost out in the woods. He thinks, well, he *says* he thinks only fools and dogs ever get lost, but that's 'cause he thinks he knows everything 'bout everything."

"Well, he's right. We were stupid."

"Arild'll tell you you shoulda brought a map along."

"Well, we had a map. We got lost anyway."

"Well," she said.

Abruptly she got up, clutching her robe around her. "My name's Carla," she said, "just like the little girl. We're both Carla. I thought it was kinda cute, don't you think? You know how old I am? I'm twenty-one. I thought I'd just better tell you, just in case."

She moved out of the kitchen and lay down with the sleeping child.

Perry went outside. He was not sleepy. He thought about Harvey and felt some guilt, but he went inside and blew out the kerosene lamp and passed through the curtains to the soft bed. Lush, illiterate sounds came from behind the curtains. The young woman's child was awake. The child was talking about the lost dog, then the young woman hushed her.

Perry wanted another cigarette. He lay on his back, listening to the shushing sounds of the young woman, thinking about one of the filtered cigarettes, then thinking again about Harvey.

His legs and arms itched, soap film.

Harvey would be all right.

He'd done his best. In the morning he'd leave early.

He scratched himself hard.

Feeling guilty, knowing the young woman was awake and listening and wondering, he got up and passed through the curtain and padded outside and urinated off the porch. The night was very cold. His penis shriveled in the cold air. He urinated and smiled at his skis and rucksack, drew some long breaths of cold air, then went back to the bed.

A long time passed. He scratched himself up and down. He took off the robe and lay naked. He could not stop scratching himself.

The bed was too soft, sagging wherever he turned, too soft and too warm.

He felt dangerous. He put a hand over his heart and felt it beating. He had a great wealth of strength. He felt like a tree, very tall and strong and deeply rooted and fatless, tough hard fibers that an electric saw could cut. Safe, now. Safe and sound.

He heard the young woman get up and hover in the dark somewhere in the center of the main room.

He listened to her try for silence.

Then he saw her shadow on the curtain. She was standing very still, her shadow straight, her headshadow cocked as if listening.

When the curtain at last parted, he pretended to be asleep. He heard her straining for absolute silence.

After a time, he heard the curtain close, heard her lie down with the child, then he slept.

In the morning she brought him coffee in bed. "Don't spill it now, you hear? No fun washin' blankets, you know." She smiled at him and he smiled back. "I heard y' havin' a bad time tryin' to sleep," she said, watching him drink, standing over him with her arms folded. "Know just how it is. Strange place, strange bed and all that."

"I slept fine once I got to sleep. What time is it?"

"Oh, I let you sleep some. Guess it's almost noon or so. You just have some breakfast, though."

Perry hurried, dressing in the bathroom. The young woman had pancakes ready. He wasn't hungry but he ate anyway. The little girl ate silently beside him.

"No need to hurry so," the woman said. "Anyhow, you should eat another pancake. It ain't, it isn't puttin' me out any if you want one more."

Perry shook his head and got up to look at the map. The young woman played with her wrists. "Well, then, you just better drink some hot coffee, that's all."

"No," Perry said. He put on his parka.

"You just goin' then?"

"I've got to. I want to say . . ."

"I ain't gonna tell Arild nothin'. Don't worry about nothin'." She smiled straight at him.

The little girl was waiting outside in her snowsuit. She held the sled by its rope. She watched Perry get into his skis. The young woman stood on the porch without a coat, hugging herself.

Perry threw on his rucksack. "Hope you find that dog, Carla."

"He's good as caught right now." And the little girl went down the road one way and Perry went the other, and the young woman stood hugging herself and watching.

———

Almost immediately, fences appeared along the road, then a summer fishing resort with a locked gate and No Trespassing signs. Perry skied in the righthand ditch. He was vaguely proud of himself, proud in a general sort of way, and soon he heard the long rush of automobiles on a paved road ahead. Then the forest changed. The trees shrank to half their forest size, turning brown and shabby looking. The change could have been drawn by a straight line. Behind him lay millions of green pines, and before him were nothing more than city trees, separate and tenuous and sparse. Things seemed somehow wilted and diseased. He passed a sprawling old junkyard circled by a peeling fence that advertised the Lake County Fair in huge red letters.

Then the road made a final violent twist, as if strangling itself out of revulsion, and then there was the highway.

Perry stopped before leaving the woods.

The snow was mushy.

He made a snowball, packing it hard in his bare hands, then he picked out a decent-sized evergreen and threw the snowball, missing the tree by a few inches, and the snowball sailed out of sight.

He turned on to the highway and skied along the shoulder. There was no ditch. He put his head down and went slowly, letting the dirty snow pass under his skis. A gray monotonous day, and except for a single station wagon that sped past without stopping, the road was desolate and empty. Ahead was Tofte, a half-mile down the road.

His neck ached. It was all dull and routine and perfectly ordinary.

He stopped at a gas station outside the town.

He clapped the skis together, knocking off wet snow, then he tied them together and rested them against the pump.

A pickup was parked in the open garage.

An old sedan stood on its head under an elm.

Inside, the light was bad. Two men in flannel shirts and jeans were drinking beer and playing an electric bowling game.

The place smelled good. It was wood and spilt beer and groceries and gasoline. A woman sat on a stool watching the men play the bowling game. She got up and brushed her hands on her apron. Perry asked for a pay phone.

"Sorry," she said. "No phone unless for emergencies, and it's a private phone, too." Her accent was frontier Swedish, hitting her last syllables with the precision of a fine bell.

Perry told her it was indeed an emergency.

She looked at him suspiciously, then went over to one of the flannel-shirted men, then came back and pulled a phone from under the counter.

Perry called the state police first. The duty officer didn't sound much surprised. He sounded old. "Hot damn! We been looking for you, fella. Where the hell you been?"

Perry told him. The old-sounding officer took down the details. It seemed to last to eternity. Finally he told Perry to hold the line and there was a short pause, then the line buzzed and another officer was on the phone, this one younger and less friendly and more efficient, and Perry repeated the story, giving Harvey's approximate location, trying to visualize the old shanty as he talked. When he finished, the efficient-sounding officer told him to stay put and not worry, a car was being dispatched from Grand Marais. The conversation ended with a long clanging buzz.

Next he called Grace. He rang four times without luck, then he tried Addie's boarding house, then the library, then Grace again. He thought he might have forgotten the numbers. He got the operator and she called and still no answer.

He hung up and stood with his arms folded.

The woman with the Swedish accent stood across the counter from him.

"Would you want a hamburger, Mr. Perry?" she said.

He nodded and sat down. Lights on the electric bowling game sparkled and bells rang.

When his hamburger came, Perry ate it down without stop. Then the woman brought him a beer without asking, staring at him with a kind of familiar astonishment. Perry drank the beer and asked for another. He drank it slowly. When it was half gone, one of the flannel-shirted men sat beside him, letting his beer bottle clank with authority. Soon the second man sat on Perry's right, bracketing him.

"What you doing out in them woods?" said the first man, allowing the question to fall more as a derisive comment.

The woman, again without asking, brought him another hamburger.

"You was the guy that got lost," said the first man. "Thought there was two of you."

"There were. My brother."

"Where'd they found you?"

"Well, they haven't yet. I found you, I guess. It's pretty complicated."

The man picked up a salt shaker and sprinkled grains on to the counter and balanced the shaker on its edge. He let it rest at the precarious angle, watching it balance with a practised eye. Perry watched it, too. The shaker rested on invisible square grains. "I was lookin' for you myself," the man said slowly. "Whole town was lookin' for you. Whole state was."

Perry nodded and kept after his hamburger.

"So," the man said, "where was you all the while?" He grinned a bit.

"I don't know. Off in the woods somewhere."

"Lost?"

"I'd say so. That about describes it."

"Shoot!" the flannel-shirted man said, making the word sound both malicious and obscene.

"Yeah."

"You out in that blizzard?"

"The whole time," Perry said.

The man grinned at his buddy. "You was lucky then. Shoot. You was lucky."

Perry nodded and smiled and kept at his hamburger.

The man grunted, pausing as though carefully considering what to say next. His buddy sat grinning. "How the hell'd you get lost?"

"We just did. I don't know. It's a big wood and everything."

"Shoot. I guess I'd say you was just awful lucky, that's what I'd say if somebody asked me. You was awful lucky, that's all. Shoot, after the blizzard, couple days after, everybody stopped lookin'. Figured you was kinda dead."

Perry tried to smile pleasantly.

The man poked a finger at the salt shaker, stabbed it like a fly and laughed as it toppled and fell and scattered white salt. He was familiar. One of the northern men. Their vices were secret. "So," the first man said carefully, "where's the other guy? There was two of you."

"My brother?"

"Yepper. Where's *he*?"

"He's all right . . ."

"He dead or something?"

"No," Perry said stiffly. "No, he's fine. He's okay. We found a shed out there, maybe twenty miles from here. He's okay, I know it."

"How come he ain't here?"

"Well, he got sick. But he'll be all right."

"Shoot."

The second man started grinning again. There was something secret between them, something that they knew about or had talked about before.

"So," said the first man, again balancing his shaker on the counter. "You left him out there then? I got it now, I reckon."

Perry shrugged. He decided not to let them rile him. "I guess Harvey'll be all right."

The second man started giggling. He got up and put a dime in the bowling game.

The first man smiled. "How come you didn't just build a big fire? That's what I woulda done, I expect."

Perry shrugged. "We did. We built a hundred fires."

The second man giggled and flung a silver disc at the maze of pins.

The first man shook his head. Perry guessed he was a farmer out of business. "Don't know how you coulda got lost in the first place," the man was saying. "But I sure would've built me a big fire, first thing."

"We did that."

"A *big* fire."

"Well, next time you can get lost," Perry said.

The man kept shaking his head. "Not me. I never once been lost." Suddenly he slammed his hand on the counter. The shaker fell. Salt spilled into the man's lap. The pinball-playing man laughed a high-pitched, shrieking laugh that was almost womanly. "I'da never got myself lost all that time. I'll tell you that. But if I did, just if I did and I didn't, I'da built me a big fire, lots of smoke. Then I would have found me a bunch of boulders and spelled out SOS in the snow with 'em, and then, then I would've set fire on a big tree or something, got a big tree burnin' at night so the planes could see it real easy. I woulda been out of there in no time flat, all right. Bill! Didn't I tell you that's exactly what I'da done? So. Anyhow. Shoot. So where's the other guy?"

"My brother." Perry sighed. "He's out there in a shed. I told you that once already. He's okay. They'll get him out fast."

"Sick, huh?"

Perry nodded.

The man shook his head. "Stupid," he finally said.

Perry nodded again. "Pretty dumb."

"Stupid, that's what."

"Well, you won't have to worry about me doing it again."

The man swiveled off his stool. "Won't be lookin' for you again, neither." He licked his hand clean of salt, then put it out for Perry to shake. "You don't play bowlin' pinball, do you?"

"No," Perry said.

"Well. Okay then. Keep your pecker up."

"I will."

The man marched out of the store and his friend Bill followed him with a giggle and grin. Perry heard them drive away in the pickup.

He sat at the counter and waited. At last the woman brought him another beer and a fresh glass. Perry found two five-dollar bills in his pocket. They were stuck together, and he peeled them apart and put one on the counter. He was depressed and still hungry. He bought a candy bar, brought it outside and sat on the steps to eat it. Snow melted off the roof. Now and then a car passed by, speeding north or south, spraying water off into the ditches. A wave of the old melancholia passed through him and he got up and went inside and called Grace again. There was no answer. Outside, he retrieved his skis and wiped them off and stacked them in a dry spot by the garage. He was depressed. There ought to have been crowds. The highway should have been jammed with well-wishers. He took up the branch that he had used as a pole, gripped it hard and flung it across the highway and into the woods. A clod of wet snow slid off the roof. Inside again, he had another beer. He watched the clock on the wall: a Hamms beer clock with a canoe floating in twilight blue waters, the moon just up and shining, the lake water twinkling, the forest green behind it, the hands of the clock saying it was almost noon. He went to the phone and tried Grace again. He let it ring twice then hung up. He was restless. He went to the electric bowling game and slid a dime into the slot. The lights flashed and the pins came down. A clown's face lit up. Lucky, he thought. He sent a metal disc whizzing up the polished alley. Four pins shot out of sight. The clown's face lit in a frown. The disc bounced back, and again he sent it flashing towards the gleaming pins, and they all shot out of sight, all but one, and the clown frowned at him. *Lucky, plain stupid lucky this time.* He fired the disc again, and it bounced back, and he fired it again, again, and the lights flashed and buzzers shrieked, and the clown's face lit in alternating smiles and frowns and tears and grins, randomly, and he kept shooting the disc up the alley until the game went silent.

Both hands on the wheel, the patrolman drove carefully. He chewed gum and wore sunglasses and he searched the road with the mechanical rhythm of radar.

They drove through Schroeder and Taconite Harbor. It was a fine, slow drive.

Perry was mildly and pleasurably drunk.

Heat poured out of ducts below the dash. The police radio now and then buzzed.

Perry felt fine. He was smiling and watching the scenery and feeling the heat and creeping alcohol.

He watched the road bend towards him. The forest grew right to the shoulders.

Inside the car, air-light dust drifted in waves, warm gentle currents. The sun was just to the west. The car hummed along at a steady even pace, and the patrolman was blind behind his sunglasses, and Perry felt fine.

A blue Chevy swept by, heading in the opposite direction. The patrolman let up slightly on the accelerator, watched the car in his rear view mirror: "Sixty-five miles an hour," he said.

"What?" Perry half turned.

"Sixty-five, sixty-seven miles an hour."

"Jesus Christ."

They continued south.

The woods finally opened and Perry saw the silver water tower of Sawmill Landing.

They turned on to Route 18. They passed the drive-in theater, the Dairy Queen, Franz's tavern, a meadow high with snow. They crossed Apple Street and turned into Mainstreet, the library, the first houses, the stone foundation of the town's first bank. It was a bright busy Saturday. They passed the farm extension office and Perry looked at it with the dull disinterest of a tourist. The venetian blinds were partly closed, but he saw the outline of his desk and the filing cabinets. The town was a jumble of artifacts. The patrolman slowed to twenty-five miles an hour, and the car glided unseen to the far side of town. Snow lay in great melting heaps along the streets. Listlessly, the road twisted along the lake shore. The patrolman smiled under his sunglasses and said it was a nice little town. Perry nodded and watched the trees go by.

Grace was waiting on the porch. She took his arm and he bent and let her kiss him, then he kissed her cheek. He saw her hair and a fast image of her eyes.

The patrolman stood holding his skis. His eyes were far away behind his sunglasses. Perry took the skis and the officer touched his cap and said so long and walked with long strides to his car and drove away. At the end of the lane he honked twice.

They went inside. The place was dark. The carpets were soft. They stood in the kitchen. Grace made coffee and together they listened to it percolate and bubble and drain down. Then he grinned with a genuine relief and embarrassment. "Harvey's all right," he finally said. "They've got him in a hospital down in Duluth. Took him out by helicopter. I guess we can drive down to visit him tomorrow."

They drank coffee standing up. Perry leaned against the counter. The kitchen curtains were drawn. He grinned and looked up and Grace looked away. "Well. There's nothing I can say. I . . . Harvey's okay and I'm okay."

"What about you, Paul?" She was whispering.

"I'm okay." He saw her completely. "I'm fine, really. It's dumb, isn't it?"

She opened the curtains. "I better make something. You must be famished."

"I'm really . . . Okay, eggs or something. I'm fine. I tried calling you. I called quite a few times."

"I was out shopping."

"Oh."

Then they went to the living room. Perry sat with her on the sofa. After a while she took his hand. "I don't want to explain it all now," he said.

"That's fine. That's fine now."

"I want to rest."

"I know," she whispered. "I know you do."

Blood Moon

That spring, Harvey took a fancy to gin. In the evenings, sitting by the fire or on the porch, they drank gin fizzes or gin and tonic. All through April, they drank gin. Harvey bought a crate of limes and filled a cabinet with expensive gin, and Addie would mix the drinks in half-gallon jugs and they would all sit and drink and plan for summer.

Harvey wanted to leave Minnesota. And he wanted everyone to leave with him. For a while he talked about Boston, then he talked about Key West, then about Seattle but eventually he settled on Nassau and stuck with it, reasoning and cajoling and orating with his special flair and whimsy. The more gin he drank, the more persuasive and beguiling he became. He talked in broad colorful images. Illusive pictures: blue water, warm skies, fans spinning slowly on lofty hotel ceilings. Deep-sea fishing, golf and tennis, fine tans and good health and shining teeth and lovely women and adventure.

He did not talk about the long days of being lost. The same

way he never talked about the war, or how he lost his eye, or other bad things. He would not talk about it. "Yes, we'll go to Nassau," he would say instead. "Where it's warm. By God, we'll have us a lovely time, won't we? Buy a sailboat and sail the islands, see the sights, sleep at night on the beaches. Doesn't it sound great?"

"What about typhoons?"

"By Gawd!" he would grin. "I *hope* so! We'll hold tight under the weather. Just think about it, will you? Buy us a house with an open courtyard and colored bricks and palm trees, and we'll chip in for an air conditioner, and we'll drink rum out of big kegs, through straws and we'll swim, and we'll go to native dances, and we'll fish the sea dry. We'll do it, we will."

"At least," said Addie, "you can't very well get yourself lost on an island."

Harvey would shrug. "No imagination."

"How about a holiday out to California?" said Grace.

"Too easy."

"Such a scout," cooed Addie.

"I thought I was a pirate?"

"No," she grinned. "Now you're a great frontier scout." She laughed. "Like Davy Crockett and Daniel Boone, you know. Never get lost, always on track, a real woodsman. A scout."

"What about California?" Grace said. "Whatever you can do in Nassau you can do there, and it's closer and not so expensive and we can come back."

"Exactly!" Harvey crowed. "Come back, come back. The idea is to go and *not* come back. Just go."

"To Nassau!" cried Addie, hoisting high her glass. "Friends forever."

"You might stop teasing. I'm serious about it."

"Actually," Addie said, "I understand that Nassau is positively crawling with creeps now. You know? Real creeps. Crooks and gamblers and politicians and students and people who never bathe."

"We'll drive them out."

"Hooray," Addie said. "Hooray!" she shouted. "Hooray for Nassau and Harvey and a bloodbath!"

Like history, he thought. He thought.

Or histories. Mawkishly the same, as repetitive as a church rhyme.

A job, though. A preacher, perhaps. Like the old man. Return to Damascus Lutheran, filled with new religion, sparkling ice insight seen on the road to Damascus Lutheran, delayed and detoured by years of mawkish melancholy. Wear the old man's vestments. Put on the garb in the attic, and be a man. And preach neither salvation nor love, preach only endurance to be ended by the end.

He was getting fat again.

A kind of mushy, nervous atrophy that settled in like a disease, and he could see it in round numbers on the bathroom scale. Sleeping, eating, television and Harvey's expensive gin.

He was defenseless.

He had until the end of June to phase out his county operations, but the deadline only added to the sleepy edginess. So he took his time. Cleaned out the files, working slowly and systematically, preparing stacks of paper work which he tied into neat bundles to be either burned or stored in boxes for shipment to Duluth. Without planning or forethought, he was going through a motion that would sooner or later make its own decision. On one productive Thursday afternoon he stacked four years' worth of futile farm loan applications, carried them to the incinerator and burned them up without regret. It even made sense.

A job, he thought. Preacher, guide, confidant, teller of winter tales, saved from the deep forest.

Near the middle of May, he bought new glasses. For more than three months he had gone squinting under the illusion that he no longer needed them, and while there were no ill effects, Grace kept pestering until one sunny day he mistook the ditch for his own driveway. Next day he got the glasses. They were fancy wire-rims. "You look older," Grace said. "Like a professor."

"A preacher?"

"No," she said. "Like a teacher. They make you look wise."

"I am wise," he said.

"Tell me something wise, then. Explain everything to me."

"You want a child," he said wisely.

"Yes?"

"You want love and a warm home and a child. You want serenity. You want a loving husband," he said.

"Yes!"

"Patience, then," he said wisely.

And she had patience. It was as though nothing had changed or ever would change, and partly she was right. In the winter, in the blizzard, there had been no sudden revelation, and things were the same, no epiphany or sudden shining of light to awaken and comfort and make happy, and things were the same, the old man was still down there alive in his grave, frozen and not dead, and in the house the cold was always there, except for patience and Grace and the pond, which were the same, everything the same. Harvey was quiet. Like twin oxen struggling in different directions against the same old yoke, they could not talk, for there was only the long history: the town, the place, the forest and religion, partly a combination of human beings and events, partly a genetic fix, an alchemy of circumstance.

The days of waiting were quiet. Grace attended him with love, and they drank gin on the porch and listened to Harvey's

dreams and Addie's teasing, and they were a comfortable waiting band, knowing it would change, but knowing they would not
see the change, but rather the effects.

The new glasses sometimes gave him headaches, even dizzy
spells. At night the glasses would seem to emit their own special
rays, millions of dots of hard white light, and he would be suddenly back in the forest, looking into the cold sky and seeing the
universe with such horrible and chaotic brilliance that he got
sick. On Memorial Day, there was a parade. Harvey decided to
participate.

"You're being a dumb scout," Addie teased, but it did no
good. Grace ironed his army greens and they drove together into
town. Harvey held a fifth of gin in his lap. "What this town needs
for its parade is a genuine war hero," he kept saying. Perry parked
in front of the bank and Harvey dashed up the street to where
the parade was forming. The sky was dark and it was going to
rain. Perry and Grace and Addie had coffee in the Confectionery.
They sat in a booth and watched the clouds mass. Perry ordered
cream pie.

"Positively fat"; Addie said. "I won't go to the badlands with
any fat man, I'll tell you that right now."

"All the better, then."

"Such a day. It's depressing. Look, there's Jud. Look at him."

Jud Harmor was standing all alone in the middle of the
street. His straw hat was in place and his hands were on his hips.
Alternately, he was scanning the gray sky and the parade route.

"Poor Jud."

"Jud's all right. Poor Harvey, you mean. Where does he get
these obstinate ideas about parades?"

"He's a character, all right. He does look dashing in his uniform, though," Grace said.

"Positively silly."

"Addie."

"I must stop teasing." She frowned at Perry. "But really! That pie. You're becoming a can of Crisco, really."

They drank coffee until noon. Then they heard the drums booming and they went out to the street.

Clouds were rolling and massing and the air was cold. Grace sent Perry to the car for a jacket. It was a dreary, nothing kind of day. Perry wished he were sleeping.

The parade started at the northern end of Mainstreet and went south, ending at the cemetery for the commemorative services. Half the town lined the street to watch the other half march. Addie stood with her arms folded, smiling. She wore a skirt and a T-shirt. A few drops of rain fell as the drums took up the cadence, and Perry stood between Grace and Addie. Addie grabbed his hand like a child. "Here, look. Here they come," she said.

The high-school band led the parade. Perry recognized some of the kids. Grace recognized all of them, and she waved and called out their names. Even with the clouds and chill, most of the town was there. There was respect and polite applause and civic pride.

The Lake County VFW commander rode by in a new Chevy. He waved and Grace waved back.

Then a troop of World War II veterans. Lars Nielson and many others. They wore their old uniforms, olive drab and khaki and navy white and flier brown and blue. Many of the coats were open at the belly. Two of them held rifles over their shoulders. A third carried the flag.

Then the junior high band.

Then the American Legion float.

Then the DFL and Republican county chairmen, riding in separate cars, both waving.

Then the Korean War veterans, then the Girl Scouts.

Then Harvey. Marching alone in his uniform, following the troop of green Girl Scouts.

The Girl Scouts carried a large banner and sang campfire songs. Harvey was behind them chanting "A-left. A-left. A-left, right, left." He marched erect, the only veteran of Vietnam. He did not seem much different from all the others, except that he fit his uniform and he was alone.

Addie shouted and gave him wild applause. Harvey went by without looking. "Such a scout," she cried. "Now *that*. That is what I call a frontier scout."

Jud Harmor finished the parade. He, too, marched alone. He carried a sword in his right hand. On his chest dangled a single faded battle ribbon. He wore instead of his straw hat a World War I doughboy's helmet.

"Good Lord," Perry said.

"We haven't heard the last of him," Addie said.

Grace took Perry's hand. He was holding the hands of two women.

"Let's get a drink somewhere," he said. "Where's Harvey?" Then he saw him coming back up the street.

"Miserable parade. No class at all."

"You're supposed to march out to the cemetery."

"Miserable parade."

Addie took Harvey's hand, and, linked together, they went to the car. The rain came. Harvey opened the gin while Perry drove out towards the cemetery.

"Fine miserable parade," Harvey said. "You ought to have had more sense, letting me march in the miserable parade. I swear. Addie, give me that bottle. I swear, I swear they have better parades on the losing side of wars. We all ought to move to Italy. What do you think? Seriously. Italy. I hadn't thought of it before. We could live cheap, really. They've got all kinds of inflation over there and we could probably be kings and queens and all that rot, what do you think?"

Perry steered the car up Mainstreet. The rain was white. Orange and blue crepe paper lay plastered in wet gobs on the street.

"Yes. Italy. I think that's it. Addie, give me that frigging bottle, will you? Italy! I can see it. We've got to get out of here."

"You hate tomatoes."

"What? I love tomatoes. I love sausage and tomatoes and noodles. I love women with big tits. No offense, Addie. Really. Ha! Touché! I love pizza and Van Gogh and women with big tits!"

"Van Gogh?"

"Sure. And I love losing wars and I love lasagna. I love big boobs and Fascists and inflation, I love it all. Addie, give me that bottle or I'm going to . . ."

"Let's go home," Grace said.

"No! The cemetery. We must honor the dead. Onward. First the cemetery. Then Italy. Addie!"

"Hip-hip!" Addie crowed.

"Look at that bloody rain. Does it rain in Italy like this? Who cares?"

"Harvey."

"Yes, that's it. Italy. No question about it. I'll get the passports tomorrow. How much does a villa cost? No problem, I'll find that out, too. Italy, it is. Will you just look at that bloody rain? Some miserable parade. I still haven't gotten a decent parade out of all this. Some miserable town, not giving me a decent warm sunny parade. Italy! I think that's the final answer. Yes. Addie? I don't know about Addie, though. Grace will fit in just fine in Italy, but Addie, I don't know. Poor Addie. I don't think the Fascists allow in half-breeds, do they? I don't know. I'll find that out tomorrow."

The car filled with wet air. Perry turned the wheel and they went up the dirt road towards the cemetery. They passed two orange school buses filled with kids in wet band uniforms. Cars and pickups were parked along the muddy road.

"Got to hurry," Harvey said. "Can't miss the ceremony to honor all the dead."

"Calm down."

Harvey opened his window and rain poured in. "Miserable parade," he moaned. "Some miserable way to honor the dead and wounded."

"You were magnificent, Harvey."

"I did my best. But a miserable parade except for me."

"Jud was good, too."

"Me and Jud. We'll maybe have to take Jud to our new villa in Italy. But he pays his own bloody way."

"Hush up."

"Some totally rotten way to honor the dead. Where are my medals, for God's sake?"

Perry turned into the cemetery. He parked and they trooped out into the rain and thunder. Grace was shivering and Perry took her arm. Harvey quieted down.

The band played the national anthem. Then Hal Bennett the dentist climbed on a raised platform in the center of the burial ground and gave a speech of some sort, and the veterans stood in groups according to their war. Later, Reverend Stenberg offered a prayer and everything was wet and peaceful, then Jud Harmor got up and gave a short speech, then the band played "Yankee Doodle" and it was over.

"Some miserable way to honor the dead," Harvey said.

"Let's go now."

Harvey coughed. "First I must honor all the fucking dead. Look at all those dead people, will you just look? Take me all day."

The band was playing taps.

"Let's go," Perry said. "We'll build a nice fire and have supper."

"No, I'm gonna go around here and honor all these dead and deceased."

Perry tagged after him. He was cold. Grace and Addie went to wait in the car.

The graves were arranged in long rows. The dead people were buried head to head, then an aisle, then another long row of dead people buried head to head. Randomly, Harvey stopped at some of the graves. He knelt down to read the epitaphs and names and dates. At last they stopped at their father's grave.

"I guess . . ."

"Let's go, Harv."

Harvey removed his army cap. Perry stood blankly and waited.

"The old man's pretty dead by now," Harvey said.

"Grace will put some flowers here tomorrow."

Harvey's face was red. "I don't know. He was a bastard, wasn't he?"

"It's raining, Harv. Come on."

They dropped Addie at her boarding house and went home. Grace drew a bath for Harvey. Later the three of them had sandwiches and cocoa. It was still raining.

"Well," Harvey glowed, "I want to thank you for a fine day."

"Lovely."

"We have to have more miserable parades. Afterward everybody gets so cheery. Now. Who's coming into town with me?"

"We all have to go to bed," Grace said.

"Too cheap. Much too cheap and easy. No, we all must honor with the rest of the partying mourners."

"If you had any sense . . ."

Harvey wrapped an arm around her. "You're a wonderful mother, Grace. And we love you. I love you. But you know how honoring the dead goes. Many sacrifices."

Harvey borrowed a raincoat and went into the storm. The headlights of the car fanned briefly across the kitchen window.

In the morning, it was still drizzling. Perry drove Grace to the cemetery and walked among the headstones while she planted flowers at his father's grave. She was absorbed in her work. Placid and quiet, she was digging out weeds along his father's headstone. She was on her knees in the rain, her face set in its sane and perfect way, her hands deep in the mud. She'd dug three holes for the plants, and when the weeds were gone, she set the plants in and covered the roots and packed the mud down. "There," she said. "That should do it." She stood beside him. The plants had dark red flowers growing. "That should do it," she said.

It was Friday evening. The stores were open till nine. Though it was not quite dusk, some of the shops had already turned on their evening lights. Perry watched through his office window: greetings, buying and selling, handshakes and nods, jerky movements. He watched a giant shadow grow in from the western forest, gradually engulf the town and move off to the east. The office was dark. It smelled of manure dropped from farmers' boots, stale corn and pine. The day's stacks of paper work were lined up on his desk. One pile was for burning, the other for boxing and shipment. Without reason, he swept the floor. Then he sat in the dark and waited for Harvey. The office already seemed deserted and worthless. A picture of the President looked down on him from a plastered wall. He waited until nearly six, and when Harvey didn't come he locked the office and stepped outside, glancing by reflex through the familiar window, then walked up to Wolff's drugstore. He brought Grace a birthday card and candy. It was too early to go home.

He waited until six thirty. When he went back onto the street, it was again drizzling. He tucked the card and candy under his coat and trotted to the car. He drove past Addie's boarding house, but her windows were dark.

When he got home, Grace was waiting alone in the kitchen.

"Addie called," she said quietly. She'd been crying. She smiled anyway. "She says she has a headache."

"What about my lovely brother?"

"I don't know," she said. "You were supposed to bring him."

Perry gave her a kiss, the card, the candy. "I waited for him . . . No matter. Happy birthday."

Grace smiled weakly. The table was set for four people. A big birthday cake stood as a centerpiece.

"Here, take it easy. Harvey'll be along. Maybe they'll both come. Or we'll just celebrate together. How would you like that?"

"Addie won't. She says she has a headache. I get aches, too."

"Don't worry about her. You know how she can be if she wants."

"Well . . . She's my friend," she whispered. "I guess she's my best friend and now she can't come because she gets a headache."

"Maybe they'll come later on." Perry kissed her and went into the bedroom and pulled out the sweater he'd hidden under the bed. It was still in its J. C. Penney sack. He looked at it and realized how utterly unimaginative and fitting it was. He wrapped

it up in Christmas paper and glued on a bow and brought it out
to her.

She seemed happy. She kissed him and she was smiling. They
had their supper, then Perry carried the cake into the living
room, where he built a fire and cut the cake and served her while
singing "Happy Birthday." And she seemed happy. She opened
up the gift, showing great surprise, and she immediately tried on
the sweater. "I love it, I love it." she said, pulling it over her shoulders and breasts, "I do love it." She made the J. C. Penney sweater
look much better. "I love it," she cooed, turning for him before
the fire, and he knew she would soon be bringing it into the store
to exchange for something not quite so tight, and he knew she
would not mention it and he knew he would never notice. "It's
marvelous, it is, it is," she whispered.

Later he had a warm shower. He found Grace in bed,
wrapped in her flannel nightgown. The lights were out.

"Feel good?" she said. She warmed against him.

"Pretty good. Those glasses gave me a headache this afternoon."

"Better now?"

"Headache's gone."

"Maybe Addie caught your headache."

"Maybe so. I'm sorry it was such a rotten birthday."

"Oh, no. It was beautiful. It was better just to be alone.
Wasn't it? Don't you think so? I was . . . I was disappointed at
first but now I'm glad they didn't come. We never get to be alone
and I thought it was beautiful just to have you and me and nobody else mucking it up."

The rain had stopped. Water still dripped from the eaves.

"You warm enough?" she whispered.

"Fine."

"Really," she sighed. "Really, I'm happy that they didn't

come. Maybe I'm too shy. I don't know. I just can't keep up with all their teasing and games and everything. But . . . I'll be glad when Harvey gets a job and goes to work somewhere. He's talking about it again, you know. He hasn't said anything but I'm sure, I'm sure from the way he talks about a job, that he's thinking about asking Addie to get married again. He's acting the same way. You think so? Anyway, I'll be glad when he gets a job and goes off to work. Or when we do, whichever it is. At first . . . at first I was feeling bad because you lost your job. Not bad, really. I didn't mean it that way. I mean, it wasn't as if you were fired or anything, was it? But I felt kind of down in the dumps. I didn't try to show it, I just kind of felt that way because I knew you were feeling down, too. But now I don't. Now I don't feel that way. I wouldn't mind moving to another place, would you? Really. Would you?"

"I suppose not. There isn't much else to do."

"Oh, it'll be better maybe. In the long run. I can find a teaching job anywhere we go, so you don't have to worry about it, about finding a job right away. I know you're a little worried, even if you don't talk about it. I . . ."

"I'm not worried," he said.

"All right. If you say so, then you're not worried."

"I'm not. I just want to take my time and find something decent. I was thinking for a while about maybe going back to school."

She sat up. "Really? Oh! I think that would be wonderful. I do. I love the idea. Really?"

"Maybe. It's an idea."

"We could go down to Iowa," she said.

"That's part of it."

"Oh. Oh, I like that idea."

"We'll see what happens."

He heard her turning and thinking. He wished he hadn't mentioned it. Water was still running off the roof and dripping from the eaves. The bed was very warm. After a time, she curled close to him. "Hmmmm," she sighed. "Are you warm enough? I'm happy. This is a beautiful birthday. Everything's getting better, isn't it? I knew everything would get better." She was touching him. "Do you want me to rub you?"

"No, not tonight."

He held her and listened to water drip from the roof. When she was asleep, he turned to his stomach and faced the wall.

He awoke once, feeling restless. He was hungry. He was always getting hungry now, ever since getting out of the woods. He tried to sleep but the hunger kept growing, and at last he got up and went to the kitchen. He ate birthday cake and drank milk. Then he went up the stairs to look in on Harvey. The bed was empty and the window was open and a puddle of water had formed on the floor. He wiped it up with a sheet and went back to bed. Grace was mumbling from her dreams and he listened. She never said much. He curled around her and slept late into Saturday. It was peaceful. The house was quiet and there was spring sun. He slept through the weekend, and on Monday, hopelessly sluggish, he drove into town to continue changing his life.

Harvey had disappeared. He tried calling Addie's boarding house, but there was no answer. Grace was sure they'd got married.

The spring sun continued into the second week of June. The fat was coming back and he had no power to defend himself, and his waist and hips quivered with the old gelatinous slime. He was either hungry or sleepy, and there was no other sensation.

He began going again to Pliney's Pond, sitting on the rocks and staring with sleepy eyes into the thick water, never going in, now and then dipping into the pond and letting the green water trickle through his fingers. The water was always warm.

Once he shed his clothes: a bright Thursday morning.

He stood naked over the pond, put his foot in, let it sink into the mud.

But he stopped.

He dressed quickly and hurried back to the house to get ready for work.

That afternoon Bishop Markham stopped in to say old Jud Harmor was dead.

"Cancer," Bishop said, sitting on the edge of Perry's desk.

"Lord."

"Old Jud."

"Well," said Bishop, "it has to happen. You're right, he was awful old. It was all over him, I'm told. Started in his throat, and I'll bet that will teach him to smoke. Well. I just wanted to fill you in. I got things to do. With Jud gone, I guess I'm temporary mayor. Seeing as how . . . town council and so on. It's no fun getting it this way, I'll tell you. You want anything done, let me know."

"Right, Bishop."

"Okay. Have a good day now."

"Congratulations."

"Thanks," Bishop grinned.

"You're a hell of a man, Bishop."

It was the way he'd felt when . . . a lot of times. He sat at his desk. He realized he was grinning and tried to stop. He finally got up and locked the office and went to have his tooth repaired. Hal Bennett leaned over him, working like a garage mechanic. Poor old Jud, Perry was thinking, but not in words, gripping the chair. Bennett drilled the cavity and smeared the hole with medication and thumped a filling home. Poor old Jud, Perry was thinking. His mouth was braced in a grin. The light was brilliant overhead, the silver instruments gleamed in Bennett's hand. "Jud's dead," said the dentist as he hit the filling. "Just like— that," and he hammered Perry's tooth. "Brush your gums," he said. "You got to take better care of them teeth, you're gonna lose them otherwise." He handed Perry a new toothbrush. Outside, Perry threw the brush away in disgust. Poor old Jud, he was thinking, but not in words.

His mouth hurt all night. He woke up with a savage headache. It started in his jaw and rolled in tremors along his skull. In the morning he had orange juice and aspirin, looked at the sun, then returned to bed.

Grace finally shook him. "Jud Harmor's dead," she said.

"I know it."

"You ought to get up."

"All right. I'm hungry."

"Well, you should be, you should be. Sleeping Beauty. Go get a shower. And you should have told me about poor Jud."

"I forgot. I'm sorry. What time is it?"

"Supper time, that's what. Go get a hot shower. Sleeping Beauty in person."

Perry sat on the rocks at Pliney's Pond. Thick steam rose from the waters. Bacterial wastes, decaying plant life, dead and living animals. Microorganisms that flourished and multiplied. Floating algae, tiny capsules of cellulose, lower-level plant life, ripe and rich and hot. Frogs and newts and creatures with beady eyes dangling from optic nerves. Continuity. Spores in the air. Chemical life, chemical transformations, growth and decay. Bacteria feeding, insects feeding, frogs feeding. The processes of protoplasm. Respiration, oxygenation, reproduction, metabolism, conversion and reconversion, excretion and growth and decay. Such a fountain, he thought. And poor old Jud. And poor old Harvey and poor old Addie, and poor old Grace. And: "Poooooor me," he sighed. Simple multiplication and division, asexual continuity, spores in the air, dispassionate life: "Poor me."

He drove into town. He stopped first at the office. Working steadily until noon, he finished cleaning out the files. He took two maps from the wall and rolled them up and stuffed them into a box for shipment. Then he emptied out his drawers, saving some personal papers and a box of staples. The rest he threw away, one by one turning the drawers upside down over the waste basket.

When the noon whistle blew, he walked to the church. The bells were chiming. He couldn't remember the last time he had gone inside. The pulpit was in the familiar place. The apse was high cold stone. He walked up the center aisle and looked down on old Jud. Behind him, the custodian was sweeping. Jud looked all right.

Perry stood awhile then went out into the sun.

He had lunch in the drugstore, then went back to finish his work. Billowing from nowhere, dust filled the air in the old office and he began sweeping the place down, taking great care to sweep in the corners and under the desk.

Then he took out the razor blade.

It was cool and slim.

He went to the window. Outside, the streets were dizzy white. To his left he could see as far as the railroad tracks. To his right, the drugstore and a corner of the bank.

He held up the blade and began scratching his name from the glass. It took him most of the afternoon: first erasing his name, then the title, then everything.

He swept the paint chips out into the street. He washed the glass clean and pulled the blinds.

———

He was sleeping when Harvey came in. His feet had fallen from the desk.

He heard the door open, and the light fanned through his dream, and he heard the boots, the rush of hot air.

"Addie's gone," Harvey whispered. "She's flown off."

"Sit down."

"Addie's gone."

Harvey sat in a hard-backed chair. His bad eye was red. The blinds were drawn and the office was dark. It still smelled of dust. Harvey sat still a long while. Then he put his elbows on his knees, leaned forward, cupped his face in his hands. Outside a tractor went by.

"Addie's gone."

"We were worried about you, Harv."

"She's flown off. She's gone to Minneapolis. I asked her to get married again and then she went to Minneapolis. She's just gone."

"It's a bad show."

"She was making the plans for two weeks. I found out she got bus tickets two whole weeks ago. She didn't say anything to anybody."

"Where were you?"

"So I found out. So I got on the next bus and went down to find her . . . makes me sick."

"You look rough, Harv. How about us going home now?"

"I tell you it makes me *sick*! She's got this apartment down there. The city, I can't believe it. I had to sleep on the floor. Can you believe that? Makes me sick."

"Let's go home."

"Let's get a drink someplace."

"You want to?"

"Sure."

"I swear to God, it all makes me sick. Almost killed me. You couldn't believe it. How nice she was. Lets me stay there and listens and smiles and says I can come and visit whenever I want, and says no, she can't marry me, and I say why the hell not, and she just smiles and says no, and it goes on and on I don't know how long, forever I guess. The goddamn city. It's not even the city. A goddamn suburb. Can you believe that? Richfield, a goddamn suburb. That's where Addie's living if you can believe that. Took me a whole day to find her. Scalped. I feel rotten, Paul. You ever feel this rotten?"

"I guess not."

"I feel rotten."

"You look it. You need sleep and supper."

"Goddamn city. Goddamn bus. So I knock on her door, and she comes to the door and, you can't believe it, she knows it's me, I don't know how, and she's smiling in that same bloody way, and she's even got a *roommate*. It's all been planned for . . . And I was talking about Nassau and Italy, and she's cheering me on, and all the while . . . I feel rotten."

"I know it."

"It's all falling apart."

"I know it."

"I could feel it coming. It's all falling apart, you know that?

"She says I can visit whenever I want."

"That's a good sign."

Grace drove into town for Jud Harmor's funeral. Perry slept late, had a long breakfast alone, then went outside to rake dead grass. It was not such a bad day. He carted the grass into the woods using Harvey's wheelbarrow. It was the first day of summer. He worked steadily until noon, then Harvey came out and they worked together. Perry told him about Jud Harmor and Harvey nodded and kept working.

After a time, Harvey dropped his rake and walked without a word into the bomb shelter. Perry carted grass into the woods, dumped it, then went to the shelter. Harvey was sitting in the old rocker. The place smelled wet. "Have a seat," Harvey said. He motioned to a bank of cardboard boxes.

"How you feeling?"

"Rotten. Addie's a witch."

"That's no way."

"I know. I've been thinking." Harvey made a vague twisting motion with his head, encompassing everything. "I think we ought to sell the place."

"Maybe so."

"Do you think so?"

"Maybe," Perry said carefully. "It's something to think about."

"We should. I'm decided on it. I decided last night. I'm ready to go, I've had enough of the place, the whole thing. We can sell it and move away, maybe to Florida or something. What do you think?"

"You were talking yesterday about . . ."

"Forget that. This is today. Today I've decided we should sell the whole joint and all of us go to Florida. I don't care where." Harvey had a hammer. Still rocking, he hammered lightly at the concrete wall, shooting sparks and tiny cement flakes. "What do you think?"

"I think it's something to think about, Harv."

"Not for long. I'm tired of thinking. Everything's falling apart. Let's just do it."

Indifferently, as if he were waving a fan, Harvey hammered at the concrete wall, striking it each time he rocked forward. "Do you remember when I built this shelter?"

"Sure."

"Well, now I want to sell it. Everything."

"That's one way," Perry said.

"You bet it is. What are you going to do? Your job, I mean."

"I don't know."

"There you are then. You see? We sell the place, then you have to do something."

"You have a way of tackling things, don't you?"

"You bet I do." His hammering chimed in the autumn-like dark, a gentle persistent chiming, and a pile of loose concrete formed on the floor.

"All right then," Perry said, getting up. "Let's both of us think about it. I'm not saying yes or no."

"That's your style, isn't it?"

"Right," Perry said. "Going to help me rake?"

"In a few minutes. You go ahead."

That evening Perry talked it over with Grace. She pretended to toss the idea around, weighing it with a frown as she dried her hair, asking drawn-out questions. But she wanted to sell. He waited until she went to bed. Then he went upstairs. Harvey was lying on his bed, awake and dressed.

"Okay," Perry said. "We'll sell."

"You sure?"

"Tomorrow. I'll talk to Bishop Markham in the morning."

"What does lovely Grace say?"

"She's for it."

"What will you do afterward?"

"I don't know."

"I guess there's not another way," Harvey said.

It was mosquito season. They were everywhere. Swarming in the kitchen at night. Around the yard light. Downtown. At the ball park. Electrocuting themselves in static buzzes against the special pest-rid machine installed at the Dairy Queen. Masses of mosquitoes. Blood-crazy and rattling against the bedroom screens as he tried to sleep and breeding in the heat of Pliney's Pond. Perry smelled the pond. He dreamed of it, dreamed that he was at last going in, lolling in the algal ripeness, joining the heated thick waters in a final search for the start of things, dreaming as the mosquitoes called for his blood against the screen windows, the aroma of Pliney's Pond drifting into the bedroom and bludgeoning him into long, dreaming, sweating sleeps.

There was nothing to do.

He wanted to talk to Jud Harmor, but Jud Harmor was dead.

"Selling!" Bishop said with delight. "Well, I guess I can sell the old place for you as well as anybody. I guess I can! You came to the right man, Paul."

"I know it."

"That's what I'm here for."

"Selling out."

"I wouldn't put it quite that way," Bishop said cheerfully. "Nobody's going to blame you."

"That's what you're here for."

"Right. Broker for the emigrants."

"I know it."

"I'll get you a good price, don't worry about that. We'll do it right."

"I'll bet you will."

There was nothing to do.

On the first day of July, he cashed his final Treasury pay check. As a ritual, he went to the office and swept it down, locked the door and posted the key to St. Paul. Then he ambled down to the barber shop. It was air-conditioned. The clippers hummed sweetly, the scissors clicked along his neck cool and precise. After the haircut, he asked the barber to shave him. It was an afterthought. He took a last look at the beard, remembering with dispassion the forest and the snow and the days of being lost, then he closed his eyes and smelled the lime-scented shaving cream and heard the razor scratch along his neck, his chin, his cheeks, clean and fast. The barber's name was Andrew but everyone called him Silent Andy. He talced Perry's face, swept the linen away, whisked the stray hairs and returned his instruments to an ultraviolet sterilizer.

Swiveling him to face the mirror, the barber surveyed his work like a farmer admiring fresh-plowed land.

"Looking forward to this a long time," the barber said.

"Good job."

"You want a shampoo? Might as well do her right."

"Sure. Why not?"

Sitting back, Perry opened a newspaper and found Bishop Markham's ad for the house. "Vintage dwelling," the copy read, "ten rooms, fireplace, twenty choice acres, pond and bomb shelter. A real buy. Peace and quiet." The photographer had captured the house at its best angle, looking in from Route 18, and the place seemed much bigger and older and more tenacious than reality.

The barber massaged his hair, then pulled his head back over the sink for rinsing, then briskly toweled him dry.

"So I see you're selling," the barber said.

"Maybe."

"Maybe? What's the ad for then?"

"Yes," Perry said. "We're selling."

"Too slow for you around here?"

"Too fast," Perry said.

"It's a shame."

"I know," Perry said. "It's a real shame."

———

The days were all slow. Perry tried not to think about it. In mid-July Harvey left for a visit to Minneapolis and when he returned he was in a bad mood. He did not talk about Addie, and Perry did not ask. There was nothing unspoken. The trip simply hadn't happened.

Sleepwalking season. Impartial events dragged him from hour to hour, and there was nothing to do but wait.

To differentiate the days he sometimes took short walks in the forest, trying to see it objectively now that he was leaving. But he stayed away from the pond. Sometimes Grace would come along. They would hold hands and stay on the well-worn paths.

Once they found a rotting tree stump. It was coated with ivory fungus that overlapped in lobes like leather armor, and inside the stump were the hallways of a dark forest castle, maggots and other insects that scurried through the decaying wreckage. He reached into the interior of the stump to touch the stuff. It was warm and lush.

Once they found a fallen tree. They scraped away matted leaves and saw spider webs with beads of captured dew.

They saw oak leaves with both sharp and rounded lobes, each representing a different species.

With the mechanisms of departure in motion, he began feeling older. There was nothing so terrible about the place.

With a fingernail, Grace broke open a sassafras leaf and held it to him to smell. "Root beer?" she said. "No," he said, "lime. More like lime." And she frowned and held it to her nose and smiled and shrugged.

She showed him the underbelly of the forest, the quiet and safe spots. Much of the forest, she noted, was neither pine nor birch, but rather soft tangles of weed and fern and moss and simple things. She showed him a delicate fern which she called maidenhair, plucking it from the soil.

Perry followed her through the waiting days.

He helped her with the gardening and shopping. Near the end of the month they drove down to Two Harbors for the county fair, and he followed her through the pavilions of women's work, quilts and mason jars filled with preserves and stewed tomatoes, needlepoint and aprons and apple pies. She went into a tent to have her fortune read and Perry waited outside.

"What did they say?"

"That's for me to know."

"Tell me."

"Well," she smiled, "they say I have a deep lifeline."

"I thought it was supposed to be long."

"For me it was deep," she smiled.

He did not worry about finding new work. Content to potter about the house, he avoided Harvey and waited for word about the house, sleeping late and performing minor chores with the old detached and sleepy languor. There were frequent rains. The grass grew fast and the woods filled with steam, and there was no threat of fire.

He did not see much of Harvey. Sometimes it would go for days at a time, long days with Grace, quiet suppers, television and Scrabble, a movie. One morning he found his brother sleeping in the bomb shelter, wrapped in one of the wool blankets stored there. He touched him and Harvey sat up blinking.

"What time is it?"

"Daytime," Perry said gently. "You were here all night. You'll get sick keeping this up."

"Couldn't sleep inside."

"Grace has breakfast ready. Come on."

"We're really leaving, aren't we?"

"That's what you wanted. I suppose . . ."

"All night I kept thinking . . . the blasted house." Harvey lay back and stared with an empty eye. "I guess I was dreaming. You know? It was strange but I kept thinking that the house was getting blown to pieces. Falling apart like a bomb hit it, except it was the wind and not a bomb. You know?"

"I know. It's tough."

"I guess it's best, though."

"Sure."

"But it's tough. I kept thinking the house was blowing apart. Pow, down she went. This incredible wind and everything was falling apart."

"I know, Harv."

"So I came out here. Lord. I'll be glad when it's sold."

"What you need is some breakfast."

Harvey sighed. "You ever get the feeling you're doing the same things over and over again? It's like . . . I don't know. The old man, all the outdoor crap. It's really a lot of crap, isn't it? But it's not the old man anymore, it's me. Now it's in me and I can't get it out. Doing crazy things. Over and over. Maybe selling the house will end it. I don't know. Do you think so?"

"I think so, Harv."

"You don't mind, do you?"

"No. I don't mind."

Harvey nodded. "That crazy dream about the house falling in. It was awful. Addie, the house. It's too much. I guess getting lost out in the woods taught you a lesson."

"I don't know what," Perry said.

"Leaving. Don't you see? You don't mind leaving now."

"Maybe that's it."

"I have a tough hide. I haven't learned any lessons."

"You're a good man, Harv."

"It's just hard to get it out of my system. All the crap. It really is a lot of crap, isn't it? I ought to get a job and make some money. That's what I should do."

"Maybe so, Harv. What you need now is breakfast."

"Or go to Mexico."

"Come on, Harv."

In the afternoon Bishop Markham brought out a young couple to see the house. Harvey watched them come up the lane. He hurried up to his room, and Perry and Grace were left to show them around.

"A grand house!" Bishop was saying. "It has all sorts of architecture and doesn't show it. Looks thrown together, but in fact it's a beauty. A real buy, I'd say." He talked like his newspaper ads. He wore a bow tie and corduroy jacket.

The couple seemed nice and friendly and very rich. The fellow said his name was Maglione. He worked as a bonds broker in St. Paul but he was giving it up to paint pictures. Clean-cut and talkative and straight, he seemed to Perry more of a bonds broker than a painter. His wife was extraordinarily pretty, and Perry guessed she'd once worked as a stewardess or model or something similar to capitalize on her looks. With her chin forward and high, she also had a bit of the aristocrat in her, nodding at things that won her approval. She was nice, too.

Bishop guided them through the house as if he owned it.

In the back yard, he pointed out towards the woods. "Now, if you want to paint pictures, I guess you won't find a much better place to do it. Real scenery. Genuine stuff, I might add. Just like the house."

"Dick paints mostly abstracts," the woman said.

Maglione blushed a little. "That abstract business is hard to swallow, I know. It doesn't mean I don't make use of nature. Actually, the idea is to expand on what you see in nature. Extend reality, if you see what I mean."

"Well," Bishop grinned, bringing him back to the house, "you aren't about to find a better place to extend reality than right here. Right, Paul?"

"Right," Perry said.

"Lovely," Maglione said.

Grace nodded and kept smiling.

Maglione's wife walked to the bomb shelter. Somewhat gingerly, she put a hand on the concrete as though testing whether it were real.

"It's a bomb shelter," Perry said.

"Yes?"

"In case of nuclear war."

"Yes, I see."

"Let's not dwell on it," Bishop said cheerfully.

"It'll keep the fallout off of you," Perry said solemnly. "My brother built it himself. He'll vouch for the construction. Meets all the government standards."

"Yes?" The woman stared at it.

"Never been used," Perry said.

"I should hope not."

"And it could come in handy. Forest fires and so on."

"God." The woman looked at him suspiciously. She said the word again as if she learned it in school. "God," she said again.

"Harvey—my brother—Harvey can tell you all about it if you'd like."

"I don't think so," Maglione smiled. He hooked his wife by the arm. "Not that I don't like it. I can see it's a solid bomb shelter, no question about it."

"You can paint it."

"Now there's not a bad idea," the man said enthusiastically.

"I mean, you can paint a mural on it or something. Like in the caves. Make an interesting relic after the . . ."

"Paul! Stop that." Grace took his arm.

Bishop guided the couple inside. They tested the water and walls and floors. Upstairs, they tried Harvey's door but it was locked. Bishop talked nonstop. He seemed to know the house better than Perry, as though he'd been waiting years for the chance to sell it off.

"Anyhow," Bishop said as they went outside, "you won't find a much better place for painting abstracts."

They stood in a broken line in the back yard. Maglione and his wife looked around randomly as if trying to sight the future.

"I can see it's beautiful," Maglione said. He had a bright, disarming way of smiling. His wife continued to eye the bomb shelter.

Finally they walked to their car. Everyone shook hands and Maglione said he'd be in touch within a few days. Bishop honked twice as they left.

"There," Grace said.

"What do you think?"

"You were ghastly about the bomb shelter." She laughed and took his arm. "I think they loved it. It was obvious."

Perry shrugged. "That woman's a real tiger."

"You were awful!"

Harvey was waiting in the kitchen. He looked shaken.

"They fell in love with it," Grace said. "And they were nice people. We've got ourselves a sale."

"Is that right?"

"Probably," Perry said.

"Charming."

"You should have said hello to them."

"Who were they? Never seen them."

"From St. Paul. Name's Maglione and he's a broker and she's some sort of beauty queen. Actually, they were all right. He wants to paint abstract pictures."

"Italians," Harvey muttered. "I can't believe it. Here we were all going to Italy and instead the miserable Italians are invading us. I don't like it. They didn't look right."

"They were very nice," Grace said firmly.

"Creeps. I was watching from the window. The guy looked like a creep to me."

Perry was disgusted. "If you don't want to sell, just say the word. You keep it. It's yours."

"I was only saying they didn't look right."

"Just let me know."

Harvey went back to his room, and that night Perry heard him pacing. The wind was from the south and he smelled the pond. It was hard to give a damn about anything except selling and leaving and finding a new place and forgetting the rest. He listened to the pacing and the mosquitoes.

"Poor Harvey," whispered Grace.

"Tough on him."

"Don't you have pity?"

"Sure. I have pity for myself, too."

"Well." She was quiet and the pacing continued. "I'm sorry," she said.

"Forget it. I'll be glad when it's sold. I was just being cranky. I'm glad we're selling. We'll find a good place somewhere else."

Grace rolled close. "You know," she said, "you do spend a lot of time feeling sorry for yourself. You and Harvey both."

"A family trait."

"Paul?"

"What?"

"Paul, what do *you* think?"

"Jesus Christ."

"No, I mean what do you think about selling? Are you . . . ? You never tell me anything of what you're thinking."

"I never know what I'm thinking." He was thinking of his father.

She sighed. "I can't read minds, you know. If you don't think you want to sell, if you changed your mind, well then just tell me. I won't mind, really. Really. I can't read minds."

"We'll sell," he said softly. "I never said we wouldn't."

"I just want you to be happy," she finally said. "I thought you'd maybe changed your mind and didn't want to tell me. I can't read minds. I like it better when we talk about things. Don't you? I do. I do. So if you changed your mind . . . I'm not going to care. I just want you to be happy. I worry over you."

"All right," he said.

"You know?"

"Yes."

"Do you want a nice rub?"

"No. I want to sleep."

He faced the wall, lying on his side, and trying to be still. The mosquitoes were buzzing against the screens. He wasn't sure of anything: Harvey's restless pacing, Grace lying awake and listening and too afraid to talk, the smell of Pliney's Pond drifting with the breeze from the woods. Once, forever, he thought he'd hated the house. Penance for not loving enough, the old man or the woods. A circumstance. He was hot. The sheets seemed to tie him down.

Wide awake and restless, he swung out of bed, his fists clenching and closing like a pulse. He sat still a moment. He listened to the July heat, mosquitoes screeching at the screen windows, inchworms in the back pines, the old house, the forest, a close-seeming flock of loons. What he did not hear, he imagined.

———

"Paul?"

"Go to sleep."

"What's wrong?"

"Nothing. I'm going for a walk."

"Did I make you angry? I'm sorry."

"No."

"Paul . . ."

"Stop that infernal whispering."

"Paul."

"I'm sorry." He got dressed. "I'm in a rotten mood. Mosquitoes, the heat, everything. I'm sorry. I'm taking a walk."

He'd forgotten his glasses. He blundered down the path, groping with his hands, thinking: she will be crying now, worrying, wishing he were happy, happy. Couldn't be helped. Selling the damned and cursed house, selling out of the great histories. He smelled the pond before him. Involuntarily, with the laxity of forgetfulness, his bowels moistened. Sweet anticipation. Selling out of the house and woods, it was time.

He blundered off the path and felt the underbush climb around him. He turned back, found the path by memory, and hurried towards the thick smell of the pond.

He was grinning and his bowels were wet and loose.

Blind anyway, his eyes were squeezed shut and he followed the path down and down. His belly was warm.

The night was warm.

A mosquito was trapped in his ear, dancing madly. He dug it out and another entered, buzzing in its frantic death dance, dancing madly, his father ringing in the death bucket, the hollow tinkle in Harvey's voice, the bells of Damascus Lutheran, the stone cold apse.

He did not notice the northern lights. He did not look up. He did not see the rocketing, wavering, plummeting red in the sky. The mosquito rattled in his ear and he plunged towards Pliney's Pond. He was blind and cold in the steaming woods. "Here we are," he said, coming to the pond. He could smell it and hear it, the soft muds and insects. It was sullen and hot, and he listened, his fists clenching and closing, and he was thinking suicide. He did not see the northern lights, but he heard the mosquito shrieking in his ear. "So, at last, here we are," he said.

He shed his clothes and at last went in.

At last.

He glided inch by inch into Pliney's Pond.

It seemed almost a ritual, but he knew it was neither a ritual nor an armistice, for his universe was fear and memories, and as he waded inch by inch into the hot algaed waters he said, "Here we are, at last."

The water drew around his belly and bowels, and he was wet and warm, releasing as he waded deeper, the whole architecture of his northern world flowing sweetly to ruin in the hot waters.

He glided through the thick water, aiming for the center of Pliney's Pond, letting his arms go out, his palms touching the surface of the waters and slowly rising in float. The mosquito still rattled in his ear and he went deeper. Expecting to sink, he was instead buoyed high. He was careful to hold his shoulders and neck and head above water. His eyes were now open. His stomach and intestines had lost all feeling, and he thought with a smile of a pricked sac of black bile that now flowed like kitchen syrup into warm Pliney's Pond. He bounced lightly on his toes, wading deeper towards the center. It was curious thick water with the odor of purity. Dead insects floated around him. Live insects swarmed around his head.

At the center of Pliney's Pond, he closed his eyes. Then he lay back, drowning the mosquito in his ear.

Eyes closed, ears closed, there were no sounds and no lights. He lay still in a bath of secondine, blood and motherwarmth.

There was no wind. The waters were stagnant. There was nothing to carry him in one direction or another, and he floated dead still as a waiting embryo. In an infant's unborn dream, the future was neither certain nor even coming, not even the future, and the past was swimming like so many chemicals around him, his own black bile running like diarrhea into the pool of elements.

He opened his eyes, rolled over, face down, submerged, put his feet into the mud bottom and submerged like a turtle, opened his eyes again, relaxed, calm, warm, suspended, at home. Things moved around him. He pushed towards the bottom and took a handful of slime and squeezed it between his fingers. Then his breath left him.

Coming out, emerging, he saw the great lights.

He waded to the rocks and sat still. He smelled the pond in his lungs. The old man's crazy illusions seemed dull and threadbare, as though their vitality and old importance had somehow flowed with the black bile into Pliney's Pond. Everything was quiet. There were mosquitoes but they were not hungry, and everything was very quiet and peaceful and things were not really so bad or so urgent as the old man had preached. And there was still Grace. He had no more memories. Not so bad, he thought. Not so bad, at all. Buck up, boy. Buck up, he either said or thought, because it's good to sell and there are better and more comfortable illusions to live under. The old man *was* crazy. That was the terrible hell of it. And there was still Grace. Warm deepdown Grace, the ripe deep pond. He would tell her that he loved her and mean it, mean it at precisely the moment he said it, rather than not saying it or saying it and not meaning it, meaning it later when he did not say it. Someday he would say it and mean it at precisely the same time. Not so bad, he thought. He smelled the pond inside him. Not so bad, at all. At last he dressed and moved without hurry along the path to the house.

He made hot chocolate and sat at the kitchen table to drink it. Grace came out in her robe.

"I was worried," she said.

"I'm better now." He looked straight at her and smiled, almost meaning it. "I'm sorry. I was feeling rotten but I'm better now. Hot chocolate?"

"You stink," she smiled.

"I know it. I went for a swim in the pond."

"What?"

"I did."

"You *hate* that pond!"

"No more. It wasn't so bad. Not bad, at all." Again he smiled and almost meant it. "I need a shower now."

"No," she said. "No, that can wait till morning. Come along with me."

So he followed her down the hallway. Already, sensing it in the bare hollow hallway, he was thinking of the house as sold. Foreign and too cold. Not so bad, he thought.

"There," she said, "aren't you lucky to have me?"

"Yes."

She pulled down the sheets. For a while he just held her, then before knowing it and without forethought, he was ready to make real love. He smiled at an image of the old man, banishing it, and it was like the warm pond. "You want a son or daughter?" he said.

"A son, of course." It was as though she were thinking of the same possibility at the same time, but the way she said "of course" had great surprise.

"A son?"

"Of course," she said.

"All right then."

"What?"

"Son," he said. "The son frame of mind." Clumsy but not embarrassed, he helped her with the robe.

"Phew!" she laughed. "What a stinker."

"It's just the pond."

"Phew."

"Should I shower?"

"Oh, no. It's lovely."

Soft as the pond, he thought. Except for certain things, such as resilience. So, "Don't stop," she said in a loud voice that was not a whisper, but still like the pond which was always so rich-smelling and mud-deep and unconscious, scaring him away and still attracting as if to a natural element, attracting until in calm desperation, with nothing to lose, he relented and went in. She examined him like a toy. "Don't stop," she said, and I won't, he thought, I won't. Two sides, he also thought. Selling and staying, and it was as much negative as positive, selling, selling and denying the crazy stuff of the old man and the histories . . . "I won't," he whispered to her because she was pleading so loudly . . . A son, he thought. He thought son, son, son, son. He would be kind to his son. Have him read all the classic books and the *Atlantic Monthly*, and give him just enough of everything and not too much of anything. Huge breasts, he thought. Flattened now on her chest, spilling over her ribs where he could not see in the dark. There was a lull of waiting and rebuilding and floating in restless waters. He smelled the pond with them. "Paul?" she said loudly. Chlorophyllrich and algathick and deep to the very bottom of things. Such breasts, he thought. She began to move again, restlessly. She threw her legs behind him and seemed to suck him in. "Ow," she said loudly but not complaining, and "All right?" he whispered and "Perfect," she said loudly, "don't stop." I won't, he thought, thinking she's pregnant already, because he'd been coiled like a snake for years and the tension had gone slack and when he was ready to spring the spring wasn't there, but it could be recoiled, slowly, slowly he thought. Unimaginative, he also thought. Clumsy, out of practice, docile for too long. Unimaginative.

He smelled the rich pond. She held his head. "There," she said in a loud voice. "Now come here," and again there was a long time of rebuilding and recoiling, and he did not think of anything. "Ah, shame," she said. "There, do you like that there?"

He could not say anything and barely heard. The weight seemed to press on his ears.

"Are my breasts too big for you?" she laughed.

"No," he said.

"Are you sure?" And she started to say something else, a kind of fresh tease in her voice, but she was cut off and said something else very loudly, and again he was not thinking, and as though sinking she moved away from him and down but he caught up and held her by her breasts until she shook, then he held her while they were quiet, then she held him.

"What a stinker," she finally laughed.

"I can shower."

"No. I think it's lovely, I do. We can sleep like this always."

"Shall I get you some hot chocolate?" he said.

"Yes. Then we can have more energy. Do you think we made a son?"

"Three of them, I'll bet."

"I have the same feeling."

"But I don't care about the son right now."

"Good."

"Are you thinking of anything? I can't think of a thing to think about."

"Shhhhh."

"I feel good."

"Shhhhh. Where's my hot chocolate?"

"Are you glad we're selling?" he asked.

"Yes, but where's my hot chocolate? Yes, I'm glad. I'm happy now."

In the morning, Bishop Markham called to say the house was sold. He was cheerful and congratulatory. "You know what really sold 'em? The darned bomb shelter! Can you believe that? It's true, I swear. The darned bomb shelter. Can you . . . Maglione says he's gonna make it into a studio. Can't get more abstract than a bomb shelter, right? Hee, hee. Anyhow, I guess it's a load off your shoulders."

"A real load. Thanks, Bishop. When do they want . . . ?"

"Easy, easy. Plenty of time for all that. Mortgages and deeds and banks. You know how that is. Never easy selling a house. But that's what you got me for, right, so just take her easy and let me handle it. You're a lucky man, buddy."

Bishop talked in a faraway voice about the finances and paper work, then Perry thanked him and hung up. Grace was out working in the garden. Pregnant already, he thought. Not so bad, after all.

He watched her through the gauze curtains.

It was cool and she was wearing a sweater, the one he gave her for her birthday, and she looked terrific, he thought, and he was grateful and felt very lucky. She was on her knees, her hands deep in dirt as she planted flowers for the spring, when they would no longer be there, her hands deep in the garden dirt. She saw him watching and waved and he waved back, then went upstairs.

Harvey was in bed, watching television with a towel wrapped around his waist and his hair slicked down. He was smoking.

"Guess that was our good and loyal friend Bishop on the phone," he said without looking up. It was Saturday morning and the cartoons were on.

"He sold it. The Maglione people fell in love with your bomb shelter."

"Charming people."

"They're all right, Harv."

"When do we get booted out? Imagine they're already coming with truckloads of easels and paints to boot us out."

"No."

"Italians."

"No. Bishop says there's a lot of papers to sign. Lots of time, he said."

Wistfully, Harvey blew smoke towards the ceiling. "We don't have to sign, do we?" He looked at Perry with a sober eye. "There's no crummy law that says we have to sign the papers."

"No. I guess there's not a law."

"I built that bomb shelter with my own hands. Solid as rock. It'll take anything. Hate like the devil to leave it, you know. Bad news getting caught in a nuclear war without your trusty bomb shelter."

"Sounds terrible to me."

"Terrible? My God, think of your testicles."

"Rotten thought."

"Think of Grace."

"I am."

"What if we don't sell?" Harvey said. "We don't have to sell just because some miserable Italians want to take over."

"No," Perry said. "No, we're selling."

"You've decided, huh?"

"Yes."

"Taking charge," Harvey laughed. "Taking the old bull by the horns."

"It's best, Harv."

"Falling apart," Harvey said, still laughing. "It's all falling apart, isn't it? The whole thing blowing up into pieces."

"Yeah. Want to take a walk?"

Harvey shook his head. He lit a fresh cigarette and leaned back in bed. "I'll just watch the cartoons. Nothing like some good cartoons to cheer things up as the world comes to an end."

"It's not that bad."

"You don't understand, do you? Even now you don't understand."

"I guess I don't," Perry said.

That evening Harvey was talkative and falsely cheerful.

He drank gin and tonic, then after supper switched to beer. "What we should do is go into town for a last party," he said with bravado, his voice nasal and phoney and too high-pitched and certain. "That's what we should do. Celebrate my brother's great and lovely cop-out and sellout."

"It's all for the best, Harv."

"Then let's celebrate! Right? Celebrate the end. Go out with cheer and good humor, right? Not with a bang but a beer."

"We'll do it tomorrow."

"Tomorrow?" Harvey said loudly. "What tomorrow? What bloody tomorrow is this? You don't understand, do you?"

"I don't want to argue."

"Argue? Argue! You've taken the old bull by the horns and

who's to argue? Celebrate. We have to celebrate my brother's decision."

"Cut it out, Harv."

"After a beer to celebrate. Then I'll cut it out. Be my old easygoing self again."

"Nope."

"Just one? Just a lousy beer to celebrate? I promise to behave."

"All right," Perry said. "Just one."

He showered and put on clean clothes and they drove into town. Franz's tavern was closed and the streets were nearly empty.

"Park the car and let's take a walk," Harvey said. "I didn't want a lousy beer anyway."

Perry stopped in front of the library. They walked up past the old sawmill, around the hub and up Mainstreet towards the church. June bugs swirled around the electric lights. They passed Damascus Lutheran and the farm implement store where, during the daylight hours, old men sat to talk and spit and watch.

Perry wondered if he should be nostalgic about anything and decided not, decided that maybe he would be nostalgic another time.

Harvey was very quiet.

They turned up Acorn Street.

Lights burned behind curtains and the sounds of radios and televisions flowed out like running water. There was no traffic. An elderly couple came towards them, holding each other by the arms and talking softly, and there were crickets in the grass.

"I don't want to sell," Harvey finally said.

"I know."

Harvey was quiet. He kicked a stone in front of him, caught up to it and kicked it again. "We could stay, couldn't we? Old times again. We could do a lot of things."

"No."

"You never loved the old man, did you?"

"Yes," Perry said. "I loved him."

"Shit."

"I don't want to argue."

"Who's arguing?" Harvey said, kicking the stone again. "You never loved him. You think he didn't know it? Shit. You could've done something to show you loved him if you say you loved him. He wasn't so bad."

"I know, Harv."

"The hell you do. I'm not selling."

"Yes. You are. You're selling and we're getting out of here."

They were in front of the church again.

Harvey stopped and took Perry's collar, fingering it as though deciding something.

"You're a coward," he said.

"Maybe so, Harv."

"Not maybe. The old man was right."

"The old man was crazy."

"What?"

Perry was shaking. "Nothing. I'm sorry."

"How can I hit a coward?"

"Harvey."

"Tell me you're just a coward."

"No."

Harvey tugged his collar, almost gently, but hard enough to mean something. "We're not selling, are we?"

"Yes. We're selling."

"Not me."

"Then you'll have to buy my half. I'm finished with it."

"Shit," Harvey laughed. "A coward from the start. The old man was right. Wasn't he?"

"Harvey, I'm sorry."

"Sorry?" Harvey laughed. He started to cough. "Ha. You just don't tell me you loved him. You hear? Selling! I wish he could hear it, I do. I wish he could just be here and listen to you lamming like a bloody little girl. He was right all along."

"Harvey, it's . . ."

"Don't call me Harvey or I'll belt you. You hear?"

"All right." Harvey's voice had that nasal tinkle that came when he got excited, as if he were talking through his nose and not his mouth. The bad eye was going crazy.

"We're not selling," he said. "You hear that?"

"No. We're selling, Harv."

"You don't understand a bloody thing about it, do you?"

"Enough to know we're selling."

"Selling?" Harvey said bitterly. "You don't understand a thing, do you? Nothing. You haven't learned a thing."

"Let go of my collar."

"Sure. Sure, there's your collar. All yours."

"Harvey."

"Shut up. Just shut up."

Harvey kicked his stone, starting walking again, fast, and they crossed over on to Apple Street. The movies were letting out and a gang of eager kids hurried past them, talking and laughing and running towards some secret adventure. It was warm and quiet. They walked to the end of the street, then turned and walked back again.

"Where will you go?" Harvey said.

"Duluth maybe. I haven't decided. Grace likes the idea of Iowa."

"Lord."

"I know."

"Look. I'm sorry."

"I know, Harv."

"I can be a first-class bum, can't I? I'm sorry. Honest. It's just the whole bloody mess . . . everything. Everything falling apart like it is. But I can say some rotten things and I'm sorry."

"Forget it."

Harvey stopped again. He put out his hand and Perry thought what the hell and shook it. Things would never be right again, anyway. Harvey smiled shallowly. "I'm sorry," he said. "It just scares me a little. The same with Addie. I can say some miserable things."

"It's tough. Forget it."

"You're a good brother. You are, I mean it." He kicked once again at the stone. "It was the same bloody scene with Addie. Everything's blowing to bits and I just say some rotten miserable things. You really going to Iowa?"

"Grace seems to like the idea. We'll see what happens."

"Well," Harvey grinned, "there's always Mexico City, isn't there? How does Mexico City sound?"

"Sure."

"It's always a possibility. Mexico City or Juneau or something. I could get a job and maybe send for Addie. What do you think? You and Grace could come to visit and it would be old times again."

Perry decided to stay quiet. Too bad, he thought, but nothing could be done.

"Mexico City. We could all go for a trip into the mountains. The four of us all together again. Sun and jungle. Mountains. We could hire us some donkeys and slaves." Harvey was talking and walking fast, kicking his stone. "I've actually never had my own slave. Wow, we could search for ancient civilizations that got destroyed by earthquakes. Or gold. Gold! We could search for bloody gold, how's that? Addie could fill our teeth with it. What do you think? Miserable, isn't it? I feel miserable. Really, I'm sorry. I am. Wish I had a beer, that's what . . . That Addie. She said she didn't want to go to Mexico City with me. Can you believe that nonsense? Said she didn't want to go. I guess old Addie's lost the spirit. Too bad for her. I feel miserable, Paul. Some hero."

Perry couldn't think of anything to say. They crossed the tennis courts and came back on to Mainstreet. Everything was quiet. He wanted to get home.

Harvey kicked his stone up the street. "You know what we should do?"

"What?"

"We should go fishing tomorrow. You and me. How would that be?"

"Maybe."

Harvey laughed. "You are a good brother. Wish I had a brother like you. A good secure and down-to-earth brother. That's what I need. I wonder how you get to be secure and down-to-earth . . . That Addie. It's a crime, isn't it? I suppose I shouldn't have been such a pirate. Right? Except I'm not really a pirate. Did I ever tell you that?"

They walked past the drugstore and Perry's office. There was no traffic. Harvey kept kicking at his stone, his bad eye shining, and they walked down the center of Mainstreet. "That's it," he said. "We'll go fishing tomorrow. Fish the crummy lake dry. How does that sound? Just you and me . . . And maybe later we can take a trip up north in canoes or something. God, we could do us some fishing then, I'll guarantee it! Wilderness. The old man says you can catch fish with your bloody *hands* there's so many of them. And water so clean you can drink it straight from the lake. How does it sound? It's what we need . . . We could . . . we could fish our way into Canada, eat what we catch. Lakes and portages the whole way . . . Not a man in sight. Nobody. Real wilderness, no more of this crap. Just go and go and go. The devil can care, how's that? The devil can care. Addie can try to find me. We'll just go and go. Take canoes and tents and sleeping bags . . . I can just see it, getting out of all this crap and . . . and the devil can care. How's that? How does that sound? Doesn't that sound fine? Doesn't it?" Harvey walked faster, kicking his stone down the center of Mainstreet. He shivered as if closing the circuit on a great electrical current. "What do you think? We'll go way the hell up there, into the woods, fish with our bloody *hands*!"

They came out at the sawmill. The streets were empty. They turned up towards the library and Harvey hurried ahead, kicking at the stone. The town smelled clean. Someone had forgotten to pull down the flag in front of the library, and it was wrapped around its pole, flapping softly. Too bad, Perry thought. He caught up with his brother and put an arm around him.

"What do you think?" Harvey said. "We'll have us a fine time, won't we? Then later we'll go to Mexico City. We'll have a terrific time. You'll see. Yes. Yes, we'll go into the mountains and have us a *great* time! Really. And who needs Addie? Who needs a squaw, anyway? We don't need any of that. No women, just us. It'll be a great time, you'll see. You'll see."

An engine started somewhere behind them and a dog barked at the sound. Softly and endlessly, the flag flapped at its steel pole. Harvey's stone rattled away down Mainstreet.

"How does it sound? Doesn't it sound great? Addie . . . Who needs her? Always running around barefoot. Who needs that? We'll have us a great time. The Big A, right?"

Perry shut his eyes.

"Doesn't it sound great?" Harvey kept saying. "Doesn't it?"

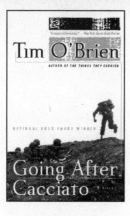

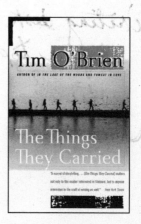

Mr. Hislop :
- Glue D/R chairs
- Writing desk –
    Repair top
    stain ?
- Hall table